THE HAUNTING

RUBY JEAN JENSEN

GAYLE J FOSTER

PROLOGUE

CREATURES OF THE NIGHT

*E*rica couldn't breathe. She felt her eyes getting larger and larger, as if they were going to explode in her head. She began to weep in silence.

The door eased open. Something black slid into view on the floor, like darkness from the third floor stairway coming down, swelling, rising up to stand almost as tall as the ghost woman. Darkness, as black as all of outer space, swirled into the room with that sound. It writhed, and separated, and Erica saw eyes with narrow slits for pupils, in faces that glittered in the weakening candlelight. Faces that were almost formless, long and thin and shiny—black and slimy. Dark tongues darted from narrow snouts, and the slanted and soul-less eyes searched the room and then found her.

They came forward, one, two, more, blending, separating. And behind them, in the doorway, stood the ghost woman.

First Printing: February 1994 in the United States of America

Published by: Gayle J. Foster, Carrollton, Texas

Library of Congress Control Number: 2021905551

Cover art: SelfPubBookCovers.com/ Shardel

❀ Created with Vellum

PART ONE: KATRINA

CHAPTER 1

"*D*on't let that face fool you!" the prosecuting attorney shouted. "That face that looks so pure and so fine and so handsome, eyelashes as long as a girl's! Hair as thick and curly as a girl's! That is the face of a killer, my good people. The most vicious kind of killer you will ever see, if the Good Lord will protect you from further exposures to his kind of evil."

Prosecutor Orville Rowson paused to wipe sweat from his face with a big red handkerchief. In the crowded courtroom the sounds of handheld fans made a soft swoosh, swoosh, feebly moving overheated air. Open windows, lined along each wall like the windows in the schoolhouse not far away, had flies buzzing against the screens, some of them inside.

Orville Rowson huffed with the heat and his sincere convictions of the young man's guilt. Orville stood no taller than the sixteen-year-old defendant but weighed a hundred pounds more. He wore a black suit, no vest, the coat hanging open and revealing a shirt that gaped over his paunch when he lifted his arms, which, like a preacher, he did often. Sweat rolled down his forehead and into heavy eyebrows. He reached up the large red handkerchief now and then and wiped the sweat and took frequent drinks of cold water from the pitcher on the prosecutor's table.

Both the defendant's table and the table of the prosecution were angled so the faces of those who sat there were visible not only to the judge and jury, but to the spectators. They watched with one expression on their set faces. Tight lips, stunned, horrified, and angry eyes.

"The most heinous crime our county could ever have, has now happened.

A small child, Katrina Etchens, five years old. Brutally murdered, stabbed so many times she ... *no*—chopped. Yes, chopped, is the word ..."

Orville Rowson's voice failed. He swallowed, looked at the dusty toes of his shoes, wiped his face. Again his voice rose.

"But before he did that final injury to her, ladies and gentlemen of the jury, he did the worst thing a young man can do to a young girl. He—mistreated her. He hurt her. If you listen to your heart, you can hear her crying."

The sounds of weeping came from a bench behind the railing near the prosecution's table. A woman buried her face in her hands. Her bony shoulders trembled. Beside her, a man's thin, pained face was white as schoolroom chalk. They were the parents of the dead girl. Their two sons, carbon copies of the father, hunched beside them like small twigs.

Orville pounded the table in front of them. Both boys jerked back, pressing against the rails of the bench.

"And this was done, ladies and gentleman, by someone the little girl trusted. Who her parents trusted! The great-nephew by marriage of the kind lady whose porches she played on, whose home she had access to. The kind lady who gave home and hire to that child's parents. Little Katrina followed Edward Wickham about as he did his chores. She trusted him. And what did he do to her in return?"

The boy on trial shook as if he were cold. No sweat rolled down his face. He wore bibbed overalls that sagged loosely on his gaunt frame. His face was thin and angular, but his eyes were alert, jumping from the prosecutor to the crowd that watched. At times they went to the stern face of his aunt, one of the crowd that sat on the benches beyond the railing that separated the court from the spectators.

"This boy, Eddie, as he is called," the prosecutor shouted, "does not have what we call good sense. He is dumb. He can't speak a word. He can't learn to read or write. But that does not excuse him from what he has done!"

He whirled toward the jury, and they flinched slightly and drew back into their chairs.

He angrily shook his fist toward the defendant.

"This boy, this Edward Wickham, aged only sixteen, is as guilty as sin. The state will show that it was he who took the knife from his pocket and killed with it! He chopped that small child to death ... after he had finished with her." His voice eased away. "This, ladies and gentlemen of the jury," he wound down breathlessly, softly, pointing at Eddie, "is your killer!"

CHAPTER 2

"*No, no!*" It was a whisper, unheard.

He was not a killer. He had never killed. He loved Katrina. She was like the little sisters he hadn't seen since he'd come to live with Aunt Theodora. When he closed his eyes he saw Katrina's fine, spun-silver hair matted with dark blood. Finding her tiny, bloody body tortured him, the vision of her burned behind his eyelids. He had never seen even an animal so bloody and mutilated. It hurt him that anyone could think he was capable of such an act. The vision of Katrina never left him. He would never be free of it, the pain, the rage. Most of all, he felt, every moment, Katrina's pain and fear. It almost didn't matter that he would be punished for something he hadn't done, for that which had been done to Katrina.

Eddie shook his head, back and forth, and struggled to speak. "No." The one word left his throat with great effort, after long, hard concentration to form a word, any word. No, no, no, it wasn't true that he had killed.

His eyes found his aunt Theodora, and the cold drew his skin tightly around him again. Nervous twitches jerked his fingers. He looked quickly away, lowering his gaze to stare at the floor.

The prosecutor was calling forth the first witness, a man who had come to help search, the first man to come to Eddie's painful, croaking cry when he'd found the torn little body.

Eddie felt Theodora's stare on the side of his face. He couldn't get away from that stare. He was more afraid of her, of Aunt Theodora, than he was of the men who hated and wanted to hang him because they thought he was the killer.

On the witness stand the man said, "I was watching this young feller, him with not enough sense to speak. He didn't know I was watching, and he went right straight to the body. He knowed right where she laid."

Eddie heard a deep breath drawn, as if the building itself had gasped in horror.

"Oh, he walked about some first, to try to fool me, like an animal will do to draw you away from its den. But then he went to her body. Half buried in leaves. I watched him through the woods because he was acting strange. He didn't talk. I didn't know at that time the boy just didn't have good sense, and that he couldn't talk. Then he stopped. I saw him stop. He got down on his knees, and began to pull leaves and sticks around. Maybe, I thought later, he was trying to bury her better, so that she wouldn't be found."

No, no, no!

"But then, he just kind of fell back, his mouth open, like people of that kind will do. And he kind of cried out ... like an animal." The man took a deep breath and twisted in the chair. "And it was her. That pitiful little thing."

Eddie, too, twisted in his chair, turning, seeking an escape from the memory of that day. Even in the stuffy odors of the courtroom he still smelled the cool damp of the woods beyond the barn. And the smell of decay, working like maggots through her flesh.

He was surprised to find the next witness was his aunt. She strode forward, her long, dark skirt brushing the tops of her shoes. Her dark hair was pulled back from her face, as always, and tightly plaited and wound at the back of her head. The tightness of her hair pulled her eyebrows upward. In contrast, her thin lips drooped at each corner. He didn't know how old she was. She might have been fifty. Or seventy. Or more.

She sat down in the witness chair, straight as the back of the chair. She put her hand on the Bible and said something that Eddie lost in the murmur that rose from beyond him. Snatches of the murmurs came to his ears instead, saying some things he hadn't known.

"That rich old lady—all alone now—no children— poor soul—has helped so many children find their way on in the world, and now, to be rewarded with this? Terrible."

"—that mansion, set back in the trees, belonged to her husband, owned that lumberyard and sawmill? Forty or fifty years ago he came to town. Built that big house—took a couple of years—"

"Brought her as a bride, didn't he?"

"Where'd she ever come from, anyway?"

"I don't know where she came from. If she has any family of her own, I never heard of it."

The voices hissed behind Eddie, carrying to him through the swearing-in of the new witness.

"Goes to church regularly—where Esther goes—but she don't associate much—Miss Theodora, that is." The prosecutor's voice rose suddenly to a higher pitch, and the ladies' voices hushed.

"Your name, Madam?"

"Theodora Wickham."

"And your relation to the young man on trial?"

"He is my late husband's great-nephew."

"How did he happen to be living with you, Mrs. Wickham?"

"I had heard of his family through my deceased husband. I knew he was the oldest of many children, and that the family was very poor. I knew he would never be able to take care of himself, being dumb and perhaps even deaf; though I found out he is not deaf. I traveled over two hundred miles there and back, in the spring six weeks ago, to bring him home with me, to give him a better opportunity in life ..."

No, no, no.

Her eyes, as black as the wings of a crow, glanced Eddie's way. He cringed against his chair. Couldn't the folks see that her eyes were cruel? Couldn't they *see*? They picked at him like a savage beak.

He had seen, that day of which she spoke, in the spring. He was in the freshly turned garden earth at home, putting in the peas one by one, three inches apart. He had heard of Aunt Theodora, Uncle Emmett's wife, his father's great-uncle's wife. But he had never seen her. He knew Uncle Emmett had died, through news that traveled in the family from one branch to another. But that was a long time ago, and had not affected him. He never expected to see Great-Aunt Theodora.

Then, one day, a strange lady came to the house, and he saw Aunt Theodora for the first time. She had smiled at him, but it was like a mask smiling, while behind the mask the soul in her eyes was missing.

EDDIE ENJOYED GARDENING. First there had been the plowing with Juniper, the mule. He liked that part, too, holding onto the handles of the plow as Juniper took her time down the length of the garden spot ... as worms, fat and juicy, were turned up, and the robins and blackbirds came flocking in to gather them up. He felt sorry for the worms, even as he enjoyed seeing the birds. The worms, after all, had things to do, he supposed, just as he did, just as the robins did. The worms were the first to plow the earth, keeping it moist and loose and fertile.

Then, after Juniper was turned loose in the pasture with the cows, the garden smooth with having been plowed and then dragged, he made rows with a hoe. At the edge of the garden, two of his little sisters played while the baby sat on a quilt in the shade. One of the boys was bringing out a little bag of corn to plant when he stopped, put the bag down on the ground, and went running. Sylvia and Rosie went running too, and the baby took his fist out of his mouth and stared.

A strange buggy was coming into the yard. It was the buggy from the depot in the village. The man who sold train tickets there, where Eddie often went to watch the train go by, was driving the buggy. A lady dressed in black rode like a queen on the seat behind the driver.

Eddie left the cup of garden peas and with the other children went to stare at the strange lady.

Papa came from the barn, and Mama from the house, and took the lady into the house, shutting the door in their faces. Eddie had a feeling then, as he waited on the porch, that something was changing in his life, and he was afraid. The lady had looked at him, only him, with those soul-less eyes, even as she'd reached down to pat Rosie's head.

HE HAD NEVER RIDDEN in a buggy. He had wanted to, but now his heart pounded, and he didn't want to get up on the buggy seat. He hung back, trying to become one of his family again.

The lady's eyes were so black. They seemed, beneath the shade of her black bonnet, to have no pupils.

His brothers and sisters hung back, silent Mama held the baby, and tears eased down her cheeks. She brushed them away with the back of one wrist. Papa patted Eddie's shoulder awkwardly, because Papa wasn't used to patting the shoulders of his children.

It had been barely an hour since Aunt Theodora had arrived, and already they were leaving. Eddie hadn't known he was going, too, until his papa had come out with a small bundle of clothes.

"It's better this way," Papa said to him, as they stood near the buggy.

The man from the train depot helped Aunt Theodora into the back seat. Her long skirt, gathered at her large, thick waist, swung behind her as she stepped upward. The buggy creaked with her weight, and sagged. She settled, a tall, large woman in black, her face shadowed by the long brim of her bonnet. The bonnet was heavily embroidered in black satin threads, as was the skirt of her garment. Black upon black. Her skin, in contrast, was like death.

Papa patted Eddie's shoulder again, and cleared his voice. There was a frog there, somewhere. Just as there was a knot in Eddie's throat. Though he felt like crying, his eyes were dry. They hurt and burned, instead.

"It's better this way," Papa said again. "Aunt Theodora is a very rich lady, and lives near a large city where there are special schools. She has promised to send you to one of them schools. You'll learn to read and write, and you'll be able to do great things. I told her you wasn't dumb, that you only had this affliction. It's better this way. Go now, listen to your great-aunt, always do what she says. She's going to send you to school, educate you." He cleared his throat again. "And then, someday, you come back and see us. If you want to."

Eddie climbed into the buggy to sit in front with the driver. He looked back once, but it was a mistake. He wanted, he *needed* to jump out of that buggy and run back. He had to finish planting the garden. He had to watch after his little sisters, and the baby, and the boys. They needed him. Didn't they know they needed him?

He needed them.

He saw her eyes again in his homeward glance, and her mouth that turned down, and he was so scared. Even though she smiled at him.

MANY TIMES he had stood still in the field waiting for the train to come into sight. The whistle wailed far beyond the trees like a big, wild wolf who knew he controlled his territory. Eddie always waited, his heart pounding with excitement. Then he'd hear the *chug, chug* on the rails, and he'd feel the ground quiver, then the long black engine would come huffing along, trailing behind it a plume of smoke. The engineer always waved, and so did the hobos who rode the freight cars, lying so leisurely on top, watching the world go by. In the passenger trains the people in the cars would look out at him and sometimes wave. When the train was gone, and the earth had stopped trembling, Eddie would sigh and go back to work. Someday, he promised himself, *someday*, he'd ride that train.

On this day when Aunt Theodora came, he rode the train. He sat in a passenger seat across from his aunt. He stared out the window, and he yearned for the field where he could watch the trains go by.

Inside, the train was different. He was in the bowels of a monster. It held him in. It gurgled as it churned him about. And across from him were the black eyes of the stranger that his Pa had said was his great-uncle's wife.

He had never seen the great-uncle, but it was known in the family that Uncle Emmett was the only member of the family to become rich. He had died long ago, perhaps before Eddie was born. He had never had any children. But he was talked about because he was the one to become successful, with a lumberyard and a lumber industry in a city a hundred or more miles away.

It was growing dark when the train entered the town whose name Aunt Theodora responded to. The conductor came down the aisle, holding to the tops of seats as the train swayed.

"Coming up," he said, "Deasville. Next stop, Deas-ville."

Aunt Theodora rose. "Come along, Edward."

They were the first words she had spoken to him during the long afternoon ride. Eddie got up and followed her as the train jogged to a halt. He could hear the steam huffing and blowing. He saw people rising. He was among those who walked down the little black stairway to the platform of the train depot, but the thrill he had always anticipated was not there. He wanted to turn and run back into the train, hide somewhere in a baggage car, perhaps. Somehow follow it home. But he followed Aunt Theodora as his papa had told him to do.

He saw the lights of a city glowing in the sky, and understood that Deasville was only a tiny arm of a much larger population. He felt drawn in, as if the glow were made of webs, sticky and perilous, sucking away his life, consuming him.

They rode in another hired hack. Two lanterns hung on the sides. Again, he rode up front with the driver. As soon as the horse was trotting away from the depot, down a cobbled road lined with trees, the driver looked at Eddie and said, "Well, young man, are you come to stay, or just a-visiting?"

Eddie opened his mouth and struggled to speak his one word, no, but nothing came out. So often, his throat closed against all efforts, and the blood veins in his temples bulged with the effort to speak.

Behind them, in the deep shadows of the buggy, Aunt Theodora said, "This is my late husband's great-nephew. He is unable to speak. He is called Eddie."

"Oh. Too bad he can't talk."

"Yes. He's going to be working for me."

Working, for Aunt Theodora? Eddie had understood she was going to send him to a special school somewhere, because his Pa had told her he wasn't dumb.

They rode down streets made of stone and brick, past stores closed for the night. They rode past a town square with large trees and a pale statue in the center near a bandstand, and turned right. Eddie saw lights in windows, and then the town was left behind and they were on a dark road with trees crowding the sides like beings from dark, unknown worlds. Eddie loved trees, but these seemed darker, taller. The only light came from the lanterns that hung rigid on each side of the buggy.

After a while the driver turned into a driveway that led even deeper into the trees. The horse walked slower. In a break in the trees to the left Eddie saw a dim light in a small window.

The driver said over his shoulder, "How're the Etchenses getting along, Miss Theodora?"

"They seem to be working out fine. Charlie cuts the grass, and Nellie does laundry, for rent. They both work for families in town, too. She takes in wash, or goes there to do their wash. They're a hardworking family, even to the children. Except, of course, for the youngest."

"I've seen Charlie around town cutting grass for folks, his boys helping. He swings that scythe like it was nothing.

"Yes, they're all good workers."

"Got quite a few young'uns?"

"The two boys, who work with Charlie, and the little girl. You can stop by the back porch, Bates."

Eddie saw they were passing the stone walls of a huge house. It seemed to go on and on, like a store building in town, except that occasionally there was a porch with railings. The windows were narrow and dark, catching the lantern lights like animal eyes.

Bates drew the horse to a stop with a pull on the reins and a soft "Whoa."

Eddie got down, clutching his possessions. One pair of overalls, one shirt, a pair of drawers, and one pair of shoes and socks that he wore only to church on Sundays. During the week he went barefoot. Mama had also added a comb, he had seen while he was still on the train—the comb Marybelle had gotten from Santa Claus at the church Christmas tree last winter.

Bates helped Aunt Theodora down. She paid him, and he asked if she wanted him to go ahead of her and light a lamp. She said no, and the driver left, turning the horse around in the dark area behind the house. Eddie watched him go.

No dogs barked, Eddie noticed. No cat came to rub against his legs.

"Come along, Edward," Aunt Theodora said, from somewhere in the darkness. Eddie heard her steps across a board porch.

She opened a door, as if she could see in the dark. He followed, as steps upward onto a porch became faintly visible in starlight

By the time he was walking blindly across the porch, a dim light rose. He saw an open door ahead of him.

He had never seen such a large kitchen. It was larger than the house where his family lived. On his left was a huge black cookstove, not a small one with four lids, like Mama's. This one even had shelves at the top, and the stovepipe didn't rise through the ceiling, it curved back into a stone chimney. At the opposite end of the room, against the outside wall, was a fireplace even bigger than the stove. In between were cabinets and cook counters.

In the center of the room was a large table, and on it several candles in holders. Near the fireplace was one rocking chair and a library table.

"You may eat," she said. "Wash your hands over there in the kitchen sink tonight. But after this, you go into the washroom there, through that door, to wash. You'll find a sink there, and running water from the faucet."

He had turned on faucets only in town once. But he knew how they worked. He washed. Even after all the long hours since breakfast, he wasn't hungry. His stomach felt as if it had shriveled to the size and consistency of a field rock.

He found a towel on a rack near the sink and dried carefully. When he turned he saw that Aunt Theodora was ladling out a bowl of stew from the large, black cast-iron cooking pot on the stove. She set the bowl of stew on the table and smiled at him. Her smiles were tight, as if they didn't touch her heart.

"There, now, you just eat all you want."

He sat down. She left the room, going through one of the many closed doors.

The stew was warm. The stove, he decided, was so huge it would hold heat all day. Or perhaps she had a maid who had kept the fire going. Or maybe it was Mr. or Mrs. Etchens, who lived in the little house in the woods across the driveway.

He forced the food down. Then took his dish to the sink and washed it.

"Come, and I'll show you to your room."

Eddie jumped. He hadn't heard her come back into the kitchen.

"Bring a candle," she said.

He chose a candle from the group on the table and followed behind her. They went into a long hall that was lighted at intervals with candles in wall brackets. Aunt Theodora opened a door on the right. She paused.

"The lighted hallway goes on to the foyer at the front. You won't need to use the front stairs, ever. These are the servant stairs. Come this way."

The hall beyond the door was narrow and unlighted. Along its way a stair rose on the left. It was long and steep, confined between two walls. He climbed. Ahead of him Aunt Theodora's long black skirt brushed the steps.

They came to a landing. It was like a room, with chairs and a table. Doors on the landing were closed. Stairs rose higher into the darkness.

They climbed another flight.

Finally, on the third floor, the stairs ended, and a hallway led straight off like a tunnel into darkness. Aunt Theodora opened the first door on the right.

It was a square room with a long, narrow window, a bed made of wood with a straw tick, and a small table at the bedside.

"This will be your room," she said. "Do not leave your room at night."

She unfolded two quilts that lay on the straw mattress and spread them one atop the other. There was no pillow.

"You will find a chamberpot beneath your bed. You can carry it out in the morning to empty it. I will knock once on your door when it's time to get up. At that time, you must go down to the kitchen and build a fire in the cookstove. Then you'll find wood in the backyard that needs to be split. There's a cow to milk, chickens and pigs to feed. Wood to cut for winter."

She closed the door.

Eddie stood still, the bundle of his belongings under his arm. There was a hook on the wall for his Sunday shirt. There too, he saw, was a washstand. Eddie placed the candle on the stand beside a water pitcher and washbowl, then he fell across the bed. He heard the crunch of straw in the mattress, a comforting and familiar sound. Some folks had feather mattresses, but in his house they were straw. He hadn't thought of it before, but it seemed strange that in this great mansion the mattresses were not feather. Of course, Aunt Theodora's mattress would be made of feathers.

He had a feeling her rooms were somewhere far away in the house.

He slept, exhausted, but he dreamed, and it seemed in his dreams he heard a wolf howling. But when he woke the howling was not in the woods, far beyond his window, but somewhere close.

It sounded as if it were a soft howl just beyond his closed door. He moved, sat up to lean on his elbow, and heard the straw whisper. A deep warning edged up his spine and into his hair.

He had never feared an animal howl before. He listened. No, it wasn't a howl, it was more a wail, soft and near and searching.

Afraid of its strangeness and its nearness, he eased between the quilts and covered his head. Silence came.

Twice during the night he went to the window. Once he saw stars in a patch of sky. The second time he saw a streak of the distant light of dawn. So beautiful, so welcome.

He hadn't gone back to sleep when the loud, hard knock sounded on his door. His heart leaped, and thundered in his throat. The food he had eaten last night quivered in his stomach.

He quickly got up, glad to leave the room that felt like a jail cell.

The candle had burned to a stub, and now, too late, he saw matches on the stand. Would Aunt Theodora be angry because he had let a candle burn all night and waste away?

His room was turning pink with the dawn.

He went downstairs, careful to remember the way. The candle stub trembled with its last light, but showed him the steps down. When at last he came to the kitchen he let out a long sigh of relief.

Candles still burned in the center of the kitchen table. He took one, found the washroom and the sink, and washed his face. With the comb he had put in his overalls bib pocket, he carefully combed his hair, but it sprang up again, coiling this way and that.

The box beside the big cookstove contained enough wood to get the fire going. He felt at home with this chore. He had built many fires for his mama, and also he had built fires in the church-house stove.

When the fire was steadily burning he went outside, going through the back door he had entered last night when he'd arrived, and across the long, wide porch. Vines grew on the porch posts and along the railings. Birds sang in the trees. The steps led down to a stone walk. Back toward a shed he saw the woodpile, the chopping block, the ax. He went toward it. Somewhere down in the barn a cow bawled.

It wasn't so scary today. Today the sounds were familiar. The bawl of the cow for her morning food, the bawl to be milked.

"Good morning," a small voice said importantly.

Eddie whirled.

A little girl, no older than his little sister Rosie, stood a few feet away. She was barefoot, wearing a dress that hung from her shoulders to her ankles, washed so many times it had faded to a dim pinkish-white. She had long, pale, almost white hair that hung in natural curls to her waist. One tube of silken-silver hair hung forward down her chest. Her eyes were the color of the sky above, dark blue, tinged with lavender. When she smiled dimples showed in her cheeks.

"My name is Katrina," she said clearly. "What's yours?"

CHAPTER 3

*E*ddie smiled at the little girl. Her presence pushed aside for a moment the feeling of being alone in a world that was no longer friendly. He responded as he had learned to with strangers who spoke to him. He touched his lips briefly, and struggled to speak his one word.

"No. No."

It came softly, and a frown dimpled briefly on her brow, then her eyes grew large and round.

He smiled again to reassure her, to keep her from running away in fright, as some children had done, as if he were the boogeyman they had been warned of. He squatted on one heel and with his hand smoothed a tablet in the dirt beneath the wood chips. With one finger he wrote, *E D D...*

Then he looked at Katrina and remembered: she probably hadn't been to school yet and didn't know what he was trying to write. He had learned from his brother how to write his name, with his finger, in the dirt. Alone, he had practiced. He hadn't written yet with a pencil. His parents had bought him one pencil the day they'd taken him to school for the first and only time, when he was six. The teacher had sent the family away, saying she could not teach a child like him. So the pencil was put away for Harry to use the next year, when he would start school.

Deadly sober, Katrina stared at Eddie, her eyes rounded and following his every move. Eddie's smile wavered. He was suddenly afraid she would run away and become lost in the mists that rose from the forests. It was a sudden, dark, hurting thought, like a premonition. He took a deep breath, and finished writing his name. *E D D I E.*

"Katrina!"

Eddie jumped to his feet. Aunt Theodora stood on the porch, a shadowy figure darkened by the thick vines that grew on the posts. She came on down, her heels tapping on the stone walk. She was carrying a milk bucket in her left hand.

"What are you doing out so early, dear?"

She put her right hand on Katrina's hair and brushed downward in a stroking manner. The way one strokes a fine piece of material, Eddie thought. But her smile toward Katrina brought one in return. Katrina no longer looked as if she were ready to run away.

"I don't know what his name is." She pointed at Eddie.

Eddie brushed his hands down the rough fabric of his overalls.

Still smiling, bending slightly over the little girl, Aunt Theodora said, "His name is Edward. But he can't talk to you."

"Why not?"

"Because ... he can't speak. He doesn't know how to talk."

"Why?"

"Because God made him that way, just like he made you a nosy little girl who should be home in bed yet. Now, run along. Go home where you belong."

"Can I come back later?"

"Later, maybe. But don't bother Edward. He has work to do."

"What's he going to do?"

"He's going out now to milk the cow, and feed the animals, then he's going to split wood and put it in the woodbox by the stove. Then he's going to the woods to cut winter wood."

Katrina ran, going beneath the tall trees that edged the driveway. She ducked through the shrubs and trees limbs, and ran on toward the small shack where Eddie had seen the light in the window.

In front of the shack was a long yard planted with vegetables. A couple of young boys worked there, hoeing. Eddie hadn't seen them before. They were half hidden beyond the trees. Now he heard an occasional *ping* as a hoe struck a rock. Before Katrina reached the yard, a man came out the front door, and the two boys dropped their hoes. Together the three went toward the road, toward town, and Katrina disappeared somewhere near the shack.

"That's Mr. Etchens and his two sons. They'll be working in town all day, probably. The boys are very good workers for tykes only nine and ten years old." Aunt Theodora handed Eddie the pail. She was not wearing the long black dress today. Instead she was dressed much like Eddie's own mother, in a print dress with a long, bibbed print apron covering most of the front. The two large pockets were outlined with the same narrow tape as the rest of the apron.

"I'll tell you your chores, Edward. You'll be expected to do them night and morning. When you milk the cow, give her one cup of grain in the manger.

You'll find the cup in the sack of feed. Give the pigs each two cups mixed into a bucket of water. The cracked corn is for the chickens. Turn the cow out to pasture, behind the barn. In the evening, of course, you'll have to get the cow in and milk her, and bring me the milk. Always, of course, bring in the milk. Do you understand?"

She spoke to him slowly and clearly, as if he were also deaf. Perhaps, too, as if he were incapable of understanding. He nodded, and reached out his hand for the milk bucket. He still felt a need to avoid her eyes, though she seemed more human today, less frightening.

"When you have finished the barnyard chores, come to the house and sweep the porches. Leaves fall, even in spring. Then you must cut wood. Take the ax and go into the woods and cut up the trees that are already fallen, the ones you can handle. Keep plenty of wood split for the cookstove. Keep the fires built. You may come in and eat three times a day. Do you understand?"

Eddie nodded.

"After you have milked the cow, bring the milk in and you can eat breakfast. And when the little girl comes over, shoo her home."

Eddie nodded.

Aunt Theodora went back toward the house, her thick leather heels clunking on the stone walk and the wooden floor of the porch.

Eddie drew a long, deep breath. The smothering in his chest eased away. With the bucket in his hand, he went toward the barn.

This was a familiar chore, and he was comfortable with it. He looked for a vegetable garden where he could work, the way he had at home, but saw none other than the neighbors' garden.

He passed the long shed where the driveway made a circle back upon itself. A buggy took up one section of the shed. Behind the shed, beyond trees tall and spreading, was a hip-roofed red barn. Behind the barn was a pasture no larger than an acre. A gray horse grazed contentedly.

A trail, not of stone and brick, but like twin paths through the grass, branched off from the driveway and went past the barn, angling off into the forest trees.

Eddie stopped and stared in awe. A strange and wonderful feeling came over him of ... enchantment? It was like looking into the lands in the fairy tales his school-aged brother and sister had read to him. He had a sudden longing to walk that road forever, for it never to end ...

"Hi!" a small voice said.

He looked around. Katrina had climbed the board fence in the barn lot and was hanging over the top board on her stomach.

Eddie laughed. He motioned toward her house, and gave a sweeping motion with his free hand. *Go home. You're supposed to go home.* But still he was delighted.

"That road," she said, "leads to a magic land, but you're not supposed to go there."

Eddie looked at the road, looked at Katrina, and raised his eyebrows questioningly. How strange, he thought, that she had called it a magic land, just after he had thought in his heart it led to a land of enchantment. Had someone read fairy stories to her?

"Miss Theodora told me so. She said, don't ever follow that road. Because if you do, you will never be able to come back."

Eddie watched her. The way her lips pursed, like a baby's, like his little brother Bobby's. The way the dimple came and went in her cheeks. And the way her eyes were so serious. He nodded to encourage her to talk more.

"But my papa says that's nonsense. It was made by the logging wagons, and it really goes to a meadow on the hill, and to the woods on the other side. A nice hill with a big shade tree, and a bluff on the other side where you can stand and look out over the countryside. He's going to take me there someday." She paused, her eyes following the road. "But I'm afraid to go because I might never come back."

She sighed deeply and climbed down from the fence.

"The cow's in here." She fumbled at a latch on a gate in the stockade fence. "And the mare, Miss Gray, is in the pasture. She just gets a cup of corn in the evenings, because it's springtime now and the grass is growing. You turn the cow out to be with her. There's a branch where they drink water. You have to carry water to the pigs."

Eddie reached over her and opened the gate. She scooted through beneath his arm and skipped and danced into the barn lot.

"Here, piggy ... here, piggy," she sang.

Three pigs, black-and-white Poland China, came from behind a trough to meet her, grunting, wiggling their curly little tails like dogs. Katrina scratched them, one then the next, and all three flopped over onto their backs, grunting for more. Eddie went to join her. He felt an added warmth in his surroundings. He'd once had a pet pig. A little runt, given to him by a neighbor. It was so tiny it fit in the palms of Eddie's cupped hands. He wished he could tell Katrina about it, about how his memories of it were both very happy and very sad.

He had raised it on a bottle, feeding it milk like a baby. It slept by his bed, and followed him wherever he went. It was with a broken heart that Eddie heard it had to die. It was going to be used for food, for the family. Eddie cried, hard and long, that day in the winter three years ago. *Why?* he had struggled to ask. *We have vegetables from the garden, beans, corn, peas, potatoes, enough to feed us until next year. We have apples from the orchard. Why does my pig have to be killed?*

Papa had left Eddie alone with the pig that had grown large and was ready to be butchered, to feed him one last apple. Wee Willie Winkle, Eddie had named him in his own mind. After the boy in the fairy tale. Wee Willie crunched trustingly on the apple. Juice dripped off his lower lip.

Then Papa let Eddie go behind the barn and cover his head, so he wouldn't hear so clearly the screams of the pig when it was killed. Still he heard Wee Willie Winkle's cries of fear and terror, then, and even now.

In his heart Eddie still felt the betrayal. Wee Willie had looked to him for everything, for love, for food, for life. And Eddie had let him down. He hadn't meant to, but he had. He had never thought he would have to, but he had. After Wee Willie, he had vowed never to love another pig, never to allow it to love and trust him. Because if the pig trusted him, it would trust every human. And one of them, somewhere, would kill it.

He had never been able to eat the bacon that had come from his pet pig.

Nor could he ever eat another apple.

He wanted to tell Katrina about Wee Willie Winkle, but the only sound that came from his throat was a soft "No, no," as he bent beside her to scratch the bellies of the pigs. He wanted desperately to tell Katrina these three pigs all looked just like his own, with the white stripe around the neck like a fancy collar.

The cow bawled, and Eddie remembered he had to milk her. He rose. Katrina ran ahead of him to a door in the side of the barn. The pigs came running behind, squealing for more attention.

They stepped over a threshold into a cool interior where the cow waited. She was a pretty little yellow Jersey with a white star on her dished face. She had big, soft brown eyes and lashes that curved out and up to protect them. She also had a big udder, tight with milk. She had entered from an open door on the left, Eddie saw, where pasture grass was green and lush. The cow lifted her nose and mooed softly as if questioning Eddie's presence.

Katrina rubbed the cow's face and ears, then ran to the manger and climbed up, pointing over.

"There's the feed. If we don't feed the pigs first, they'll lie down against the door. There's the cow feed, too. And the chicken feed. I'll help you. I'll show you the way Miss Theodora does it. The way she likes it done."

Aunt Theodora, that rich lady who lived in a house as big or bigger than a county courthouse, did the chores herself sometimes? Eddie wished he could ask.

"If you want it done right," Katrina said, as if she were trying to sound like someone old and wise, "you have to do it yourself. Miss Theodora says so. Or get yourself a right-handed man."

She looked up with her head tipped. "Are you her right-handed man? My papa is sometimes. He cuts her yard grass just the way she wants it cut. She gives us our house to live in because she likes the way he cuts her grass. And my mama washes and irons Miss Theodora's aprons and dresses just the way she likes, too."

Katrina ran around trying to help, showing him where the feed went, pausing at Eddie's side to watch the pigs and chickens eat.

Just as he pulled the stool beneath the cow and started to milk, he heard Aunt Theodora's voice in the barn lot, ordering Katrina home. Her voice grew faint and distant, as if she were leading Katrina away.

When Aunt Theodora came into the barn, she was alone.

"That child," she said with a soft chuckle. "Send her home, turn around twice, and there she is again. Into everything. Curious about everything."

With a basket she went on to gather eggs, then with the basket over her arm she went back to the house.

Eddie milked, surprised that a rich lady like Aunt Theodora would work, gather her own eggs, and feed her own chickens.

He turned the cow out into the pasture behind the barn and carried the full bucket of milk into the kitchen. When he crossed the porch, he smelled the food.

"Just put the milk bucket on the counter, Edward. Then wash and sit down and eat. Then go out and gather up the wood for morning."

Yes, thought Eddie, perhaps I am Miss Theodora's new handyman.

Awkward and embarrassed, Eddie washed his face and hands in the washroom sink. He sat alone at the large table. A glass of milk stood by a fork and a knife. From the stove she brought him a plate with a biscuit, two eggs, and a strip of bacon.

He ate the biscuits and eggs, but pushed the bacon aside. A nervous quiver crossed his shoulders and gripped his throat. Would she be angry and demand he clean his plate? Or would she not notice? He looked for a slop bucket behind the stove in which to scrape out his plate and saw none.

She noticed, and asked, "Why didn't you eat the bacon, Edward? Don't you like bacon?"

The word came as if speaking were natural and easy for him. "No, no."

She looked at him, startled, for just a moment. "You can talk?"

"No, no," he said again, his throat tightening, the single word feeling as if it were a fist clogging his windpipe. He gulped.

"Oh, yes," she said. "I recall your mother saying something about your ability to make a few sounds. She voiced some kind of hope that perhaps a doctor could help you, opening something up, or something to that effect. Which, of course, is ridiculous. Here, I'll take the plate. You may go do your work now."

Eddie was relieved to be out of the house again. He found the ax, and split the wood already in the woodpile. Katrina came and went like a little mouse, peeping in, peeping out.

She led the way into the forest to the nearest fallen tree, and returned with him to the shed, where she pointed out the woodcutter's tools. Then, crying happily, "Here comes my mama home! I have to go now!" She skipped away to meet the thin woman that walked the path from the road.

Eddie gathered up a saw, a wedge, and two axes. Carrying them, he returned to the fallen tree and began work.

The sound of the ax and the saw filled his ears. He could imagine the sounds ringing through the depths of an old forest, long and deep, where nothing lived to hear but the animals and the birds. Though his arms were thin, with only the measliest of muscles, nothing like Papa's, still, they were strong. The work did not tire him.

He worked till sundown, until during a pause he heard the Jersey cow bawl for food and relief in her aching udder, now again filled with milk.

Reluctantly he carried the woodcutter's tools back to the woodshed and went to do the chores.

Again he ate alone, while Aunt Theodora peeled a large bowl of fresh vegetables and dropped them into the black cookpot on the stove. Heat radiated out from the stove as she fed the firebox more of the wood he had carried in.

Though she seemed never to look at him, she knew the minute he stopped eating.

"Take one candle," she said. "Remember to go down the first hallway that branches to the right, and up the back service stairs."

With a candle in his hand, he went into the hall where the service stairs rose between two walls, and climbed to his room on the third floor. He discovered that his window looked out over the peaked rooflines, and over some of the trees that grew close to the house. He had a view of the sky and the stars, and tonight, his second night in the house, the moon hanging fat and bright in the west.

He sat on his bed, sleepless, and watched the moon inch downward through the trees, its light split and scattered by branches and leaves. He didn't know what time it was. Dark, but not late. Aunt Theodora, he thought, must be expecting company. He didn't know what she was cooking in the pot on the stove, but it must have been a great lot of food, for a great lot of people.

He wished for a book, and the ability to read. He wished for paper and pen so he could write. Write a letter to his family, and tell them of the little road he saw, the enchanted road that if you walked it you would never come back. Perhaps heaven was at its end. He'd tell them of the little girl, who was about Rosie's size and age, and every bit as pretty as Rosie, though Katrina's hair was pale, not dark like Rosie's.

He'd tell them about the pigs, Wee Willie Winkle come back to live again, tripled. As if every time something died or was killed, three came to take its place.

He'd tell them how every time he felt as if he would collapse to the ground and start crying for loneliness, Katrina would appear, peeping out at him from somewhere and saying, "Hi." It didn't seem to bother her that he couldn't answer. She talked anyway, and told him all about everything. Where the pig and cow feed was. Where to cut wood. How Aunt Theodora wanted him to stack the wood he split, *after* he had filled the woodbox behind the big kitchen stove.

"Make sure you *always* keep the woodbox filled," Katrina told him at one point, leaning close in conspiracy, lowering her voice. "You see, the last boy Miss Theodora had here didn't keep it filled well, and she only kept him a week. Then—he was gone."

She motioned upward with her hands and hunched her shoulder in a little shrug.

"My papa wondered where he'd gone. He said he reckoned he must have left in the middle of the night. When it was dark."

Eddie blinked at her, picking up on her alarm, yet feeling some hope rising in his heart. Only a week? Then she sent him home? His lips moved, but he couldn't ask. Katrina seemed almost to read his mind.

Still in a low whisper, she said, "I don't know what happened to him. My pa wondered. He just disappeared. One day he was here, and the next he was gone. I asked her where Johnny was, but she didn't tell me. She just gave me a sweet from her pocket." She paused, frowning as if in deep thought. "Sometimes she carries sweets in her apron pocket."

She threw a glance behind her and said, "I think the Bad Things got him!"

Then she had run home, and Eddie hadn't seen her since. He didn't know what she meant by bad things, unless she meant sprites and goblins and elves, and things of that nature that old fairy tales talk of and small children might believe.

So, he'd tell his family, if he could write, that maybe he'd get to come home in a week.

The bed on which he sat had been crudely made from pine. On the frame was a straw tick, and on that two quilts, one for the bottom, and one to cover. There was no pillow. The bed sagged in the middle. The wash-stand, in strange, ornate contrast, was of dark, fancy-carved wood with delicate legs and a marble top, like other furniture he had seen in the house. The pitcher and washbowl had fluted edges and thin touches of gold among green vining leaves and tiny blue flowers. Aunt Theodora had filled the water pitcher sometime during the day.

Eddie drank a glass of water, then took off his overalls and hung them over the bedpost. He blew out the candle and lay down on the bed, hearing the crackle of the straw beneath him, feeling its uneasy surface. He squirmed to get comfortable, to find a place where straw ends didn't stick like needles through the ticking and the quilt.

He was not so afraid of Aunt Theodora today.

Maybe it was because of her treatment of Katrina, which seemed loving and kind. And yet ...

... And yet there was something about the way she had stroked Katrina's hair that ...

... Gave him a different kind of fear. A deep, swelling dread.

For Katrina.

CHAPTER 4

*W*ith his hands cradling his cheek he fell asleep, and dreamed of strange landscapes and shadowy figures that held a vague danger. He woke, thinking he heard voices, not voices that spoke a language, but voices that cried like wind through deep, dark caves, sounds not human nor animal.

He rolled over and slept again, and dreamed of strange movements in a long, dark tunnel. He woke, his heart pounding, smothering, his breath trapped. He sat up. Somewhere beyond the crackle of the straw tick beneath him was the sound of something rubbing against the wall, of a presence sensed. And a warning. *Do not leave your room at night.*

His lungs swelled with his trapped breath. The sounds were real, not part of his wild, disturbed dreams. He listened in the dark, glad he had blown out his candle, yet wishing for light, blinded by the darkness. Something was in the hall outside his door. It touched the door, causing the door to rattle on its hinges. Then it moved on, a strange and frightening sound of smooth heaviness slipping past the wood of the door.

It came back again, and the door rattled. The knob moved just a bit, as if pushed by something other than hands. The dim nether-light of the moon made the white doorknob gleam like a round, white eyeball staring at him in the dark room.

Another sound came in the silence, one he recognized instantly—three quick, inward breaths. Sniffing.

Something sniffing the crack beneath his door, like an animal. He visualized large dogs, or even wolves. Yet there was no padding sound, no footsteps. Only the strange sliding, as if the thing crawled on its belly. He felt more threatened than he ever had in his life, with only the thin door for protection.

Do not leave your room at night.

Did Aunt Theodora know there was something that roamed her house at night? Or was he only having waking nightmares?

Then, suddenly from somewhere distant in the house came a call. No distinct, spoken word, but an *"Oooie,"* strangely soft but echoing, as if it came from a deep well, or a cave. The call, more than the sound in the hallway, sent a frenzy of trembling over Eddie's body.

The long, soft rubbing against the door moved away and along the hall, down the stairs, and left silence behind. Whatever it was had not walked like a dog. It had made no sound of footsteps.

After a long while Eddie lay down. He stared at the doorknob until it was only a blur that lulled him with its stillness. The moonlight slipped away and the doorknob disappeared in the dark. Nothing crawled against his door, or sniffed at the crack, or lifted its head and made that strange, ungodly wail.

It was a dream, he told himself. Just another part of his bad dreams since he had come to this house.

DURING THE DEEPEST of his fitful sleep he was brought suddenly and heart-crashingly awake by a single loud knock. He sat up, desperately trying to orient himself. Then he heard her voice.

"Edward! Time to get up."

The voice seemed to come from all around him. He blinked at the pale rectangle of the window and immediately swung his feet to the floor. He ran his hands through his hair to erase the unruliness of tossing back and forth on his straw tick all night. He felt for the matches he had left beside the candle and struck a light. He touched it to the blackened, curled wick on the candle. A tiny flame rose and glowed and opened up his room.

Never again, he promised himself, would he put out his candle at night, though he might always think about the waste. Never again, until he got used to the sounds here in Aunt Theodora's great, large house, would he sleep in the dark.

He pulled on his overalls, and stepped out into the dark hall, the tiny flame of the candle making a dim path of light near his feet.

Something small and dark lay on the floor just outside his door.

He bent slowly and picked it up. It crumbled in his fingers. A lump of clay. Still damp on the inside, but drying. The kind of mud that came from a cave.

Then it wasn't a dream. He brushed the mud crumbs into a small ball and stuffed it deeply into his pocket. He would look at it later, in better light. He was sure it wasn't black soil from the surface of the earth, but red clay from underground.

When he reached the downstairs, a faint pink was lighting the sky in the east. He took a deep breath of the new dawn, thankful night had ended. He wished he would never have to spend another night in his room. The thought that he must made him feel like crying, and so he pushed it away. His Pa would not approve of him breaking down like a baby.

He went into the kitchen to fetch the milk bucket, relieved to see Aunt Theodora was not there. She had left candles burning on the table. The stove had grown cold, and he built a new fire before he left to do the chores.

He looked for Katrina to join him at the barn, but she didn't. He fed the pigs and scratched their bellies. He turned the cow out into her pasture behind the barn. He did all the chores carefully, taking his time, dreading to return to the house. Dreading the day to pass away and night to come again.

He learned he would never sleep easily and deeply in this house. This huge house made of stone and steep rooflines, and thick walls. Of many, many hallways and stairways and rooms he only glimpsed. Of corridors and stairs from which he swept those strange bits of red clay.

Each morning, after the chores were finished, he swept the porches. So many porches it took him a while to remember them all. Little porches tucked in where a door was almost hidden back in the shadows beneath the roof, darkened by trees that grew close on the east side of the house. How, he wondered as he swept, did they get so dirty? Woodland trash and debris littered the porch floors as if things were dragged in from the woods at night.

But the most disturbing was the red clay inside the house. Who—what— tracked it in? There must be a cellar in the house, though he hadn't seen it. Whatever it was must be kept there during the day and released at night. By Aunt Theodora.

Do not leave your room at night.

Eddie snorted inside his head. *Don't worry,* he wished he could say to her. I ain't about to.

Strange, sickening smells filled the kitchen each morning, and bubbled at night in the large, black cast-iron pot on the stove.

Aunt Theodora never fed him from that pot. For him she cooked eggs, and biscuits, and gave him jam in a small bowl. And large glasses of milk, saying, "Milk makes boys grow tall and strong." As if she really cared.

In the evening, he sat uneasily trying to eat what she had prepared for him.

Potatoes, green beans, bread. Some kind of meat cooked hard and tough and damp. Perhaps, he thought as he looked at it, it had come from the strange pot on the stove after all. In the silence of the room he could hear the soft blurp, blurp as it slowly boiled.

He tried to ignore the smell as he ate potatoes and hot bread with butter.

Sometimes she came to sit at the table with a cup of coffee which she poured into the saucer in small dribbles and then daintily sipped. She never talked to him, but sat staring beyond, or at the wall, or somewhere.

The candles burning in the middle of the table shot beams of dim, wavering light onto her face, making her cheekbones look sharp, and her nose long and pointed. Her dark hair gleamed, and in profile the lumps of her braid took on little red lights, as if a fire burned somewhere beyond her.

Fear clogged Eddie's throat. Homesickness made him ill.

And the smell of the stuff bubbling on the stove upset his stomach.

NEAR THE END of the first week in his new home, a distant, metallic sound made him jump. Aunt Theodore put down the large rag with which she had been wiping a counter, smoothed her apron, and left the room, walking briskly. Eddie sat tense and still. Several silent moments passed. He became aware of a ticking sound and turned his head. On the mantel above the large fireplace at the end of the room a tall old clock sat, its pendulum swinging slowly back and forth, back and forth. The ticking came each time the pendulum reached its apex and swung in reverse. He watched it. Then his gaze slid to the fireplace below the mantel. There was no fire on the hearth. The weather was too warm. The inside was like a black cave. A hook hung down from somewhere within, black and empty. The black pot on the stove, he thought, was the pot that would hang in the fireplace when cold weather came again.

"Edward."

Eddie jerked around. Aunt Theodora stood in the open door to the front hall.

"Come, Edward. I have someone for you to meet."

Eddie got up and followed his great-aunt. For the first time he went down the hall that led to the front of the house. Brackets that looked like they were made of gold were spaced at intervals along the hall, and new candles burned in them. The smell of candle wax was heavy in the long, narrow hallway with the high ceiling where darkness lived always.

They came to a large entry. A wide stairway took up the middle, with fat newel posts and carved banisters. It rose to a landing that was like a furnished room, then turned and rose higher to a balcony overhead. That, too, was lighted dimly by candles in wall brackets. Their tiny, glowing flames reflected in the sleek wood of the banister. This part of the house was much nicer than

28

all the rest that Eddie had seen. Here, the polished wood floor was like dark satin.

"This way, Edward."

Aunt Theodora's tone was faintly critical. Eddie turned quickly away from staring upward toward the mysterious second floor.

He followed her through a door.

It was a parlor, with the finest furniture Eddie had ever seen. Even in the store windows in town he had never seen such a fine sofa, with polished wood all along the edges of the back, outlining each cushion, and down each arm to the floor. The material looked like satin. His mama, he thought suddenly, would never have a sofa like that. Unless he could somehow manage to earn it for her.

On the other side of the large room was movement that Eddie saw from the corner of his eye. He turned.

A man in a black suit stood in front of a chair. He wore a closely buttoned vest, a white collar. He held a Bible in his left hand. He came forward, his right hand extended.

Eddie put out his hand. The grip of the stranger's hand was dry and cold. His eyes held an accusing slant that made Eddie drop his own gaze. A preacher, Eddie thought immediately.

"Edward," Aunt Theodora said, "This is Reverend Cheney. Reverend Cheney, Edward cannot speak, as I told you before. But he understands most instructions."

"I'm sure he does. How are you, my boy? How blessed you are to have an aunt like Miss Theodora. She has helped many unfortunate children like yourself. Now, you'll be sure to come to our church and Sunday school, won't you?"

Edward nodded eagerly, looking up. Sunday school? Church? A chance to go somewhere besides into the woods to cut firewood? His life would not be so confined after all. There would be church, and Sunday school. He nodded eagerly again, and smiled at the reverend, and looked at the pleasant wrinkles of a face that had been living as long as, or perhaps even longer than, Aunt Theodora.

"You may go back to your supper now, Edward," Aunt Theodora said, as the reverend resumed his seat on the high-backed chair and balanced the Bible precisely on both long hands.

Eddie nodded again and backed toward the door. He turned. As he went into the hall he heard Aunt Theodora add, "When you have finished your supper, go on up to bed. Dawn comes early these days."

"Ah, yes," said the preacher. "With the singing of the birds, the sky turns pink, and our good Lord gives us another day."

... *with the singing of the birds*. Eddie went down the long hall, their voices fading away to silence behind him. In the kitchen he stood looking down at the plate of food he hadn't finished eating and thought of something. The only birds he remembered hearing since he had come to Aunt Theodora's were crows.

Tomorrow, he told himself, he would notice.

At home, many birds sang.

Why, here, were there only crows?

At the end of the stove on the floor sat a large slop bucket. Scraps of peeling, of leftovers, were put into the bucket and fed to the pigs each morning. Eddie carried his plate to the bucket, paused, and listened. There were no footsteps in the hall outside the kitchen door. Hurriedly he scraped the large chunk of strange meat into the slop bucket.

He washed his plate and put it away. Then, in the laundry room, he took what his mama had always called a sponge bath. With a cloth he bathed as well as he could without removing his overalls.

As he did every night, he took a fresh candle from the table and went up the back stairs to his room on the third floor.

Lying on his bed, he watched the pale, flickering lights of the candle. It was like a race, where one tongue of light raced a shadow up the wall, trying to reach the ceiling. Always it failed, and fell back only to try again, racing, racing, struggling, struggling, to reach the distant ceiling.

Eddie listened. At home this time of year the whippoorwills sang, their voices loud and clear in the distance. This time of year the frogs in the pond peeped. But Eddie heard nothing beyond the creak of a board somewhere in the house, and the brush of tree limbs against the side of the house.

LIKE THE BLACK *eyes of something he had seen in the swamp once.*

A reptile he hadn't recognized.

It had lifted its head from the dark mixture of water, leaves, and vines, and looked at him with dark, cold, unblinking eyes before he had run away.

That was what Aunt Theodora's eyes were like.

He frowned.

Why had he thought of that? What would the preacher say if he knew the evil thoughts that were coming to Eddie's mind lately?

More came. Unbidden.

Not lizard eyes, nor even a snake's, but something as old as Satan himself. That was what Aunt Theodora's eyes were like.

"No, no," Eddie said softly aloud. "No, no."

He slipped out of bed and onto his knees. He closed his eyes and put his palms together beneath his chin.

Our Father, who are in Heaven … forgive me my evil thoughts.

Aunt Theodora is giving me a home, he thought, pushing away his doubts. She is going to send me to a special school.

He murmured in silence, his lips moving, his eyes closed. "Bless all my loved ones at home, bless Katrina and her family, bless the animals at the mercy of cruel people, and bless Aunt Theodora."

CHAPTER 5

*K*atrina climbed the long, curved staircase. It had been a busy morning, the kind she liked best. She had hung over the fence and watched Edward feed the pigs. She had gone into the barn where he was milking the cow and he had squirted warm milk in her mouth, right out of the cow's teat. Both of them had laughed and laughed as the milk ran down her chin and dampened the collar of her dress. Then, he had let her help him scatter corn on the ground for the chickens and turn the cow out into the pasture behind the barn, where dandelions grew like little round suns.

"Are these baby suns?" she had asked him, picking one, forgetting that he couldn't answer in words, like other people. But he had smiled and motioned with his hands, palms up. Then he peered through the treetops at the sun and nodded his head, his mouth making a round shape, then a longer one. She understood. *Why not?* he had said to her, without speaking.

She was glad Edward had come to live with Miss Theodora. It wasn't so lonesome now. With her papa and brothers gone all day, and lots of time, like today, her mama gone, too, it was nice that Edward was here. She had left him cutting wood. Chips had flown, and he had motioned her to stand farther away. So finally she'd come into the house to see Miss Theodora.

Miss Theodora wasn't in the kitchen, where she so often sat in her big wood rocking chair near the fireplace, even when there was no fire. Where she sat and sewed or tatted or embroidered. Her basket was there, with her embroidery hoop stretched tight over a piece of white material on which she was making strange shapes in colors brown, black, and dark red. Katrina hadn't touched it, she'd only looked.

Nor was Miss Theodora in the parlor.

Katrina didn't call out as she climbed the staircase. A few times before she had called for Miss Theodora, and she had heard strange, repeated answers that didn't sound like Miss Theodora, but like herself, like many of herselves, answering on and on, farther and farther away. It had scared her, but then, Miss Theodora had said they were only echoes. Only her own call coming back from different walls, different rooms. Nevertheless, Katrina no longer called or shouted, or raised her voice when she was climbing the stairs.

She stood a moment on the landing of the second floor. A hallway crossed, like the cross on which Jesus had died. One of the halls went straight through toward the back of the house, but Katrina knew that it came to a landing, and went down to the lower floor, and up to the third floor. Many doors closed off rooms, but Katrina had seen most of them. Alone, she had peeked in, many times before, looking for Miss Theodora. Looking, too, to see what was in the room.

She turned left now, and knocked on the door to Miss Theodora's sitting room. The room that joined the big bedroom where Miss Theodora slept.

Katrina heard a sound, a soft murmur that might have been the winds in the walls or Miss Theodora saying, "Come in."

Katrina opened the door, heard the long squeak of the hinges, and crossed the threshold. The room was empty. Miss Theodora was not sitting in the pretty chair by the window where she sometimes rested. She was not at the organ against the wall where she had played music for Katrina in times before.

The door to Miss Theodora's bedroom was closed. It was a dark, heavy reminder that she should not enter unless she was invited. Of course, there were many doors in the house that were dark and closed and which Katrina was not supposed to open, but she liked very much to see what was beyond the doors. Most of the time she found only a bed, a dresser, maybe, or a wardrobe, with the bedspread covering only a tick, and no sheets or quilts. Beds that stood on legs, high off the floor, so high she could sit under them. Not like the wood frame beds on the ground in her house. So many beds, so many rooms. Rooms that no one ever came to stay in.

"Why," Katrina heard Papa say to Mama last year, when they'd first come to live in the shed that belonged to Miss Theodora, "Why would anyone want such a big house? And no children to fill those rooms?"

From her place against the wall, in her parents' bed, Katrina sleepily heard her mother laugh. "Lord-a-mercy, Charlie, enough children to fill that house would make it an orphanage, not a home."

An orphanage. What was an orphanage? When she had thought to ask her mother, Nellie had said, "Run along, sweetheart, Mama has work to do. But don't bother Miss Theodora!"

Many weeks later Katrina had remembered and asked Miss Theodora, as she'd stood at her knee and watched the tiny stitches the lady's long, thin fingers were putting in the material stretched tight in the embroidery hoop. "What's an orphanage?"

"An orphanage is a place where many children live. Children who don't have a mother and father."

"Who don't have a mother and father!" Katrina cried. "But why don't they have a mother and father?"

"Many reasons. Usually death."

"Death."

It sounded very bad, whatever it was. Oh yes, cows died, when they were turned into meat for the table. Chickens died when they had their heads cut or wrung from their bodies, so they could be eaten. Did the parents of some children die the same way?

"Haven't you ever been to a funeral?" Miss Theodora asked, in answer to her many questions.

"A funeral?"

"Good Lord, child, run along. You're making me stick my own fingers. Go play somewhere."

It was that day, as she'd roamed through the house, that she'd found the doll. The beautiful, beautiful doll that sat on the dresser, in front of the mirror with the gold frame. The mirror showed Katrina the back of the doll, the long hair, that looked as real as Katrina's own hair, but which was dark, like Miss Theodora's. The hair hung down the doll's back, and touched the dresser scarf on which it sat. The scarf stretched across the dark, glossy top of the dresser and hung off each end, embroidered with dainty figures and many colors. Something Miss Theodora must have made just for the doll to sit on.

It had such a pretty face that Katrina stood and stared at it that day. And many times afterward. And now.

She stood on the rug that covered the middle of Miss Theodora's upstairs sitting room and stared at the face of the doll. Sometimes, she found the doll was dressed in a different dress. Today the dress was different. Instead of the white-and-blue dress of the last time Katrina had stood and admired the doll, it was wearing a long, dark gown with strange figures embroidered along the bottom, and around the high waist. The dark material of the gown made the cheeks of the doll look like the pale pink roses that bloomed at the side of the shed, and her forehead was white as the daisies out at the roadside.

Katrina went forward. The doll smiled down at her. Katrina's hands reached up. At night sometimes she dreamed that Miss Theodora gave her the doll. "Here, child," she would say. "She wants you to have her. She asked me if she could go live with you and be your doll."

Katrina stood on tiptoe against the front of the dresser. For the first time her hands touched the doll. She had very carefully touched the doll's dress before, other dresses, but never the body of the doll. Beneath her fingers she felt a soft body, like a real body of a real person. She pulled it forward.

It toppled suddenly, unexpectedly heavy, its arms and head falling toward her. Katrina grabbed at it, her arms encircling the doll, its carved face with the small nose and the long eyelashes coming to rest on her shoulder. She hugged it tightly, her heart pounding. What if it had fallen to the floor and broken its face?

"Katrina!"

Katrina gasped and whirled, the doll tight in her arms, its hands slipping down her arms as if caressing her.

Miss Theodora stood in the doorway of the bedroom.

"Haven't I told you never to touch that doll!"

She had never before spoken to Katrina with so angry a voice. She crossed the room and pulled the doll from Katrina's arms. She smoothed the gown down. It was so long it covered the doll's black, buttoned shoes.

"Don't you ever touch this doll again, Katrina! Don't come into this room again unless I'm here."

Katrina's chin had begun to quiver. Her hands shook, her whole body shook with the tears she tried so hard to hold back. She stared up through the tears at Miss Theodora's face.

"You could break her," Miss Theodora said more gently, as she smoothed the hair back from the smiling face of the doll. "You see, her head, her arms, and the lower part of her legs are made of china, and if you dropped her, she would break. Also, you must learn that you are never to touch anything that does not belong to you. Do you understand?"

Miss Theodora's face was suddenly in front of her, and Katrina could no longer keep the tears from overflowing. She ran, out the door, into the hall.

"Katrina," Miss Theodora called. "Child ..."

But Katrina ran on. Blinded by her tears, she searched for a door that would let her out of the house. She found an open door, and stairs set between two walls. She ran down them, one hand on the wall. She opened a door and found herself in a strange hall. Narrow and long, with a high ceiling, it was like being in a ditch that was shadowed even when the sun was shining. She crumpled in the corner behind a tall wardrobe. In the wall at the end, almost within reach beside her, was a door. She stood up, reached high, and cupped her hands on the knob.

She could barely reach it, and the knob turned slowly, then flopped back. It was not white, like those along the main halls, but shiny black.

She tried again, stretching taller. The door opened, and she slipped through, then stopped.

35

Dark.

She smelled earth, and dampness. Beneath her bare feet the rough stones of a stair led downward. But it was very, very dark there, below. She felt dampness licking her skin, the icy cold raising bumps on her arms, as if the dark here were something that reared up and ate little girls.

In the silent dark something moved. She heard a sound of sliding, along the floor, or up a wall, or along the steps rising toward her. Unable to move, she stared into the darkness below, where the edge of the stone steps disappeared. The sliding sound came closer, closer.

Part of the dark moved.

Suddenly, out of the darkness, eyes appeared, slitted, narrow, blacker than the darkness of this unknown place. She saw a face that was not a face. It darted from the darkness, hissing. A thin tongue lashed at her.

The Bad Things.

The Bad Things whose voices rose at night in her dreams and made her cry. The Bad Things—she had opened the door to the place where they lived.

She sucked in her breath, a scream drawn to silence inward, and spun backward. She whirled through the door into the hall and slammed it shut. She ran along the shadowed hall, through a door she had left open, through other doors, until she found a way into the kitchen. With tears in her eyes, making the outlines of familiar things look wavery and strange, she ran out of the house and crawled behind a bush that grew by the back porch. She huddled, hugging her arms across her chest.

Something touched her shoulder.

The scream erupted, then, cut to silence when she saw the face above her. *Edward.* Bending forward, with sympathy, concern, questions on his silent lips. Katrina flung her arms around his knees. The weeping erupted and she cried with her face pushed against the rough overalls bib on his chest as he bent and picked her up.

He patted her, held her, whispered, "No, no."

He carried her away from the sharp thorns of the bush.

Footsteps crossed the porch, and Eddie looked up to see Aunt Theodora glaring at him with disapproval on her tight, thin lips. He set the weeping child down, and unloosened her fingers from his galluses.

"There, there," Aunt Theodora said, reaching over and patting Katrina on the head. "You simply cannot have the big doll to play with, Katrina, dear. Someday I'll let you hold her. But you must never, never try to get the doll down from the dresser yourself. Nor must you ever allow anyone else to touch it, either, Edward."

Eddie shook his head, even though he didn't know what doll she was talking about, or where it was.

"I'll tell you what I'll let Edward do for you, Katrina. Hush your crying now. Edward can make you a dolly. I imagine, what with all the younger sisters Edward has, that he had made more than one doll, right, Edward?"

Eddie nodded. Yes, little dolls formed of clay from the bank of the creek. With eyes made of pebbles. Little dolls that fell apart as they dried, but which the little girls loved. Dolls made of long, slender stones, on which Eddie etched eyes, nose, mouth, with soft, white chalky stones from the creek bed.

"Come with me," Aunt Theodora ordered.

They went ahead of Eddie, Katrina's hand held in the long thin hand of the tall woman who wore her hair pulled back into a knot on the back of her head, and an apron that almost covered her dress. Eddie followed them, through the kitchen, into a hall beyond, and up a stairway to a small, cluttered room.

The room was not arranged like most of the rooms Eddie had seen. A broken chair stood in the corner, with another broken chair upended and resting upon its seat. Trunks stood here and there about in the room, and discarded furniture rested even in the middle of the floor.

Aunt Theodora bent over a trunk. It appeared to be full of discarded clothing. She began sorting through it. Katrina stood at her elbow, tears gone, an occasional sob jerking her body.

"A rag doll," Aunt Theodora said. "We're going to let Edward make you a dolly of your very own, Katrina. With these old clothes."

Aunt Theodora stood up, then took a deep breath and a step toward the door.

"THERE, Edward, use whatever you need to, then perhaps Katrina will feel better."

The door closed. The footsteps came like echoes, once, twice, then were gone.

Katrina stood looking at the old things in the trunk, sobs still causing her chin to jerk, her shoulders to twitch.

All these tears over a doll? Eddie looked at her face as he knelt beside the trunk. There was something in her face that seemed distant, as if her thoughts were elsewhere. Dark memories, like bad dreams, as he had seen on the face of little Rosie after she'd screamed at night with the kind of strange terrors that sometimes visit little children. Those horrible, terrifying dreams that God must have no part of, that the mind of a little child reaches, somewhere in the layered depths of sleep, that older children and grownups have lost.

He wished he could speak to her, ask her, "What frightens you so much? In the daytime, while the sun is shining, and the crows are cawing above the treetops? It's not a mere doll that troubles you and makes those big tears. What is it?"

He gathered an armload of old rags, then motioned her to follow him. The sun shined beyond the walls.

They would find a sunny spot outdoors in which to make Katrina's doll.

CHAPTER 6

*E*ddie found a spot of sunshine where only yesterday Katrina's papa had scythed the grass and made it short and velvety. He sat down and patted the grass beside him. Katrina sat down, her knees making tent poles in the long skirt of her dress. He could hear her take deep, shuddering breaths now and then, with the sighs like fading light. He wanted to ask her, did Aunt Theodora scare you so much?

From his pocket he drew the small knife that had been a birthday present from his papa, and opened a blade.

"You've got a knife?" Katrina asked.

He was glad to hear the question. It meant she wasn't so afraid now. He nodded.

With the knife he cut narrow strips from one old heavy garment, then he arranged several large pieces, put them together, doubled them over, and used a narrow strip to tie near the top, forming a head. He worked with the material until two small flowers were situated right where eyes should be, and a larger arrangement of flowers made a mouth.

Katrina rose to her feet as Eddie worked; she stood with her hand on his shoulder and watched. He could feel her calming, and it delighted him. He laughed, looking up over his shoulder at her, but she stared wide-eyed at the face of the doll.

Eddie held it up. The sun had moved, and he was in the shade. He held the doll over where it caught the sunlight. The blue flowers that made the eyes had little stems leading away from the lower edges. Too late Eddie saw it looked almost as if the doll were crying. He pointed to the stems, then to his own eyes as he crinkled them in a big smile.

"No, no," he said softly. Not tears, but laughter.

Katrina looked soberly from him to the doll.

He had made a large head, and a long skirt. He made the doll dance, and Katrina smiled.

He extended the doll to her. When she put out her hands for it, the skirt touched the ground. She clasped it around the neck. Its flowery mouth smiled at her. She looked at it, her chin puckering.

"Ain't got no arms ..."

She spoke tremulously, as if she was about to cry again. Nothing had ever made Eddie feel so helpless as when one of his little sisters cried.

"No, no, no, no, no." *Awwwww,* Eddie longed to say in sympathy and protest. *The dolly has something much better than arms.*

He picked up the upper layer of the many skirts the doll was made of and spread them. See. *She has wings.*

He found a bare spot on the ground near the path, took out his knife, and drew the shape of an angel. He pointed. Katrina leaned over and looked.

"Wings?" she asked.

Eddie nodded vigorously. Then he etched again with the tip of his knife the outline of the angel.

"An angel?"

Eddie nodded.

Katrina hugged the doll around its neck. The wings fell to its side, and the bottom of the skirt came to the length of Katrina's own skirt.

"Will she protect me?"

Eddie nodded.

"Even from the Bad Things in the dungeon?"

Eddie felt his smile waver. What bad things? What dungeon? Still, he nodded. Slowly, wondering.

The kitchen door opened and Aunt Theodora crossed the porch and stood on the steps. In her hand was a clean milk bucket. Was it time to do chores before the sun was below the trees?

"Let me see your doll, Katrina."

Katrina dutifully carried her doll over to Theodora, and the tall woman took the bundle of rags and looked at it, smiling. Eddie went to stand quietly and wait for her to pass him the bucket and tell him what she wanted. Perhaps some berries from the blackberry patch in the pasture.

"What a fine job!" Theodora exclaimed, and Eddie felt his face and neck grow warm. "Why, it has eyes, and a mouth. Katrina, how could a little girl want for a better doll than this? This is the kind of doll a little girl can play with."

"She's an angel," Katrina said. "She don't have no arms, she's got wings instead. And she can protect me."

"Of course she can. Now here, run along and build a playhouse."

"How do I build a playhouse?"

"Edward can show you. As good as he can build a doll, I'm sure he knows how to build playhouses, too." She extended the bucket toward Eddie and he took it, watching her for some sign of what was expected.

"We're going to church tonight, Edward, so the chores have to be done early. Then I'll want you to harness the horse to the buggy and bring it up to the driveway here beside the house."

Eddie nodded and took the bucket toward the barn. He had looked in the shed that held the buggy and thought what a grand thing it would be to be able to ride in it. He had even climbed into the seat and bounced, finding good, strong springs. It was made of fine, heavy leather and black wrought-iron. The steps up to the seat looked hardly used.

"Will you help me build a playhouse?" Katrina asked, as she trotted along, the doll's skirt bobbing as she skipped and ran.

"No, no," Eddie said, holding the bucket out so that she could see it. He motioned over the barn with a wave of his hand, then to the sun that was dropping low in the west now. Then he made a motion toward the east, as if toward a rising sun.

'Tomorrow?" she asked.

Eddie nodded.

She whirled and skipped away. But Eddie knew that in five minutes she could be back again, ready to talk, telling him all about her mother and all the washings and ironings she did for people in town. At those times, her mother left, trusting that Katrina was safe on the grounds of Miss Theodora's home.

She had told him, too, about her papa, and that when he got enough money saved, he was going to buy a place that would be their very own. Her two brothers, who helped her papa, would then have time to go to school. And she, too, could go to school.

As Eddie fed the animals, as he brought the old mare and hitched her to the buggy, even as he got to drive the buggy out into the driveway where Maggie the mare would stand resting on two feet, balancing on the toes of the other two, her chin hanging and her eyes closed, even then he realized his pleasure in this was small. And temporary. He couldn't stay outside all night. He had to go back into the house now, and he was afraid.

He had to leave, get away. As he had so often this past week, he studied how it could be done. And the only chance he had was to teach himself to read and write, so he could let folks know his thoughts, and tell them in writing the work he was willing to do.

There were schools for boys like him. If he could only manage to find one …

41

Church was the first step. There he would have access to a book. The Bible. He needed a Bible so he could learn to read.

There was no way he could get a book of his own, even a Bible. It took money to buy even a Bible. But church lasted two hours, sometimes longer, and maybe there would be a Bible he could copy words from.

He hurried to the barn, where there was a small heap of shingles left over from the last time it had been roofed. Some in the pile had been discarded because they were too thin; others had been too thick. It was a thin shingle he selected, one he could slip beneath the bib of his overalls.

Supper this evening was light. A glass of milk, a square of cornbread. Aunt Theodora disappeared, and returned after Eddie had put away his clean glass. She was wearing her black dress with the black embroidery around the skirt, and a black knitted shawl over her shoulders.

"It's time to go, Edward."

She lit one candle in the middle of the table. The long kitchen had grown nearly dark. The window was a narrow slit, almost hidden by a dark drapery. When Eddie stepped out onto the porch, he saw the sinking sun like a red twin of the rising moon, laced by the forests surrounding the house.

He had hoped she might want him to drive, but she climbed without waiting for help to the driver's seat. She picked up the reins, and Maggie the mare lifted her head and placed all four feet flat on the ground. Just before she took the first slow step, Eddie climbed up to sit on the springy seat next to his aunt. He could feel the thin slab of wood between his shirt and his overall bib.

They went out onto the road, and turned toward town. They passed a farm on the right where lights gleamed yellow in windows. They looked brighter than the lights of candles, and Eddie presumed the folks used kerosene, the way of his own mama and papa.

His folks owned one lamp, carried from room to room as it was needed. At Aunt Theodora's he had found, when he'd swept hallways on the second floor, lamps much fancier than he'd ever seen before. With tassled shades, and deep bowls for holding kerosene. Yet Aunt Theodora, to his knowledge, used only candles.

They passed a small white house. There was a bit of cleared land behind it, as there was behind Aunt Theodora's barn for the pasturing of a cow, three pigs, and a horse. The white house had a friendly porch, with rockers and other chairs. But no one sat there.

Aunt Theodora saw him looking past her, and said, "That is where the Beckleys live. They have a small farm, and Mr. Beckley has a barbershop in town. Two older sons are grown now, and work somewhere in the city. There are daughters yet at home. They belong to our church."

Our church?

Did she really consider him one of her family now? Some part of Eddie's heart responded warmly. Still, that didn't change his need to learn to read and write.

Now that they were away from the house, now that he didn't have to look directly into her eyes, he could feel grateful that she might include him. Even though she had told Papa a falsehood about sending him to school.

Could it be she had only wanted him to come stay with her because she had no children of her own and wanted him for company?

But if that was the reason, why hadn't she chosen John, for instance. John, the brother just younger than himself, was able to speak. He talked, went to school, had learned to read and write and cipher. Why hadn't she chosen John?

No, he decided ... it wasn't for company that he was here. He rarely saw her. His days were spent cutting wood, doing chores. Only the chores were things that had to be done at certain times. He was free, many hours, to do nothing but such things as make a doll for Katrina, and now to build her playhouse.

Why does she want my company when I cannot talk to her? Why does she want me in her house when she sees me only to give instructions?

The church came in view, tall and narrow, brick on the walls and glistening stained glass in tall windows with rounded tops. A thin spire reached even higher than the forest trees that crowded against the small churchyard. With the view of the church came Eddie's determination to work quickly, learn what he had to in order to leave. To run away, if he must.

He felt a great urgency as he climbed down from the buggy. He took the reins and secured them at the hitching posts near the church, his hands fumbling with the sudden feel of urgency. Something behind him, coming out of the dark of the forest, something that seemed to have followed from the old mansion, was reaching for him. He had to hurry. Hurry. Learn. Leave. Before he was drawn back and held forever.

AUNT THEODORA WENT FORWARD down the aisle, tall and imposing in her black dress and black shawl, with her black hair pulled tightly from her face and plaited into a bun. She went to the front bench and sat down, but she didn't motion Eddie to follow her.

Several folks were already seated here and there in the long, silent room. Families sat together on long benches with solid seats and solid backs. Dark polished wood, like the wood in the mansion. Unlike the small church at home, where Eddie had gone since he could remember, this church was large. Long, it was tunnel-like, with a high, rounded ceiling. Candles in brackets all around the walls whispered softly.

Left to choose his own seat, Eddie slid into place several benches back from the front. In pockets made of wood, spaced regularly along the back of each bench, were Bibles. That was what he was looking for.

He took a Bible and spread it open on his knees, bending over it. His mother had read to him, and so had John. There were a few words he remembered. He searched for them. Jesus. God. Savior.

Someone sat down on the same bench at the distant end. Eddie moved as far left as he could.

He pulled the thin slab of wood from behind his overall bib and placed it on one knee. He opened his knife to the smallest blade. Using the point, he attempted to make letters in the wood.

He had to rise for singing, silently mouthing words he had listened to before. The church was filling, and the bench he had chosen was getting more crowded. He noticed that the girl who had sat down at the far end, seen at first only from beneath his corner lashes, was now against his arm as they stood. The rest of the bench was filled with other young people.

The girl beside him was almost as tall as he. Without looking directly at her, he saw a smooth, pale cheek with just a touch of pink high on her cheekbones. Her hair was long, and much like Katrina's, though darker, as if among its sunny lights it had captured shadows. It hung forward over her shoulder and down onto the rounded part of her bodice.

He realized he was looking slantwise at that rounding beneath the white bodice, and he pulled his eyes away and stared with deliberation at the woman on stage who played the big organ. He hadn't heard the song end, but then everyone sat down, and he became aware of the silence. He smelled roses, and then again realized it was the girl who sat next to him. He felt as if the world were spinning ahead of him, leaving him behind. It *was* the girl, he decided. The girl was bothering him, in some strange way. A way he had never thought would happen to him. She was, after all, a total stranger. He would never speak to her, even though they sat side by side. He *couldn't* speak to her.

Regret hit him, like a horse kick in the middle of his chest. He couldn't speak to her, ever.

He stole a glance at her, and was startled to see her smiling at him. He returned her smile and ducked his head. What would she think of his efforts on the shingle with a penknife, during church? Would she think he was just playing, not listening? Whittling?

He stood up again with the congregation and heard the girl's silver voice, like a cord reaching to heaven. He mouthed the words, old familiar words.

"He put a little joy and gladness, where sadness once had been ..."

A glance sideways toward the girl met a glance at him in return. Without missing a note, she continued to sing. He was relieved when it was time to sit down and lower his head in silence for the long prayer that Reverend Cheney spoke, almost sang, his voice rising and falling in the way of many preachers Eddie had heard.

"Ask and it shall be given you; seek, and ye shall find; knock, and it shall be opened unto you. For every one that asketh receiveth—"

Why did preachers always go to that part of the Scripture? Hearing it made Eddie feel sad and lonely. So many times he had asked, on his knees in the woods, on his knees in a silent prayer beside his bed, Please God, give me speech. Please ... please ... so I can be like others.

He had even made promises, when he became desperate that God was not listening to him. Jesus hadn't come with the promise he had made on the Mount. So Eddie made promises.

Please Lord, please Jesus, give me speech, and I will carry the Word to the world, just as you did, as much as it will be in my power. Ask God to give me speech.

He had finally stopped asking. His fourteenth birthday had passed, his fifteenth, and now his sixteenth. The time had come when he must learn on his own to read, and to write, so he could write to people his intentions. *I can fix fences. I can milk cows. I can raise gardens and farm products.*

I can make rag dolls for little girls who cry.

He hadn't realized he'd laughed, that low sound that came in his throat sometimes when he was least expecting it. The girl ducked her head beside his and whispered.

"What's funny?"

He sobered instantly. The preacher's voice had risen now and quivered from the beams in the high ceiling of the church and bounded from the wall.

He shook his head and drew farther away from her, bending his nose closer to the Bible. He knew the alphabet. John had taught it to him as he himself learned it. ABC ... on to Z. A few words were familiar. The. And. Of. But all the other words were like bird tracks made in sand. Though he knew the individual letters, arranged together, they made no sense.

The sermon went on and on. Eddie carved small letters in the shingle. Katrina? How was it spelled? K? He carved the K. Ah? Could it be an A? And Angel, didn't it also start with A? Yes. Angel. An ... he found it, the only thing it could mean. Angel. But Katrina? K-A-T-R-E-E-N-A. He drew a long breath and sat up, looking at the name he had carved. Yes, he could teach himself. If he sounded out the words, found the letter that matched ...

But then the girl beside him handed him a folded sheet of paper. On the outside was written. KATRIN A, the letter I underlined. Eddie's eyes met hers, questioning, open in awe. Did she know what he was trying to do?

Her hands touched his as she unfolded the note. She pointed at the message written there. He stared miserably at it, unable to respond.

She took it back, folding it into an even smaller note. "It says I'm glad you're here."

Her giggle was soft. Someone, an older sister, perhaps, on the other side, looked critically at her, but the girl ignored her.

She whispered, "My name is Angie."

Angie! Almost like an angel.

Then again she whispered, her lips even closer to his ear, "You're the new boy at Miss Theodora's?"

He nodded.

She pointed to his crudely carved letters on the shingle. "You were spelling Katrina? The little girl who lives near there? In one of Miss Theodora's sheds?"

He nodded again.

"Don't you have a pencil and paper?"

"No, no." The word came out louder than he intended, as often it did. His control over those few sounds he could make became even less when he was excited, or happy, or frightened. With this beautiful girl whose name was Angie, he was both excited and happy. A bit of fright edged in, too, as if he stood on the brink of something unknown. Marvelously unknown, marvelously wonderful.

The older girl on the other side of Angie poked her with her elbow. Angie only smiled at Eddie, leaned shoulder to shoulder with him, and whispered, "I'll bring you one. I'll show you how to use it. My house is next door to yours. Behind your house is a little road. It leads to a meadow on the hill. I'll meet you there, tomorrow. At ... let's see, in the afternoon. After dinner."

He stared wide-eyed at her, his soul drinking in her flawless skin, her long, thick lashes, the perfect blue of her eyes. The kindness he saw in the depths of her eyes.

The pity ...?

CHAPTER 7

For the first time in Eddie's life, church ended too soon. Long-winded preachers had at times been a bane in Eddie's hours off from work, when he'd have preferred to be at work. He had heard the same stories over and over, it seemed, and they all ended with something about sin, and if that sin weren't absolved and forgiven, then the poor fool would sit all eternity with his feet in fire. In the beginning, when Eddie heard that threat, it had worried him. He was only about five or six at the time. He became afraid of fire, afraid it would reach out fiery fingers and grab him, because he had sinned just by being born. Later on, when he was older, the threat seemed a little ridiculous. Feet in fire? Forever? For being born? Of sin? What sin?

After Angie's older sister had poked her for the third time, Angie lifted her head and listened to the preacher, and after a moment Eddie tried, though his mind kept wandering away ... home. His brothers and sisters, Mama and Papa. He had never before been to church without them.

He wondered if Katrina's family came to this church.

But most of all, he was aware of the girl whose arm touched his.

The sermon ended, and he didn't know what the preacher had said. They stood for prayers. Angie reached over and took the shingle from Eddie and whispered, "Tomorrow. Don't forget."

How could he ever forget?

They went out into a night bright with stars. People milled about in different directions. Katydids and jarflies made steady, loud buzzings in the dark woods. Eddie followed Aunt Theodora after she shook hands with the

47

reverend and mentioned how lovely his sermon was. The reverend reached for Eddie's hand and held it a moment.

On the walk to the buggy, Eddie tried to remember what the sermon was about, but all he clearly remembered was the pretty girl, with the pretty smile and nice name, and how friendly she was. Had she really meant what she'd said about meeting him tomorrow? Was she really going to bring him a pencil and paper and show him how to write?

He wanted to ask her questions, so many questions. Did she go to the school he would go to? If he could go to school ...

It was enough that they went to the same church.

Did Angie really like him, or only feel sorry for him?

He wanted to ask his aunt, how often do we go to church? Is it every Sunday, Wednesday, and Friday, the way it was at home?

Except for the sound of the horse's hooves against the gravel of the road, they rode in silence.

In the driveway, Aunt Theodora turned the reins over to Eddie.

"Put the rig away, Edward. There'll be a candle on the table for you. Good night."

Under starlight Eddie led the mare back to pasture. In the dusky corner of the barn lot the pigs stirred and grunted, disturbed about something. Eddie went over to give them a pat, and found only two pigs where three had been just hours ago.

Down on his knees in the pigpen, he felt about with growing concern. His hands roamed the dark corner of the pen, going again and again from the feeding trough to the watering trough, and to the fresh straw he had put down for their beds.

Two pigs, not three. Betsy and Reba were here, but Solomon was gone.

He checked the gate. It was closed, latched, as he had left it. The outlines of the barn, the railings of the stockade fence, became gradually more visible as his eyes adjusted to the dark. The white rings around the necks of the pigs were visible when they stood, grunting, milling restlessly about. He wanted to ask them, where is Solomon? What happened to Solomon?

He hurried out of the pigpen. Bypassing the gate, he climbed over the fence. Starlight glowed on the path, shadowed at points by the trees. Eddie ran. *Aunt Theodora!*

He entered the kitchen. On the stove the big pot bubbled softly, fed by the fire that Aunt Theodora always built up in the evening at bedtime. Eddie knew that was probably the last thing she did before she went to bed, because in the morning there were always red coals in the firebox. Tonight the smell of something cooking was stronger than ever. Cabbage? Onions? He never knew. Sometimes the smells were subtle, like mushrooms on a damp forest floor.

Sometimes they were dank, like old wood rotted and falling away. Sometimes there seemed to be the smell of peppers, or some strong spice.

She was gone. The candles burned on the table, three of them. Eddie ignored them and ran on. The long front hall was always lighted, dimly, between long strips of deep shadows. He had to find Aunt Theodora. Something had happened to one of the pigs.

He ran into the hall. The strangely sickening smell that came from the pot on the stove was shut away. Here, there was only the smell of old walls, and burning candles.

Aunt Theodora!

His voice refused to work. Not even a cry escaped his lips. He had never been to Aunt Theodora's private rooms. He didn't know where she went when she left the kitchen. Other than the time she had taken him into the parlor to meet the reverend, and upstairs to the storage room, he had not gone with her to any other room. When he swept the porches, he went around the house, outdoors. When he swept the halls, it was always the back halls. He didn't know where the doors led.

He came to the foyer, where a candle burned faintly in a single bracket. The ceiling was high, and seemed to be peaked, like a crown. A large chandelier hung down, filled with candles, but they weren't burning. The banister of the wide stairs glistened darkly in the dim light of the candle. At the landing above he saw another candle, and farther on, another.

He climbed, hoping the lighted candles led the way to Aunt Theodora.

He reached the landing halfway up the stairs. It was like an open room, furnished with a short sofa with a curved back, a table, and a lamp with fringe on the shade. As he hesitated, he heard his name spoken harshly from above. He looked up. Aunt Theodora stood above, looking down over the banister.

"Edward! Go immediately to your room! What are you doing here?"

His mouth working in silence, he began motioning toward the barn. She stared down at him, the distant light of the candle below making her face look as if it hung alone in the darkness.

He tried to draw with his hands the shape of a pig. He held up three fingers, then folded down one. Three pigs, now two. With the two fingers he motioned frantically toward the barn.

Aunt Theodora gave a sigh of exasperation and walked along the balcony to the stairway and came down. Eddie turned and ran ahead of her, looking back frequently to see that she was coming.

In the kitchen Aunt Theodora paused, then from the washroom took a lantern and lighted it. She followed Eddie outside.

He ran ahead of her, then waited for her to catch up. When she drew near, he ran on again. She came with quick steps behind him, the lantern swinging at her side, the light reaching down the path, moving back and forth in the darkness.

He opened the barn lot gate for her. The horse stood beyond the fence at the corner, head down, resting. Nearby the cow lay. Eddie ran on to the corner where the pigpen was closed off from the rest of the barn loft. He motioned, lifting three fingers, then bending down one.

"Oh, for goodness' sake," Aunt Theodora said in disgust, turning immediately away. The lantern light disappeared for a moment beyond the sweep of her long, dark skirt.

Eddie followed her, his palms opened toward the sky. What happened? Where is Solomon?

"A man came and got the third pig," Aunt Theodora said, as if she now understood clearly the desperate motions Eddie was making. "If I had known you would have such a fit about this, I would have sent you to bed and put the horse in the barn myself."

A man came and got the pig?

Eddie's hands fell.

He followed behind Aunt Theodora, hearing the swish of her skirts, a shhishh, shhishh sound in the night as if she were angry at being disturbed. All the pleasure of the evening was gone for Eddie.

He swallowed a knot that swelled in his throat, took a candle from the table, and went up the narrow backstairs to his bed.

He lay staring at the ceiling. Solomon was gone. A man had taken him. That meant only one thing: Solomon was going to be butchered. Though he was still small, he would be eaten.

Eddie stared at the ceiling. He had to get away. He had to learn to cypher, so, perhaps, he could keep books for a business. He had to get away from animals, from working with animals. Solomon had liked to follow him around at chore time, before the pigpen gate was closed. Solomon always hurried and ate, then, squealing, followed Eddie, and lay down nearby while Eddie milked the cow. Squealing softly then, he followed Eddie into the henhouse while Eddie gathered eggs.

Now Solomon was gone. A man came and took him away. While they were at church.

Perhaps Solomon would have a nice pasture to roam in, to eat and root and live in. But no—things didn't happen that way for pigs.

Tomorrow, Eddie was going to see Angie.

With the memory of her face closed into the darkness behind his eyelids, he went to sleep.

Wee Willie Winkle was screaming, not the wee, wee, wee of a small pig running behind him, begging to be held, to be petted. He was screaming, a cry of horror and fear, of seeing for a moment his trust in mankind was a futile trust. Eddie stood with his hands covering his face, hiding his tears, the screams of his pet pig tearing the soul of his heart. As the scream turned to gurgles, a throat filled with blood, Eddie sank to his knees in his helplessness to save something he loved.

He woke weeping. Dry tears, deep, silent sobs, hurting his chest. Then he froze.

Wee Willie Winkle—no—another pig—a tortured cry distant, dim, chopped to silence.

Solomon!

He was out of bed and to the door. Then remembered.

Do not leave your room at night.

He stopped, listening. The house, the night, was silent.

Perhaps it was his dream after all.

IN THE NIGHT he woke again and drew the quilt up from the foot of the bed and covered himself. He slept restlessly.

The sounds were in the house again. Sounds he couldn't put a name to, that were nothing he had ever heard before. Not the grunting sounds of pigs, nor their squeals. Not the howl of a dog. Yet somewhere in the house, sounding as if it were muffled by distance, came the voices.

Eddie listened. He got up and put his ear against the door. There was no sound in the hall. Not tonight. Not since the first few nights he had slept here had he heard that movement in the hall outside his door.

He put his hand on the knob, but he didn't turn it.

The sounds faded way, and after long minutes, Eddie went back to bed.

Sleep came again, near dawn, not long before the knock on his door.

HE SLIPPED AWAY FROM KATRINA. Twice during the morning she had suddenly appeared. Like Solomon had done, she followed him when he did chores. This morning, with her rag doll in the crook of one arm, she was suddenly behind him.

"Where's the other piggy?" she asked through the fence as Eddie poured water into the trough.

She didn't know that Eddie had given the pigs names. No one knew. The man who had taken Solomon didn't know the pig had a name.

Eddie motioned with one hand, up, away. Katrina watched him carefully.

"Where?" she asked.

Eddie measured higher than himself, then tugged on his overall bib. Katrina stared at him. She didn't understand. Eddie tried again, indicating wide shoulders. Katrina frowned.

"A man?"

Eddie nodded, and motioned away again.

Katrina shook her head, looking about.

Eddie went on with the chores. Feeding the chickens, milking the cow, turning all the animals out to pasture. Katrina followed. When Eddie took the milk to Aunt Theodora in the kitchen, Katrina stayed.

As he got the broom to sweep, he heard her asking Aunt Theodora, "What happened to the other piggy?"

He heard Aunt Theodora's answer, more difficult to understand as Eddie moved from sweeping the kitchen floor to sweeping the washroom.

"A man came and got him."

"I didn't see no man." Her voice sounded aggrieved, as Eddie felt, as if the pig they'd fed and petted was theirs, not Aunt Theodora's.

"Well, I expect you were in bed asleep. If you weren't, you should have been."

Eddie moved on to the narrow, long inner hall from which the service stairs rose. The red clay was there again, more than it had been lately, drying, powdering. Bits of dried mud as large as beans clattered like small stones when he swept them up into the dustpan.

He stood leaning a moment on the broom, looking into the dark shadows, seeing in his mind beyond the walls. He knew now that beyond a width of forest, there was a cleared area. And on that cleared land was a small farm. Was that where Angie lived? She had said she was his closest neighbor.

THE AFTERNOON FINALLY ARRIVED, and with his ax in hand, Eddie slipped away. With the barn between him and the house, he ran into the woods. Then, safely out of sight, he found the little trail that led through the trees. The old road looked as if it had been made by a magic, golden chariot, rather than by logging wagons.

He followed the road to a hill. The road curved upward, around a bluff, through trees. A meadow, she had said, at the top of the hill.

He passed small bluffs in the hillside, hiding tiny dens of tiny animals. Larger bluffs held small caves, like doors, their entries swept clean, as if whatever lived there had a desire for orderliness.

He reached sunshine. Trees rimmed the edge of the flat, hilltop meadow. She was nowhere in sight.

He waited.

"Hello."

Eddie whirled. The voice was close. To his right. It took a moment for him to find her. She stood close to a tree, and held in her arms a book and writing tablet. Smiling, she came toward him. Her hair hung in curls over her shoulders, pinned back on each side behind her ears. Her dark blue dress, hanging to her ankles, was worn closely at her small waist. Her breasts pushed against the bodice, straining the buttons. Eddie tore his eyes away, and made sure that from now on he looked only at her eyes.

"I don't even know your name," she said. "I've heard of you only as the new boy at Miss Theodora's. I also heard," she added with a soft apology in her voice, "that you could not speak."

He gulped the fist that seemed permanently lodged in his throat whenever he looked at her, and nodded.

The root of the tree beside her grew above ground, and she sat down on it, arranging her skirt carefully. Arranging, too, on her lap the tablet and book.

He sat near her. Then with a small stick he tried writing his name in the soil near the base of the tree. But moss grew in the way. Soil was sparse. She nudged him and handed him the tablet and new penny pencil.

"You can write?"

Only my name, he wanted to tell her.

On the tablet he printed awkwardly, EDDIE. That was the way his brother had taught him. Eddie, not Edward. He didn't know how to spell Edward.

"Eddie," she said softly, her eyes meeting his, her voice like music. Then, "Can you read this book?"

It was a schoolbook, such as Johnny had brought home, a book with stories. Eddie shook his head.

She looked at him with tenderness and sympathy.

"I had heard more about you, Eddie. They say in the neighborhood that you are deaf and dumb. But I saw in church right away that you aren't deaf, and even though you can't talk, you aren't dumb. Not the kind of dumb that you can't learn. I was wondering at first if perhaps you can read, then I saw—I felt—that you wanted very much to read. And to write."

He nodded eagerly, though he wished this pretty girl had never seen his afflictions. He could visualize himself older, wider of shoulder, wearing a new suit and polished shoes, educated, holding a job, meeting Angie. Not a skinny-shouldered youth, such as he was now, who could only print his name.

"Well," she glanced away, her cheeks taking on more color. "I want to be a teacher, you see. And you're going to be my first student."

He waited. After a moment she looked up again. "The problem is, no one must ever know I've come here, or I'll be severely punished. My family would never understand."

Eddie shook his head, and with his right hand crossed his heart.

They smiled at each other.

CHAPTER 8

"*E*dward?"

Katrina opened a door and looked into a shadowed room where there was nothing but a bedstead, the straw tick rolled against the head, and a tall wardrobe across the room. Dark curtains covered the window. Pretty rugs were only in Miss Theodora's rooms down on the second floor, and on the ground floor. The high ceiling was like a great dungeon overhead where the strange Bad Things might crawl when they came up from below. She backed out and closed the door.

She was in a long corridor, so narrow she could almost touch each wall. She'd been looking and looking but hadn't been able to find Edward.

She had seen him when he fed the animals this morning, but she wanted to see him again now. She wanted to tell him about the baby frog she had seen on the path. When it jumped into the grass in front of her feet it turned green, like the grass. On the walk it was brown, like the stones. Was it a magic frog? There was no one to ask but Edward. Mama and Papa and her brothers were all gone to work in town today. And sometimes she was afraid of Miss Theodora. Especially now, after she told Miss Theodora about the Bad Things that came up from the dungeon.

Miss Theodora had looked at her with her eyes very tight and strange. "*Bad things?* Then you'd better be careful, or they might get you." And Miss Theodora had laughed and laughed.

"Ain't you afraid?" Katrina had asked, standing at Miss Theodora's knee while she embroidered.

Miss Theodora put her face close to Katrina's, and said in a low, deep voice

54

that didn't sound like hers, "The bad things are *mine*. They won't eat me, they only eat nosy little children, like *you!*"

Katrina ran. To find Edward. Who'd protect her. Miss Theodora's strange, frightening laughter followed her through the halls, up the stairs.

Then she remembered her angel doll. It would protect her. She adjusted it in her arms and held it against her chest, its face close to hers.

"Edward?"

She only wanted to tell him about the frog, not about Miss Theodora. She knew, because her papa had told her before this, that Miss Theodora was only funning with her when she laughed at something Katrina had said or done.

"Edward?"

Her voice came again, again, *Edward, Edward*, and mingled with the remnants of Miss Theodora's laughter. Was her laughter only funning her too?

She went outside and looked everywhere, in the barn, in the woodshed, on the porches. She listened to hear the sound of the ax, and heard nothing but the crows. For several days now she had looked for Edward after she'd had her nap in the afternoon. Where was he?

Miss Theodora had her nap, too, Katrina thought, now that the house was quiet. She often napped this time of day. Once she'd gone into Miss Theodora's bedroom and seen her sleeping. She had hurried out. "Don't bother Miss Theodora, Katrina," her mama had said. More than once, she remembered when she saw Miss Theodora asleep. But most of the time Miss Theodora didn't mind. She had told her mama that.

"She doesn't mind, Mama."

"Oh, and how do you know that, little miss?"

"Because ..." She wasn't sure how she knew that. "Her doors are always open."

Her mama laughed, and looked at Papa. They smiled together. That was before the Bad Things.

Her brothers never came to Miss Theodora's house. They had never even been on the steps to the porches.

Katrina drew a long sigh, and heard it in the shadowed hall behind her. It was so quiet in the house. Even though Edward couldn't talk, when he was around it didn't seem quiet.

She put her angel doll under her arm so she could hold onto the railing, and went down the stairs to the first floor. She wanted to tell Edward also that she slept with her doll every night, and it protected her from bad dreams. Before Edward had made her the doll, she'd often dreamed of the Bad Things.

"Edward?"

She stood in the big hall that went to the front stairway and the front door. Her voice came back at her, softly. *Edward. Edward. Ed ... Eddie.*

She started back, turning the corner toward the kitchen, when she heard a door close somewhere. She stopped. It had sounded like the echoes of her voice. Close, yet very far away.

She almost called out again when she heard the murmuring sound. She listened carefully, her head tipped.

Miss Theodora was upstairs, asleep.

Sometimes, Edward could make sounds. She had heard him laugh out loud. And he could speak one word. She had heard him cry out once when he'd hurt his thumb in the gate, a strange squawking sound like the chickens made when they were disturbed. Then he had looked at her and laughed and motioned with his hands out and his lips turned down like the clown she'd seen on the town square last winter. Edward could be so funny.

She liked to slip up behind him and scare him. He'd jump and make his mouth into a big O, as if he were screaming. Of course, she knew he only pretended to be scared. Still, she liked to slip up on him.

Instead of going on into the rear of the house, she chose the hall toward the east porch. It was long and dim, like other hallways in the house. It was the hall where she had glimpsed stone steps beyond a door at the end. Where she had seen the dungeon, where the Bad Things lived. But if she was quiet ... very quiet ...

She slipped along on her tiptoes. She came to the tall wardrobe and peeked around it. The door to the dungeon stood open slightly. Did Edward dare go down there? Was it Edward she had heard? She had looked everywhere else for him.

She tiptoed around the wardrobe and hid in the corner it made against the wall. Had Edward gone down those steps? It was so silent now, and was dark behind the opened inches of the door.

She edged forward, straining to see through a doorway she had looked through only once before.

But if Edward had gone there ... someone was there, she knew ... she had heard a sound, she had heard a door ... and Miss Theodora was asleep upstairs ...

"Edward?" she called timidly.

She saw a movement in the darkness beyond the door, a shifting of the dark. Was Edward trying to scare her, or was it the Bad Things she had glimpsed before?

Without going closer she leaned away from the wall and strained harder to see in the dark. The Bad Things were only her imagination, her papa had told her as he'd held her on his lap, the way he did every night. Bad things that come in dreams, and which only *seem* real. But she had seen them in Miss Theodora's house, she told him. Once, she had seen them.

"So what were you doing in Miss Theodora's house? Snooping about where you didn't belong?"

She had decided it was better not to talk about it than to have her papa getting angry. So there were a lot of things she no longer told Papa. Nor did she tell Edward everything.

She hadn't told about seeing the pig's face.

... Staring at her ... trying to cry ... crying for her help ...

She couldn't talk about it because she wanted to think it was a bad dream.

Perhaps she hadn't really seen Bad Things, either. But ...

The door inched open, softly, silently. She started to call Edward's name, but stopped, her breath held.

Beyond the opening now the stone steps became visible. The darkness that gathered there took shape and moved. Like a huge lizard, it eased upward along the steps. There were a head, arms, legs short and thick. Its head lifted, turning this way and that, searching, sniffing. The top of the head was flat and tapered toward a long, broad nose. Thin fingers clasped the edge of the door, and a forked red tongue flicked the air. She heard the sliding of the body over the stone steps. It stood upright then, almost as tall as the door. Its eyes were black slits, long and cold, like ice in winter ponds. They found her and settled. Its long fingers darted like the tongue toward her.

She screamed, a low cry that was cut off in her throat as she gasped for breath.

Whirling away, she ran.

Bad Things—real—not made from her dreams. Miss Theodora had not been funning, after all.

THE AFTERNOONS HAD SPED AWAY like magic. At night, under the light of his candle, he worked. He had learned to print the ABCs, all of them, right down to Z. He had learned the words in the little primer Angie had brought for him. But sometimes as they sat together, they learned more how to communicate with each other, and almost forgot his studies.

"What happened?" she had asked him, after several afternoons together. "Were you ... injured?"

"No, no," he told her, and motioned with his hands. Baby. He made a cradle with his hands and rocked them back and forth. I was born this way.

She looked at him, that soft sympathy on her face. Yet at other times he had seen something else in her face, in her eyes, a darkening—a teasing, perhaps—that excited him in ways he had never dreamed of. It embarrassed him, too, as he realized his manhood, afraid that she would see. He had never known; no one had ever told him. And his yearning toward her both delighted and frightened him. His breathing grew short, and he had to edge away so that even her skirt did not touch him.

They carried on a sort of dialogue, and she seemed to understand the motionings of his hands.

I came to live with Aunt Theodora because she said she would send me to a special school. But she must have changed her mind. I don't know why she wanted me here.

"Perhaps she does send boys on to schools," Angie said softly, understanding. "Last year a boy was here for a while. He came to church with her, just as you have. But he wasn't bright like you. And soon he was gone. It's said in the neighborhood that Miss Theodora is ..." She searched her memory and mind for the word she wanted. Eddie watched her, seeing the way her long, dark lashes threw shadows across her cheeks as she glanced up, down, to the side. "She's philanthropic."

Eddie smiled, and motioned with his palms upward. No wonder she had to search her mind. What a word! He drew a question mark in the air.

Angie giggled, the way she could at rare times. "I think it means she does good things for poor people. I'm not sure. To my mind—well, perhaps I shouldn't say this, but there's something about her ..." She shuddered.

Eddie nodded desperately, seriously. For the first time he had someone to whom he could tell his feelings of uneasiness about Aunt Theodora. He pointed to his eyes, narrowed them, and stared piercingly at her. He made a sign of darkness, of no color, by cupping his hands. These signs would mean nothing to people who used real sign language, but he knew, he hoped, Angie understood them.

"Yes," she whispered, leaning closer. "The way she looks at you—at me. And they're like they have no pupils. Or maybe it's they have no irises. They're so black."

Angie sat back, looking down. Eddie understood. She was uncomfortable with criticism of anyone. She was too kind to say what they both felt.

"Of course," Angie said after a moment, "maybe it's because she's been alone so much. Maybe that's why she wants you there. Maybe she's lonely. She can't help the way her eyes are, can she? Like, your eyes are a lovely brown." She smiled softly at him. "And mine ..." She opened them wide. "Are sometimes blue, sometimes green. Miss Theodora would probably say they're strange eyes, too. She probably thinks I look weird."

She laughed, but Eddie didn't smile. He glanced toward the road that led back to the house.

I'm afraid. The house scares me. Aunt Theodora makes me uncomfortable. How could he express these feelings?

I don't want to go back. Ever. When I'm with you, I wish I could stay here forever.

He sat still, his hands motionless. These were things he couldn't tell her. She was only being kind.

I love you.

She jumped suddenly to her feet. "Oh, dear. The sun is going down. I have to hurry. I mustn't make my sister or Mama suspicious."

He helped her gather up her books, her writing paper, her pencils.

"They think I'm studying alone in the woods somewhere."

She gave him a smile and turned away. Then abruptly she swung back, stood on her toes, and kissed him. He was so startled he only gaped at her. It had been a soft brushing of her lips against his, a shock that went through his heart, his whole system, and then settled embarrassingly, reminding him that they were male and female. And he loved her.

She ran, and he stood watching her.

Then he hurried.

He hid his tablet, book, and pencil in the barn until after chores were done; then, with them hidden in his bib, he took them to his room.

AT NIGHT lately he was given to daydreams about Angie. About himself being an educated man who wore suits to work, who kept books for big businesses, who supported his lovely wife. Then he'd have to remind himself to study. Study the words, practice the letters, the numbers. The numbers were easier. They came so naturally.

Angie had called him a mathematical genius.

THE SOUNDS that had disturbed him when he'd first come to live with Aunt Theodora no longer reached him.

He slept soundly.

CHAPTER 9

*W*here was Katrina?

He hadn't even thought of her yesterday evening, he realized, as he did the chores. He had been drifting under the spell of love, thinking only of Angie. This morning as he finished feeding the two pigs, he wondered: *Where's Katrina?*

As if his thoughts created her, he saw her peering through the fence at him. He stopped, looking at her small, perfect face.

He motioned a question mark in the air, then pointed to his lips. *Why are you so silent? Where were you last night when I did chores? You usually are underfoot, getting in the way, talking all the time. What's wrong?*

She climbed through the fence and came to him, reaching her hand up to his. He felt it, small and soft—almost boneless, it seemed. He squeezed it and drew a question mark in the air again, then pointed to his own turned-down mouth. *Why are you so sad?*

She didn't laugh and tell him he looked like a clown. Instead, she turned her eyes solemnly toward the house. His gaze followed hers. Beyond the barn, beyond the woodshed and the trees, it loomed, large, dark, heavy green vines growing on its stone walls. Beyond the trunks of big oak trees the back porch was visible like broken sticks, the fluted columns curled round with deep green vines, and ivy growing along the banisters.

"I saw the Bad Thing yesterday, Edward," she said, as if the barn walls had ears. She pushed nearer to him, looking back over her shoulder, then again to the house. There was a slight tug. "I didn't tell my papa, because he would tell me I only dreamed it and I should stay away from the house. But there are so many nice places in the house to play. I don't want to stay away."

Eddie bent to see her face. He read fear in her eyes, yet she tugged again toward the house. He made a questioning face at her, eyebrows lifted.

"I want you to see it," she said. "It's in the dungeon. Tell Miss Theodora to make it go away."

Dungeon?

She had mentioned the dungeon to him once before, he remembered. *Where?*

He shaped the word carefully with his lips. She had begun to try to read his silent words, the way his brothers and sisters had, the way Angie did. She tugged sharply again on his hand.

"I'll show you," she said.

They went toward the house. Above the trees of the forest behind the barn the crows screamed, their voices shrill and ear-splitting, as if they had discovered something dangerous in their nests. No other birds chirped or sang, not even a sparrow, or a pigeon in the barn.

Katrina began to tiptoe softly as they went up the steps to the long, ivy-shadowed back porch. Windows of the kitchen reflected the green of the ivy, and the white columns of the porch. Not even the curtains beyond were visible. Eddie remembered the night he had first entered the house, coming across this porch, and the fear he had felt. Even now, after living here going on three weeks and crossing this porch many times, still his throat tightened and something bade him run, run away, before it was too late. As if, indeed, the house contained a Bad Thing.

The long, dim kitchen was vacant. Aunt Theodora was not striding about, dust cloth or wash cloth or drying cloth in hand. She was not at the stove stirring something in the big pot, or adding vegetables to it. It simmered slowly, that stomach-wrenching smell of meat spoiled, of rotten food. Eddie had decided that was what it was, something for the pigs, perhaps, that would be added to the slop bucket at the end of the big iron stove later on. Yet when Eddie carried out the slop each evening with its floating potatoes, carrots, and other recognizable vegetables, it didn't have that spoiled smell of the pot on the stove.

Katrina didn't seem to notice the smell. As if it hovered like fog near the stove, they moved away from it, Katrina still tiptoeing, her bare feet making no sound.

Eddie let her lead the way, humoring her, a smile tugging at the corners of his lips, trying to pretend that he felt no reluctance. Trying to forget those sounds he often heard in the middle of the night, in the deepest hours before dawn. Sounds that the logical front of his mind tried to find reasons for. Perhaps even a family of nocturnal animals, who had made their homes in the thick walls low in the house. Perhaps that, he had soothed himself many times. Perhaps their grunting, hissing sounds traveled through the walls, like sound through a pipe. Perhaps Katrina had seen one of those animals somewhere low in the house. Maybe there was a room without light that to a five-year-old child looked like a dungeon.

In the shadows of an inner hall she pulled him toward a corner. It led eastward, toward the porch that each morning had to be swept again, as if it hadn't been swept yesterday ... that each morning had torn vines and damp forest leaves, as if something had been dragged through the forest floor and across the porch sometime during the night. The porch that had a solid door, without glass. He had never tried to open it. He only swept off the debris, which gathered on the ground beneath the edge of the porch and rotted there. On that side of the house the trees grew close, there was no cut grass, no lawn. No path. No reason for the porch.

Katrina pulled him into the strange hall. It was narrow and high, and almost dark. Light came only from an open door behind them.

She pulled him on in silence. They passed a door that stood open and issued a small amount of light. A glance showed him that it connected to the kitchen, and was a large pantry and storage room with shelves to the ceiling and a long wood table in the center. A door in the opposite wall opened near the large kitchen range. He glimpsed the black iron corner of the reservoir as Katrina pulled him on past.

Shadows returned as they passed on by. They came to a tall wardrobe near the end of this long, narrow hall which seemed to lead nowhere. Then he saw the door at the end.

Katrina went around the wardrobe, and stopped at the closed door.

She pointed, whispering, "There. That door was open, and I saw the Bad Things, coming up out of the dungeon."

Eddie had never been in this part of the house.

The silence seemed total. His ears rang with the sounds of his own body, rushing blood, pounding heart, ragged breathing. He was in a place he didn't belong. Aunt Theodora wouldn't approve.

"Open the door," Katrina whispered, her voice a shock to Eddie.

It was like being in a cave, this long, narrow passageway between its thick, hollow walls. Going where? Obviously to this dark, closed door. There was much of the house that to Eddie seemed cave-like. Even the shorter, lighter hallway on the third floor by his room. This big useless house, known locally as the Wickham House, he had learned from Angie, was like a cave above ground, a cave with long, narrow windows of glass that were never opened. Just enough windows to let in slivers of light, leaving corners in perpetual shadow. Leaving them holding things that were never seen, things that a person felt stared through invisible eyes.

Stop it, Eddie ordered himself. Be a man. Be brave. Katrina thinks you're a brave warrior who can fix the Bad Things and make them go away, so she can play in the house, in all the dark corners and under the fancy tables with the curved legs and lion's feet, and behind the couches with the fringes. She's not afraid of dark corners.

Eddie turned the knob on the door, and discovered it opened inward, over what at first looked like the dark dungeon Katrina had described.

Then he saw a dim light somewhere below.

Visible now, as if growing slowly in front of his eyes, the steps came. Made of stone, they dropped away toward the pale light. Odors of dampness, of earth never exposed to sunlight, met him like a wall.

The light below was not natural light, but soft, yellowish, like a candle. Was Aunt Theodora down here? This, perhaps, was her root cellar, the place where she kept potatoes, apples, turnips, other things grown in gardens and stored beneath ground. Yet he detected no sweet fragrance, only the cool, damp earth.

Then, something else.

At first he didn't recognize the rotted smell. A mouse ... a burial place, perhaps, for some little rodent.

Then he knew what it was: the food in the pot that Aunt Theodora cooked.

The stink of it touched him and was gone, as if it had only lingered from a past time. From the night, perhaps.

Though Katrina kept tight against his leg, she urged him forward, onto the stone landing in the place she called the dungeon.

"Here," she whispered, and Eddie bent to her, to hear her clearly, because now her whisper was growing softer. With her smooth cheek brushing his, she said, "It was right here, on this big step. Only it was dark behind it. I saw its face."

What did it look like?

Her answer to his silent, useless question startled him and made him wonder, made him remember sounds he had heard during the long nights he had spent in his room, sleepless, before he'd met Angie.

"It hissed at me."

He hesitated. Snakes. Why hadn't he thought of snakes? Snakes crawling in the hall at night outside his door, that first night he was in the house. That slithering sound he had heard. Snakes here in the cellar. Of course.

Snakes were not bad, though. Even the poisonous snakes were only trying to protect themselves, their territory. Keep away from me, its hissing warned. Go away, leave me alone. Unaggressive snakes got out of the way, if possible. They bit only if cornered or pushed, if they were stepped on unexpectedly or were otherwise frightened.

He squeezed her hand, then pulled his free. She reached up desperately, making a soft crying sound in her throat. But Eddie needed both hands to show her what he meant, to ask her if this was what she'd seen.

He spread his hands for length. Some harmless black snakes were longer than he could reach. They hissed, even though they had no poison sacs.

Then he cupped his hands for size. Not large. Native snakes never were larger around than his hands could measure.

Katrina watched him, her lips parted, eyes large and round, waiting hand hanging in the air.

From his mouth Eddie motioned with two fingers for the forked tongue, and the hiss.

Snake?

Katrina only stared at him, blinking a bit, her hand reaching with determination. She didn't feel safe if he wasn't holding her hand.

He relented. She hadn't understood exactly what he meant. Perhaps she'd never seen a snake, except the one she had seen on this stone landing.

A black snake would be hard to see on the dark floor of earth, whose odor rose so cloyingly. Still, he took her hand firmly in his and went forward.

When they passed beyond the edge of the standing door, he saw the cellar below was indeed lighted by candles. Two of them, placed on rocks that jutted from the basement walls. The floor looked damp, the streaks of candlelight touching upon it like lost starlight on a still, black lake.

He saw no baskets of vegetables or fruit. There was nothing but the stone walls, the glistening floor, and a stone, slab-like table against the wall, as if it had been chiseled out of the rock.

He would have turned back, taken Katrina, and tried to explain to her, out in the sunlight, on the ground where he could draw with a stick, that she had seen a snake ... that to be safe, she should stay away from the stone steps, the door that led to her dungeon. It was no place to play, no place to explore.

He would have hurried out—but he looked again at the wall above the table, between the burning candles.

There was something strange about it.

He went down another step, then another and another. He was only vaguely aware that Katrina came at his side, squeezed tight against his leg, her fingers pinching the material of his overalls leg.

He stared at the stone wall.

Unlike the rest of the wall, with its jutting rocks like bricks, the rocks were flat and seemed to form some kind of symbol. Not a cross, as there was in churches, not a symbol of the death of Christ, but something else. It was like a puzzle, where one must figure out the face, or the meaning. Flat, smooth stones, glistening with dampness, made a strange star-like shape. Within the star, gradually becoming visible among all the stones, all the lines leading from one stone to another of its kind, Eddie found the cross. But it was upside down, with the crossbar low on the pole.

He stepped off the last step, his bare feet feeling that the floor was cold to the touch, but not wet, as it had looked from above. With snakes only peripherally on his mind, he slowly went closer to the strange, long table.

He stopped, Katrina pushing against him.

Then he noticed something else.

The table was too low for a real table, too long and narrow, yet too wide for a shelf. It was more like a bed of some kind.

It was the size of a coffin, he suddenly saw. Solid, at least seven feet long, a yard high, and a yard wide, with a top made of one long piece of smooth stone, like a stone used for a house step. There were faint depressions in it, and in those depressions was something still red in the center, as if it had pooled, drying to brownish red at the edges. Brown-red streaks stained the cobbled sides and disappeared into the black ground beneath.

Blood.

Something had been killed here!

"What are you doing here?" a voice behind them demanded harshly, so harshly that at first Eddie did not recognize the speaker.

Katrina's gasp was sharply audible in the moments of silence that followed the sound of Aunt Theodora's voice. Eddie whirled.

She stood on the stone landing at the top of the steps, and in that first glance she looked huge, threatening, looming in the open door. In her right hand she carried a large butcher knife. Something white dangled from her left hand.

"You children should never come down here," she said in a less severe tone as she came on down the steps. "There could be snakes here. Now run along, and never come here again."

The white object in her left hand began suddenly to struggle, its wings reaching out as if they might help it fly away from the impending danger. But its feet were caught tight in Aunt Theodora's hand. It was one of the hens from the barn lot, Eddie saw in horror. An hour ago it had been feeding contentedly on the corn he had scattered on the ground.

With Katrina's fingers digging into his, Eddie paused long enough to lift her into his arms. He carried her quickly up the steps.

At the top of the steps his eyes followed hers, and he glanced back. Aunt Theodora had laid the terrified chicken on the bloody table. It squawked and screamed in agony and terror as the butcher knife bore down on its straining neck.

Katrina cried out, and strained against Eddie, to get down, to run back. "No! No!" she screamed. "Don't hurt it!"

"Edward!" Aunt Theodora demanded, looking up, the knife poised before finishing its job. "Get that child out of here! Shut the door when you go out."

The white wings of the chicken flapped against the bloody stone table. Katrina screamed and cried, and strained to get down. Eddie held onto her, tighter.

When he reached back to pull the door shut, he glanced once more, against his will, back at the strange, horrible scene in the cellar.

The chicken lay still on the table, its head hanging by a strip of skin at the neck, its wings inert. Aunt Theodora had knelt. Her head was lowered, as if she were looking for something on the floor.

Or as if she were in prayer.

Praying to the strange configurations on the wall.

CHAPTER 10

*A*ngie was waiting, wearing a plaid dress, the waist small, the long, gathered skirt ending in a ruffled hem just above her ankles. Though she stood against the tree where they always sat, her hair gleamed as if it contained the sun itself. Eddie wanted to drop to her feet, he was so glad to see her. His mind cried to push away the dark cloak of the morning, but even the sight of Angie did not rid him of the memory of the past hours.

"What's wrong?" Angie asked, the moment she saw him. Her smile died, her eyes searched his face for an answer.

He struggled to find expression to explain what had happened. Katrina— he motioned a short, little girl, long hair. He reached into his overalls bib for his pencil and tablet, and realized he had forgotten them. His hands motioned, his mouth twisted in frustration.

Trying to keep Katrina from running back into the house. Trying to comfort her. *"I'm going to tell that Miss Theodora. I'm going to tell her!"* Katrina had raged, weeping, struggling to pull away from Eddie after he had carried her out of the house. While he tried to hold her from running back, she fought against him in fury at what she had seen. *"I'm going to tell that bad old Miss Theodora! I'm going to tell her! She hurt my chicken! She was hurting my chicken! I'm going to tell her she can't do that!"*

"No, no!"

Eddie tried hard to breathe normally, to calm down, even now, remembering. He had to explain to Angie about Katrina's tears, her struggles, her anger at Aunt Theodora. He had to explain how finally he had carried her

67

home. For the first time he had crossed the area between the old mansion and the little shed where the family lived.

With Katrina weeping in his arms, he went into the shed. How could he explain to Katrina's mother what had happened? Would Katrina's mother think Eddie had hurt Katrina? But of course Katrina could talk ... she would tell.

On his shoulder Katrina wept. "She hurt my chicken. She made it bleed. She cut its head off. Why did she do that?"

Her mother, Eddie thought anxiously, Katrina's mother could tell Katrina. That was what people did to chickens, to pigs, to lambs, to calves. That was what they did, in order to cook and eat their bodies. Katrina's mother would know what to say.

The shed was quiet and shadowed. The only light came through the open door and one high, tiny window. Beds made of straw ticks lay in wood frames on the floor in two corners. In the center of the room was a rough, hand-hewn table with benches on the sides. There was a little black iron cookstove in another corner, the pipe rising through the roof. It was a stove like Eddie's own mother's, and he took a moment to look at it longingly. There was a granite teakettle and a coffeepot on its flat surface.

But no one was home.

Katrina wept against him.

Eddie slowly lowered her to the dirt floor of the shed.

He made a motion with his hands, a sweeping motion that asked where her mother was. Then he remembered: this morning he had seen her going away, carrying a bundle of clothes she had washed and ironed for someone in town. Sometimes she stayed away all day, cleaning houses, or doing laundry for people who wanted their laundry done at home. She wasn't always back by noon, but usually soon after ... back home to feed Katrina, and see that she took a nap. Katrina had many times run joyfully through the trees toward the shed, calling back to Eddie, "Here comes Mama! Here comes Mama!"

Angie asked now, inserting herself into his dark memory, "The little girl? Did something happen to the little girl?"

Eddie motioned to his eyes, trailing a finger down his cheek.

Angie asked, "She was crying?"

Eddie nodded.

Angie took his arm and pulled him to their usual seat on the rough, exposed roots of the tree. Her hands covered his a moment, then she handed him her tablet and pencil.

"Can you ...?"

He picked up the pencil then dropped it in frustration. He had learned to print all the letters of the alphabet, but he didn't know enough words yet to express himself. How could he write "chicken," or "stone table in the cellar with dried blood," with a small pool of blood not yet dried? He picked up the pencil again to try to draw what he had seen, and his fingers gripped it hard suddenly as a memory returned.

His nightmare about Wee Willie Winkle—reliving the actual slaughter, years ago.

The pig, the sound of the pig in the night, the cry he had thought was part of the dream. Aunt Theodora had lied. A man hadn't come and taken the pig away, she had killed it. On the stone table ...

Why had she lied?

He began to draw. Bent over the tablet, for the first time drawing a picture for Angie. He drew a door. He drew steps made of cobblestones.

"A door," Angie said, "Stone steps going down."

Eddie motioned to the ground and pointed with a finger downward.

"In the ground? A cellar?"

Eddie nodded vigorously. Then made a motion of a huge house, and drew on the paper the outlines of a house.

"Beneath Wickham House?"

He nodded, and bent to draw again, his hand trembling with the urgency to let Angie see. He drew the table, made of stone, against the stone wall with the strange figures in it.

"An altar?" she asked.

He stared at her. An altar? He hadn't thought of that before. An altar? As if in a church, yet not in a real church, but in a dark, dank cellar.

"An altar in a cellar?" she said, her eyes narrowing, her stare straight and steady.

Eddie drew the shapes of a pig and a chicken. Then a butcher knife. He made a mark that severed the heads of the animals, and made drops falling like teardrops.

"Blood?" she whispered. "Butchering? Killing?"

He nodded.

"Your aunt Theodora makes animal sacrifices on an altar in the cellar beneath Wickham House?" She was still whispering, her eyes darker as they narrowed, her lashes shadowing.

Sacrifices? Eddie stopped drawing and returned her stare. It was as if she understood something he did not. He could see the expression of horror in her eyes.

"Eddie... if that's what she was doing, Eddie, do you know what that means?"

He shook his head.

"It has something to do with the devil, Eddie."

He felt a coldness move over his skin, rapidly, like water turning to ice. It tightened around him. He had a deep fear of the devil, and the powers of the devil. If unleashed, those powers were beyond imagination, as strong perhaps as the powers of God. He had heard preachers talk about those powers all his life. He feared the devil even more than he feared death.

"I don't think you should go back there, Eddie." Her hand clasped his wrist and held it. "If she's calling forth the devil, if she's seeking its evil for some reason—you know," she whispered close to him, "there are old rumors. I heard my grandmother talking once, years ago, when Miss Theodora took in a child and kept it a while. The rumors were that Mr. Wickham found her in some faraway place, that she was part of a Satanic church, or something. She was a young woman, and others of the group were sentenced to hang because they had been sacrificing humans. So he rescued her, and married her. It was said she was the daughter of the leader of the church, and he was hanged."

Eddie held his breath, listening. Ice covered his scalp. She said, "I was told never to repeat it. That it was only gossip. But—I don't know."

His lips had turned dry. He licked them. Their eyes held.

She said, "You should leave, Eddie. Just walk away, now. I wish I could take you home with me, but I can't. Not yet. But you could go," she paused, and her tongue moistened her own lower lip. "You could go into town. Maybe to the sheriff's office."

Eddie shook his head and motioned. *Little girl.* Katrina. He couldn't leave Katrina. She would be there alone with Theodora, every day. And now, she knew too much.

The sheriff would say, too, it was only a chicken. Or a pig. They didn't count.

The sheriff would do nothing. Nor would anyone else.

He hadn't even told her yet about Katrina seeing what she had called the Bad Things. But how could he tell her that? He had no way of expressing the fears of a little girl. He had thought she saw black snakes, large and fat, perhaps from eating sacrificial food. But had they been snakes? Or something far worse?

"You don't want to leave Katrina?" Angie asked.

Eddie shook his head. "No, no."

"Does she play often around the house? Wickham House?"

Eddie nodded. He motioned, *Katrina, eyes, cellar. Steps down. Tears. Chicken. Pet. Killed.*

Angie watched him in silence, then said, "Katrina saw the cellar ... the chicken ..."

Eddie nodded. *Yes, yes, yes.*

"Katrina was frightened."

Eddie stopped, then smiled faintly. "No, no." He made a face of rage, and claws of his fingers.

Angie laughed softly, a sound sad, not happy. "Yes, so she wasn't so afraid as she was angry."

Eddie nodded, and made a cutting sweep with the edge of his hand. The steps, back to Aunt Theodora. His touched his lips, then indicated *talk, talk*.

Angie smiled again. "So Katrina was ready to tell Miss Theodora what she thought about it."

Eddie nodded. He had carried her home, held her there as she'd continued to weep alternately with trying angrily to go back and tell Miss Theodora that she was bad, bad for hurting Katrina's chicken.

Finally, after a long time, Katrina had gone to sleep. Eddie had left her there, on one of the beds, sleeping. Then, without going into the kitchen for his noon meal as he always had before, he hurried instead to meet Angie.

Angie sat still, in silence, looking down at her hands. For a long time she just sat.

"I don't know what to do," she finally said. "If we went to Reverend Cheney, he would probably say she's making her sacrifices to God. He'd say if she only sacrifices animals ... after all, it's only animals ... I mean, that's what Reverend says, that's what the grownups say, and I suppose they know. Animals don't have souls, the reverend says, Papa says. People do, animals don't. To me ... even animals ... it doesn't seem right. Why would God want a creature killed for *him*? If all things come from God, then the life of the animal is *important*." She paused, looking off into the forest, her eyes squinted. Eddie understood. The logic of grownups sometimes seemed cruelly unreasonable to him.

"But—she's sacrificing to the devil, it sounds to me. And that's very dangerous. She's her father's daughter. I want you to leave, Eddie."

Angie sighed, drew back to him, her eyes coming to meet his. "But if you don't want to leave Katrina ...?"

Eddie shook his head. *Not yet.* Not until ... until when? Perhaps her parents would soon make enough money to move. To find a real house, where Katrina's mother wouldn't have to leave her all morning when she went to work. Then ... by then, maybe Eddie would have learned to write, so that he could communicate better, and find a job.

Angie looked into his eyes. "Are you afraid, Eddie?"

He hesitated. Pride stepped in. He didn't want Angie to see how scared he was, that he had been scared the moment he had to go with Aunt Theodora. He was, after all, struggling to become a man. A man who could support a wife and children, buy a home for them, make a happy life.

He shook his head. "No, no." *Not for myself*, he motioned, *only for Katrina*.

The lie settled like bitter almonds in his stomach.

CHAPTER 11

*H*e milked the cow by the light of the lantern, one of the last jobs of the evening. Aunt Theodora hadn't questioned him when he came in past sundown. She didn't ask him why he had not come to eat his noon meal. She seemed distracted instead as she stirred something in the big pot on the stove. Eddie smelled the familiar odor of chicken cooking. But beyond that was the other odor, the faint smell of rotten meat, or rotten potatoes or some other root, perhaps dug from the forest floor. He had seen her coming from the forest at times, something gathered into the basket she carried. She never explained to him what it was. He had seen mushrooms, but also other roots that looked strangely like tiny men with twisted bodies.

He sat on the little one-legged stool, the milk bucket held firmly between his knees, his head against the cow's flank. His hands squeezed milk from two fat, warm teats. The cow stood still, her jaws rhythmically grinding corn from the manger. Above the noise of the milk squirting into a half bucket of milk he heard the call.

"Katrina?"

It sounded far away, beyond the barn walls, the sounds of the cow munching grain, beyond the sounds of chickens clucking and their babies peeping as they settled to bed beneath the feathers of their mothers.

Eddie lifted his head and listened. Katrina had hardly been off his mind. Their morning together blended with his afternoon with Angie, and their efforts to make sense of what Eddie had so laboriously described to her. Still, when Katrina hadn't come to watch him feed the animals, he had thought of her as being with her family. And that was good; she was safe. Sometimes, through the trees, he had glimpsed her in evenings past with her older brothers, or with her mother and father. Especially in the evening, they sat outside the shed, on blocks of wood they used for chairs. Sometimes, he had seen them cooking over a small fire. They were only glimpses, people a hundred yards away through trees that mostly obscured the view.

"*Katrina?*"

The voice was closer. A man's deep voice, lifted in a questioning call.

Eddie got up. He hung the bucket of milk safely on a peg on the wall, and went out into the barn lot. The sun had gone down, but its glow lit the sky, and darkness had not yet claimed all the land. Only the forest was dark.

It was Katrina's papa, coming out of the trees and toward the barn lot. He was a slightly built man, narrow in the shoulders, who stooped already like an old man, even though he still had a young family, a young wife. His eyes darted this way and that, searching, worried.

"Edward," he said, "have you seen my little girl, Katrina?"

Eddie opened his mouth. Nothing, not even his one word, no, came forth. The man stared at him, his dark eyes miserable, narrowed into flesh that was only now beginning to show wrinkles.

Eddie pointed upward. The man's eyes glanced up and saw nothing but the open sky, where a few stars had begun to blink.

Noon. I saw her at noon. Eddie tried to explain with his hands.

Mr. Etchens stared at him.

Eddie pointed toward the man's house, and then cradled his cheek. Nap. Katrina was asleep, the last time he saw her.

The man continued to stare at him, eyes squinting. He stood in silence. Eddie grew increasingly uncomfortable as he went through the motions again. At noon, he saw her. He took her home, and when he left, she was sleeping.

Mr. Etchens finally said, "She went home to take a nap?"

Eddie nodded eagerly. That was close enough. He made a circle with his fingers and pointed up again.

"At noon," the man said, turning, looking into the woods. "That was the last time you saw her?"

Eddie nodded, and nodded, uncertain that Mr. Etchens could see him from the corner of his eyes.

"Well," the man said, moving off toward the rear of the barn, "she's probably only playing, and forgot to come in. Much obliged, young man."

Eddie watched him climb the fence into the open pasture behind the barn. He went out of sight, and Eddie returned to finish milking the cow. He turned her out to pasture with the mare, and patted the two pigs.

He blew out the barn lantern and carried the bucket of milk to Aunt Theodora in the kitchen, wanting desperately to tell her that Katrina's papa was calling for Katrina. But she worked diligently at the cabinet counter near the stove, wiping the countertop with such vigor her whole body shook.

Eddie went into the washroom. He pumped water into the sink and washed his face and hands. With damp hands he pushed his hair back, combing through it with his fingers. He listened, but heard nothing beyond the thick walls. The washroom was nearly dark. By the time he returned to the kitchen, Aunt Theodora had lighted several candles in the middle of the table.

At the one place setting was his plate. She never ate with him. In the beginning, Angie had suggested that she wanted him to live with her because she was lonely. But what good was he to her when she so seldom sat down with him, when he couldn't talk to her?

There was a large glass of milk, a thick slice of home-baked bread, and a plate of food. It had not come from the pot on the stove. On his plate was a variety of cooked vegetables. He was relieved to see that she had not offered him pork, or chicken.

He hadn't eaten since morning. Still, his throat seemed closed against this food, his stomach in revolt. He longed to leave the kitchen and go see if Katrina had been found.

He forced down the milk and bread. Aunt Theodora baked her own bread, and now he saw her getting out the big wooden bowl in which she measured some flour. In the center of the flour she vigorously made a valley, and into the valley she poured milk, yeast, salt and grease from the copper container that always sat on the reservoir of the stove where it was kept liquid. With her right hand she began rolling the mixture into a ball.

Eddie rose and hesitated. Aunt Theodora appeared not to notice him. He took himself to be excused, and went out onto the porch, where he could listen for the call for Katrina.

But the night was quiet now, except for the night insects and a dog barking somewhere far away.

Eddie drew a long breath of relief. Katrina had been found, surely. Maybe she had only been hiding, playing, the way children sometimes did.

Eddie returned to the kitchen and, unnoticed, emptied most of his plate of food into the slop bucket at the back of the cookstove.

He washed his dishes and put them away. In the sink, he saw, was the butcher knife, blood still damp and thick on its long, wide blade. Feeling as if he pulled into his skin like a turtle hiding, he washed the bloody knife, too, because he couldn't stand the sight of the blood. He dried it carefully and laid it on the counter. Aunt Theodora seemed not to notice.

He stood awkwardly then, waiting. Aunt Theodora always told him good night, and he always nodded and smiled at her in return. But tonight, she was intent on mixing the bread, moving the ball of dough onto the kneading board.

At last she noticed him, and nodded curtly.

"That's fine, Edward. You can go to bed now. Good night."

He took a candle from the kitchen table and passed through the door into the silence and darkness of the house beyond. With a long sigh of relief, he turned right, into the hall that led to the narrow service stairs to the third floor.

In his room, the door closed, he felt safe. For the first time he realized that when he closed that door behind him, it was like shutting himself into another world. His den. His safe place.

The room was small, with no more than enough space for the nightstand, the chest at the foot of the bed, where he kept what few clothes he had, and the bed. The one window was open, as far as he had managed to push it. Through it came the sounds of crickets and katydids.

Eddie pulled off his overalls and sat down on the bed, his back against the headboard. He pulled out from beneath his quilt the tablet and pencil, and the storybook. Although it was hard to concentrate, he had to. Even though his thoughts kept returning to the morning, to Katrina, her hurt and anger, and then to the afternoon and Angie, still he must work. There were words he knew now. In the silence of his mind he could read, from memory, the few paragraphs of the short story in the front of the book. The story Angie had read to him over and over, pointing out words.

On his own he had found those same words in other stories, and even in the Bible she had given him. He could write those words now, in careful block letters. But they didn't make a sentence, or explain a thought, or express a meaning. Numbers were easier, and he longed to go to his arithmetic book, but he had to learn words, so he could write notes to the men he asked for employment.

You'll learn, Eddie, he could hear Angie say. *None of us learns in a few days, or even weeks. It takes time, Eddie, but you'll learn.*

Time? Tonight he felt as if he had no time.

He could tell by the night sounds the approximate time. By the heaviness of his eyes, and their need for sleep. Midnight, he was thinking, as he finally put his books, tablet, and pencil back under the quilt.

He had slid down into bed and closed his eyes when he heard the cry. It was a sad, desperate, plaintive cry. Like the sound of an animal wailing helplessly.

Eddie sat up. This time the cry was not in the house, but outside somewhere, in the woods. He went to the window and felt the cool night air wash against his face. He listened carefully, holding his breath. Somewhere beneath him the house creaked. Boards within the house often creaked, soft, distant sounds, as if the house murmured to itself, night and day, on and on. But outside the night had grown quiet. The katydids that earlier had made such a racket, the jarflies with their loud buzzing, the crickets, had almost stopped.

The cry came again, out in the woods, and something made of sick dread caught in Eddie's throat.

"*Katrina!*"

"*Katrina ... Katrina ... Katrina ...*"

Like thinning echoes, the calls came.

My God, no, no.

Katrina's papa was still trying to find her. Now, too, her brothers were calling, their voices echoing their papa's. He had to go help.

Don't leave your room at night. This time, he had to disobey. They still hadn't found Katrina.

He pulled on his overalls hastily and rushed out into the hall, finding a wall of blackness. He hurried back into his room and grabbed up the candle, almost blowing out the flame. He steadied his hand and cupped his free palm to protect the flame. With his bare feet thumping on the stairs, he hurried down both flights, into the narrow hall, and from there into the kitchen.

Several candles still burned on the kitchen table, lighting the cabinets, the stove.

Aunt Theodora stood between the stove and table, staring at him severely.

"Edward! What are you doing up at this time of night? Go to bed!"

Eddie motioned desperately toward the door. He pointed toward the home of the Etchens, then held up three fingers. He touched his fingers to his open mouth to indicate calling. *Hadn't Aunt Theodora heard them calling?* Katrina ... little girl this high.

Lost.

He had to go help find her.

"What could you do?" Aunt Theodora said, dismissing it with a slash of her hand. "Go back to your room, Edward, and stay there until I call you in the morning!"

He stared at her defiantly. For the first time since he had come to live with her, he returned her stare. Katrina was lost. Didn't she know Katrina was lost?

"They'll find her," Aunt Theodora said. "She's only wandered away. Children do that occasionally. They follow an animal, or something, then they lie down and go to sleep and don't hear the calls. They'll find her without your help. Even if you went out there, and even if you found her, how could you let them know?"

I could bring her home!

Aunt Theodora went to the stove and opened the big oven door. The smell of fresh-baked bread wafted into the room. She drew out a large black pan that held four loaves of bread, their tops rounded high and brown. She turned the pan upside down over the kneading board, and the loaves tumbled out in one. She pulled them apart, and steam rose from the white inner sides.

"Would you like a slice of hot bread and butter to take up to bed with you,

Edward?"

He shook his head, but she was already slicing it from the end, with the butcher knife he had washed at suppertime. The one with the dried blood staining it, turning the wood handle permanently dark.

It's only an animal ... they're only animals, Angie had said, with no conviction in her voice. *They don't have souls.*

But the heel of the bread was his favorite part. Especially when it was hot from the oven, and when it had a thick slab of butter melting on it.

He watched her use the same butcher knife to slice the butter from the covered bowl on the table. The butter slid across the hot knife and onto the bread. Aunt Theodora replaced the top of the butter dish and smiled at Eddie as she handed him the bread. Her smile was tight, as if it pained her.

But her voice was almost gentle as she said, "Don't worry. I'm sure everything will be all right."

Eddie went back upstairs.

Sitting on the side of his bed, he ate the bread and butter, in that act deliberately keeping his mind only on the food, trying to forget the knife that had cut it, trying to forget what connected to the knife ... the cellar, Katrina, the reason she had taken him to the cellar ...

... The strange table ...

... The altar ...

Katrina, missing, lost, somewhere in the woods?

Katrina, lost?

No, not Katrina. She knew the woods better than he. No matter where he went to chop wood, she could find him, and then find her way home. She had never followed him in the afternoon, though, when he met Angie. Because her mother was always home. When her mother was home, most of the time Katrina also stayed home. In the afternoons she took a nap. She had told Eddie that, many times, and sometimes her mother took a nap, too. Or sometimes she ironed, making pretty the clothes she had washed for other people. Then she folded them into the basket she carried each morning when she walked into town, and to the homes of the people she worked for.

This afternoon, Katrina had been sleeping. Hadn't she been sleeping when her mother had come home? Her mother came home at noon, or soon after, most days.

Eddie wanted to know, find out from Katrina's mother. Hadn't she been on the bed in the corner, taking a nap, when Mrs. Etchens had come home?

But he had orders to stay in his room until he was called, in the morning. Even then, who could he ask? How could he make his questions understood?

He listened for the calls, for her name, echoed in the night by the voices of those who loved her.

But at last, the night was silent.

CHAPTER 12

*E*ddie lay on his bed, staring at the ceiling. The night beyond the window seemed warily silent. No dogs barked in the distance. Cricket sounds had softened and nearly stopped. Eddie listened and heard no voice calling for Katrina.

He prayed to the Lord they had found her. He had to make himself believe that was why the night had become silent: Katrina had been found. In his mind's eye he could see her, curled beside a log near the little stream of water she had wanted Eddie to help her find, her rag doll in her arms. Asleep in the arms of nature, and then carried home in the arms of her papa. Eddie had to believe that.

He turned onto his side. Beneath him, the straw in the mattress crackled dryly, masking at first the other sound.

When the cry reached him, Eddie reared up, tense, listening hard.

As if a door had opened and closed, as if continual screams and cries had been released for just a breath, Eddie heard it. Shrill, high-pitched, brief. A tortured animal? Katrina? Then, as if the door had solidly closed, it was gone again.

He wanted it to be part of his own mind, created by his fears. Part of the night in this big house, with so many rooms he had never seen. He wanted it to be an owl in the woods, a death screech of something wild. But he was afraid. The distorted sound, dimmed by distance, still seemed too near to have been in the woods. Now the scream was gone, and only its memory remained, like fine wires twanging through him.

His thoughts kept going back to Katrina, rebelling: no, not Katrina. She was safe at home in bed, between her mama and papa. Maybe Aunt Theodora herself was calling for help. It was not a man, not the hoarse misery of a man's cry.

Eddie got up again, pulling on his overalls with one hand and reaching for the candle stub with the other. This time he didn't go down the backstairs, but turned at the landing on the second floor and opened the door into the front bedroom hallway.

It was longer, wider than the third-floor hall. Doors along the way stood open, like doors upon dungeons as dark as the darkest midnight sky. The tiny flame of his candle barely burned, flickering weakly. Its dim light showed him the walls, the outlines of doorways, and furniture along the hall.

He came to the balcony, and saw a polished railing around the drop into the foyer below. To his right, on the balcony, a door stood open, revealing a room lighted softly.

He went toward it. Aunt Theodora's private rooms?

He stood on the threshold, looking into a small hallway where two doors stood open. Both rooms were dimly lighted with candles. One was a sitting room, with sofa and chairs and a chest against the wall with a gold-framed mirror above it.

The other was a bedroom, with a large bed like a fat spider against the wall. It had not been slept in. It was still made up, its fringed hand-crocheted bedspread hanging almost to the floor. At the side of the bed, whose headboard reached halfway to the high ceiling, was a small ladder, for climbing into the bed. Eddie backed uneasily out of the room.

He glanced into the sitting room, enough to see that its only occupant was the doll Katrina had thought so grand. It sat almost like a small person, a smile on its pale pink-cheeked face. He gave it a second glance, then stared. It had fat cheeks, and a sharp, thin nose. Its mouth was tiny and pursed, like a spoiled child's. It was like a gnome, he thought. Ugly and evil in their hearts, they came from the center of the earth to do harm to humans. They attracted children, especially.

It was good that Aunt Theodora had kept it from Katrina. Much better that she have a rag doll.

He edged out. Aunt Theodora was not in her rooms.

Candles below lighted the stairway down to the first floor. Eddie hurried, almost forgetting the candle stub in his hand.

In the lower hall, above the whispery squeaks his bare feet made on the polished wood, a sound reached him again. He stopped. Not a cry this time, but those unnerving noises he had heard before, which seemed to rise through the hollow walls that surrounded his room. Utterances he had tried to identify with something familiar, the whinings or gruntings of animals, the hissings of snakes, the voiceless groan of wind through broken shingles. But it was none of those.

The cellar!

He hurried to the back hall and turned right, where Katrina had led him to see the "Bad Things" she had been so afraid of. The long hall ahead of him seemed at first dark and empty. Not even the wardrobe was visible. Yet in the darkness something moved. Outlines changed, dark figures replaced things less dark.

Then, a light, dim, almost nonexistent, came from the room between this long, dark hall and the kitchen, and as Eddie stared he saw Aunt Theodora, carrying a candle in her left hand and the butcher knife in her right. He instinctively pinched to darkness the tiny flame of the candle stub he carried, so she would not see him.

As she entered the hall he saw her face, lighted by her candle, features shadowed and made huge, her eyes narrow, dark slits, her mouth a tight band. She entered the hall where Eddie stood, but did not look his way. He pushed back against the wall, melting, he hoped, into the protection of the dark corner. Then he saw Theodora was not alone. He stared at the creatures following her.

Stared, stunned, stupefied by horror.

Behind Aunt Theodora they came. Men, dressed in Halloween costumes? No. There were no costumes, no dress, no clothing. The only light was in the woman's hand, and the shadows cast behind her touched upon the glistening bodies of creatures that moved on two hind legs, claws clicking faintly against the floor. Their black skin glistened in the dancing shadows and feeble light as if they had been oiled. Eddie glimpsed hands with strange, long, rubbery fingers—clawed, like their feet. He saw faces that sloped to snouts, curled back to sharp, long teeth, eyes slitted and as black as the bottom of a well.

They moved together, blending in darkness. Eddie heard mutterings, moanings, low, unearthly cries—the sounds that had risen through his walls. Or that had come from the hall outside his door.

Briefly they were in his view, and then they were going through the door into the cellar. And in that moment Eddie glimpsed a pale body, hanging limp, in the arms of one of them.

The door closed. The hall was dark and still, and Eddie heard only his own gasps. He felt smothered by the dark, unable to breathe, as if he were lost in hell itself.

Then he saw a pale, dim light through the edge of the pantry door. He crept forward. Through the doorway of the food storage room he could see the kitchen. The light there indicated that the candles on the table were still burning.

He slipped forward, past the wardrobe, and paused by the cellar door. He heard his heart sounds in his ears. Sounds of rushing blood, of fear and terror.

Beyond that, silence. Then, the almost soundless licking murmurs of the candles in the kitchen.

In the pale light that reached the end of the hall, the outline of the cellar door became visible. Eddie touched the knob. It seemed strangely warm, as if some inner thing heated it.

His mind swirled with what he had seen. Indescribable beings. How could he tell Angie so that she would see what he had seen? *What were they?* Was it they who brought soil from underground into the halls? Was it they whom Aunt Theodora fed, from the pot of stinking food on the stove, as if they were pets? Pets? Creatures almost as tall as Aunt Theodora herself, with skins oily and glistening ... were they what he had seen?

And a small white body in the arms of one?

Was that what he had seen?

Or was it something else, a part of the creature itself? Something that rose out of the caves beneath the house and dotted the cliffs, even back by the hill where the meadow was, where he had met Angie so many times ...

What had he seen?

The sounds came softly at first, almost like a congregation singing in a churchyard somewhere. The sounds of varying voices, of animals deep in their dens, of snakes hissing, of bodies tangling. The sounds gathered and rose, and rising faintly above them came Aunt Theodora's voice. Her words indistinct, they came in a tone monotonous and even, as if she were chanting.

Unaware of having moved, Eddie found he had opened the door. On silent hinges it swung toward the cellar, away from his hand.

They had gathered below, close to the table against the wall, so that it was hidden by their bodies from Eddie's view. The two candles on the wall, separated by ten feet, barely lighted their movements. They jostled, one against the other, their sounds rising eerily toward Eddie, freezing him where he stood. In front of them, standing near the table, was Aunt Theodora, her back toward him. Her chant still was not understandable, and suddenly Eddie knew why: foreign words. Or jabberings, like someone speaking in tongues. Or perhaps a language understood only by the creatures with her.

As if she sensed him watching her, suddenly Aunt Theodora paused and looked sharply upward over her right shoulder, straight at the half-open door.

Eddie stepped back, squeezing into the darkness of the corner.

Aunt Theodora gave a brief command.

Eddie heard a soft, watery movement on the stone steps, and saw an arm-like projection, a tentacle, long fingers reaching. Its clawed end clutched the door and swung it closed. The thud was soft and close.

As if the closing of the door released Eddie, he ran. Guided by the faraway, dim light of the kitchen, he found the hallway to his room. Fumbling in the dark, his hand on the wall, he climbed. When he found his room, he fell to his knees against the closed door, and in his mind, with his palms together, he began to pray.

Stumbling for words of his own, he chose the Lord's Prayer.

Our Father, Who are in Heaven, hallowed be thy name, they kingdom come ... deliver us from evil ...

... Deliver us from evil ...

... *Deliver us from evil* ...

HE CURLED up at last on the floor against the door, as if his body would stop the entry of the horrors he had seen this night. He waited for the dawn, weeping, terrified. He had to talk to Angie; she would give him courage. She would tell him what he had seen.

Oh, God, he whispered in his mind, *deliver us from evil* ...

Outside in the night, as dawn came, the silence held. The calls for Katrina had stopped long ago.

Inside, the walls were silent. As if the creatures he had seen were the creatures of nightmare, put aside now with the rising of the sun.

The knock came at his door.

CHAPTER 13

*E*ddie went downstairs, feeling his way along the lightless stairwell, into the hall below. His breath came jaggedly. He had to act as always, do the chores as always, then he would pretend to go to work cutting wood. Once into the woods he would be free to run and find Angie. He had never been to her house, but he had walked with her to the edge of the woodland that separated her papa's land from the land of Wickham House.

Not Aunt Theodora. Not *aunt*; he could never think of her again as *aunt*. Not the woman he had seen, with the ... whatever they were. *Whatever they were.*

Angie might help him to understand.

He had to hurry to see her.

The kitchen was quiet and still, the candles on the table out. Dark shadows hovered in corners. The door to the pantry, the storage room, was closed. Working hurriedly, Eddie took the front lid off the stove. He saw coals glowing in the firebox. From the wood box behind the stove he put kindling in first, and watched it catch fire and begin to flame, making the soft eating murmurs that fire makes when it starts. He added sticks of wood until the firebox was filled, then he closed the stove.

The milk bucket sat, as it did every morning, bottom side up on the cabinet beside the sink. Eddie went to pick it up. Light from the rising sun came bleak and filtered through the window over the sink, and Eddie's eyes were drawn downward.

The butcher knife lay in the sink, crusted with blood.

Eddie backed away, then turned and hurried out, the milk bucket in his hand. This time he couldn't wash the knife. He couldn't touch it, or bear to leave its image in his mind.

He looked for Katrina. Katrina, where are you? Please, Katrina, come climbing through the fence. Come get in my way when I feed the cow and the horse and pigs. Help me with the chickens.

But he reminded himself she seldom came out so early. He was usually finishing the chores, in the morning, ready to carry the milk back to the house, when she showed up. With her rag doll under her arm. Her angel doll, she called it, because it had wings. Wings to protect her.

He looked toward the shed where she lived. Across the driveway, beyond the carriage house and the strip of woods, only parts of it were visible. It was the same shaded gray as the tree trunks. It was hard to separate building from forest; the shed looked deserted. No one walked about outside, not even into the open garden in front. Had the family loaded up their few things in the middle of the night after they'd found Katrina and left?

Eddie hoped they had.

He hoped for anything but the fears that ate at him, deep in his heart, far back in his mind. That turned his bones weak and clumsy like an old, old person's, or those of a baby yet unable to control his movements.

He had started yesterday to count the animals. Making sure they were all there, every morning, every evening. In the pig pen, two pigs now. In the pasture behind the barn, one horse and one cow. They all came at sight of him, to eat the feed he put out. The cow came into the barn and went straight to her stall in the manger. She never went to the wrong stall.

He counted the chickens. Exactly twelve hens, two roosters, and fifteen baby chicks. What went through their minds, he wondered, when one of their group was cornered and picked up by its feet and carried off? For hours afterward they remained wary and easily scared. He had seen that himself at home. He knew that folks educated in book ways would laugh at him for even thinking chickens had minds. But he knew they were easily scared, and each learned their name quickly, if given one. They responded to love and attention. How could they if they didn't have minds?

His own mind wondered, and worried, and darted this way and that, as if caught in a trap. The future he had been struggling for might never happen, he realized in cold futility. He was here, he was part of last night. He was here today, the present. And he was trapped.

He must reach Angie before it was too late.

He took the milk back to the kitchen. He slipped in quietly, looking before he stepped, his eyes searching for the woman.

She was not there. He saw signs that she had been there. His plate was on the table, as always, with cooked eggs, and strips of bacon, and a biscuit. A tall glass of milk stood precisely at the tip of the knife, as always. The spoon lay perfectly beside the knife. The fork, on the other side of the white plate with the gold trim and gold vines, lay on a folded napkin. Without sitting down he drank part of the milk. Then, watching carefully, hoping she did not walk in and see him, he emptied the rest of the food into the slop bucket.

The bucket was over half full. He carried it with him when he left the kitchen. In the barn he paused at a feed sack and put three cups of ground grains into the slop. He stirred it all into a kind of thick gruel. The pigs began to squeal and whine eagerly, running about in the pen, hungry for breakfast.

Eddie poured the gruel into the trough. The pigs dug in, their little snouts wiggling. Grunting in little noises of satisfaction, they ate.

Katrina did not come. He looked for her, for the small body slipping up behind him to make him jump, and listened for her laugh. He had jumped in great exaggeration just to hear the tinkle of her laughter. But that was days ago, before she had grown so fearful.

Eddie left the slop bucket sitting at the side of the barn and began to run.

He fought through underbrush that slapped back into his face when he pushed it away. He stumbled over rocks hidden beneath moss. Ordinarily, when he walked through a woodland that was an unknown area to him, he went more carefully. But all he knew was the direction of her house, as she had shown him. The path she followed led from the meadow on the hill, and he needed to take a shortcut now.

Breathless, he came suddenly to the edge of the woods. A white house, with screened porches and flowers growing in beds, sat in a clearing a few yards away. Between him and the house a vegetable garden grew.

He darted behind a tree and stood watching.

Three women were in the garden. One of them was Angie. Although a bonnet covered her face, he recognized the grace of her body as she stooped, the movement of her hands as she picked cucumbers and put them into a basket.

He waited, staring at her, hoping she'd be drawn to his stare.

The other two were her sister and mother. The older lady straightened and carried a basket of green beans toward the screen porch. She said something, and the older girl picked up her basket and followed.

Angie stayed. She squatted on her heels, her head turning to watch her mother and sister go into the house. A dog, lying on the porch step, got up, wagged his tail, and went into the porch with the sister.

Angie stood up, and Eddie held his breath, willing her to look at him. *Don't go into the house. Don't go.* If she did, he would have to follow her, even though her parents would not approve of her talking to him.

She turned toward him, and her hand lifted and pushed her bonnet back. Her eyes looked straight at him, but she wasn't smiling. Was she angry that he had come so close to her house? She made no motion that she saw him.

She stooped, picked up her basket, and with her skirt lifted above her ankles, ran to the porch and disappeared.

Eddie felt crushed. She had seen him. She had looked straight into his eyes. Didn't she want to talk to him?

He moved back. Go back to Wickham House, he told himself. Go back. Find out if Katrina is all right. Go to her house and see for yourself if she is there. Or if they have moved away. If they've moved, then start walking. Go to the train depot and climb into a boxcar when the train slows. Go home. *Go home.*

Tell Mama and Papa what you've seen.

He could hear his papa's voice, once he understood. "You must have been mistaken, son." And life would go on as always. Papa would not waste time twice on the crazy notions of a son who could speak only one word that usually was inappropriate.

He was hesitant to leave. Angie, the girl he loved. Could he walk back to a life she would never be a part of? But if she had turned from him, this meant she had only felt sorry for him. She was only being friendly. His love for her was unwanted, surely. She would go away to a fine school, and she would meet someone meant for her. Not him, not a skinny, ugly feller with two pairs of overalls to his name, and two shirts, one pair of shoes that he had to save for church. A feller who couldn't even talk.

The screen door closed softly, but Eddie heard it and looked again, from the protection of the trees.

Angie.

She ran down the steps, the bonnet swinging from her hand. She walked casually around the edge of the garden and then quickly straight into the woods toward him.

The moment she reached him she clutched his arm and pulled him deeper into the woods. She stretched up on her toes and kissed him softly on the lips. As before, he was too startled, too awed, to respond. His arms hung at his sides, his fingers trembled. His shoulders trembled. But too late, as finally he wished he had lifted his arms in time to catch her to him, she was apart from him and pulling him deeper into the woods.

"I've been so worried about you, Eddie," she said in a soft, urgent voice, her gaze going cautiously back toward the house. "Hurry. Let's get farther away. I'm surprised Henry, our dog, didn't hear or see you. He's really a pretty good watchdog. The moment I glimpsed you beside the tree, I held my breath. I was afraid Henry would start barking. Of course, he would have run straight to you, too, because he considers all these trees his, even though they're part of Wickham House property."

Her hand on his arm, she walked slightly ahead, pulling him deeper into the woods.

"We have to get far enough away that we won't be heard or seen. I asked Mama if I could go for a walk. She said yes, but not far. She said I must be home at noon. My sister wasn't happy. She wanted to know why I always manage to get out of work. So Mama said I have to work this afternoon. We're canning green beans and putting cucumbers in brine."

They hurried along in silence, their steps stirring dead winter leaves that turned up damp undersides. Angie seemed to have in mind a certain place. She led him as if along a path visible only to her, where the underbrush was less dense, the vines were less tangling, the trees older and taller, with no low limbs to catch their hair.

They came to a dry ravine where rainwater had uncovered stones and gravel. She drew him down into its protection. Sitting on the ground, her knees touching him, she leaned toward him.

"I've been so worried. I was afraid I wouldn't get to see you today. What's happened?"

He didn't know where to start. He had forgotten to bring his tablet. She had none with her. The ground on which they sat in the bottom of the ravine was rocky. There was no soil on which he could draw.

"I know you wouldn't have come to my house, Eddie, if something terrible hadn't happened."

Her face came close, her blue eyes almost crossed as they peered so desperately into his, as if she were trying to reach into his mind for his thoughts.

He nodded and nodded. *Yes, something terrible has happened, I'm afraid.* He made the sign that meant Katrina. *Short person, tiny girl, long, silly hair—gone.* Papa—tall, Eddie reached up to indicate height, and then touched his own smooth chin to mean whiskers.

Angie murmured, "Katrina. Gone? A man. Her papa?"

Eddie nodded vigorously. Then he touched his mouth. Last night. Calling.

A frown made a lump between Angie's eyes. She gazed hard at him, putting words to the motions of his hands.

"What happened to her?"

Eddie shrugged, his hands lifted, palm up. *I don't know. I hope they found her.*

"Did they find her?"

He hesitated, then nodded indecisively. With his lips he mouthed, Maybe.

"You don't know."

Eddie shook his head. *Maybe they moved away.* Their shed looked deserted.

Angie nodded.

But ...

"Something else?" Angie said slowly.

Eddie nodded. This was going to be the hard part.

Last night, midnight, later, much later. When most folks are sleeping. *I heard a cry, a scream. I went downstairs, to the cellar door, and I saw ... Theodora.*

Angie watched his lips carefully, and the motions of his hands. She repeated, softly, "Theodora."

He nodded. Then ...

The horrors.

Skin like snakes. Many teeth, sharp, like needles. Eyes cold, black, like pools of oil, no feeling, only hunger. Strange, dark shapes. Voices without words, grunts, hisses, little squeals and howls. Arms, with snakelike movements, as if the arms themselves were different creatures. Hands, long fingers, coiling. These things I saw, but in shadows and darkness, with only the flame from the candle she carried touching here, touching there. Light and dark, moving so fast, making puzzles.

Then, *down into the cellar.*

Angie had stopped talking, making words of Eddie's lip and hand motions. She stared hard, concentrating, her frown deepening, her lips parted.

Something, Eddie said with his lips, his hands out, palms up. *They carried something ... something white ... perhaps a person, a small person ...*

He did not make the signs that meant Katrina. That he could never do. Only in the far reaches of his terror could he say, they carried Katrina. Limp, pale. They laid her on the table.

"The altar," Angie murmured.

Eddie made a motion. *Whatever it was, they laid it on the—yes, altar.*

"You saw!"

Yes, I saw.

"They let you escape!"

Yes. No. They didn't see him. He drew a question mark in the air. What were they? What had he seen?

"Eddie," Angie said, her hand reaching again to grip his wrist. "I've been thinking about all that. Now, this makes it almost certain that Miss Theodora is conducting some sort of black mass, or devil worship."

From the distance, back the way they had come, a voice called, "Angie!"

"Oh, Lord," Angie cried softly. "That's Geraldine. She can't stand it that I'm not helping. I have to go, or she'll come looking for me."

Angie got up, brushed her skirt. Eddie stood as she did, waiting for her to make the first move, to turn and run away. He drew a deep breath. He had told her. Together they would figure it out.

"Listen, Eddie. This afternoon I'll go see the reverend. And I'll tell him what you've told me. Maybe he can do something about this. You must leave there— leave that house!"

Eddie nodded yes.

"Where will you go?"

Eddie shrugged. Not home, not now. Not now that she had kissed him again.

Her face softened and a faint smile appeared briefly on her lips. "I love you, Eddie."

He blinked. His chin shook with his effort to speak. *I love you.*

She ran up the bank, stopped, and looked back at him. "This afternoon, I promise. Then I'll see you. This evening. Soon. I'll talk to the reverend first, then I'll tell my parents."

Eddie nodded.

He watched her go, a slender girl in a dark blue dress, the skirt lifted above her ankles, her fair hair pulled into a thick braid that hung down her back to her waist.

He stood still and stared at the spot where he'd last seen her, then turned back toward Wickham House.

A sudden, deep wish struck him with such force that he felt ill: he wished, *wished* he hadn't told Angie. That Angie had not been made part of it, whatever was happening in Wickham House.

By telling her, he had pulled her in.

And now, she, too, was trapped.

ANGIE ENTERED THE KITCHEN. The cat uncurled herself from a soft spot in a rocking chair near the window. Angie noticed with growing alarm that the sunshine had moved away from the chair. She looked around. Where were her mother and sister?

Faintly, then, from the front room, came voices. A man, talking to Mama. Angie opened the door into the dining room. Through the wide door that joined dining room to living room she glimpsed the shadow of a man as the front room door closed.

Footsteps crossed the living room, and Geraldine appeared. The expression on her face warned Angie that something terrible had happened.

"A child has disappeared," her sister said.

Katrina, Angie thought; *they're looking for Katrina.* She said nothing. Her mother came through the room, brushing her apron down. She'd had it rolled at her waist, the way she often did when she wanted it out of her way. She stopped when she saw Angie, relief evident on her face.

"Thank the Lord you're here," she said.

Angie followed them back into the kitchen, forcing herself to be patient, to wait.

"It's the little girl who lives in the shack on the Wickham House land," their mother said. "The man wanted to know if we had seen her. She disappeared yesterday afternoon. Her people looked for her all night. Today there's a search party out, led by the sheriff." Her mother kept talking as she returned to the chore of snapping beans and filling jars. Angie dared say nothing yet. Her eyes sought the clock on the shelf. Minutes stood still. She stood at the table, snapping beans.

"I told Mama," Geraldine said, "It's not safe for you to be out in the woods."

"Of course it's safe," Angie replied quickly, her heartstrings tightening. Geraldine didn't approve of her sitting always beside Eddie in church, even though she made a point of sitting wherever Angie sat. To spy on her, Angie thought, feeling again the resentment of being watched so closely by her older sister. Because Geraldine was three years older, she thought she had a right to see that Angie behaved according to her own religiously conceived ideas. Sometimes Angie had wondered at the differences between them. But today, she was too worried to be very concerned about Geraldine. She had to go see the reverend.

"I thought it was safe, too," Mama said. "But not now."

"It's that strange dumb boy," Geraldine said. "He's done something to her."

"No!" Angie said quickly, adding less stridently, "No, I'm sure you're wrong."

"See, Mama?" Geraldine said. "I told you Angie would stand up for him. I think you should forbid her to see him."

Mama said, "For goodness' sake, Geraldine, she only sees him in church."

Angie barely heard their conversation. She looked at the clock. Only three minutes had passed? It was not yet eleven o'clock. She thought of the things Eddie had told her, fear dark in his eyes. She could almost see the strange altar in the cellar of Wickham House. She was afraid. For the little girl, for Eddie.

"Mama," she said, waiting no longer. "May I go see the reverend? It's not yet noon."

"Go see the reverend? What on earth for, Angie?" Angie tried to think of an excuse that would be accepted. She had been so worried, she hadn't anticipated this moment, and the need to have a reason she could use.

"It's—uh—it's about young people's meeting Wednesday night, Mama. It's —uh—very important that I see him this morning."

Geraldine cried in alarm, "You want to walk through the woods to the church and rectory even as there's a search party for a missing child?"

"Please, Mama," Angie begged.

"Absolutely not," Mama said. "You aren't to go anywhere alone from now on. I don't want either of you girls going out alone anymore."

Angie looked again at the clock, tears clouding her vision. Another minute, slowly moving by.

Where was Katrina?

Where was Eddie?

CHAPTER 14

He saw them long before he left the haven of the woods: a group of men, some of them in overalls, two in suits, two with badges pinned to their lapels. Among them was Katrina's papa, Charlie Etchens. There, too, were his sons—Paul, short and thin, years younger than Eddie himself, and the younger son, Ralph, only a few years older than Katrina. Still, they went every day to work cutting weeds and grass, doing odd jobs. Perhaps in the winter they sometimes went to school. Eddie had never seen them playing.

Theodora stood on the top step of the back porch, head and shoulders above the men scattered below, as if she were queen. She wore a big, cheerful apron over her print dress. Every day she put on a clean, freshly washed and ironed apron, and tied it in a bow at the small of her back. The bib reached up over her chest, sometimes made like a heart, or a diamond, sometimes plain and square, but always trimmed in bright edging. On the ample skirt were two roomy pockets, trimmed like the bib. The skirt, too, was edged with the same color. She removed her apron only to go to town, or to church. Or when the reverend came to visit.

It was the younger boy who first saw Eddie. With his hands deep in his pockets he had been kicking at the stone walk, then his eyes were suddenly drawn to Eddie, standing in the edge of the woods.

The boy pointed and shouted, "There he is!"

Eddie felt his muscles jerk and tighten, an instinctive urge to run, to try to escape. As if in the pointing of the little boy's finger he had been accused of a terrible crime.

The man in the suit with the badge on the lapel came halfway across the backyard as Eddie forced himself forward. The rest of the small crowd stood quietly, their eyes on Eddie.

"I'm Sheriff Archer, son. What's your name?"

Eddie opened his mouth, his eyes darting from the man who stood halfway between him and the others to Theodora as she came off the step and toward the sheriff. The movement of the men and boys as Theodora passed through was like the shifting of a storm cloud as it gathered. Eddie put a hand to his mouth.

Theodora's voice carried strongly. "This is my late husband's nephew, Sheriff. His name is Edward, but he won't be able to converse with you. As you've probably heard, Edward doesn't have good sense and is incapable of speech."

The sheriff looked at Eddie again, his eyes piercing, doubtful, as he studied Eddie's eyes. "Is that a fact," he said, as if speaking to himself.

Eddie dropped his hands.

Theodora said, "Edward, these men are looking for Katrina. They want to know if you've seen her."

Oh God, Katrina. They had not found her last evening.

Eddie turned his palm upward. "No, no," he said. His eyes sought the woodland behind the barn, beyond the pasture. If she was lost in the woods, she might be hungry, but she would be safe. Not even the wolves or bears would hurt her if she stayed still against a tree.

The sheriff scowled. "Did I hear you speak? What did you say?"

Eddie tried to speak again, but his throat closed, and only strange, small grunts of effort escaped. Theodora took a couple of steps closer, almost as if she were coming to protect him. Eddie looked at her, surprised, astonished that she might stand up for him, but then he saw the look in her eyes. Dark, cold, and in some terrible way, pleased.

"He can make some sounds, Sheriff, but only one word, which is hardly any help. No matter what you ask him, he says no, even when he means yes."

Sheriff Archer turned, sighed deeply and followed the way of Eddie's instinctive glance toward the woods. Then he turned back. "Young man, do you understand what I'm saying?"

Eddie nodded.

"I hear that the little Etchens girl spent quite a lot of time with you."

Eddie nodded again, slowly.

"When was the last time you saw her?"

Eddie looked from face to face. Stern faces, accusing faces. The papa of Katrina worried, the skin drawn tight over his sharp bones. His eyes, blue, like Katrina's, begging for an answer.

Eddie wondered how to communicate. He glanced at Theodora. Yesterday morning, when Theodora had killed the chicken, Eddie had carried Katrina, angry, weeping, wounded Katrina, carried her home and sat with her until she fell asleep. That, and all since, one long, vivid memory that seemed made of the fires of hell and the coldness of endless ice. None of it did Eddie dare try to tell. Not now, not with Theodora's eyes on him.

She said, "The last I saw Katrina, Edward was carrying her. Yesterday morning, near noon. She was crying. I supposed she had fallen and hurt herself."

Eddie stared hard at Theodora. She had seen him carrying Katrina home? She had come up from the cellar and watched?

All faces of men and boys turned toward Theodora. "You hadn't mentioned that, Mrs. Wickham," the sheriff said, but not accusingly. "I don't believe you mentioned that."

Others shook their heads. A few murmurs rose. Theodora said, "He was always carrying her around."

No, no. Only a couple of times. But he dared not dispute her word even with a shake of his head.

"I had forgotten it until now," Theodora went on, "that the last time I actually saw her was when I saw Edward carrying her away from the house yesterday, near noon. Of course, I assumed the child went home to spend the afternoon with her mother, as she always did. At least, to my knowledge."

"Mrs. Etchens," the sheriff explained, "arrived home much later than she usually does, she has said. It was getting late."

He looked at Charlie Etchens, who nodded, then fixed his stare on the ground at his feet.

Eddie looked toward the shack and saw Katrina's mother standing near it, watching through the trees.

"The child was not at home when her mother got there, and has not been seen since. So," the sheriff said, turning again toward Eddie, "I believe, Edward, that makes you the last person to have seen Katrina."

He only looked at Eddie, then said to Theodora, "Is there any way to find out anything from him?"

Theodora said, "Not to my knowledge, Sheriff. He doesn't take orders well. He does chores for me. He milks, feeds the animals, cuts wood. Of course, there is no real communication." She added, as if the sheriff would not be able to understand what she had meant, "No talking, that is, because of course, he's dumb. Except for the one word, he is dumb."

The sheriff fixed a steady look on Eddie.

Eddie felt his chin beginning to jerk. Katrina, still missing. Little Katrina, whom he had grown to love as he loved his own sisters.

The sheriff said, "Have you seen Katrina since yesterday morning, son?"

Eddie shook his head.

"Did you carry her somewhere?"

Eddie nodded. Then he pointed toward the shed that was the Etchens' home. Toward the mother who stood there in its shade.

"You carried her home?"

Eddie nodded.

All eyes stared at him. Theodora's burrowed into him, but then, again as if she were trying to protect him, she said, "I'm sure he was only trying to help."

The sheriff asked, "Why did you carry her home, Ed?"

Eddie touched one finger to his eye, and then down his cheek. His lips turned down.

"She was crying?" the sheriff asked.

Theodora said, her eyes boring into Eddie, "Just as likely, Edward doesn't know what you're talking about. I doubt very much that he carried her home. Perhaps he carried her into the woods."

Eddie looked at his feet. Had he expected that she would stand up for him? That she would say that she watched him carry her home and minutes later come away without her? He turned toward the woods behind the pasture.

The sheriff asked, "Did you carry her into the woods, Edward?" His voice seemed more gentle than Theodora's.

Eddie pointed toward the strip of woodland between the driveway of Wickham House and the shed beyond. Toward the mother.

"You carried her home?" the sheriff repeated.

Eddie nodded.

Charlie Etchens cried in a voice edging on hysteria, "Why would he be carrying my little girl home? Or anywhere else? She's big enough to walk. She ain't been carried since she was two years old! It ain't right that he touched her!"

The sheriff said gently, "We're only trying to find out what he might have done with her, Charlie."

Eddie pointed at the shed. Three points with his finger, as if throwing darts. *I didn't do anything with her. I took her home. I put her to bed.* What were they trying to say he had done?

The sheriff asked, "Edward, what time was that?"

Theodora said, "Edward certainly can't tell time, Sheriff."

Eddie nodded adamantly. Yes, yes. He pointed to the sky, a few degrees off straight up noon.

"I think we would like you to help us search, Edward," the sheriff said. "It won't hurt to go deeper into the woods. If the child often played in the woods, Edward, would you show us where?"

Eddie walked, going toward the barn, keeping well away from the group of men and boys.

In the shadow of the barn Eddie glanced back and saw Theodora standing

94

on the walk, halfway between the back porch and the carriage house. She seemed even now to be staring at him, sending a silent message that made him feel like shrinking into his inner soul, searching for a place that might be safe from her, from whatever evil she wished him. But even there, would she not be able to reach him?

Katrina ...

Katrina was here somewhere. In silences between words Theodora had told him so. By her words to the sheriff she had sent them to look for Katrina where she knew Katrina would be.

Katrina, whose voice was silent. Eddie walked on wooden legs, his skin tight and cold with fear. Why hadn't he taken Katrina with him yesterday when he met Angie?

She had seen the Bad Things. He had seen them, too. Theodora knew they had seen them—those creatures of the cellar and the night. But he couldn't describe them to the sheriff, or suggest that maybe Theodora had sent them after Katrina. Maybe Theodora herself had gone after Katrina, and she was not in the woods, but down in the cellar.

But please, Lord, better that she be in the woods.

Eddie heard the orders the sheriff gave, on the edge of his awareness, but he didn't pause. He kept walking.

"Scatter out, men. Though we looked here a piece this morning, let's go deeper and wider into these woods. She didn't wander there alone, she was carried there!"

Eddie walked toward the little road that led to the meadow on top of the hill. He stopped, still within sight of the barn. His eyes followed the road. It wound through the trees, paced leisurely by horses and a wagon long ago. It was his private road to the happiness of being with Angie. Like twin paths it wandered through tall trees. Sunshine fell like drops of gold here and there on the paths, leading away to paradise. He would not take the men along his private road.

He turned westward, into the woods. To his right the others spread, going two by two. No one came with Eddie, though he saw several yards behind him a heavy-set man in overalls. Watching. Watching. Never letting Eddie out of sight.

Eddie looked ahead, into the shadows and silence of the woods. Far over the trees the crows cawed, as always, as if disturbed by the presence this time of men.

Images of what he had seen in the cellar yesterday came like nightmares. Flashes of moving figures, as black as the darkness of their background and hard to define.

Eddie felt frozen. What would happen, he wondered, if he tried to lead the sheriff down into the cellar beneath Wickham House?

He pushed aside undergrowth, bending low to avoid the slap of young bush limbs. He stepped over the fallen log of a half-grown tree, one he had started cutting for winter wood.

To his left was the corner of the pasture, where sunlight fell on green grass, where the cow stood, near the horse. The heads of both were lifted. They watched, curious. The cow mooed softly, recognizing Eddie. The horse watched him a moment, then lowered her head and began to graze again.

Eddie turned deeper into the woods, going away from the grazing ground of the animals. Trees here had never been cleared away. They stood centuries old, leafy tops creating a roof of green. Eddie walked on ground he had never walked on before. When he had gone into the woods to cut dead trees, he had gone eastward, in the direction of the sheriff and others, beyond the private road.

The underbrush was growing thicker, less penetrable. Eddie bent under a hazelnut bush and then straightened. He stared. At the base of a huge, old tree, fern grew, deep green against old brown. But within those natural colors there was another: pale, white, and a touch of bright blue.

Eddie stared, his heart thundering in his throat, his mouth dry, his tongue filling his mouth with dry bristles. His eyes burned. Something deep in his head raged, a river of emotion broken through a dam. Katrina had been wearing a print dress with blue flowers. Blue on white.

He stumbled forward and fell to his knees.

His fingers closed on the tall, curved fronds of fern and pulled them aside.

Her blue eyes, milky pale and staring, looked up past him. The bodice of the pretty dress was slit and ripped, and from the rip blood had spilled. He saw the strange rope-like coil of intestines through the gaping holes in her dress ... body ...

A shout rose behind him.

"Hey! Here, Sheriff! I think he's finally led us to her!"

Eddie felt his arm grasped, and his body jerked up as if he were a sack of feed for an animal. The heavyset man in overalls pulled him back through the hazelnut bush, his hand on Eddie's arm a tight band of pain. Eddie gasped for breath. Through the limbs of the hazelnut bush he still saw Katrina's small body, so still, so torn and ripped, so bloody ...

... And something else.

Beneath her arm was the rag doll, soaked in blood. Its "wings," as she had called them, were folded under it.

It had not protected her after all.

CHAPTER 15

A knife had been the weapon used.

That was determined as Eddie stood in the woods, his head down, no longer able to bear looking at the terrible things that had been done to Katrina. He heard Charlie Etchens weeping, sobbing, swearing. He heard some of the men suggesting getting a rope from the barn, stringing him up, and ending it right there.

"That's enough," the sheriff snapped. "The hanging will be done legally. I don't want no more of that kind of talk."

The sheriff searched Eddie's pockets, found his small pocketknife, and took it away. They led him past the pasture, where the cow and horse watched. They went past the barn and onto the driveway.

Filled with burning pain that pushed dryly up behind his eyes, Eddie walked beside the deputy whose hand clutched his arm.

In the small front yard of the shed beyond the lane of trees, Katrina's mother came forward in silence. Eddie longed to break loose and run to her and tell her he hadn't hurt Katrina. He would never have hurt Katrina.

But there was no way he could reach her, and there was no way he could tell her.

Theodora stood watching on the stone walk that led from the screened porch.

A scene of horror came before Eddie's eyes, blotting out the sheriff, his searchers. He was in the long hallway again where the only light came from candles. She was there, the candle in her left hand, the butcher knife in her right. He saw the dark arms of the creatures that had no name, and the white, limp body they carried. A small, thin arm hung downward. A foot, bare, candlelight glancing off the soft curves of small toes, swung gently.

Katrina.

Deep in the back of his mind he had seen and known. It was Katrina who was carried into the cellar.

Eddie lifted his eyes and looked at the face of the woman. Her high cheekbones caught a glint of sunshine, creating a hollow beneath that was shadowed and dark. Her eyes, black as night, stared steadily at Eddie.

Shocked, Eddie returned the stare. Her eyes ... the eyes of the creatures that had followed her ... they were the same. What were they? What was she, this person he had known as Aunt Theodora?

The handcuffs no longer frightened him. He was less afraid of those who would hang him them he was of Theodora.

She had killed Katrina, but even if he could tell the sheriff what he had seen, he would not be believed.

He tore his eyes away from her hard, dark stare. He was less afraid of jail, of going away forever to prison, of being hanged.

The sheriff went over to talk to her.

"Ma'am, I'm sorry you had to see this," the sheriff said, his voice carrying clearly to Eddie. "You see, we found the child's body. She's dead, of course. This boy went straight to her. I have confiscated the murder weapon. I'm sorry. The law will have to take its course."

"I'm only thankful you caught him, Sheriff, before he did such a thing again. I had no idea I was bringing such danger into the neighborhood."

"You can't be blamed for that, Miss Theodora. You couldn't have known."

"No, but he is, after all, my nephew. By marriage."

"No blood relation to you. None of this your fault, ma'am."

"Katrina was such a lovely child. So friendly. I'll miss her."

"Yes, ma'am."

"Such a loss for the family."

"That's true, ma'am."

"I'll certainly do what I can to help them."

"That's kind of you, ma'am."

"Of course, they can have more children."

The sheriff didn't answer. He turned away.

EDDIE SAT at the table of the defense and listened to the evidence against him. They said he had taken her out that afternoon, and he had done terrible things to her before he'd killed her. They said his knife, which was shown to the jury, had been washed clean. There was no blood. They said he had tried to cover her.

98

They implied that he was a half-wit, who was so dumb, so stupid as to think she wouldn't be found, that her decomposing body would remain hidden by the leaves pulled over her.

The case had come to trial quickly, for Edward's protection, it was said, because the people of the neighborhood, and even the people of the nearby city, demanded a quick trial. Eddie had lived the past three weeks in the jail cell, separated from other prisoners. No one had come to see him.

He felt at times like he was dead, and already in hell, and at other times the pain was so intense he wished he were dead. When he slept he saw Katrina. She ran and laughed in his dreams, and always the dream ended with the vision in the woods. He woke many times during the night, trying to cry. Sometimes the guard banged on the bars of the cell.

"Hey, there! What's the matter with you? I thought they said you couldn't make any sounds!"

Now he sat at the defense table, sometimes numbed, incapable of feeling the pain.

On the last day of the trial, as the lawyers began their summation, it happened.

Daily, as he was led to the defense table, Eddie had looked at the faces in the crowded courtroom. Only one face mattered: Angie's. He was relieved, daily, to see that she was not there. He didn't want her to see him this way.

But on the last day, as the defense lawyer stood up and said, "Your honor, ladies and gentlemen of the jury, our only defense is that this young man does not know right from wrong. We ask only that his life be spared."

The man's voice was not strong. His defense was forced upon him by some quirk of the law that Eddie did not understand. Every accused person was entitled to a defense; he understood that. But if a young lawyer was forced, what good did it do?

Eddie barely knew his name. He had come to the jail, where Eddie had been taken to the waiting room, and he had told Eddie, "I am your attorney, appointed by the state. I understand you can't talk, so asking you questions will waste everyone's time. I'll just do what I can."

He got up to leave, then turned back. "Oh, yes, I should ask, are you guilty?"

Eddie saw in the young attorney's face that he already knew the answer. Of course Eddie was guilty. There was no one else who could be.

Eddie only stared at him, and the lawyer turned and walked through the door. The question had been asked, and answered, to the lawyer's mind.

Now, after the defense offered no defense, the courthouse seemed to breathe. People shifted. Murmurs rose softly. Papers rustled at the table of the prosecution. The judge leaned forward and put his elbows on the desk.

Murmurs rose louder, then ended abruptly.

Eddie turned his head, following the eyes of everyone he saw. The attention of the judge, the lawyers, the court reporter were riveted suddenly toward the aisle beyond the gate.

Angie.

She stood just beyond the gate, bonnet in hand, her bright, pale hair braided and coiled around her head. She looked thinner, her cheeks not as rounded as they had been three weeks ago.

"Your Honor," she said, and her voice carried clearly in the strained hush of the room. "May I come forward?"

The silence lasted another moment, then the judge nodded.

The gate squeaked softly as the prosecutor stepped forward and unlatched and opened it. Angie walked through, looking straight ahead, her eyes on the judge.

"Your Honor," she said, looking up at the judge behind the desk on the platform. "I have something to say in defense of Edward Wickham."

"No, no," Eddie said softly.

Go back, Angie, don't let Theodora know you know me. Go home, Angie.

Who knew where Theodora's creatures went in the dark of night, in those hours when perhaps they went into the woods, to bring back onto the porches damp leaves, sticks, moss that clung to their strange, damp bodies? Angie's house was only across the woods from Wickham House. Her bedroom window, she had told him, looked out into the woods. At night, she had said in a soft, sweet voice one day when they'd sat together beneath the tree at the edge of the meadow on the hill, sometimes she gazed toward the woods and dreamed of walking with him, her hand in his. In the moonlight. He dreamed of it, too, a dream he would carry with him to prison, that he would hold in his heart forever. But now that dream was drowned in fear.

Angie, don't let Theodora know that you know me.

He started to rise, but his lawyer's hand pushed him down. Why was she here? What could she say that wouldn't harm her?

Already Angie was going through the swearing-in. She laid her hand on the Bible and said she would tell the truth, under God. It seemed that no one in the courtroom breathed.

Angie Beckley? they seemed to be saying in the aisles behind Eddie. *Angie Beckley, that nice girl from that nice family that lives on the small place between Wickham House and the white church with the spire? The church Miss Theodora belongs to, the one the Beckley s belong to ...*

The defense lawyer opened the gate to the witness stand and Angie walked in. Her hands curved around the railing, holding tightly, as if she were on a high cliff from which she could fall.

"Your Honor," she said clearly, her voice carrying to the corners of the courtroom, and burrowing into Eddie's heart. "Many people have sworn that

Katrina Etchens was murdered on the afternoon of the thirteenth. Edward Wickham stands accused. But I know that Edward Wickham is not guilty."

The courtroom gasped softly. Eddie heard clearly the inward breath that Angie drew. He saw the rise of her breast, and the pulse throbbing in her temple.

No, Angie, no.

"Yes, Miss Beckley?" the judge said. "How do you know?"

"Because ... he was with me that afternoon, from noon till sundown. He was with me. He couldn't have killed that little girl."

The noise burst. People's voices. A cry came from behind Eddie. "Oh, my God!" Eddie knew without looking that it came from Angie's mother.

The faces of the jury looked oddly blank, then stunned. They stared at Angie.

They stared at Eddie.

CHAPTER 16

The black-robed judge seemed finally to become aware that it was he who had to restore order to the courtroom. He pounded fiercely with the gavel. "Silence!" he bellowed. "*Silence!*"

The noise receded. Softly, behind Eddie, Angie's mother wept.

The defense lawyer turned and stared at Eddie. It was as if suddenly Eddie had become a person. A curious smile tucked one corner of the young lawyer's mouth. He turned back toward the judge and hollered, "The defense rests!"

He returned to the table with the grin blinking on and off. He glanced at Eddie, patted his shoulder. But Eddie was too frightened to respond. *No, no, Angie.* She thought she was doing him a favor, but a jail cell was safer than Wickham House. Hanging by a rope would be an easier death than the one Katrina had suffered. Theodora could not let him live to tell what he had seen in her cellar. She must know that someday he would find a way to communicate. Perhaps she wondered even now about Angie, how much he had managed to tell her.

Theodora stared hard at Angie. Eddie saw how thin and tight her lips had grown.

The judge said to a courtroom that was buzzing again, "Silence! Let the prosecutor respond."

The prosecutor rose from his table. He was no longer sweating. His face looked pale and cold. His eyes were on Angie in disbelief.

"Miss Beckley, I'm afraid you're going to have to explain yourself. How is it that you are so certain that Edward was in your company the whole of that afternoon?"

"Because ... we were together every afternoon, sir. From the evening I met Eddie, shortly after he came to Wickham House, we spent time together every afternoon. Sometimes only an hour or two, but on the last day, many hours."

Eddie no longer heard the gasps, the murmurs. He turned his eyes from Angie to Theodora.

She sat at the end of the bench directly behind the railing on the side of the prosecution. She sat upright, stiff, and her black eyes looked narrowed and dangerous. They were the eyes of the beings whose arms had carried the limp body of Katrina.

Perhaps, he thought suddenly, she, too, was a gnome from the center of the earth that had achieved human form. Perhaps they were all gnomes—the doll, and the creatures that Theodora fed.

Perhaps their favorite food was human flesh.

Angie, don't tell. Don't let her know that you know. He struggled to send her the mental message. Her eyes didn't meet his. She sat upright in the chair, her body stiffly controlled, and looked only at her questioner.

She doesn't know about the cellar, he wanted to shout at Theodora, *or the things that live there.* His throat choked with the silent cry. He wished—he wished he hadn't told her—about those beings that pulled dead leaves onto the porches at night, their bodies slithering at times like reptiles, at times standing like men.

They were in Theodora's command, somehow. They could be sent for Angie, if Theodora knew she was a threat.

The prosecutor's voice held Angie's attention. She looked at no one else.

"And why was that, Miss Beckley? If the young man can't talk, can't speak, whatever possessed a young lady like you to spend time with him?"

"Eddie can't talk, but it isn't true that he is incapable of understanding what's said to him, or of communicating. The first night I met him in church, I could see that he wanted to learn to read and write—"

Oh God, Angie.

The crowd murmured again, then grew silent.

"Eddie is not stupid," Angie said, small spots of color coming for a moment to her pale cheeks. Her blue eyes flashed darker, like the sky at sundown. Eddie watched her with sinking hope, willing her in silence to *hush, hush, Angie.* But she continued.

"I understand him very well. He uses a form of sign language that I grew to read well."

"No, no," he cried loudly, surprising even himself. All eyes turned upon him. Angie gave him a glimmer of a smile.

"He can only speak one word, and sometimes not that. But he was able to write his name, print. I saw he wanted to learn. So I began meeting Eddie in the afternoons. I took him a tablet and pencil, and books. And we studied. At night he studied. He was with me all that afternoon. Longer than usual."

Longer than usual because I told her about Katrina's tears, and the animals killed on the terrible stone table beneath the symbol on the wall. She called it an altar, where animals were sacrificed to something evil. She understood things I had not. I drew her a map of the house.

The next morning he'd told her of hearing Katrina's name called deep into the night, and that he had not seen Katrina after he'd put her to bed the noonday before. They talked about the horrible things that walked with Theodora in the dark halls of the house—when one of them carried something into the cellar—to the altar.

Then, he hadn't been able to accept what he had seen. Shocked by the horror, he had not recognized the dangling small foot, or the swinging white arm. But now he knew, and when Angie's eyes met his, he saw she knew, too.

And oh, God, how he wished he had told her nothing, ever. How he wished she had not been drawn into this. That she was still as innocent as the night he'd met her.

The prosecutor asked, "And why did it happen to be longer than usual on that particular day, Miss Beckley?" He spoke with sarcasm dripping off his words like soured cream. "Could it be that you're just making all this up in some misguided effort to help someone you *think* is innocent?"

Angie's stare clung to Eddie's. He saw the terrified widening of her eyes. The killer of the child was no longer some unknown person; it was Theodora, or her followers, whatever they were. *Angie, don't tell ...*

Angie drew a deep breath and turned her eyes to the prosecutor. "Sir, I know he's innocent, because he was with me, from noon until sundown that day. He was with me."

She said nothing more.

Her lips had tightened, pressed together so firmly Eddie could see little creases formed at the corners. She wasn't going to tell what he had told her, not yet, not today. He caught her glance once more as she walked back to her seat in the courtroom.

Eddie didn't turn to watch her, though the effort to restrain himself caused him to clench his hands until he felt the thin muscles in his upper arms bunch painfully. Let her go, he warned himself. Don't show that you love her.

They might send him to prison, saying he could have killed Katrina before noon, just before he went to meet Angie. Even though the medical examiner had said Katrina was killed sometime in the afternoon, probably around three o'clock. They would send him to prison, but perhaps, under reasonable doubt, supplied by Angie's testimony, he would not be hanged.

The jury had left the courtroom. Eddie sat still. Many of the others waited.

Groups of people talked, some left, others returned. Eddie sat with bowed head.

Two hours later the jury returned. The judge came back from the room where he had gone to wait, and took his seat behind the desk that overlooked the room.

Eddie did not lift his head.

He only half listened to the voices. The judge asking if the jury had reached a decision. The shuffling of feet and papers, and then the silence. Eddie looked up. One of the jurors was standing.

"We have, Your Honor. We find Edward Wickham not guilty."

The silence lasted several heartbeats in the courtroom, and far longer in Eddie's mind. He continued sitting, stunned. They were setting him free? *Free?*

The judge's gavel struck the top of the desk when the uproar began.

"Silence, please! Since Edward Wickham is only sixteen years old, I am returning him to the custody of his aunt, Theodora Wickham. Court dismissed."

The custody of Theodora Wickham ...

"No, no," Eddie said aloud, not realizing at first that his voice expressed his thoughts. "No. No."

The young defense lawyer patted his shoulder, and pulled Eddie to his feet.

"What do you mean, no? Boy, you're free. You've been exonerated. You can go home now with your aunt."

Hands touched Eddie as people congratulated him, and one of them lingered, holding to his upper arm.

"Come along, Edward," Theodora said, as she smiled at this person, that person, nodding and smiling, all the while talking to Eddie. "This terrible ordeal has lasted much too long. Let's go home, Edward."

He was less afraid of prison, less afraid of the hangman's noose. But he had no choice at the moment but to walk beside the woman who was responsible for the death of Katrina.

As they walked through the crowd, a man's voice rose hysterically.

"If that boy didn't kill my little girl, then who did? Tell me, *who did?*"

CHAPTER 17

*A*ngie got into the family buggy, directed into the backseat beside her mother by her father's strong, angry hand. The gesture was silent, but rough and jerky. She felt their anger. She had humiliated them in the neighborhood, in front of their relatives and friends, in front of their church. But she had heard the jury's decision: not guilty. They weren't going to hang Eddie. And at first, she had felt faint with relief.

Then, when the judge sent Eddie into the custody of his aunt, she had heard his words: "No, no." And the consequences struck her. Eddie would not be hanged, but he was going home with a woman in whose house terrible things were happening. She felt ill with helplessness. Her parents hadn't allowed her to go talk to the reverend. Did she dare talk to them? No, not yet. She saw their unhappiness with her, felt their anger. Even Geraldine either glared at her, or turned away.

Papa drove the team in silence, though she saw him slap the reins against the horses' rumps unnecessarily, causing them to jump with the sting and walk faster. Geraldine sat as stiff as if she were made of iron. Beside Angie, her mother wept on and on, softly, into her embroidered handkerchief.

She'd catch it when they reached home, Angie knew.

She didn't know what they would do. Never before had she done anything that deserved punishment—nor, she felt, did this. She should have told them. She should have asked for Eddie to come to the house so they could study in the parlor, or out on the lawn. But she'd known immediately their reaction to him. Their answer would have been no.

Would Eddie have been better off if she had never suggested they meet?

No. He had learned much. Although his writing abilities were those of a first grader yet, at least he was very good with figures. And, she thought, he understood many printed words, because in the days before he began to tell her about the cellar in Wickham House, and the altar and blood and the strangeness of the *beings* ... those things that Angie in her mind now thought of as demons ... *demons* ... what else could they be? ... before those last two days, he had pointed out words that were similar in meaning. He had been learning.

But he needed her. Together perhaps they could go away and face the world alone. She had to help him get away from Wickham House.

She followed her mother and sister into the house while Papa went to put away the horses and buggy.

She hung her shawl on the hall peg. "Mama, I'm sorry to have put you through this, but—"

Geraldine said, "I told you, Mama, she was going out into the woods too much."

"Geraldine, please. Angie, how could you have lied to us like this?"

Papa came into the hall, his face dark and stern. "Come into the parlor, Angie."

Angie looked for her mother, but she had taken Geraldine out of the hall. They would go to the kitchen, probably, where they would get to work snapping beans too long in their baskets and now probably tough, perhaps ruined. Because of Angie, and the trial she had insisted on going to.

In a way, Angie was glad to be alone with her papa. She had to tell someone what Eddie had told her, and if she weren't allowed to go see the reverend, perhaps Papa would know what to do.

The door closed.

"I have never whipped one of my girls," Papa said as he motioned for Angie to sit down. "But with you, Angie, I'm apt to do just that. I see no repentance in you. You have disobeyed your mother—"

"No, Papa," she dared interrupt. "I was given permission—"

"You know that's not enough of an excuse, young lady! Did you for one minute tell the truth about where you were going? Who you were meeting? No. It was thought that you'd been studying. By yourself."

"Papa, I have something very important to talk to you about."

He paced in silence. With his dark beard and his angry eyes, Angie was reminded of the angry men of the Bible.

"I think there's nothing more to be said." He stopped pacing and, standing near the closed door, looked at her. "I think the best thing is for you to be confined to your room."

Angie stood up. "Papa! Listen to me. I have something to tell you. I wanted to go talk to the reverend, the morning after the child disappeared, but wasn't allowed to leave the house. Now please, sir, I beg you, listen to me."

He stood still. Angie returned his stare, her heart smothering her in anxiety. She had never stood up to her father before.

"Well!" he finally said, "What?"

"Oh ... thank you, Papa. I didn't know ..."

He nodded. "Sit down. Tell me what it is, and be quick, chores are waiting."

"Papa, Eddie saw terrible things at Wickham House. I think, Papa, that Miss Theodora must be involved in something very dangerous. She—she has demons, Papa, that are not human, not animal, nor even reptile. They're large, like apes, or men, and stand upright. But their skin is hairless and snakelike, and these creatures carried something small into the cellar, where there's a sacrificial altar—"

Her words tumbled faster and faster as she saw the narrowing of his eyes. She felt his stunned disbelief, saw the horror and disgust on his face. She had never seen him look at anything the way he was now looking at her.

"That boy claimed he saw that?"

"Yes, Papa," she cried in desperation. He must believe; he must. "It was they who killed Katrina, and Papa, if Eddie isn't taken away from there, they'll kill him—"

"He saw it, he claims?" He stared, disgust deep in his eyes.

She must be careful how she spoke, to make sure it wouldn't be construed as an argument. Papa would never allow her to argue with him. She nodded.

"And if he saw such a thing, how did he tell you about it?" he demanded, his frown deep.

"By sign language, Papa."

A faint, derisive smile appeared on the man's face. "And since when do either of you know sign language? Sign language is a very complicated thing, and must be studied and learned, like any other language."

"I know that, Papa. But we had our own. And—"

"Oh, you had your own. In a couple of weeks you developed this fancy way of talking that made you understand he had seen in Wickham House things that haven't existed since the old days, and perhaps never did."

She said nothing. Blinking back tears, she stared up at him.

He gazed at her thoughtfully for a silent moment, then he said, "You stay with your mother and sister, and say nothing. As soon as the chores are finished, I'll get the reverend."

He spun round on one foot, and with heavy steps went out the door and toward the kitchen. She was afraid to hope. Had he listened to her after all?

Angie went to the window and looked toward the woods that joined her yard to Wickham House. The sun was going down. Darkness would soon fall, mixing with the rising mists in the woods. These were nights of full moon. Last night, sleepless, she had sat on her bed and looked at the moonlight on the narrow strip of grass between the house and the woods.

Tonight Eddie was there. Tonight they had to get him away from there. She had hopes now that Papa was really going to get the reverend. Did that mean he had believed her story? Eddie's story?

She felt ashamed she had at first been doubtful of Eddie's story. With his hands once, early in their visits, he had tried to explain something she couldn't comprehend, to describe something outside his door. Something that slid along without footsteps, a steady sound, and paused, pushing against the door. Like an animal, it sniffed, but rattled the knob, as with a hand.

Other nights he had heard muffled cries, howls, that were more like a soul lost in hell than like an animal. And once he heard footsteps, not graceful and easy, like a wolf or dog's, but more like a man who walked upon padded feet with claws that clicked faintly against the wood. He had heard whines and groans and sometimes hissings. Through his lips and teeth he made the hissing sound.

Those nights she had nightmares, of a huge, shadowy, featureless thing that hovered over her, hissing.

She had told him of her dream, and he had been worried. He shook his head and touched her hair gently and said, "No, no."

He told her nothing more about his nights, until the last day.

She left the parlor, used only for special occasions, and went into the hall. Lamps had been lighted in the living room and dining room, and the door to the kitchen was open.

Though her mother's eyes were red, and almost silent sobs jerked her body now and then like hiccups, her hands were quite steady as she poured glasses of milk. Geraldine worked silently at the stove, dishing up mashed potatoes.

Angie began her own part of supper preparation. She brought plates down from the safe, and set the table for four.

Papa brought in a pail of milk, and Angie took it to the cook table in the corner and strained it into two-gallon pottery jugs that were used only for milk.

It was almost dark when she took the warm jugs and went outside. The dog went with her, to the cellar that was a hump of grass above a door sunk into the ground. At the door she hesitated. She would have to go down in the dark, because it was so much later than usual. The sun had gone down, leaving a red streak beyond the treetops west of the house, and the moon was rising like a huge red eye in the east.

The big red dog with long, silky hair stood quietly by her side, looking up into her face. His plumy tail waved against her. She looked at him. There was nothing around to cause him alarm; therefore, it was safe to go into the cellar.

She didn't need a light. She knew where the milk went. On the first shelf to the right.

She set one jug aside and opened the cellar door. What if ... she wondered ... what if all cellars were connected by underground tunnels, and in the dark the demons roamed from cellar to cellar ...

Stop it, she told herself. Quickly she went down the stone steps. For just an instant she paused, and in the silence something scurried, something moved. Angie squealed softly, without meaning to. Henry came down the steps, his tail wagging against her skirt. She could hear him sniffing in the dark corner of the cellar, around the baskets of fruit and potatoes, turnips and cabbages, but he didn't growl. Of course the cellars weren't connected, of course this familiar old place, which she had been coming down into as long as she could remember, of course it was safe. When wind and electrical storms swept the world above, where did she, Geraldine, and their mother come but to the cellar? And Henry with them, though Papa always stayed in the house to watch.

She found the shelves and quickly placed the milk jugs in their usual places. Then, with darkness catching at her heels and skirt, she ran up the steps into brightening moonlight, the dog beside her. She closed the cellar door and locked it.

In the woods toward Wickham House an owl screamed. Not a soft *hoot-who*, but the loud cry that always sent rivulets of ice through Angie's body.

She ran to the house and into the lighted safety of the kitchen.

Her family was already seated at the table. Angie sat down at her plate. They ate in silence. If it weren't that her papa had promised to help her, that he had listened to her and was going to bring the reverend, she would feel she was being shunned by her family. That particular religious punishment that could break a heart.

Papa stood up, pushed his chair back under the table. He picked his hat from the rack of pegs near the outer door.

"Where are you going?" Mama asked.

"I'll be back soon. I'm only going to get the reverend."

Angie heard him washing at the hydrant just outside the porch. Then, with a brief whistle for the dog, he was gone.

"What does he want with the reverend?" Geraldine asked. "Oh, yes, Angie was wanting to see the reverend. Is that why?"

"I wasn't told, Geraldine," Mama said. "I have a terrible headache. I'm going to bed. You girls wash up the dishes and put them away."

Angie washed, while Geraldine dried and put away. Angie felt Geraldine eyeing her at times and knew she wanted to ask questions. Angie was relieved that she didn't, until their chores were finished and they were wiping up table and countertops.

"Why did you want to see the reverend?" Geraldine asked. "To ask forgiveness of God for what you've done?"

"There was just something I didn't feel anyone else would be able to help with, that's all."

"No one? Not even Papa?"

Angie paused, wondering. Papa, help? No. Not Papa, not even the sheriff. Only the reverend. The reverend would know what to do about demons. But she couldn't tell Geraldine.

As if her thoughts of him caused a materialization, she heard the front door open, and men's voices. She heard footsteps go into the parlor. The familiar footsteps of her papa separated from the other and came to the kitchen door. He looked in.

"Angie, come. Geraldine, please go to your room when you've finished here. The reverend hasn't come on a social visit."

Angie followed her papa down the central hall to the parlor.

The Reverend Cheney had been in their parlor a few times before in the two years since he'd come to replace Reverend Styles. But never before had he been there when the room was lighted only by a lamp.

"This is my daughter Angie, Reverend, who wants to talk to you."

"Yes. Angie. A faithful church member."

Angie had never thought him so tall before. Although in church, as he stood on the stage behind the podium, he had looked very tall, she had thought it was because he was elevated above the congregation. Even at the door of the church, where, with her family, she dutifully shook hands with him and told him she enjoyed the sermon, he had not seemed as tall as tonight.

He stooped a bit, as if to avoid the ceiling, to hover above her when he took her hand. She found herself recoiling from him.

"Take this chair, Reverend," Papa said, and the reverend moved aside from Angie.

She closed off the part of her mind that was trying to find a reason for her sudden distrust of him. Was she becoming afraid even of the only person she had felt she could trust?

"Angie can sit here."

Papa placed a chair with a straight back near the reverend, then he chose one farther back and to the side. It was almost like being in court again, Angie thought, as she sat down. She, on the high chair, faced the reverend, and Papa, the audience, sat in the shadows.

The reverend sat bent forward, his long hands overlapping each other, his hooded eyes on Angie.

Papa said, "It seems my daughter feels she has seen demons, Reverend."

Angie felt a jolt. She couldn't see Papa's face, but there was derision in his voice. He was making fun of her.

"She's having all kinds of imaginings lately. Not only did she imagine that she's spent every afternoon with the Wickham boy, who as everyone knows is an imbecile, but she's been imagining that she's been teaching him to read and write."

"Tsk, tsk," Reverend Cheney said between his teeth. His smile seemed the kind that was supposed to comfort, placate.

Angie stared from her papa's shadowed face to the reverend's.

"So you think you've been seeing demons?" the reverend asked.

She had lost trust in both of them. Papa had mocked her. With a few words he had turned her confession in court, her defense that had freed Eddie, into the imaginings of a romantic child, herself a half-wit.

"I—" How could she make herself sound believable now, after what her papa had done? "It wasn't I who saw them. It was Eddie. Edward."

"Ah," said the Reverend. "And he told you about them?"

"Yes, sir."

"This imbecilic young man who can't speak told you?"

Angie heard the deep chuckling of her papa. Anger arched through her and she stood up, putting herself in a position where she could face both men. Her fists clenched at her sides.

"I'm telling you, and you can make fun of me if that pleases you. But Eddie is not an imbecile, and I am not an empty-headed dreamer! We were together, and we had been, and he was learning to read and write. And I understood him when he told me things!"

She had started to cry, but forced back the tears. Neither man spoke.

"The day Katrina disappeared, he told me. He told me about the altar in the cellar of Wickham House where Miss Theodora made animal sacrifices—perhaps—to the devil—"

Papa jumped to his feet. "Now wait a minute! That's a direct accusation, and must be retracted!"

The reverend held up his hand. He had stopped smiling. "Let her speak, Arthur."

"He saw her," Angie cried. "Katrina saw. It was Katrina's pet chicken, one she had petted."

"Miss Theodora's own chicken, however," the reverend smiled again.

"Well ... yes, but ..."

"My dear child, killing a chicken doesn't mean an evil sacrifice. Chickens are killed daily, for food."

"But ... but she knelt in prayer at the altar—Eddie saw her, Katrina saw her."

"How lovely," the Reverend said. "Giving thanks for food. All good Christians should do the same."

"You don't understand," Angie pleaded, holding her hands out as if with an offering. An offering of her trust, that at last they would listen.

"What is it we don't understand? I see no demons in this."

"But that afternoon, that was when Katrina disappeared. Eddie was with me, you see, and he told me about the morning. About the—the killing of the chicken in the cellar of the house, and Katrina's tears. Eddie took her home, and she went to sleep. He left her there."

Papa said, "I knew nothing about this. I thought my daughter was at home with her mother and sister, where she belonged."

The reverend had stopped smiling. Angie took heart from that, though his eyes seemed to be more lost beneath the heavy lids.

"That night, Eddie heard Katrina's papa and brothers calling for her. And deep in the night he heard a cry, a scream. His aunt had ordered him never to leave his room at night, but he did. And in the downstairs hall that leads into the cellar, he saw them. He was so shocked he didn't take notice clearly of what they were carrying."

"And what were they carrying?" the reverend asked softly.

Angie drew a long breath. "I haven't talked to Eddie since then, Reverend. But I think they were carrying Katrina. I think it was Miss Theodora, and her—her demons, that killed the child."

Papa was oddly silent.

The reverend said, after clearing his voice and leaning back in his chair, "The belief in demons, Miss Angie, ended long, long ago. It ended with witches and all those old pagan religions. Such simple creatures as snakes, and goats, harmless, for the most part, were turned into devils by some. They tried to cure evil by creating ever more evil. There are no more such things as demons than there are little fairies that are an inch tall and live in the grass."

Angie sat down. What more could she do? They weren't going to help her. Her eyes sought the window pane. Between the still lace curtains the night lay beyond the glass. Behind the moonlit yard the woods were dark. But her eyes would adjust, and there would be touches of moonlight among the trees, just enough to light her way. She was eager now to end this farce. She had to find Eddie.

Suddenly Papa said, "You didn't ask her to describe those demons, Reverend."

"It wasn't necessary. All demons have been described as having horns, and forked tails, like their master, the devil. Part goat, part man. It dates back to when goats were sacrificed and their skins worn in ceremonies. Demons don't exist, that's all Angie needs to remember."

Angie frowned. There was something in the air of the room that puzzled her. The reverend hadn't wanted to hear what Eddie had told her. But Papa did?

She said, "No, that isn't what Eddie saw. And what Katrina had seen before that."

She felt the stares of both men.

"Yes, Katrina," she said. "She came several times to Eddie and told him about something she called the Bad Things."

"Edward told you this?"

"Yes."

"How did you understand what he meant?"

"He could mouth words in silence. And he had learned to write some words. But he thought Katrina had been dreaming, or frightened by snakes in the cellar beneath the house. She said it hissed. Then, he saw them, that night before he found her body. They weren't horned demons, Reverend, they weren't half animal. It was more as if they were—if they're like anything of nature—they were reptilian, with manlike characteristics, because they could walk, on very small legs and feet They had long bodies, unclothed, with smooth skin, and long forearms with very long fingers, shiny and black. One of them was carrying something small and light in color. Theodora was leading the way, carrying a candle. They went down into the cellar, to the altar ..."

The reverend stood up abruptly. The Bible fell off his lap and landed with a splat on the floor. Arthur Beckley bent in silence and picked it up.

"Miss Angie," the reverend said in quick, low, precise words that sounded like a rubber band snapping. "Don't ever repeat anything of this nature outside this room, do you hear? You are maligning the kindest, most wonderful woman in our area. Why, child, don't you know the very church was built by her and her late husband? Don't you know the Wickham money supports not only the church, but many indigent families in the area? The family of Katrina, for one. Don't you know that Miss Theodora has taken in many young people and kept them and fed them and given them jobs until they could move on?"

Young people ... like Eddie ... who then, according to the neighborhood news, left to find their own way. Young people who disappeared.

Angie closed her mouth firmly.

"I'm sure she'll think carefully before she speaks again of such outrageous nonsense," Papa said, and offered the Bible to the reverend. "We are grateful that you have come to talk with Angie."

The reverend, somewhat calmed, nodded, took his Bible, and tucked it beneath his arm.

Angie edged toward the door.

"May I go now, Papa?"

"Yes, go to your room, and stay there until you're called."

"I believe," Reverend Cheney said with a long breath, "that her punishment at this point should be confinement. But if she persists in talking about something as threatening to Miss Theodora as she has tonight, then something more should be done."

Papa nodded.

"We'll discuss this further in a few days, Arthur. You've no idea how grateful I am that you came to me, rather than to some of the law people. Who, at the least, would go and embarrass Miss Theodora."

Angie slipped through the door, hurried down the hall, and went into her own room. She pulled the door firmly shut behind her. Moonlight gilded the window and lighted the sill. The moon was reaching up, full and bright.

Hours would tick by slowly, the moonlight would inch farther into her room, until that last moment, when Papa opened the door to check to see if she was in bed asleep.

Then ... until then ... she would wait.

CHAPTER 18

"You will eat your supper as usual," Theodora said, as they entered the house. As shadows fell across him. As for the first time she walked with her hand gripping his shoulder, pushing him ahead of her. Her fingers dug like coffin nails. "We will live much as we did before, except I'll have to decide how much freedom you deserve."

They stood in the cavern of the kitchen, the ceiling filled with darkness twenty feet above. She removed her hand from his shoulder as she bent to light the group of fresh candles she put on the table each day.

Eddie thought about running, going into the woods, crossing over into the village beyond and from there into the city. But his feet were like blocks of iron.

Light fluttered up, like a feeble life struggling to be. Theodora's shadowed face hovered over the row of candles on the table as she lit each one.

She hadn't spoken to him on the way home. When they reached the driveway, in growing dark relieved only by moon patches through the trees, a silent strange man came to take the horse and buggy.

Theodora didn't introduce them, and the heavy, broad man said nothing. The horse jerked her head sideways, as if she didn't want to go with him. With a hard yank on her reins, he led her away.

After the candles were lit, Theodora said, "The chores have been done, and will be done by Kester. He's another itinerant who happened by and will be taking over your chores. I might add that the Etchenses are gone. There was much sympathy for them in the city, and they had several job offers. So they have left."

He met her eyes, just a glance before he lowered his. Fear held his throat tight and dry.

Would it be tomorrow, or the next day, that she would tell the church members, the Reverend Cheney, Angie's parents, that Eddie, too, had run away? Gone. And, as now, no one would ever invade her privacy, no one would ask to search her house. No one would ever find the cellar.

Then, one day soon in the future, Theodora would take into her house another boy who needed help, and people would think her a grand and generous lady.

"Sit down, Edward, while I get you some food. What did they feed you in jail? It must have been bread and water, you're nothing but skin and bones. First, come here and wash up."

He obeyed her, going to the sink in the washroom. Water gushed cold into the basin, and before he washed, he scooped up a handful and drank it.

"Why, you poor boy," Theodora said, and her hand touched his shoulder again, but more gently. "You must be very thirsty. I'll pour you a big glass of milk."

Her voice seemed filled with dark sarcasm.

She left him alone and returned to the kitchen. He washed his face, brushed his long, curling hair back with his hands, and looked for escape. The window was closed tightly and locked. The door that led out onto the porch was within sight of the kitchen. At that moment Theodora appeared again in the doorway.

"There, you're fine," she said. "Come and eat."

He was hungry, but he was more afraid. She had cut a slice of bread and buttered it heavily, spreading a purple, lumpy jam over the butter. A tall glass of milk looked cool and thick with cream. He drank it, and ate the sandwich. He had to have strength. This was no time to allow his throat to clinch against food. He could not allow her presence as she stood over him to stop his determination to live, to escape.

She went to the other side of the table and sat down, her hands clasped together on the tablecloth in front of her. Eddie noticed there was nothing cooking in the pot on the stove. For the first time there was no whispering fire in the firebox, no simmering food in the black iron pot. He glanced at it only briefly. He had a feeling she could read his every glance and thought.

"Is this true, Edward, what the girl said?"

Eddie met her eyes. Dark, heavy-lidded, reflecting the flickering of the tiny candle flames like still, oily ponds ... suddenly the eyes of the beings he had seen in the hall, the non-human, non-animal creatures that had carried Katrina. Their eyes were as one.

His mind felt as if it were exploding. There were connections, but he didn't understand. They were alike, Theodora, and the creatures she served, or who served her. He didn't know who was the master. Was it Theodora? Or those which Angie called the demons?

Whoever, whatever was master, they were deadly. He had to escape. And Angie?

"Is it true," Theodora asked again, her face drooping in anger from the strain of trying to treat him as if he were a loved one coming home, "is it true that you were able to talk to her?"

He shook his head. His mouth trembled, his throat jerked. No, no. The words wouldn't come. He swallowed. Her hidden eyes, deep and dark, watched every movement of his face. He held his hands up, palms toward the ceiling, and shrugged. He forced a smile to his face.

"Are you telling me the truth?"

He nodded eagerly. Yes, yes, oh Lord, yes.

"She didn't meet you in the woods?"

He shook his head.

The next question should have been, then did you actually kill the child? But she knew the answer to that. The part of the murder that confounded Eddie was why Katrina's body was left in the woods. What did Theodora and her masters, or followers, ordinarily do with the bodies of those they sacrificed? It was obvious, it seemed suddenly to Eddie, that parts of them became part of the mixture in the big pot that had bubbled day and night, until now. As the chickens and pigs had ended up there, so, too, hadn't the others? They were sacrificed and used for food to fuel the demons and keep them happy. But why had Katrina been left in the woods? What was it about Katrina that had ruined the sacrifice and made her body unfit for food for the demons?

"Why did she lie for you?" Theodora asked.

Eddie moved his shoulders in a shrug.

"Who, Edward, do you suppose killed Katrina? If it wasn't you, then who was it?"

His eyes swept to hers against his will. She knew, and he knew. He didn't know how it had happened. He didn't know whether Katrina had come back to the house after she'd awakened in the afternoon, or if Theodora had gone after her. But she had been killed on the altar. Theodora knew that Eddie knew. He saw it in her eyes, in a flicker that was almost a smile.

"The law will be asking around again, won't they, Edward? It would have been much better if you had been found guilty. Wouldn't it, Edward?"

Eddie made no motion. He sat still, staring into her eyes, his eyes held by hers as if she had thrown out an invisible hook and caught his inner self.

For a long moment Theodora stared at him, then she got to her feet, chose one of the candles, and handed it to him.

"Go to your room, Edward. Stay there, as always, until you are called."

He left, gratefully, seeing that she came behind him, near enough to watch him enter the stairwell to the third floor. He closed the stairwell door, shutting himself into the narrow dark tunnel that rose upward. Darkness hovered far above. He climbed toward it, the candlelight flickering higher on the stairwell walls, climbing like a frightened, dying diaphanous moth.

On the landing of the second floor Eddie paused. The landing was like a room, furnished with a sofa and chair, with a table between them, and a lamp that was never lit. Opening off the landing were doors. One of them led into the second-floor hallway. The other two led perhaps into other halls, with other stairs going back to the ground floor.

He had to get out of the house. Morning would be too late. There would be no knock on his door at the break of dawn. She would not allow him to live through the night. And what of Angie? He had to help her; he didn't know how. Her father would never allow him near her. How could he talk to her father?

He opened the door on his left, and crossed the threshold. But it was only a room, stacked with a few pieces of old furniture and some trunks. It had a musty, closed odor that made him want to cough. A narrow window was dusty and dull, moonlight catching in the webs that were woven in the corners.

Eddie backed out and closed the door. The door to the second-floor hall had to be the one at the end. He went to the door and put his hand on the knob. His chest quivered with the thundering of his heart. He turned the knob slowly, imagining what the hallway would look like. Long, and wider than the one on the third floor, it would lead to the balcony above the foyer, and to Theodora's rooms.

Would she be coming up the stairs now? Was she still in the kitchen? Wiping the cabinets, putting on her apron again, perhaps bringing some vegetables out of the pantry and cutting them up into the pot, getting it simmering again for the meat that would be added later? Food for those that lived in her cellar, or elsewhere in the house, or beneath the ground, perhaps in natural caves, or tunnels of their making? That wove like mole tunnels beneath the woods, beneath even the house in which Angie lived?

He turned the doorknob. He had to take a chance that she had not yet come to the front of the big house. He could slip away, through the front door, and run down the driveway, in the moonlight to the road. From there he could run to Angie's house, and, together, maybe they could make her people understand.

He felt the pressure against the door from the other side when he pushed gently to open it. Something was there. The door wasn't locked, but it was blocked.

Eddie released the knob, and the pressure from the other side caused the door to click shut.

Eddie held his breath and listened. He heard a sound, a soft sliding against the wall, a murmur that was half grunt, half-hiss.

Eddie backed away from the door. He looked back down the stairwell, and something, darker than the darkness below, stirred. Black moving with darkness.

He was trapped.

Quickly, looking back over his shoulder, he climbed the tunnel stairwell to the third floor.

He stood a moment looking down the long hall, his eyes shaded from the light of the candle. Its tiny flame moved up, down, its feeble light pushed back by the darkness ahead.

He stepped into his small room and closed the door. He listened. The sound came, sliding along the hall, against the wall, causing his door to move, then it inched away and was still.

He placed the candle in the holder on the stand and went quietly to the window. It was a long drop to the ground, but perhaps he could hold onto the stones that made up the walls, and the vines that grew heavy and solid against it, and get down without breaking a leg.

The window resisted his push against it. When last he had slept here, the window was partly open. Now it was shut.

His fingers moved along the top of the bottom sash and found nail heads. The window had been nailed shut.

He was trapped in Wickham House.

CHAPTER 19

A streak of light widened across the bed in which Angie lay with her back to the door.

Papa tiptoed across the braided rug and looked down at her. She lay on her right side, trying to appear asleep, the cover pulled so high around her cheeks it didn't show that she wore her clothing.

For a long time he stood above her, and she grew afraid he was going to pull the quilt down to see what she was wearing. The night was too warm for a quilt. She was counting on him feeling it would not be proper for him to uncover his daughter.

But then he drew away. For a longer moment he stood by the door, then it softly closed.

She remained still, her breath caught, her chest tight with tension. She heard his footsteps fade down the hall.

A moment later the clock in the parlor began striking ... ten ... eleven ... twelve. The sound faded away like a train whistle in the distance.

Midnight. Papa had sat up for two hours past his bedtime, waiting for this hour. And Angie had lain in the same position in bed, the quilt pulled up, waiting for him to check on her.

She slipped out of bed. Even her shoes were on her feet, buttoned to her ankles, growing tighter and tighter and more uncomfortable. She hurriedly straightened her skirt and tiptoed to the window, grateful that Papa hadn't thought to lock it. It was still raised, the screen unhooked, so that all she had to do was push it out and climb through.

She dropped to the ground and stood outlined in moonlight against the wall. Ahead of her, thirty feet across the grass, woodland began. She lifted her skirt in both hands and ran, praying her sister wouldn't look out her bedroom window at this time. Praying that her papa or mama hadn't chosen this time to go to the back-house at the end of the moonlit garden. Hoping Henry wouldn't see her and bark, thinking her a stranger.

Hoping he wouldn't see her and follow.

She reached the shadows of the woods. Deep within them a hoot owl screamed, then dropped his call to a hoot-who, soft, coming closer. She could feel it swooping in silent flight toward her, to see what had entered its wood. It called again, very soft, only yards away.

Angie turned to face the house. White, and brightly lighted by the moon, it looked as if it would be holding a sleeping family safe, secure, none of them torn by fear or sorrow or disappointment. She looked at it with grief growing in her heart. She would never see it again.

With Eddie, she was leaving. They had no choice but lose themselves in the city. Other cities, then, farther away.

She had no doubt she would reach Eddie. She didn't allow herself to think that she could be stopped.

She faced the darkness in the woods. She had walked into these woods every day, most of her life, and knew it tree by tree. But tonight the trees were lost in darkness, and she could only guess her way. Occasional spots of moonlight lay for moments on the forest floor, and then disappeared as the moon edged westward in the sky.

Eddie had drawn the house for her, those rooms that he knew. She remembered them by heart. First, at the back, was the long porch, with the ivy-covered railings and posts. The door on the left entered the big kitchen. The door on the right went into the washroom.

The kitchen had four doors leading out of it. One went into the big pantry that opened on the other side to the hallway that ended at the wall. It was there the door led down into the cellar.

There was another door out of the kitchen that led to hallways. Connecting the main hall to the front was a large portion that was blank on Eddie's drawing, because he didn't know what was there. A narrow passage to the right held doors to the washroom, a storage room with an outside door that was locked and never used, and a door into the service stairwell. Eddie's room was up those stairs, past the second-floor landing. As if it were a small room it had furniture for some reason that neither Eddie nor Angie understood. The day he had drawn that sofa and table with its lamp, Angie had questioned his indecipherable marks. "What's that?" He motioned, then drew more carefully. Sofa. Table.

"There? Why?"

He shrugged, and they smiled. Angie said, "So the servants can rest halfway up to their rooms." They giggled, except Eddie's giggle was silent. She could see his Adam's apple moving, and the width of his smile reached his eyes and crinkled the corners.

Except in Miss Theodora's house there were no servants. She did the work herself, dusting, dusting, washing dishes, busy, busy. Angie had found herself frowning, wondering, even then. What a strange woman. It was almost as if she were someone else's servant.

Angie comforted herself as she went deeper into the dark woods. Back to the drawing of the house. Keep your mind on where you're going. Was the kitchen door locked at night? Eddie didn't know.

His room was up those service stairs, on the third floor. The first door on the right.

She had gone over it and gone over it. Although she wasn't comfortable in the dark, tonight the dark was her friend. In the dark she wouldn't be seen.

On the porch she planned to remove her shoes. Then, walking in silence, she would feel her way through the dark to his room. She had thought of all ways to reach him, and it seemed the only one.

Moonlight leaked through the trees like drops of milk. She avoided the larger spots of light that might reveal her. Yet who would be in the woods tonight? Leaves made small rustling sounds beneath her feet. Twigs snapped. She paused, listening. A warning rippled up her back. She felt layered in thorns. Her hair pulled as if fingers had tangled in it.

Someone ... something was following her.

When she stopped, it stopped.

Had she only thought she heard the rustle of leaves elsewhere in the woods, near enough that she could have reached out and touched whatever it was?

The dog! It was like him. He must have seen her cross through the moonlight by the house, and followed her.

She stared into the dark. Dribbles of moonlight moved like spots before her eyes. Somewhere deeper in the woods, northward, past the meadow on the hill, an owl hooted. A leaf fell, its touch upon others too soft to have made the sound she'd heard.

She dared use her voice. She could imagine Henry standing a few feet away, his tail wagging slowly back and forth, staring at her with his superior night vision, wondering why she was walking in the woods at night. Wondering why she hadn't sent him back to the house, as she did on her afternoon walks to spend her hours with Eddie.

"*Henry!*"

Her voice was a hissing whisper.

"Is that you, Henry?"

There was no answer. If it had been the dog, he'd have come forward now, nuzzling into her offered hand.

She sucked in her breath. Her imagination—that was all. She had to go on, hurry, try to get to Eddie. Then, she had to insist they leave, together, now, tonight. Together they must fear nothing, not even the demons of hell. There would be a way they could escape, together.

She was terrified of trying to enter the house. Yet how else could she reach him?

She wouldn't let herself think of those creatures he had seen with Theodora. They were of the underground, the cellar, whatever they were, and she knew according to his drawing of the house there was a door closing off that hall.

Demons. They don't exist, Reverend Cheney had said. Perhaps not. No, of course not. There was only Miss Theodora, in her madness, and ... perhaps the darkness in the cellar had frightened Eddie. There was nothing but Miss Theodora. With her butcher knife, and her secret altar in the cellar beneath her house.

Angie could slip quietly through the dark and find Eddie. This soon after the trial, Theodora wouldn't dare hurt him. There might be an investigation into her house, into Theodora herself. No, she wouldn't hurt Eddie now. Theodora would want Eddie to be seen with her in public first. In church, at the open market where she shopped for vegetables. A few days. Then, she could say he had run away. And Theodora would be safe from any suspicions.

She was near the house. She could see the peaks of its rooflines through the trees, reaching higher than the treetops. Moonlight highlighted and shadowed its turrets and gables.

Behind her something moved. Leaves rustled evenly, not step by step. Something crawled, sliding almost soundlessly, touching bare ground and soft moss, then coming into dead winter leaves from seasons past and gliding through them. A soft yet large sound, as if its size expanded as it came nearer to her.

Angie paused slightly and heard the sound stop, as it had before. Then she hurried, faster, breaking out of the woods and into the less wooded area near the house. The walls ahead of her rose upward, streaked by moonlight. She swerved to the right, going toward the back of the house. She saw the vines growing past dark windows that caught the moonlight and absorbed it.

Then suddenly someone stood before her. Dressed in black, the tall figure blended with the dark. Reverend Cheney?

She stopped, her hands slapping over her mouth to stop the scream that bubbled spontaneously. She only gasped.

So she had been followed after all. By the reverend, and perhaps by her papa, too.

Yet the sounds she had hurried from in the woods had not been the steps of men.

Then her being began to die inch by inch in cold horror as she stared. Not the reverend after all. Not a man dressed in black. But something changing before her eyes, as it moved, as the moonlight moved.

Its eyes ... slitted, heavy-lidded, uncovering a dark emptiness, reflecting the moonlight like black glass. Its head tapered, sloping to a jutting point. Described to her by Eddie, still the image had not formed fully in her mind, this, the unbelievable, as she stood facing something made of the nether substances of its own eyes, its lack of soul.

"Get her," a woman's voice commanded from nearby.

Angie turned to run, but dark demons surrounded her. She felt herself lifted. A cold tentacle choked off her voice.

Eddie, Run. Run, Eddie.

EDDIE HAD SLEPT, for only a moment, it seemed. Dreams were like thoughts, leaping from face to face. Katrina. Angie. Dreams took him back to the cellar, and the creatures took shape again, writhing in a diabolical impatience as Theodora prayed at the side of the stone table on which lay her sacrifice, Katrina. Katrina, still clinging to her rag doll with a hand that hung lifeless against the stone wall that shone with her own blood.

He saw her face clearly, her open eyes staring sightlessly at the ceiling on which feeble candlelight licked. The butcher knife slashed at her.

Though she lay dead on the sacrificial altar, still she screamed, screamed.

Eddie leaped up. Even as he woke, he was moving toward the door. Then he paused. Only a dream ...

Then again he heard the scream. Through the thick walls of the house, through the hallways, the closed doors. Not Katrina. *Angie!*

"Eddie! Eddddieeee ..."

There was more before her voice faded. Eddie, run, it had sounded. Eddie, run away.

They had Angie. Somehow they had stolen her, and she was here, in this house. His only comfort had been in thinking that she was safely at home, in her bedroom, protected by her papa. But instead, she was here. He had not dreamed her cries, her call to him.

He ran, through the darkness in the hallway, his hands reaching out to guard against the walls. He ran down the service stairs, stumbling over the end of the sofa on the landing of the second floor. He fell to his right knee. In the dark, he grasped the wood edging on the velvet sofa and pulled himself up and ran on, going down the steps, his hands on the walls.

He knew where she was. It was not until he had crossed the main hall and opened the door into the hall that led to the cellar that it occurred to him they had allowed her to scream. They had wanted her to call him.

He paused. He could turn back and go for help. He could run the half mile to the parsonage and get Reverend Cheney to come and help ... but by that time Angie would be dead.

He could fight. He could find a weapon.

He swerved left into the pantry. There was a stool. He remembered it standing by shelves that reached to the ceiling.

It was easy to find. Candlelight made a dim track through the open door to the kitchen. The stool stood like something threatening, on tall legs. He grabbed it, and turned toward the hall, the legs pointed outward.

The door at the end of the hall stood open.

The stone steps into the cellar glistened in flickering candlelight, dark and damp.

On bare feet he ran onto the steps.

The scene was his nightmare. But it wasn't Katrina on the altar, it was Angie.

The only sound in the cellar was a slow dripping of water, or blood. *Drip, drip.*

Angie lay on the stone table as if she had been placed in her coffin. She was stretched long and slender, her bodice torn open, her white breasts rounded. Dark red rivulets of blood ran beneath them and down her side and dripped onto the stone.

A long, raw slit between her breasts and through her stomach and flat belly oozed blood. Her skin was colorless in the flickering gold of the candlelight.

Her head had been turned so that her open eyes stared at Eddie as he came slowly down the steps. Blood ran from the corner of her mouth and soaked into her hair. Eddie descended slowly. Life ended here. When Angie died, he, too, died. He moved now only from his need to be with her.

Something moved to Eddie's left.

He tore his stare from Angie's body.

Theodora stood holding the butcher knife in her right hand. She lifted it slowly, as if to show it to him. A smile began on her lips.

Eddie screamed. He heard it, filling the underground, echoing in dark caves far beyond the light, magnified. A cry of fury, hatred, total abandonment came from his throat. With the stool lifted in both hands he rushed at her, its legs pointed at her face.

Long fingers like tentacles slid around his neck from behind, and cut his breath away.

He felt the hard thump of the ground against his head as he fell, and heard his own breath gush to silence.

He saw slitted dark eyes above him, soulless, unfeeling, creatures made for death and darkness, and powers beyond life. He tried to cry out his rage, his hatred again. But the tentacles slid around him, tighter and tighter.

Angie.

It was a whisper of a thought deep in his mind, his last thought. His last wish.

Angie, I wish I could have told you that I love you.

PART TWO: THE RETURN

CHAPTER 20

Katie Rogers sat at her desk in one corner of the Yates Real Estate
front office and leafed through the thick catalog of homes,
various properties, and general real estate for sale. Business was slow. She
hadn't had a client in two days.

She was dressed casually in a calf-length tan skirt that had a slit six inches
up the left leg and gold buttons from there to the white blouse where a loose
gold chain belt defined her small waist. Her brown boxy jacket hung over the
back of her chair. She wore her long blond hair back in a French braid. Her
high cheekbones were enhanced with a touch of the same pale pink that she
wore on her lips; otherwise, she wore no makeup. Around her neck were gold
chains of various lengths, given to her by her husband, and all worn at once so
that she would feel closer to him. Though now that Ethan had been dead six
months, the sharp pain of loss had become a calm acceptance. Sometimes she
felt like a child who had been slapped down and told to stay there.

At the receptionist's desk the phone rang, and Katie paused. The call
wasn't transferred to her.

She paged deeper into the thick catalog, marking homes she thought might
be easiest to sell now.

She felt vaguely depressed, stagnated. The almost unbearable grief she'd
lived with for several months after her husband had died in the crash of his
small rental plane had lessened—replaced, it seemed, by an anxiety like a
worry, and boredom, and restlessness. Perhaps more, she didn't know. She
knew only that when she wasn't working, she was walking, or driving. Just
wishing she knew what she wanted to do with the rest of her life, now that

Ethan was gone. Ideas came and went, nothing stuck. She had an understanding now of a woman alone. She had an added understanding of the lonely, the homeless. She wanted to help, somehow. Ethan would want her to use his insurance to help others. Though when he was alive they had been young and frivolous during their short marriage, his death had made her old at twenty-five.

He would approve, she felt, of the idea that was taking shape. She was looking for a specific property, one Ethan had flown her over the week before he died. He had been begging her to let him rent a small plane and take her up, ever since he got his license. She had resisted. She had things to do, she told him. She made excuses, until finally, he asked, "You don't trust me?"

"Oh, no-no-no, that isn't it," she assured him, all excuses crumbling in the face of the truth. It wasn't that she didn't trust him, it was that she didn't trust small planes. They were like tin cans, it seemed to her, with wings. But he had been so excited about flying that she hadn't wanted to discourage him. Logic told her the small planes were fine. But that didn't extend to that nervous inner self that said: No way am I going to ride in one of those tin cans!

So she was morally obligated to let Ethan, whom she'd do anything for, short of a few absolute no's, show her how well he could fly.

As it turned out, the flight had been pleasant. They had looked down over the western edge of the city, on small towns and farms and hills and valleys. And during that flight they had passed over a large wooded property near a small town south of the city, where wooded hills began and joined a national forest, so that the house seemed to be on the edge of civilization.

The house intrigued both of them, and Ethan flew in a circle above it several times. It was old, they decided, not a modern replica. It was taller than the surrounding trees, with sharp rooflines, turrets, peaks, angles, chimneys. She counted six chimneys. There also was an old barn, and several other outbuildings that looked as if another leaf on the rotting roofs would cave them in.

"Go back, go back," she had cried, forgetting what she was in. "See if anyone lives there. Ethan! I think that place is vacant! Wouldn't it be marvelous if we could get it?"

"What? A million dollars?"

She settled down. "Yeah, you're right."

She kept looking, though. The yard was not kept up. Big trees in the yard shaded it, but weeds grew along the almost invisible driveway. The house was perhaps three hundred feet back from the two-lane blacktop road out of the small town that was less than half a mile away. It was secluded from the road by old, massive trees. She felt a strange longing to go there, and determined that day to see if it was listed.

"I'll buy it for you tomorrow," he said casually, as he turned the plane back toward the airport.

The next morning, he was killed when the same rental plane went down in a pasture south of the city, not far from the old house in the edge of the national forest. He was alone.

In her grief, she forgot the house for several months. Then it began to come back to her, and she felt that old longing, as if only there would she ever feel at home again.

This morning she had described it hastily to her boss, Mr. Yates, as he was on his way out the door, and he had said it sounded like a place they'd had listed for years. The next minute he was gone with a client, before she had a chance to get any more information. So she had settled down and started going through the thick catalog.

She wished a potential client would walk through the door and head for her desk. Mr. Yates was still gone. Carol had taken the morning off. She had no clients either, today. The last client Katie had was last week. He'd wanted a house in the hundred-thousand-dollar range. He was willing to go up as high as one-twenty-five. So Katie had spent a couple of days showing him houses, from city to suburbs. They had looked at seven houses. Hey, he'd said at the seventh, this looks like it. He'd bring his wife over tomorrow, he said. That was three working days ago, and she hadn't heard from him since. She was still waiting. And she had marked three more houses in his price range.

The phone rang again. Katie paused. But another of the agents took the call. She went back to the catalog.

That was the thing about real estate she didn't like—it took iron nerves to handle it. The promises made and broken were worse than those of a fickle lover.

She stopped on page 110 and looked at the picture of a large house nearly hidden by trees. It was authentically old, not a reproduction. It had three stories, with sharp, peaked, angled rooflines. Although the listing called it Victorian, it looked as if it were a mixture of architectures, as so many old houses were. The walls were stone. The Victorian style was in the porches, the railings, and the gingerbread. Bits of gingerbread were dimly visible in the peaks of the rooflines, like spider webs. Whoever had taken the picture must have stood a hundred yards away, she thought, as she strained for a clearer view of the house. She had the impression that the camera had gotten more trees than house.

She read the description, excitement slowly rising. This was it. This was the house they had seen from the air. She had felt a strong attraction toward it the moment she'd spotted those peaked rooflines above the trees.

Forty-four major rooms ... *forty-four?* Good Lord, what would she do with forty-four rooms?

Well, she could figure that out later.

She continued reading the description of the house and property. Six fireplaces, water from its own two-hundred-foot well. Many outbuildings. One hundred sixty acres of wooded land. It even had one bathroom on the ground floor, a modern addition. A bargain at two hundred thousand.

What?

Two hundred thousand for one hundred sixty acres and a forty-four-room house in excellent repair? What was wrong?

She read farther down on the page. Ah! No electricity, for one thing. No heating, except for fireplaces. A house built in the 1800s that had not been modernized except for cold water, and one ground floor bathroom. *That* was what was wrong. It was probably icy cold.

However, it was not far from the city. Certainly she could commute the distance with no problem. It was almost as if she was predestined to own it.

Since Ethan's death she'd been having vague dreams about a huge house. In the dreams she saw emptiness, shadows in every corner, walls obscured by darkness. Was this the house that had triggered the dreams? She wondered if children had ever lived there, if their sounds had ever entered that house.

Her sister Nancy, with her two small children, could move in with her. She had left her husband, Perry, a week or so ago and needed some thinking time, she'd said.

Even that seemed part of the strange pattern forming around Katie since Ethan's death ... perhaps it had started earlier. It almost seemed now to have started when she first saw the house.

Nancy and her two kids were staying temporarily with Mom and Doug— and the kids were about to drive Doug mad, Mom had said. They'd certainly have lots of room to run and play at the old house without getting on anyone's nerves.

On the practical side, she needed money. The insurance company had fought payment on the death of Ethan, claiming it was suicide, which was ridiculous. She'd had to get a lawyer, but when the money came through, she'd not only be able to buy the place, but to have electricity and natural gas installed.

At that moment, as if fate were running her way, Mr. Yates came in the front door on the way to his office. The catalog folded in her hand, Katie hurried after him.

He sat down behind his desk and leaned back with a sigh as Katie entered through the open door. He looked up at her, a small, slender man in his seventies with wide-open eyes in a pixie face. The eyes were disarming. Innocent as a child's or a puppy's. She knew how shrewd he really was. This was the head office of several branch offices. He worked because he liked to work.

Katie put the catalog, folded to the old mansion, in front of him.

"What is there about this I should know? How long has it been on the market, and why?"

Yates smiled. "Ah! Wickham House again. I thought this might be the one you saw. Is it?"

Katie detected a twinkle in his eye. "There are monumental things wrong with it, right? Besides no electricity and no gas, what else is wrong?"

"Nothing, for an old house. It's even got some of the original furniture in it."

Her hopes rose a bit. She said, "I think I could do something with this place, Mr. Yates, if you would give me a good deal."

"What'd you have in mind?"

"Oh—a low down, something I can manage—"

"I mean, what would you do with it?"

"I'd fill it with people." It seemed to come off the top of her head. "Homeless, families in transition, who don't have money for rent until they get paid on their new jobs. The kind of people we've been seeing around here lately. Mothers without husbands. My sister, first of all. She's separated from her husband and staying with our parents. She has a daughter who's eight, and a son, five. They need space."

"They'd move in with you so you wouldn't be alone?"

"Yes, probably."

"What if they went home? I assume there's a place they left?"

Mr. Yates was asking odd questions. They seemed out of character. She looked at him. There was no twinkle in his eye.

She put her hand up to her face in a defensive gesture. "There are other homeless families. The shelters are overrun."

He returned her look a moment, then said, "Well, you're a sensible, strong young woman. Sure, I'll make you a good deal."

He leaned over his desk and began writing on a sheet of paper.

"Here are directions. It's almost big enough for a hotel of sorts. Some have said there are sixty rooms, not forty. I don't think anyone knows. It's been in the catalog so long I don't remember when it went in. Several people have been interested, but the sales were never completed. A few moved in but didn't stay long. The original owner, Mrs. Theodora Wickham, died in 1949, and it's been empty since then."

"No survivors?"

"No. An insurance company owns it, set the price back then, and it's never been raised. The last time it was almost sold was about six months ago. A retired couple. Those folks even put in a gas stove. A range, in the kitchen. Very modern." He almost smiled.

"There's a gas line?" She envisioned a city line of natural gas.

"No," he said. "Just a bottle of gas, Katie. Sorry. But I think those people had even moved in some canned goods. They were setting up housekeeping. They left everything there."

Mr. Yates's eyes twinkled again. A smile dipped the corners of his lips. He was sending mixed signals. At first he had seemed worried that she'd be living there alone. Now he was ready to make a special offer for her. It was as if he knew a joke he wasn't sharing. She watched him with growing suspicion. There was something he wasn't telling her.

"Why would they walk out leaving everything? That sounds like they didn't even want to go back long enough to get their things. Is it haunted?" Only joking, her smile said, as she watched him. Old houses were known for strange noises. They were usually darker than more modern places, too. She could understand that some nervous souls might have wild imaginations under those conditions.

"Could be." He extended the note paper of directions to Katie. "But you're not worried about that, are you, Katie?"

She laughed. "No."

"Good. Then it's all yours. I'll be glad to sell it to you."

CHAPTER 21

$\mathcal{T}$wo hours later Katie found the driveway.

A curving highway out of a town on the south side of the city passed through old sections that were surrounded by large, old trees, side by side to new developments. On the right grew the trees, and Katie knew from the directions she had reached the land she was looking for.

The driveway was almost hidden in the undergrowth. She pulled to the side of the road searching for it. Traffic passed sporadically.

She saw the culvert almost hidden by summer weeds, waited for a line of traffic to pass, and then pulled back onto the road to make the turn into the driveway.

The drive seemed to be no more than a logging trail following the easiest route into the trees, then she glimpsed the corner of a stone wall, far back. She drove slowly. Weeds and brush slid along the sides of her car. As she progressed, the forest appeared to fall back, and only a few large trees grew near the house and the outer buildings. Green spring weeds, uncut, grew over brown, dead weeds of seasons past. The house was visible a wall at a time. The roofline rose above the tallest trees like the peak of a cathedral. It looked even more desolate and deserted than it had from the air.

"Good Lord," she muttered aloud. "Doesn't anybody take care of this place?"

Still, it was oddly beautiful. She parked the car near a porch that reached out toward the driveway and sat a moment, windows down.

If only Ethan could be here with her, she thought. A sharp pang of loneliness, such as she had not felt in months, threatened to consume her. Then, like a pain easing, it drifted away.

She sat still, looking, listening.

A crow cawed persistently somewhere. The traffic on the road sounded distant, muffled by the trees. Through a line of trees to her left, she saw a shed-like building, its board sides grayed with years, the roof rotted and caving in near a corner. It was one of the many outbuildings that were mentioned in the description, and which she had seen from the air. It was worthless, except for firewood.

Ahead of her, its sides also gray, was the old barn, one section crumbling, the roof sagging and filled with holes. A stockade fence still stood. Beyond the barn was an opening in the forest, as if once it had been a meadow for animals. Now, it was filled mostly with young saplings. But they were so much smaller than the surrounding trees Katie could almost see the grass that had once grown in place of them.

She got out of the car and walked slowly on past the house. The driveway was vaguely visible, leading to a garage, or carriage house, open on the front. An old buggy sagged in the first compartment, shrouded under spider webs and dust, one wheel collapsed. On the walls hung various old leather items that might mean something to an antique dealer. Or a horse.

Strange, she thought, that no vandals had found this place. There had been no gate across the driveway, no sign forbidding trespassing. In this case it was probably better there wasn't. The trees along the road hid the buildings, and it was possible that over the years most people in the neighborhood were too new even to know the place was here. So many acres of trees, who would bother to explore? Not the vandals, evidently.

She went to the barn and peeked through a door that hung on one hinge. It was shadowy dark and smelled of rodents, rotted hay, and age. She backed away, went around the fence to the corner of the barn, and stood looking into the forest. A dim little road was visible among the trees, two tracks with a strip of weeds in the center. It curled in a leisurely fashion deep into the woods, toward hills and the miles of national forest.

She put her hand on the corner of the barn.

I've done this before ... I've stood here before ...

She felt the blood leech from her face, leaving it tight and tingling.

She blinked, and the strong feeling of deja-vu eased away.

For just a moment she had experienced a strange sensation that all this around her was familiar, that she had stood here before, looking at this tiny road that drifted off through the forest of old, tall trees. The feeling was gone now and she stood looking at the road through a stranger's eyes. But she would never forget the feeling.

She moved uneasily away from the old barn.

Another day, another time, she would follow the road, see where it led. On another day, she would walk the outer boundaries of the property to see if there were any old fences, see what joined on all sides.

She began to walk. Some of the smaller buildings contained rusty old junk that, like the buggy, might be important to an antique dealer. A couple more were empty. But the one she was drawn to see was the building barely visible through the trees, nearly hidden by the undergrowth.

She stood in what was once its front yard. Young trees grew tall, but it was obvious that once many years ago it had been a cleared area, judging by the older, taller trees that edged it. She pushed her way through uncut weeds by the door.

The door sagged partway open. She stepped over a high threshold onto a dirt floor. The gloom within hit her like a wall. A weight seemed to press on her chest, and she felt smothered. She drew a deep breath and stepped back outside.

What's wrong with me?

Never in her life had she been so affected, so easily changed in her moods. Even in the terrible two months after Ethan's death, before there was some relief in her grief, she had not had such sudden mood changes.

She was determined to see inside the little shack. It had been one of the first things she'd seen when she'd come into the driveway, other than trees and more trees, and she was going to go in. No mood change was going to keep her out.

She stepped over the threshold again and stood looking into the shadowy, webby interior.

One small window, nearly obscured by dust, spider webs, and dead leaves caught in the corners, emitted the only light other than a few holes in the rotting roof and the half-open door. But Katie saw immediately that this had once been used as someone's home. And the shack separated from the old mansion by a carefully planted line of trees? A caretaker's shack, probably.

There was still an old iron cookstove in the corner, with a pipe going up through the ceiling. In two corners were wooden platforms on the ground, and scraps of material and straw. She walked toward them, puzzled. What kind of furniture was this? Then it came to her, oddly clearly. Beds. Built of rough lumber on the dirt floor. Beds with straw for mattresses. Scraps of material looked as if they might once have been quilts. Something small scurried through the straw and peeked out, and she found herself looking into the eyes of a frightened mouse. As suddenly as it had appeared, it was gone.

Katie moved back toward the center of the one-room house. Shelves on the walls near the stove were probably where the pots and dishes were kept. They were empty now. An old table back in the fourth corner was little more than a heap of wood.

Such horrible poverty.

Katie felt its weight in her heart. How was it that a family—and it must have been a family, since there were two large beds—how could they live here like this, while yards away a forty- or sixty-room house held probably one person, or two at most?

She felt devastated with the weight of the long-ago misery she sensed in the one-room shack—of a shifting mood like darkness rearranging itself. Something apart from herself.

She started out, then stopped.

It was lying on the dirt floor against the wall, as if someone had dropped it there, or thrown it there on his way out. Perhaps when he'd moved.

Katie picked it up.

It was made of rags, caked with dirt, darkened with an old, dried substance that stiffened the fabric. Katie cleaned off the caked dirt as well as she could, gently. Part of the material came off with the dirt. But still, its face was there, flowers in the material, two eyes made of single violets and a mouth that was a faded rose.

A child's rag doll.

CHAPTER 22

$\mathcal{K}$atie carried the rag doll with her, protecting it from the reach of thin limbs, briars, weeds. She put it on the floor in the backseat of the car, then looked up at the house as she closed the door. She hadn't even been in the house, and she had spent almost two hours here. If she didn't hurry, she'd have to come back tomorrow. She couldn't leave without at least a quick look into the house.

The sky had grown cloudy during the afternoon. No wonder everything here seemed so lightless.

With the long, old-fashioned, skeleton-type key Mr. Yates had given her, she headed toward the porch that was closest to the driveway. It would open some of the doors, he said, but not all. If she bought the house, she should have modern locks put on, because he didn't know where the original keys were. Lost over the years, he supposed.

The boards of the side porch squeaked when she stepped on them. Once they'd held a gray paint, but it was now mostly peeled away. However, the white gingerbread that decorated the porch was still white, as if it had been repainted in recent years.

The door had a small, stained glass insert, but whatever lay beyond it was dark. She needed her flashlight. She inserted the key and was disappointed that it didn't fit.

She left the side porch and made a detour back to her car for the small flashlight she always kept in the cubbyhole. With the flashlight tucked into the hip pocket of her jeans, she walked back down the driveway looking for a path. She found it, stones laid carefully, nearly hidden by weeds. It led to the tall front door. The porch here was smaller, less welcoming, it seemed to Katie. But at least the key fit. The door screeched open.

Katie cringed. First thing—oil the damn door.

She entered a nearly dark foyer and pushed the door wide open so the dwindling daylight would enter the house.

A stairway in the center rose to a landing, then curved on up to a second-floor balcony. Brackets spaced on the wall held candles, little white sticks like tiny ghosts in the still gloom. High-backed antique chairs and a tall, narrow chest stood against the wall opposite the stairway. The chest contained an umbrella stand, a mirror, drawers.

"The house was never wired. But you won't be in the dark," Mr. Yates had said, with that teasing look that puzzled her even now. "The house is fully equipped with candles."

Katie turned on her flashlight. It looked almost comical, with its little beam making a thin track through the increasing darkness. Still, it was better than nothing. With it shining here, there, she started on down the hall, deeper into the house.

Like a warning, thunder growled from the clouds. Windows trembled, rattled faintly, like thin, fine voices complaining. She hesitated. She should leave now, come again tomorrow. But she didn't want to leave. There was something so big and so solid about the house, a sense of protection here against any storm. In her car she would feel more vulnerable.

Still, it was getting darker. She hadn't brought anything into the house with her except the key and flashlight. She should have brought her shoulder bag, in which she always carried a small emergency pouch that contained small tools and even a box of matches. She'd better hurry out before the rain started.

At that moment, she heard it strike. In waves it came against the house, a windswept sound through the open front door. The air cooled, as if she had come up against an invisible wall of ice.

She started out, then halted. Sudden rainstorms usually wore themselves out in minutes. Since she was in here, she might as well take a quick peek. There was a kitchen somewhere, at the end of the hall, probably.

She passed several closed doors, and a couple that stood open. But she saw only the dark outlines of furniture. She followed the narrow flashlight beam with her eyes, looking at tall doorways with decorative carvings, and darkened wallpaper with darker traces of pattern.

At the end of the long central hall she came to an arrangement of closed doors. She chose the one straight ahead and entered a large, high-ceilinged kitchen with tall cabinets, a large central table, chairs, knickknacks, and two stoves side-by-side, one new and white, the other huge and old, of black cast iron. On the old stove sat a big black cast-iron pot, apparently once used for cooking. Its edges had rusted brown and flakes had fallen to the surface of the stove. The rest of the stove top appeared shiny clean, as if it had been oiled and wiped recently.

She shined the flashlight around quickly, and then more slowly. In shadows beyond the light, she saw doors leading elsewhere. She shined the light again on the table, where a selection of candles stood in the center. There was something odd about the appearance of the room. She looked again, bringing her finger across the top of the table. No dust.

"This place looks as if someone lives here," she murmured.

She found herself looking over her shoulder, as if she were intruding, as if she expected to see the lady of the house standing there, returning her look with bewilderment, asking, what are you doing here in my kitchen?

The rain had either slowed, or was so completely muffled by tall ceilings and thick walls and closed doors that it was only a dull movement of sound. Thunder rumbled again. She shivered in her sweater. No heat, she remembered.

She would love to see the rest of the house, but in better light ... tomorrow. Tonight, she would call Nancy and talk to her about this, about what they might be able to do with it.

She retraced her steps down the long hall and out onto the porch. Darkness had fallen with a vengeance, relieved only by an occasional flash of lightning.

On the road beyond the trees a car light streaked past, soundless. There was a quality about it that seemed eerie and out of place, a century separated.

She held one arm over her head and ran out to the car. Rain poured steadily from a black sky. The rain wouldn't be stopping soon, she thought, as she turned the car key in the ignition switch.

It clicked, then was silent.

What the devil?

She frowned into the dark trees ahead. Lightning flashed, opening up the view, the high roof peaks above, the windows, narrow, tall, reflecting the bright lightning, then dying to blackness.

She tried starting the car again, but heard nothing now, not even a click. The battery was dead? How could that be?

She drew a deep sigh. Nothing could make her feel as helpless as something going haywire with her car. She wasn't a mechanic. She was not mechanically inclined in any way. Oh, Lord, how she missed Ethan. If Ethan were here, he'd raise the hood, look around a minute, say, "It's not the battery, it's this"—whatever—and fix it.

She sat still for several minutes, then tried the car again. It was as if there were no connection between the key and the engine.

She looked at the house.

Well, at least she hadn't been caught out somewhere with no shelter available.

She tucked the shoulder bag firmly beneath her arm, turned the joke of a flashlight back on, then ran to the porch just as the sky split and dumped a waterfall. She dodged into the house and pulled the big, solid door shut.

The rain sounded like a monster prowling, even with the door closed. But the house, at least down here, was dry. For the first time she wondered if the roof leaked.

She looked at the stairway. There might be beds up there. But she could figure out that part of her problem later. Meantime, there was the kitchen, clean, with a gas stove, and, Mr. Yates had said, some canned goods left in the pantry.

Standing near the empty umbrella rack at the side of the tall chest, she began a series of why-hadn't-shes. Why hadn't she brought someone along? She had run home long enough to change to jeans and sweater because she was planning to walk on the land, so why hadn't she gone to get Nancy and the kids to come with her?

Because it would have taken another hour.

Why hadn't she put a damned phone in her car, the way Mr. Yates had once suggested? Why hadn't she waited until tomorrow, when there might not be a threat of rain? But of course, she hadn't listened to any weather reports lately, and she didn't know there was a threat today. Why hadn't she had her car checked for some abnormality, or whatever the mechanics called it? Of course, she hadn't known it was about to create a problem.

She sighed, and someone mimicked the sigh just over her shoulder.

She jerked around, but saw only the lightning through the tall windows on each side of the door.

The sound of her footsteps followed her to the kitchen. She paused, listening. Did footsteps echo in tall, old houses?

Of course it was possible. The ceilings were very high, perhaps twenty feet, and there seemed to be many openings for stairways and in those places even more distant ceilings. She was alone, and there was no reason to be nervous.

At least she had a house, a place to stay. Not warm, but dry. She had a house, by damn, and suddenly she was feeling very good about it. There would be no problem drawing up the papers, Mr. Yates had said, if she decided she wanted it. And she did; Nancy's kids would love it. Here they could run and play without getting on Grandpa's nerves. Probably Grandma's, too, if she'd just admit it.

But how different the house seemed now, in increasing darkness, with only her skimpy flashlight. She needed to light candles.

First thing, before they moved in, they'd have to get the house wired.

Second thing, gas heat, before winter. Carrying wood to a dozen fireplaces didn't sound romantic to her.

She dug into her bag for the emergency kit, found the matches, and lighted a candle in the wall bracket halfway down the long hall.

Ignoring the sound of her footsteps, leaving the candle burning merrily in the hallway, she went back to the kitchen and began lighting the candles on the table. She lit the entire group that stood in the center of the table, each in its little holder as if waiting for whoever needed one.

She looked around.

The house seemed solid under the rain and the thunder. She looked at flashes of lightning against windows where old curtains hung. An open door at one end of the kitchen revealed tubs on legs, a long table covered with oil-cloth, and something more ... a human figure in the darkness where the candlelight dwindled away to nothing.

Katie's heart nearly burst. She stared, pulses throbbing in her temples. The figure didn't move.

It isn't real, she told herself. *Yes.* Someone stood there as still as Katie herself stood, returning her stare. It was a woman, shrouded in shadows. Only the outline of her head and body were visible. Yet she didn't move.

Something wasn't right.

Katie took a candle from the table and went with determination toward the open door. She almost fainted with relief. In the corner of the room stood a dressmaker frame, with an old gray sheet draped over the top. She could see the stand beneath, and the ribs of the frame where the sheet separated.

The room had a treadle sewing machine, ironing boards, old, sad irons on a shelf, laundry tubs, even a rusted faucet over a deep sink. It also had a window, uncovered, and an outside door that was locked.

Katie returned to the kitchen, pulling the door shut. It had a rusty squeak, too, like the front door.

She was all at once exhausted, depressed, hungry. It didn't matter if she didn't go home, now that no one was there to care whether she returned on time.

She had lost her appetite. She'd rather sleep. Sleep, she had found, was the restorative answer to emotional hurts. But she was reluctant to leave the kitchen where the light of the candles on the table filled the room with a moving shadowy dimness. But light. As opposed to the solid dark she would find in other rooms.

She looked for something to rest on. Why hadn't she carried emergency pillows and blankets in her car?

There was a large stone fireplace near one corner of the room, and near it a rocking chair. The chair held a couple of cushions, one in the seat, the other, larger, tied to the back.

She untied both, and chose a spot at the end of the raised hearth, cornered by the edge of the fireplace on one side, and the wall on the other. She sat down, leaning back against one cushion, hugging the other in her arms for warmth and comfort.

She stared morosely at the amber flames that fluttered like trapped moths above the candles. She would probably sit here awake all night. Sit and hug the cushion and wonder why she had always trusted her car to start when she needed it to. Was the oil change overdue? Probably. And the battery hadn't been checked in a while, either. Not since Ethan's death. There were so many things she had just let slide since then.

For an endless time she sat, watching the candle flames. She noticed suddenly, after what seemed hours of staring, that the candles were different colors. Most of them were white, but there were a couple of blue ones, and, like black sheep trying to hide in the center, three black candles. The black candles were different. Larger, thicker, with flames that seemed larger and steadier. Weren't black candles used by witches?

Oh, well ...

She arranged the cushions so that she could lie down. The rain still fell, but with only a steady sliding sound on the window beyond the fireplace. With her head on one cushion and her upper body on the other, she closed her eyes. The candle flames continued to flutter behind her eyelids.

She slept uneasily, feeling like an intruder, aware of thunder and rain and lightning, of a strange old house with strange sounds. Occasionally she tried to get more comfortable, but the floor was hard and the air chilled and damp. She turned over and covered her ears and face with one of the cushions.

A metallic squeak brought her instantly wide awake. She listened. Where had she heard that sound before? The door into the workroom! She sat up.

A woman disappeared through the door into the other room, carrying a candle, holding it out in front of her.

Katie gaped at the doorway, incredulous. Someone lived here? My God! Someone actually lived here!

Katie was left with a vivid image of the woman. Tall, large, thick-bodied yet not obese, her dark hair pulled severely back from her face and secured in a coil. She wore a print dress covered in front by a bibbed apron in a different floral print.

Katie couldn't move. Who was she?

Someone Mr. Yates hadn't known about, or hadn't told her about. What should she do, get up and apologize, or slip out as quietly as she could?

But no. It surely was the woman who was the intruder, not she. A homeless person, perhaps, who had found shelter. She would stand up, go into the room and talk to her, tell her it was okay, explain that she was buying the place and hoped to use it for people such as her.

Katie sat still, an eerie sensation of coldness growing, becoming fear, making her afraid even to breathe. Afraid of being seen, being heard by the woman.

An unfounded fear, she told herself, her mind passing through possibilities that further traumatized her even as she tried to reassure herself.

Who, exactly, was the intruder? Katie felt guilty.

The softening thunder was moving east. Darkness, streaked by filtered light from the other room and distant lightning, turned the kitchen into a twilight world of strange shapes. Katie smelled the dissipating odor of burnt wax, and suddenly realized all the candles she had left burning on the kitchen table were now out.

The woman must have extinguished them. Then, without seeing Katie in the corner behind the hearth, she had taken one and gone into the workroom.

Katie forced herself to rise. She should just leave, maybe. Sneak out, get in her car, and hide. Or walk away, move on. To hell with Mr. Yates and his great offer.

She gathered up her shoulder bag and flashlight and prepared to tiptoe out. The noise from the workroom stopped her.

It had a whispering squeak, rhythmic, *swish, whish, swish, whish* ...

Katie leaned forward and through the open door saw the woman sitting at the old treadle sewing machine, working busily. The candle had a place on the end of the machine near her elbow.

Katie stared, her chin drooping, her mouth drying. The machine was still visible, like inner bones, through the woman. Katie was afraid to move, afraid to breathe. She stood petrified, in an awkward leaning position, staring at the woman, watching her sew, seeing the machine's mechanisms move, beyond, through, the bulk of the woman's body.

The woman stopped working at the machine and pushed her chair back. It made a distinctive noise, wood legs scraping against wood floor. The woman rose and turned toward the ironing board. The outlines of the board showed through her as if she were made of gauze. Her hand reached out, picked up the sad iron. She turned and came toward the kitchen door.

With every hair on Katie's body pulled tighter than her skin, she watched the woman lift the candle in her left hand and bring the sad iron into the kitchen and place it on the old iron cookstove next to the modern gas range.

Clearly she saw the woman's features, a hollow-cheeked, aged face, eyes like dark slits, nothing within them. No soul, no life as Katie understood life. Yet she moved about with an energy that had power over the physical. She carried the iron and the candle.

For a while she moved about the kitchen, opening a drawer, closing it, then opening and closing another, as if she were looking for something. She paused often to look over her shoulder, and each time, Katie cringed.

The woman stood still then, in the middle of the room near the table, and looked about with a puzzled frown. She looked at the table and the collection of candles. She turned and looked behind her. She opened a door and peered inside. Then she gathered up the candles on the table and put them into a drawer. She paused again, and her eyes passed over Katie without seeing her. Katie cringed into the triangle between the wall and fireplace.

The woman went again to a drawer. She removed a large butcher knife. With the lighted candle in one hand and the knife in the other, she went into the hall. The door closed behind her.

The light of the candle was gone, and the kitchen dark. Not even the lightning flashed now.

Katie finally was able to move again. A blessed, dying last flash of lightning revealed the outer door, and Katie ran toward it. She bumped walls and doors during her frantic passage from the house.

She half fell off a back porch and ran out into a cold, soaking rain. She stumbled around the house in search of her car.

The car loomed in front of her, like a white ghost. A real ghost, not what she had seen inside. She fumbled her way into the car and after a moment of desperately fighting for breath, locked the doors. She was cold, wet, and miserable, and her teeth chattered. Part of it was unadulterated fear.

The house was a dark giant against the night, its peaked rooflines dimly visible against the mottled sky. Lightning ran like arteries of blood through the clouds. In an upstairs window a candle glowed briefly. Then it went out and the house was dark.

No wonder the house was such a bargain. Now she knew why Mr. Yates had that cream-eating grin on his face. She knew what his joke was, and she could have strangled him happily with her hands.

The damned place was haunted.

Actually haunted.

It was no longer a joke.

CHAPTER 23

*H*aunted.
It had a ghost. A real, live ...

Who in the hell ever really believed in ghosts? When she'd asked Mr. Yates if the house was haunted, she hadn't meant it. Now here she was, sitting in her car, listening to the rain on the roof, staring at the outlines of the house she was going to buy, and—

Yes, buy! Because no ghost was going to scare her out of it. The ghost had, successfully, it seemed, scared many other potential buyers away, but it wasn't going to scare Katie. Katie was going back in there and take possession of her house.

Katie sat still.

For the first time she thought of her flashlight. She had run through the dark kitchen trying to find a door through which she could escape, without once thinking of her flashlight.

She tugged it out of her pocket and turned it on, found her car keys, and tried the switch once more. Tomorrow she'd come back. In daylight. *Please, God, start, start.*

The engine turned, ground slower and slower, and then came the silence again.

So it was the battery. Why? She hadn't left anything on. Maybe batteries just wore down after a while. After all, the car was almost ten years old.

Katie listened to the rain on the roof of the car. The temperature had dropped. It was promising to be one of those cold three-day summer rains.

Katie looked around. How far was she from the road? How far from a house with a telephone?

Great, she had said, when Mr. Yates had told her it was isolated. She was sick of living in a city apartment. Especially without Ethan. "I'd love to live in the country, where I'd have lots of privacy," she had told him, while he'd grinned at her with that chessy-cat grin. Oh yeah, Mr. Yates. Funny.

She felt like crying, like banging her head on the steering wheel.

She slid down into the seat and stared morosely at the black bulk of the house. Nothing happened. No light came on in a window. No white form floated toward her. Finally, she curled up on the seat, rested her head on her arm, and tried to get comfortable.

No use. She was freezing. In the house, she remembered, was a gas range. There would be flames, and warmth. In the house were candles, for God's sake, and even they had flames. Warmth.

She hugged herself in misery and watched the house. Distant lightning flashed on windowpanes. Or was it the candlelight from within moving from room to room?

The world seemed to be less dark. It was turning a misty gray. Objects took shape. It seemed she had dozed, but she hadn't slept. The temperature had dropped further and she felt encased in ice. She turned the flashlight briefly on her wristwatch. Almost five o'clock. What time had she run out to her car? Midnight, maybe.

Rain fell, a steady sheet, straight down. Clouds overhead were a smooth gray. The thunder and lightning were gone.

She had stared at the house for hours, and nothing had happened. No face appeared in a window. No curtain moved. Maybe this ... *occupant* ... came out only at night. Maybe it was safe and dry in the house now. The house looked even larger than it had last night. A monster of wood, stone, and vines guarded by marvelous old trees.

Katie unlocked the car door and got out. Rain flattened her hair again and flooded down her neck. She pulled her head into her shoulders and ran around the house to the back door. On the porch she paused. The door was closed. Hadn't she left it wide open? Of course. She hadn't taken time to pull the damn thing shut behind her, she was in too much of a hurry to get out.

She dreaded going in, but this was now her house, and she'd be damned if something she had seen in the night was going to keep her out of it. She touched the doorknob. Maybe she had closed the door. Who remembered things like that?

She gingerly turned the knob. Locked.

Well. She certainly hadn't locked it. But then, maybe it locked automatically.

This old house? That used old-fashioned keys?

She dug among the keys in her pocket for the skeleton key Mr. Yates had given her. The door opened. She stepped into the dry kitchen with a long sigh.

Last night she had seen a woman here, dressed in an old-fashioned print dress and apron, but today, even in the gloomy light, such a sighting seemed like a bad dream.

She looked around at the kitchen. It was long and filled with shadows. It would always be filled with shadows. The windows were narrow and long, and there were only three. The old cabinets had doors that reached almost to the high ceiling. There was a sink with a single faucet, and probably cold water available. A braided rug was on the floor by the sink.

She hurried to the white gas range and turned on a burner. She smelled the distinctive odor of bottled gas briefly before it lighted with a *swhoosh*. She lingered over its warmth a moment, then turned on all the burners, including the oven. With the door down, lovely heat rolled out into the chilled air.

The room Mr. Yates had called a pantry was large and windowless, an inner room. She still had to use her flashlight. There were shelves on the walls, a few cans of vegetables, empty glass jars. A table in the center of the pantry was covered with old oilcloth that had faded and cracked. But it was surprisingly clean, with very little dust. Webs high in the corners were lost in perpetual darkness.

A closed door in the back wall probably opened onto a dining room, but she left it closed. She looked for coffee on the shelves and found none.

She returned to the kitchen and to the central hall, opening a door now and then. The rooms were small and numerous, some of them unfurnished, others furnished only with a fancy armoire or cupboard, decorative, obviously old and probably valuable. A living room joined a library and music room by means of a wide doorway with sliding doors that were almost closed. She only peeked through. Across the hall was what must have been a formal dining room. It had been stripped of all but the old draperies and a cracked china cabinet. Odds and ends of glassware were still in the tall break-front, although Katie guessed that a lot of things had probably been removed.

She hesitated in the foyer, then climbed the stairs. Bedroom doors stood open. She entered all six bedrooms and saw that some of the beds were covered, as if made up. The bedspreads were old and looked handmade. One was crocheted, or tatted; another was quilted.

This part of the house, too, was surprisingly clean. There were a few cobwebs too high to reach, and very little dust. That fact made her uneasy, increasing her feeling of being not alone in a house that was supposed to be unoccupied.

The woman she had seen last night ... a ghost. Perhaps not even that. Maybe it was her own hallucination, or maybe she had somehow picked up an image that had lived ninety years ago.

It had not been real, she reminded herself. She had been able to see objects through it. Still, the image, whatever, had done some weird things, like putting away the candles. And taking the butcher knife out of the drawer.

She returned quietly downstairs and to the kitchen. What was she going to do? She went through her choices again. Walk in the rain to a telephone, and call for a battery? For a mechanic? Call for Mr. Yates?

This house was what she had dreamed of all her life, she was now surprised to realize. In her dreams, she had roamed through large houses that seemed to have no way out, yet in her dreams she had not been afraid. She was a child in those dreams, looking into strange rooms as if she were exploring. Now that she had a chance to buy one that could have been in one of her dreams, was she going to let a ghost chase her out of it? Maybe if she got some sleep, in one of those comfortable beds, she'd have more courage.

She turned out the fires and went back upstairs. She chose the large bedroom at the front of the house. There were doors closed that she hadn't opened. She assumed they were closets, but at this point of exhaustion she wasn't interested.

The bed had a soft mattress, and was made up with bedding the last buyer must have left, thick blankets and smooth sheets. Katie took off her wet jeans and sweater and hung them over a chair to dry. She got into bed, pushing the hand-tatted bedspread to a roll at the foot. Rain slid down the windowpane in a solid sheet of water.

The pillow was thick and soft, and her head sank comfortably into it. She felt safe and warm for the first time in a long time. Sleep quickly wrapped itself around her.

She dreamed of being in a large house with many rooms, all shrouded in shadow. She saw a child running, running, trying desperately to find a way out. She watched the child, then suddenly she became the child. She ran in silence, holding something in her left arm. She ran down dark corridors, too terrified to cry out.

She snapped awake, aware of a touch.

She saw the woman clearly at the foot of the bed. Even the lines in her face seemed startlingly clear in the gray, filtered light from the window. As Katie stared, clutching the blankets to her chin, the woman in the print dress and bib apron began pulling the bedspread up, going from one side of the bed to the other, unrolling it carefully. She drew near Katie, unrolling the spread.

Katie saw the woman's eyes, deep-set under heavy lids, black and empty like bottomless holes in the ground. She was intent on her job, and appeared not to see Katie. She continued to spread the tatted cover, up over the pillows, over Katie's face.

Katie lay still. She had no problem with breathing.

There was no breath in her. The woman's footsteps clomped hollowly across the room, and the door closed.

With a gasp Katie gulped air. She threw the bedspread off her face and fell out of bed. Her clothes felt heavy and cold, still damp. She dressed faster than she'd ever dressed in her life. When she'd finished, she fixed the bedspread the way the woman wanted it. Fine, she thought to herself. You keep your previous bedroom.

She went cautiously out into the hall. All of the bedroom doors were closed now, and the hall was almost dark.

Looking over her shoulder at the hallway that reached back into darkness, she went quietly downstairs.

This lady, this ghost, did not pass through walls. Like a living person, she moved about in the house. She was able to handle the physical, though obviously she herself was no longer physical. She could pull up bedspreads, snuff out candles, carry them about. She could open doors. Her footsteps at times were faint and hollow, but as clear at other times as the closing of the doors. Yet physical objects were at times visible through her. So, if she had power over the physical, what could she do to Katie? She had taken a long-bladed, ugly butcher knife from a drawer.

Could there be a real danger here? Incredibly, Katie felt it might be possible.

Perhaps she had better give it all up, and go back to the lonely apartment. Wait for other choices.

She looked about at the kitchen, then sorrowfully she locked the back door and gathered up her shoulder bag and flashlight. Fortunately, the woman didn't seem as active in the daytime as at night, and Katie hoped she could sneak out of the house without seeing her again.

She was halfway down the hall to the foyer when her shoulder bag slid off her damp shoulder and dropped with a loud thump. As she stooped to pick it up, a nearby door opened.

The woman stood outlined there a moment, the shape of dark furniture in the room behind her dimly visible through the print of her dress, the bulk of her body.

Katie slowly straightened.

The woman's face looked clearly puzzled. She came out into the hall, the butcher knife clutched in her right hand. She looked down the hall beyond Katie, then back toward the front door.

Suddenly her eyes came to Katie and fastened upon her. They stared at each other. Katie saw hard, black pupils in the folds of flesh.

Her skin tightened and broke out in goose bumps from her cheeks to her ankles. Her eyes locked into the woman's eyes and she saw the changing expressions on the woman's face.

The woman's mouth opened wider and wider, and Katie realized she was screaming. In absolute horror the woman stared at Katie, her face contorting. Her hands raised to her cheeks and the knife clattered to the floor, the only sound. Her silent scream grew.

Katie blinked, and instantaneously the woman disintegrated. In a silent explosion of horror, she was gone.

Katie stood still, staring incredulously at the empty doorway.

She slowly sank to the floor.

For several minutes she sat on the floor, looking at the butcher knife. It lay within reach, a darkened handle with a sharp and well-honed blade.

She pushed up, her legs weak, her fingers nerveless when she tried to lift the shoulder bag.

Finally, the strap over her shoulder, she went toward the front door. It had stopped raining, she noticed.

Before she closed and locked the door, she looked back once more at the butcher knife on the floor. Then she began to laugh. Suddenly it was all hilarious.

A ghost, afraid of a living person?

She went to the car laughing, near hysteria.

Poor old soul. "Whoever you are—were—I'm sorry," she said aloud.

She couldn't wait to tell Mr. Yates that his little joke had backfired.

She inserted the key into the switch and turned it. The car began to idle regularly, gently.

She stared at the lighted dash almost in irritation as she realized this latest phenomena. Last night, when she'd needed the damned car to start, it wouldn't. Now it started as if nothing at all was wrong. Still, she'd better have the battery checked, as soon as she could.

She turned around on the circle driveway near the carriage house and drove away. At the end of the driveway she looked back at the house, large, tall, barely visible through the trees, blending like a natural outcropping from the ground into its setting.

Something occurred to her suddenly, and she sobered thoughtfully.

In the myriad expressions on the ghost woman's face, the foremost had been recognition.

CHAPTER 24

"That's not possible," Katie muttered aloud, as she drove back through town and toward the city. It wasn't possible that the ghost woman's shock and horror had been caused by recognition, because Katie had never been in that house before, and the woman had more than likely been dead for years ... since before Katie was born, surely.

Was it the original owner Mr. Yates had mentioned? If so, she had died in 1949. Katie's own mother was only about ten years old at the time.

Maybe it was all her imagination—caused by the shadowy age of the house, and her own fatigue and sleeplessness.

No. Not her imagination.

Not the ghost ... that was real enough, as ghosts go. But maybe it was only her imagination that the look on the woman's face had been recognition.

No, not that either. In memory, now, it was the most striking thing about the ghost, and certainly the most startling experience Katie had ever had.

She tried to laugh again, but it turned into a sigh.

She thought about going back to her one-room apartment, bathing, washing and drying her hair, and dressing in fresh clothing before she went to the real estate office. But on the other hand, Mr. Yates should see for himself what she looked like after a night in his haunted house.

The office was located in a shopping center wedged between two of the better suburbs in the area, where new homes were still being built, and there were usually plenty of buyers for them. Katie parked in front of the ice-cream place next door.

She entered the front office. There were six desks, one of them her own.

Three of the women were at their desks, and one man. The others were gone, probably showing property. They all looked up, and stared without speaking as she passed by. They were used to her being neat and clean, at least, usually dressed in a modest suit. Now, here she was, wearing jeans and a sweater that were trying to dry on her body, and her hair strung past her shoulders with no curl, the way she'd worn it when she was a preteen. She didn't speak, either. She could do that later. She could imagine what she looked like with her face as undone as her hair, her freckles showing, and her damp clothes lumping against her.

Mr. Yates was in his office, the door open as usual. He looked up round-eyed as she entered, then looked at his watch. Then he looked up again, and his eyes took on that mischievous twinkle. He leaned back in his chair, folded his hands across his midriff, and began to smile.

"I know I'm late," Katie said. She was aware that almost everyone from the outer office had followed her, but she didn't care if they heard. "And I know I look like last night's nightmare. But my car wouldn't start. I got caught in the rain, and I had to spend the night in that house."

His eyebrows lifted, but he said nothing.

"With that ghost!" she added.

"Oh, no," someone behind her muttered.

"Ghosts?" Terri questioned. "You're joking."

Mr. Yates said, "I'm sorry about your car, Katie. What happened?"

"This morning it started."

Daniel peeked in and suggested, "The ghost cut the wires then welded them back together."

Katie laughed with the others. "Look, Mr. Yates, why didn't you tell me that old house was really haunted?" Mr. Yates opened his mouth, but Daniel, leaning like a long strip of taffy against the door, his arms folded, said, "You're not serious about the ghost, Katie. Can't be. Nobody believes in ghosts."

Janet said, "Only on Halloween," and giggled.

Katie looked at them.

Chris, an older woman, wasn't smiling. "Were you in the old Wickham mansion, down south?"

"Yes," Katie said.

"I won't even show that house," Chris said. "Not anymore. I had a client once that wanted to buy it. They put ten thousand dollars promissory down, and were spending a lot of time out there even though the final papers hadn't been signed, the loan hadn't come through, and they couldn't legally move in. Well, there were strange things going on around there, and they left. Of course, they were going to forfeit their money, but Mr. Yates gave it back to them."

"You're joking!" Daniel scoffed, his tone claiming they were all a bunch of hysterical females.

Mr. Yates opened his mouth for the third time. "It's true that it has that reputation. That seems to be the reason that none of the sales has gone through. But I thought you, Katie, would be sophisticated enough not to believe in ghosts."

"Sophisticated! What has that got to do with it?" She leaned with her hands on his desk so that she wouldn't give in to her urge to drag him out to Wickham House and throw him in and lock the door.

He shrugged. "I thought, so what if a door swings shut as soon as you turn your back? So what if candles are blown out by some stray draft? Katie will be levelheaded enough to know there are reasons for these things happening. Got nothing to do with haunts or ghosts or whatever."

"But Mr. Yates, *I saw her!* She's—it's real. I saw her as clearly—well, almost as clearly as I see you, any of you."

"What'd she look like?" Chris asked.

"She was elderly, probably sixty, maybe even seventy. Her hair was pulled back in a bun on the back of her head. She was tall, large-bodied, and wore a longish print dress with a bib apron."

"You *saw* her?" Daniel suggested, "Maybe she's a homeless somebody who knew the house was always empty and just decided to make herself a home."

Katie said, "I thought of the same thing. But then, I saw *through* her."

"You're joking!"

"Why didn't you tell me?" Katie demanded of Mr. Yates again.

He gestured with mock helplessness, his palm toward the ceiling. He opened his mouth and closed it. The twinkle was still in his eyes.

Katie demanded, "You were enjoying thinking about me in that old haunted house, weren't you?"

Mr. Yates shrugged, then said, "It's a good buy."

"Well, I've got news for you, Mr. Yates," Katie said, and paused. Everyone was quiet. "I'm going to take it! You said I could have it with very little down, and pay it when the insurance comes through, right?"

Mr. Yates nodded, some of the twinkle sobering.

"Okay. And now I want you to know that the ghost no longer exists."

"What!" Daniel demanded. He had started to leave, but now turned back. They all paused to listen. "How do you know?"

Katie grinned at them all. "Because I scared her away."

She had their wide-eyed attention. They were like a group of kids at a party, she thought, and she was beginning to like it. The joke had been on her, so far as Mr. Yates was concerned, and now it was on him.

"She saw me, actually saw me, and she went up in smoke. More or less."

They all laughed, even Mr. Yates.

Terri went walking away, saying over her shoulder, "I don't believe a word of it. Any of it."

No, Katie thought to herself, few people would. It was too bizarre.

Someone came through the front door then, to Katie's relief, and all of the agents turned and left.

Mr. Yates got up and pushed a chair closer to Katie. "Here, sit down." He patted her on the shoulder.

He returned to his chair behind the desk and leaned over. From a drawer he pulled an arrangement of papers. "I'm not a believer in ghosts. I knew you'd be able to handle whatever problems the house has. The worst things, in my opinion, are getting electricity to it, and a gas line. You'll probably not want to move in until it's fixed."

"Does the furniture go with it?"

"Yes, of course. I think a lot of it has been removed over the years, but the last time I was in there, I estimated there'd be probably ten or twenty thousand dollars' worth, maybe more. It's yours. Well, let's get down to business."

BY THE TIME the business day had ended, with the more familiar activities of arranging the sale of a property, this time with herself as buyer, Katie felt so removed from her experiences in the old Wickham mansion that she was beginning to doubt it herself. Yet later, in her tiny bathroom, standing under the shower, the scene in the hallway when the eyes of the ghost met Katie's came back with such clarity that Katie felt it all over again, this time without the humor. Now, remembering, there had been something horribly threatening in the experience.

No! she told herself as she dried and pulled on a robe. Don't look at it that way. It was not frightening, not at the last.

She rolled her hair in large curlers and went to sit on the end of the sofa near the telephone. She looked around at the tiny apartment. After Ethan's death she'd had to move. The roomier apartment they'd been living in depended on his income also. It had been difficult but time-filling to look for another place during the height of her grief. At that time her sister, who was five years older and had been married for seven years and had two kids, was still with her husband in their inadequate apartment. But Katie remembered a remark that Nancy had made at the time, "Maybe we should pool our resources and move in together." Then she'd added, "Only, I don't have any resources."

Katie didn't remember even answering. She was too wrapped up in her loss. She knew that Nancy had been growing unhappy with Perry. Since the birth of Curtis five years ago, Nancy had talked about moving to a suburb, buying a house, having a yard for the kids to play in.

It was a dream, Katie had thought, just as she'd dreamed of a suburban home, fenced yards, kids. But with Ethan gone, gone too was the dream. She couldn't imagine marrying anyone else.

Nancy and Perry had married young. They made a good-looking couple— Nancy curvy, blond, and petite, Perry tall, square-shouldered, dark. The kids were a mixture of the two, beautiful, healthy. When Katie heard Nancy had left Perry, she couldn't believe it. "Why?" she had asked. Nancy's answer had seemed to her a bit childish, but she decided not to judge. What did she know about being cooped up with two kids in a small apartment?

Kate picked up the telephone and pushed the button that dialed her mother's number. Jane answered. The background was filled with voices that sounded as if they came partly from television and partly from playing children. Katie visualized her mother's house—small, three bedrooms, none very roomy. One and one-half baths. Not enough room for two people who were trying to retire, two children ages five and seven, and a young mother who wasn't strong on discipline.

"Mom," Katie said. "How would you like to have some peace and quiet?"

"What?"

Katie laughed. "Can I come over?"

"Can you—well, of course. If you'll hurry, you can eat with us. Have you eaten?"

"No. Come to think of it, I haven't eaten all day."

"Oh, Katie, please try to take better care of yourself. You need to eat."

Katie looked at the ceiling while her mother talked to her about food, vitamins, and keeping up her strength. Why had she spoken out loud? Stopping to eat simply had slipped her mind, that was all. She'd had several cups of coffee, and a few cans of cola, but if she told her mother that, Jane would go into hysterics.

"When you're my age," Jane ended, "you'll realize how important proper eating is. Stop eating meat, you don't need it. Eat lots of vegetables and fruit."

"Okay," Katie said, "I promise I won't stop for a hamburger and fries. Now, I have to dress, Mom. Be there as soon as I can get there."

The house where her mother lived was in one of the older developments that had been built after World War Two. She and Katie's father, a man who was only a picture to Katie, had first bought a two-bedroom frame house. That was the small place where Nancy and Katie were born and lived until Katie was ten. By that time their parents had been divorced for several years and their father was dead. Katie didn't remember him. He had been killed in a car wreck before she was two years old.

With real estate growing in value, their mother had sold that first house and bought the slightly larger brick house farther out in the same suburb. The suburb grew, encroaching onto the countryside. It was there Nancy and Katie grew up. Jane worked in a nearby nursing home as a nurse's aide and remarried when Katie was thirteen. Doug was the only father she'd ever known.

The suburbs had continued to expand, larger and larger homes, curvier streets, more countryside taken in. Now, from the apartment building where Katie lived in the north side of the city, it took about thirty minutes to get out onto the expressway around the city and off again down into the suburbs on the east side.

Katie's thoughts covered the years, jumping from one incident to another, as she drove. It had been a pleasant life, no tragedies that affected her personally until Ethan's death.

Then she had been left with a sense of emptiness, as if her life no longer had purpose or substance. She had been searching for something—anything that would return to her a feeling of meaning, if not happiness.

Then she had remembered the house they'd seen from the air, and it had all fallen into place. Like a math problem working itself out in her sleep.

Her purchase of Wickham House gave her a place where her heart could heal. And something to work with.

She was beginning to feel as if she were on the right path. *Right* within herself, for the first time in months.

She pulled into her parents' narrow driveway. It was separated from the neighbor's by a well-trimmed hedge. There were no old forest trees here. One tree Doug had planted in the front yard was about twenty feet tall.

She parked behind the old station wagon that belonged to Nancy. The wagon was half on the driveway, and otherwise on the grass, the fenders pushing against the stiff, clipped limbs of the hedge. What the heck, she could just hear Nancy saying, a few more scratches ...

What was wrong with this family, Katie wondered as she crossed to the walk. Her mother, divorced for some undisclosed reason when she was young with two small children, and Katie widowed at age twenty-five, and now Nancy, homeless with her two kids. Homeless by choice, it seemed to Katie. She was the one who had moved out of the apartment her husband had provided for her. Maybe their mother had been divorced by choice, too, though she'd never said. It was for certain Katie wasn't widowed by choice.

The front door burst open and the two kids spilled out, pushing at each other.

"Katie, Katie, Aunt Katie!"

She bowed to hug them both. Erica, as lovely as a doll, with her blond-brown curls bouncing. Curtis, as pretty as Erica, glossy brown hair in ringlets like a cap.

They went into the house, a child's hand in each of Katie's. She adored her niece and nephew, always had. She had just begun to feel stirrings for a baby of her own when Ethan was killed.

The living room was brightly lighted, warm, and comfortable, with signs of recent habitation. When her stepfather had moved in, only one thing had changed. He'd brought along his favorite chair, a big, brown recliner. It didn't match the rest of the living room furniture, and the room began to look smaller immediately, but they all loved Doug, and so the chair became a source of warmth. It was like knowing you had come home, when you looked at that chair.

"Come in here, Katie," Doug's voice called from the kitchen, "before I eat my supper and yours, too."

She entered that bright, lively area. Doug was already seated at the end of the table in the dining end of the kitchen. Jane was still dishing food up into bowls on the counter that separated the kitchen from the dinette. Nancy was filling glasses with water or milk.

Katie kissed Doug's cheek. It was slightly briary, with a new growth of whiskers, as always. He shaved every day, he said, but Katie and Nancy had always kidded him about that. "Says he shaves every day, but he really doesn't."

And he teased back, "I have to protect myself from the girls. If I got too smooth a shave, they'd all be kissing me."

The table was full, as usual. Mom had already cooked more than they needed, but then she'd mix the leftovers and they'd have a thick vegetable soup, with cornbread or muffins or biscuits. "Out of a box," Doug would tease. And Mom would reply, "I'm retired. What do you want me to do, mix it by memory?" Which gave Nancy and Katie openings. "Memory! She's used mixes all our lives."

Just nonsense. None of it serious.

'Well, Katie," Doug said, when they were all settled at the table and had started to eat. "We haven't seen you for a while. What have you been doing?"

"Pop, you'll never guess. I just bought a huge, old, haunted house today."

CHAPTER 25

$\mathcal{P}$erry let himself into the apartment, and found darkness.

He stopped, blinking. Nancy and the kids were still gone. Why the hell didn't they come on home? He was getting pissed off.

He'd been leaving her alone, letting her get whatever irked her off her chest. She usually came back after a couple of days. But this time she was staying on and on. She couldn't be serious about this. What the hell was he going to do, if she was serious?

What had he done? Bought a new van. She wanted a house. The apartment was too small, she said. It was getting to be a dangerous neighborhood.

Also, she wanted him to come home right after he closed the printing shop. But hell, man, didn't she know he had book work? And he didn't want to bring it home. Where would he put it, on the kitchen table?

That was her point, she'd said. We need a bigger place.

Also, he needed to relax with the guys after work. A couple of beers, a few discussions on the state of the world. She didn't understand that, either.

"If it's not a house they want, or a new apartment, it's something else," the guys laughed. "Give her time, she'll come home."

He snapped on the light and looked at the small room. Toys on the floor, a couple of knitted throws over the back of the couch. He nudged an old teddy bear with his toe, then stooped and picked it up.

It was flattened from being slept on. Why had Nan not taken Curtis's teddy bear along? He'd slept with it since he was six months old.

Coming home no longer gave him a good feeling. For that matter, staying out for a beer with the guys was beginning to pall.

The kids were usually asleep when he got home, but at least he'd had them here to hug and kiss before he kicked off his shoes and jeans and fell into bed.

He went into the kids' bedroom. The bunk bed took up most of the space. The rest of the floor was spotted with toys, too, just as the small living room was. The toybox against the wall stood open. The chest of drawers still had clothes, but enough had been taken out to last a while.

That first night he came home to darkness he figured they'd only be gone a couple of days. Hadn't it always been that way? Ever since Nancy had decided he wasn't spending enough time with them, she'd take the kids and go over to her mom's for a couple of days.

But then she'd come home, and life would go on as always. He had thought she'd be home in a couple of days this time, but she was still gone.

He called her mom, after the third day, when he'd kept getting the answering machine at home.

"Hi, Mom," he'd said. "Nan and the kids there?"

"Yes, but they're out at the moment. Over at the park, I think."

"Tell her I'm waiting. Tell her to call me at the office. I won't be getting home until late."

But Nancy hadn't called back. He had been put in a position of needing to go talk to her, but the advice he'd gotten from his friends, those guys Nancy called his beer buddies, was to cool it, give her time.

"Hey, man, it's not exactly like you've got some other woman. What's she got to complain about?"

The trouble was, he missed them. He missed those sleepy little guys reaching their warm arms to give him a hug good night. He even missed having Nan in bed, though lately she'd started turning her back as if she were asleep. But was she really?

He thought now she probably wasn't. But he always came in so sleepy and tired, he was ready to go to sleep, too. Sex could wait until morning.

Then, she'd begun to already be up by the time he woke, and he'd have to hurry to work. Most of the time the kids were either still asleep, or she was getting them up for school.

Sleep had not been coming easy, lately. And again, tonight, he lay in bed and stared at the patterns on the ceiling made by a light across the alley in another apartment.

He missed her soft breathing.

His stomach felt odd. Something like a fist had gathered there, getting bigger day by day. He had to face a truth: his marriage had a problem, a real problem.

Nan had been unhappier than he'd thought, maybe. What had gone wrong? He'd thought he was doing what he was supposed to do, working long hours, building his printing shop. There were so many things that might have gone wrong.

Maybe they'd gotten married too young, before Nancy'd had a chance to get around much. Well, he'd been young, too. He hadn't exactly been a virgin, though he'd been her first, but he hadn't been in love with anyone else, either.

Was she tired of being a mother? No, or she wouldn't have taken the kids.

He didn't think she had another guy. Did she?

No. She was with the kids all the time.

Well, most of the time.

Sometimes she had complained that she felt her life was headed nowhere. That she wanted a bigger place to live. That she wanted him around more.

But she had stopped complaining, and he thought she had gotten over whatever was bugging her.

Maybe, though, he hadn't been listening.

It was true that he was working long hours lately, and after work he'd stop in and have a beer with the guys.

He sat up and looked at the clock. It was still early. He had stayed for only one beer tonight. The kids might not be in bed.

But didn't Nan put them in bed by nine? He didn't even know.

If he drove over there, tonight, it would take him an hour, and they'd definitely be in bed. If he called ... What would he say? "Nan, I'm sorry. Whatever I did, I'm sorry. Come on home, okay?"

He could hear the click of the phone as she hung up.

KATIE SAID good night to Doug and Jane, and asked Nancy to walk to the car with her.

Katie leaned against the car. A street lamp beyond a tree in the next yard competed with a rising moon. Dew had settled on the car. Katie opened the door.

Nancy stood with her hands on the door as if reluctant to let Katie go.

"Let's get in the car and sit down, Nancy, and talk awhile."

As Nancy settled herself in the passenger seat, Katie wondered how to begin. She needed to talk about last night.

"I'm so glad you bought a place of your own, Katie," Nancy said. "And did you mean it when you said we could move out with you?"

"Of course I did."

Nancy sighed. "What a relief. Mom and Doug have been great. But ..."

"The only thing is, we have to wait until it has at least basic wiring. But you'll love it, Nan. If everything goes okay, it shouldn't be longer than a week or two at most. It's really beautiful, in its way. The trees are great, and there's so much privacy and freedom."

Nancy said nothing. Her eyes followed a car that drifted by on the speed limit.

Looking at Nancy, her blond hair highlighted by the light of moon and street lamp, Katie was struck by how much she resembled their mother.

When she was a growing, awkward teenager, Katie had wondered who she was like. Her father? She had only one picture of him, leaning against a car, a somewhat cocky, smiling blond with his arm around a gorgeous young Jane. It was obvious she didn't look much like Jane. Nancy, though, also gorgeous at eighteen, and at twenty, while Katie was still trying to find good balance, could have been the girl standing against the car.

Occasionally through the years, Katie had felt as if she didn't really belong in the family. She not only was physically different, taller, skinnier, with green eyes, there were other things. Though she loved Nancy and Jane with all her heart, it was usually she who had sat in a corner with a book while Nancy and Jane talked.

It was she who felt ill-at-ease when trying to carry on a one-to-one conversation with her mother. It was always a relief when Nancy came into the room and took over, leaving Katie to her own thing.

Mom used to complain to Nancy, within Katie's hearing, "Katie just won't talk. She never tells me anything."

So Katie had tried harder to talk to her mother.

But it was Nancy to whom she had turned with confidences, thoughts, hopes, dreams. And fears.

Looking now at Nancy, Katie felt an almost maternal affection. Above all, she didn't want Nancy to be unhappy, or worried, or scared. About anything.

Katie said, "If you're in a hurry to get out of here, we could live by candlelight. It might even be fun. The kids will love it out there. There's enough room for everyone." She paused. "What happened, Nan? Do you want to talk about it?"

Nancy drew a deep sigh and looked down, as if she were examining the toe of her sandal in the dark beside the car.

"I believe Mom thinks I'm being unreasonable, and I know Perry thinks so. But Katie, I feel so stifled. He doesn't really care for me, it seems. I know he loves the kids, and probably he thinks he still loves me. But whatever it was that we had is gone. I don't know if we could get it back. He's just never around."

Katie said nothing. She waited.

"Mom says, well, he's working hard. And I know that. But don't we count, too? Mom says I'm expecting too much. And maybe I am."

Still Katie waited. There was nothing she could say. Nancy had to discover her own reasons and feelings.

"I suppose I made a mistake, as usual," Nancy said softly. "I've always gone back before. I just tell the kids we're coming to Mom's for a little vacation. This time we just stayed longer. I can't tell them I don't want to go back. But I don't know what else to do, either."

Now Katie said, "You have choices, Nancy."

"Thanks, Katie. Still, I suppose I should take the kids back to the apartment, even though it was so depressing, with no place for them to play. But—"

"That's one advantage you'll have in the country: no shortage of room. No restrictions as far as space is concerned."

"I really need to get out of here. I know the kids get on their nerves. They aren't used to a couple of rowdies taking over their house. I try to keep them out in the yard or somewhere, but we can't stay out all the time."

"Of course not," Katie paused, "But Nancy, I need to tell you something— somewhat unusual—about the house."

Nancy turned her head and looked in silence at Katie.

Katie stared out over the hood of the car where dew sparkled in the varying lights. Her hands lay on the steering wheel.

"What's wrong?" Nancy asked.

"I really had a very strange experience in that house, and I just think you should know about it. It probably won't happen to you. Some buyers have been scared off. Mr. Yates just laughs at it. He thinks it's hysterical women seeing things in the dark. But the last potential buyers even left canned goods in the pantry a few months ago."

"You mean you were really serious about your new place being haunted?"

"I only know what I saw."

Katie considered telling it all, from the time she drove into the driveway until the disappearance of the specter, and the fall of the knife. But at the last moment she left out the knife. It sounded ... insane. If she found it lying on the hall floor when she returned to the house, she might believe it had really happened. But until then ... there was something insane about a ghost carrying a knife. The rest of it was funny. She preferred ending on that note.

"She—*what?*" Nancy cried incredulously.

"She went *poof.* She just disappeared."

Nancy tipped her head back and laughed and laughed. When she could talk, she said, "When she saw you it scared her to—to wherever ghosts go? You're kidding, Katie! I've never known you to make jokes before."

Katie laughed, too. Yet the memory of the sound of the knife falling to the floor stifled her sense of humor. Had it really happened? Yes. No. She didn't know. How could a ghost carry objects about?

"I saw the ghost, really. And I was scared out of my socks. But after it was over, I realized she was such a nice, gentle creature, Nan, just taking care of her house. And when she saw me, she left. There's nothing to worry about now."

"I'm not worried about a ghost, Katie. If that's all I had to worry about, it would be great. But thanks for thinking of us. For wanting us to move with you."

"I'm sure there's no danger, or I wouldn't have asked you. I wouldn't buy it if I thought that! Having good lighting might be all it needs. Perry could even come with us. We might need a man around there!"

Nancy laughed. "I wonder what he'd do, if he met your lady ghost in the hall?"

Katie laughed, too. "Well, it's gone now. All we have to worry about is electricity and gas."

Nancy got out and stood with the door open, leaning in. In the streetlight Katie saw a sad smile come to Nancy's lips.

"I don't have money to help out."

"I'll furnish the money, you take care of the house. Okay?"

"Okay." Nancy smiled, closed the car door, and stood back.

Katie turned the switch. Today, after work, she'd had the battery replaced, and now the car started on the first urge.

"I'll talk to you tomorrow, Nancy. We'll get things together and decide what we want to do."

Nancy nodded. "Good night. Drive carefully."

She was close to being dead on her feet, Katie decided, when she let herself into her apartment. Exhausted. Her brain cried for sleep. And no wonder. All the excitement today that made her the owner of her first home, plus the traumatic, almost sleepless night she had spent last night.

She took out the pins that she had used to put up her slightly damp hair earlier in the evening, and let her hair fall. Smooth and silky now, it hung in loose curls to her shoulders.

Within three minutes she had changed to pajamas and fallen into the narrow bed in the corner of the room that, in the daytime, was dressed up with a ruffled cover and became a daybed. She stretched out and nestled into the pillow, her hands cradling her cheek. She expelled a long breath and closed her eyes.

SHE WAS OBSERVING A CHILD. The little girl stood in a long, dark corridor that had walls, but seemed to have no ends or ceiling. In her arms she clutched something. She was hurrying down the hallway, faster and faster, throwing looks of terror over her shoulder.

Suddenly Katie was the child.

She heard something coming down the hall. The hollow echoes rang in her ears as it came closer, closer. She began to run and suddenly was against a wall at the end of the corridor. She tried to scream, but her voice was silent.

It was a woman, coming to get her. A woman she was terrified of. In her silent heart she cried out, and cringed. The footsteps stopped, and she saw the apron. Little dark flowers and vines tangled before her eyes.

She screamed and ...

... Screamed.

Katie woke up, trembling, her heart thundering. She felt as if the darkness in the corridor were still around her. She was afraid to put her hand into the darkness in search of the light, but more afraid to remain in the dark, where she felt the eyes could see her.

She sat up and reached, and found the lamp on the table at the end of the daybed.

Light filled her apartment.

She got up and poured herself a glass of milk.

The dream was not like any dream she'd ever had. It was more like a mental experience. Strangely, in the dream, she had seen the child as very small, smaller than Erica. Smaller, perhaps, than Curtis. No more than four years old, or five. She had long, very pale hair that hung in curls to her waist. Then, she had felt the child's fear, and seen with the child's eyes the apron the woman wore.

The dream had seemed to invade something deep and hidden within her very psyche.

She was the child, and yet ... she was only an observer.

CHAPTER 26

*N*ights were difficult for Nancy lately, especially in these nights of waiting. Waiting for daybreak. For the house to be ready so she and the kids could move. The waiting was difficult for Katie, too, she knew, but at least Katie was busy with her work. This past week she'd called only once, to say she'd let Nancy know when the electricity was in the house.

Nancy couldn't sleep. The couch was so narrow she felt trapped against a cliff, unable to turn over without falling off the edge. She got up, and went to check on the kids. They were both sideways in the double bed in the spare bedroom.

In the beginning she had slept there with Curtis, while Erica had slept on the couch. She had learned that Curtis had a habit of kicking suddenly in his sleep, as if he were playing football, then turning over and always ending with his head at the side of the bed and his feet in the middle, pushing against her back.

Mom had offered to give up her room and move in with Doug. But they had kept separate rooms for so many years, and were so comfortable that way, that Nancy had said no.

A thought had been persisting in her mind for several months now: if this is all there is in life, what's so good about life?

She loved her children, more than life, certainly. Yet the time would come when they'd be grown and no longer needing her. And what then? She faced emptiness.

Maybe, she had thought, it was the depressing place they lived. It had changed in the years since Erica was born. In the hallway, gangs were beginning to gather, selling dope, grinning at her in a lascivious manner when she passed by. Worse, she had caught one of the tall, oily-haired, skeletal drug dealers looking at Erica with that hooded, yearning look. And that was it.

The end.

That night, she told Perry. He told her to keep the kids inside. She reminded him they had to go to school. He told her she had to take them to school, and go get them. She told him it was time they put a down payment on a house in the suburbs. He told her they couldn't afford it. She found one near where her mother lived that needed work. It was an adorable small house with a weedy yard that hadn't been cared for, but it had a couple of large trees and a cracked driveway that could be patched, and even though the frame house was small, all it needed was paint and paper. Surely they could swing a loan for it.

He wouldn't even go see it. Instead, he was getting a loan to expand his small business, in the roughest part of town, within three blocks of the apartment complex that was rapidly deteriorating. He was adding the building next door to his rented space. Buying it. An hour's drive from the suburb.

"Next year, Nan. Can you hang in there one more year?"

That was two years ago. This year he needed a new van for his business. He didn't see anything dangerous about the neighborhood.

When school vacation started, she wrote Perry a note saying she couldn't face another summer in the apartment. She went to her parents', and they had no choice but take her in. She had thirty dollars in her purse.

Several times she had taken the kids on the city bus and met Katie for lunch. Katie had been looking for a place, for something. This idea of using her insurance money for a large place which they could somehow turn into a home where other desperate people could have at least a stopover left Nancy feeling depressed. How did such things work without money? Katie knew more about it than she. Nancy had tried to understand, but it was over her head.

She had married without a business education, without any education beyond high school. Literature had been her thing, not bookkeeping, not real estate, nothing practical.

Was it necessary, she wondered tonight as she sat on the cool cement step outside the front door, to wait for the electricity and gas to be installed? She wanted to move now.

She went back to the couch, planning to tell Katie she didn't care if they had to live with candles and no heat. It was still warm weather. She had to settle the children before school started.

School! What about school? She hadn't asked.

Was there a school bus, or was school within walking distance? She could drive them, of course, and get a part-time job.

She stared wide-eyed at the window where the street light made little diamonds of light in the corner. Her mind played between the too-small apartment, Perry, the kids, and the mysterious old house she hadn't seen yet.

She thought of the ghost Katie had described, and smiled. She felt laughter, like bubbles rising in a glass, rise in silence within her. A kindly old soul, Katie had said, who went around dusting, blowing out candles, spreading up beds.

She might be of help, Nancy thought. It was going to be Nancy's job to keep house, and she could use all the help she could get the way the house sounded, with forty-four rooms and numerous hallways and porches.

Too bad, Nancy thought as she drifted back to sleep, that Katie had scared her away.

ERICA LISTENED. She had heard Mama go out the door, and had made herself lie still. *Don't run after her. She's not going to leave us.*

Then, she heard her come back in and lie down again.

Erica wished she were home, in the bunk bed that had her dolls and stuffed animals on it. Where Curtis slept in the lower bunk. Where Daddy could come and kiss and hug her good night

Sometimes, in the night she cried to go home. Cried for her daddy.

But she never let Mama know. It would make her sad.

She reached over in the dark and felt for Curtis's hand.

She held it tightly.

KATIE CLOSED the blind on the window over the day bed to shut out the streetlight. She lay down again, surrounded by darkness, her face buried beneath her pillow. Finally, she slept.

The child was running in terror, something soft clutched under her arm. She was afraid to look back. Darkness moved with her. She ran as far as she could in the corridor that had walls but no ceiling, nothing but black endlessness behind her. Something bad was coming through the dark, and it was going to get her. She could hear it moving, part of the dark and cold. She could hear it breathing.

She came to a tall wood wardrobe and hid against the wall beside it. Then she saw the wall at the end of the corridor, so near. There was a closed door in the wall. She huddled down, made herself into a ball, arms folded around her knees, looking up into the darkness.

The footsteps grew louder, closer. The other sounds came too, the sliding movements of the things made of dark that stirred and moved. They came down the corridor, figures darker than the darkness, moving about one another, intertwining, like huge worms, with no sound except the sliding softness.

A glistening arm snaked out and with long, rubbery fingers opened the door just beyond her. The darkness eased, a dim light was somewhere beyond the door. She saw the figures were not human. Upright bodies, flat heads tapering to long snouts silhouetted briefly against the light. Among them walked the woman. She was wearing a long, bibbed apron.

KATIE WOKE up in her apartment, trying desperately to breathe. She, the child, had learned not to scream in these horrible dreams. It was as if she were half awake, and knew to keep her fear silent.

The dreams had been coming, one after the other. It seemed she couldn't go to sleep without seeing, and feeling within her, the terror of the child.

They were not like any nightmares she had ever experienced before. They were too vivid, too real, and filled with a terror so overpowering Katie feared for her sanity.

Light from the street lamp leaked through the Venetian slats. The room looked weirdly distorted, reality altered. The bathroom doorway in the wall across the room wavered, narrowed and deepened. Beyond it she could see the long, dark corridor in which the child had been trapped.

Katie turned on the light, and forced herself to go to the bathroom and turn on the light there. It was a moment before the awful fear receded.

She looked at the clock. It was 5:20 a.m. Thank God the night was ending. Although she was exhausted from so little rest, she'd rather just get up and get ready for work. Keep your mind on work, on your new house, on moving, she told herself.

On the future.

Life should be easier, now that she was busy.

She'd been recently inundated with customers at work, buying customers, and they had taken up her time. In the past week she had earned three thousand dollars in commissions. But that was the way with real estate. Today she had no prospective buyers coming, and she might not have another one for a month. A month of famine following a month of riches.

Yesterday she had called her lawyer, and he'd told her to be patient, he was sure the insurance money would show up one of these days. If it didn't, he'd sue.

She had paid Mr. Yates a thousand dollars on the house, and was planning on using most of the rest of her earnings getting gas and electricity in. But she had run into trouble there, too. The gas line up to the house could be put in as soon as a contractor could be found. Same with electricity. All the contractors said it would be at least a month before they could get to it. Sorry.

"Good Lord," she had said to Mr. Yates. "There isn't enough competition in this area. We need more contractors with backhoes to dig ditches. Don't people ever dig ditches by hand anymore?"

"You'd have to pay about ten times as much."

Well, forget that.

There was a shortage of electricians, too, it seemed. Although the major problem was the electric company itself. They would have to lay an underground cable from the road to the house, and there, too, a backhoe was needed. So they decided to use the same trench the gas people were using. That meant waiting a month.

A month.

She hadn't told Nancy yet.

She washed her hair, blow-dried it, then set it on electric curlers. Large, fat ones that would give her hair a slight wave to her shoulders with a flip at the bottom. Sometimes she still pulled it back and fastened it with clips, the way she had worn it when she was younger.

She went into the kitchenette and looked at the clock on the wall. Only seven?

She was dressed and ready to go to work, and it would be another hour before the office opened.

She wasn't hungry. Breakfast held no interest, not now, never had. But her head hurt. A dull ache, as if she hadn't gotten enough sleep.

It was almost a week since she had signed the papers to buy the house, and her head had been hurting ever since. Sometimes she almost wished ... but no, the house was something that both she and Nancy needed.

She took an aspirin, and made a cup of coffee. She watched the hands of the clock slowly move.

A vision flashed into her mind suddenly. She saw the back of the child, long curls swinging as she reached high. She was trying to open a door. She had to stretch to reach the knob. Using both hands, she struggled to turn it.

She entered a room that in some way caused her fear to swell to terror. She stood still. The room was spotted with furniture and deep, crawling shadows. In the corner, something moved, as if she had disturbed it ...

Katie pressed her hands to her face, and the vision was gone. Her heart raced. The intense fear of the child had returned, and with it the distortion. She looked out the window at the trees in the park across the street, and they were like the figures in the dark corridors, unfamiliar and strangely frightening. She turned quickly away, and her eyes came to the clock. She stared at it. What was happening to her? She had never been in a room like the one she'd just seen. What was it? A memory? What room? Where?

Am I losing my mind?

Suddenly, the vision returned. A woman, face in shadows, separated from the moving things in the corner and came toward her. Katie saw clearly the red piping that decorated the rounded bottom of her apron, and the cotton print of the material. Small flowers, vines.

Something within Katie seemed to snap, and she was back in her apartment. Everything was back to normal. The fear drifted away, like a soft cloud, leaving Katie weak with relief.

She felt helplessly trapped by the waking dream, the hallucination, whatever it was. It was as if something in the back of her brain had separated from her mind and was releasing bits of horror. Until now, they had come only when she was sleeping. She couldn't stand this. She was afraid—afraid of another vision paralyzing her with horror.

She left the apartment and drove slowly to the shopping center and the office. She greeted the other agents, who were preparing their desks and appointments for the day, then went to her own desk in the corner.

She opened the telephone book to the medical section. Once, after Ethan had died, she had gone to a doctor for something to help her sleep. He had recommended a therapist. Katie had marked his number in the book.

"I'd like very much to see the doctor immediately," Katie said to the woman who answered his phone. "If only for a couple of minutes."

"What seems to be the problem?"

Katie searched her mind for words to explain the terror she felt, not only in the dreams, the waking visions, but the lingering fear that stayed with her afterwards. There were none.

"I've suddenly been having horrible dreamlike images. I don't know what they are. I just need to see someone."

"Could you hold a moment, please?"

"Yes."

Katie waited. Maybe she should just hang up, she thought, and get to work. But the thought of lying down to sleep tonight terrified her. Worse was the fear that another of the visions would suddenly come forward to control her. What would happen if she was driving at the time, taking a client to see a property? She no longer could trust herself. She had to have help.

The voice came back on the line. "Dr. Firman can see you at four o'clock."

CHAPTER 27

$\mathcal{E}$rica ran through the house, Curtis behind her. Nancy heard them coming, their footsteps loud even on the carpeted floor. They came from the front bedroom, through the living room and through the kitchen. They both had their hands going over their mouths, letting out *hooo, hooo, hooos*. Nancy didn't know if they were playing Indians on the warpath or if they were a freight train. Why were her kids so rowdy? Her friend Beth's kids were always so nice and quiet.

"Stop it!" Nancy yelled, just as the back door slammed.

Jane cringed. Nancy saw the action, the way her mother had tried to draw her head into her shoulders. Although Jane had a dishwasher, she was washing pots and pans by hand. Nancy was drying and putting away.

"Sorry," Nancy said. "Didn't mean to startle you."

"Nancy," Jane said, "It's just that it doesn't seem to do a bit of good for you to scream at the kids. All you do is make me jump."

"Mom, I'm sorry."

Nancy went to the door and looked out. The kids were running in a circle in the backyard, not far from Doug, who was working with his roses.

"They're all right out there," Jane said. She spent a few seconds working on a pan that was already sparkling.

Nancy felt awkward. Did Jane always do so much housework, or was she just trying to keep busy because she wasn't free to do her own thing with Nancy and the kids here?

Nancy hadn't lived at home since she was eighteen, and here, at age thirty, she was back again. With two kids who were noisy and active at least half of the day.

She said, "I'm sorry if we're messing things up, Mom. Can you imagine living in that small apartment with these two kids?"

Excuses, she thought. She could almost see her mother thinking the same thing. They had always been much alike, not only in appearance, but in the way they thought.

Only now, Nancy was pulling away. She felt it within herself.

Then Jane surprised her.

"Maybe you need to go back to school, Nancy. Find a career. Plan ahead. Have something beyond home-making to look forward to. Is having a larger place really the problem?"

Nancy opened her mouth and closed it.

Jane was quiet.

Being with Mom and Doug for holidays, and at least one Sunday a month, as well as having her mother meet her for lunch occasionally, had given her a different relationship with her mother.

Nancy wanted to leave, but she didn't want to go home to Perry. Not yet. Maybe not ever. She wasn't sure. But that was something she didn't want to discuss with her mother. Jane would never approve, unless he was abusive, and Nancy had to admit he wasn't.

But he hadn't come through as she'd hoped he would. She had hoped when she left that he would give in and do *something*. But although he had called and called, promising next year to get a house or at least a bigger place, he hadn't offered to do anything now. She had hoped he'd offer to sell the new van.

Yesterday she had gone over to see him, in his expanded printing shop, taking the kids with her. But he wasn't there.

"Where's Perry?" she had asked James, who came forward from the back room.

"He's out on delivery. He'll probably be back soon, if you want to wait."

The kids tore through the front office, running around the copy machines behind the counter.

"Stop it!" Nancy demanded, embarrassing herself because her voice came out louder than she'd intended.

James looked embarrassed, too. He reached up and ran his fingers through his hair. Red hair, Nancy noticed. She'd seen him a couple of times before, when, with the kids in tow, she'd come down to get some money from Perry.

She shouldn't have come, she thought. Why had she come? Just to get away from Mom's house. It seemed she was always trying to get away from somewhere.

"No, we won't wait. Thanks anyway, James. Just tell Perry we dropped in, okay?"

Nancy started out, Curtis's arm clutched in one hand, and motioning to Erica with the other.

"Tell Perry his shop is looking great."

James nodded, smiled.

Since she had been here, the printing shop had been expanded, with new copy machines, a new desk. Perry seemed to want to talk about nothing but business these days, even when they did talk.

Last night, when he'd called to say he was sorry he wasn't in when she and the kids came, he turned the conversation to business. He had been out on a delivery.

"It's going good, Nan. If you'd just hang on for another few months ... come on home."

"Perry—" How could she make him understand? "Do you still have the van, Perry?"

"Nancy, you'd love it, really. We could take our whole vacation—"

Nancy had hung up. Perry didn't call back. Nancy sat by the phone for almost an hour, but it didn't ring.

Perry didn't have his priorities straight, she thought to herself. Then, as she'd cooled off, it all lost some of its importance. Perhaps, she thought, she didn't have her own priorities straight.

Nancy took a deep breath and looked out the kitchen door. Her kids had stopped running around and were watching Doug. They had been here a month. It was a month too long.

"Mom," Nancy said, "what do you think about me and the kids going on out to Katie's house? Even though it doesn't have electricity yet. We could live with candles. As Katie said, it might be fun."

Jane raised her head and looked out the window over the sink. "It's a long ways out. Nancy, are you sure you want to keep the kids away from Perry?"

"I'm not keeping them away. He can see them whenever he wants to."

"Whenever he has time, you mean. He works hard, Nancy."

"So he won't miss us much." This conversation, bordering on argument, made up Nancy's mind. She felt almost childishly stubborn now and determined to move. "I think it will be a good move for us."

Jane was quiet a moment. "Be careful," she finally said. "Candles could start a fire. The house is old. I suppose—in the beginning, anyway, until Katie has made the house into whatever she intends, she needs you and the children. But don't put Perry out of your life."

"I don't feel he's thinking of our welfare."

"Of course he is. Otherwise, why would he work so hard? Just don't be so quick to run away from every unpleasant circumstance. Divorce isn't good for children, I don't care what the experts say, so long as there isn't outright abuse. A couple who have children need to stay together. Not everything is wine and roses."

Nancy stood with her head down, feeling as if she'd just been scolded.

"Both of you need to grow up, I think," Jane said. "Think of the kids first. That doesn't mean you can't think of yourself and prepare for a future for yourself, when they're gone."

Jane turned to her and drew her into her arms.

"Nancy, don't think I'm scolding. I love you as much as you love Erica and Curtis, and I want to see you happy."

Nancy felt the pats on her back, the closeness of her mother, the hard hug.

"You know, Nancy, you can stay here as long as you need to." Jane released her and went back to scrubbing a clean pot.

"I know, Mom. Thanks."

Nancy went into the living room. She began picking up toys, tears burning her eyes.

She found herself at the telephone, and she picked it up and dialed Katie's office number. Please be there, Katie. We need the room in your new house, and the yard space. School won't start for another month.

A female voice answered the phone. "Yates Realty."

"Is Katie Rogers there?"

"No, she isn't. Could I take a message, please?"

"Just tell her Nancy called, please. Ask her to call me as soon as she can."

Dr. Jason Firman looked to be at least six-feet-three or -four. He stooped slightly. His suit jacket hung loosely from his thin shoulders. He wasn't wearing a tie. The collar of his blue shirt was open, as if to make room for his protruding Adam's apple. It bobbed when he spoke. His voice, like his hand, was surprisingly soft and gentle.

"Sit down, Mrs. Rogers. Is it all right if I call you Katie? I like to be on first-name basis with my clients." He didn't say that he wanted her to call him Jason, and in fact, she wasn't interested in being that familiar.

He sat behind his desk and smiled faintly at her. "You've been having problems with dreams?"

"Yes—uh—problems in that they cause me a lot of anxiety. Fear, actually. I didn't know such fear existed. It distorts reality, makes things look—different."

"Tell me about the dreams."

She tried to tell them as she had felt them. The child, the black moving things in the darkness, the reaching arms with the long, inhuman fingers, and the woman with the apron.

"When did these dreams begin?" Dr. Firman asked.

"Just this past week. And this morning, I had the same experience while I was awake."

"Has anything traumatic happened to you lately?"

"My husband was killed in a plane crash six months ago.

"Tell me about it."

Her fingers clasped and unclasped the purse on her lap. The sound was soft.

"He was learning to be a pilot, and he had just gotten his license. One day he rented a small plane. He crashed it. The insurance company tried to prove it was suicide. It wasn't, I know. There were no problems in Ethan's life, in our lives. We were happy. We both had good jobs, and were saving to buy a house in the suburbs. Everything was good. It was a total shock to me. I moved to a smaller place, partly because I couldn't stand being alone where Ethan and I had lived, partly to save money."

"Any children?"

"No ... that only made it worse. We'd been wanting a baby. We just hadn't had the luck."

"How long had you been married?"

"Two years. I was twenty-three and he was twenty-eight when we married. We used birth control only for the first year."

"So how are you coping now, consciously, with the loss?"

Katie looked at her hands, remembering nights when she had wept, cried, pounded her pillow. Why had it happened? And then ...

"One night a couple of months ago he came to me in a dream. There was a barrier between us, like glass, and it was foggy. I reached up and wiped away the fog. He was beautiful, smiling, young. He'd started to bald slightly, but in this dream his hair was the way it had been when he was twenty or so. In the dream he smiled at me and said, 'It's a lovely day.' "

Dr. Firman stared at her. He said nothing.

"After that," Katie said, hearing the softening of her voice, feeling the smile on her lips. "After that it was okay. It was as if he had come back just to tell me to stop grieving, that it was all okay."

"So it's been easier for you since then."

"Oh yes, much."

"Had you done anything specific to bring on the dream?"

"No. Well ... perhaps. I had gone to his grave and sat down on the grass and talked to him."

Dr. Firman nodded. His eyes seemed to narrow slightly.

"I haven't gone back since," Katie said.

"The dreams you're having now, about the child ... what do they remind you of?"

Katie paused, thinking. Remind her of?

She shook her head.

"Nothing."

"Could they be you when you were a child?"

"No," she said quickly. "I don't have that feeling at all. The child in my dream is someone I'm watching."

"Yet you feel her fear."

"Uh—yes. Or maybe my own. Because I still feel it after I wake up. And this morning, I was awake and walking around when I had another of the—dreams ... visions ... whatever."

"Can you describe the child?"

"Yes. She's small, smaller than my niece or nephew, even though I think she may be about my nephew's age, which is five. She has long blond hair that hangs in ringlets past her waist. Long tube-like curls. She's always wearing a dress ..."

Katie paused, seeing something about the dress she hadn't thought of before.

"What is it?" Dr. Firman asked softly.

"The dress ... it's long. It hangs almost to her ankles. And she's barefoot. She's holding something that's very important to her under her arm. Very important."

Dr. Firman watched her intently, but Katie frowned past him, aware of his study of her and yet more aware of the scene in her mind that was growing more vivid.

"She's afraid, and she keeps trying to hide. But the woman comes closer. The woman isn't afraid of the—the whatever they are in the darkness. The woman ..."

"Can you describe the woman?"

"No. Her face is in shadow. She's wearing an apron. The kind with a bib—oh, my God!" Katie laughed, pressing her hands over her mouth. Dr. Firman's eyebrows lifted in a silent question.

"It's the ghost!" Katie told him, feeling a release within her, as if tension had drained suddenly from her body. "The ghost was wearing an apron. I don't know why I didn't make the connection before this!"

Dr. Firman smiled. "I'm afraid you've lost me." Katie told him about her experiences in the house. "She was a wonderful old thing, actually," Katie said, "On looking back. Busy, grandmotherly. But the sight of me scared her literally to pieces."

She laughed with relief. Only the ghost, triggering strange dreams of a frightened child. She wasn't losing her mind after all. Thank God.

"That's very interesting," Dr. Firman said. "Had you never hallucinated before you had this experience, as you call it, with the ghost?"

"Hallucinated?" She felt as if he had scolded her for laughing.

"Of course you don't believe such things as ghosts exist."

"Uh—no, of course not. At least, I never had. That's what made it so strange."

"Look at it this way, Katie. Going into that house opened a door within your mind. It brought back a memory, perhaps. And the ghost, the woman, was a product of your mind. It wasn't necessarily the house that set this into motion. It could have been anything. A certain stage of your life, for example. Repressed memories seem to require a certain mental maturity in order to unfold."

She stared at him, not liking what she was hearing. He continued, "You say at first you thought the woman was real, a homeless person, perhaps, who had found the vacated house and made a way in. Did the woman have clear features?"

Katie had thought so, but now all she could remember clearly were the eyes, the hair, the shape of the face. "I saw her clearly, yes. She had hollow cheeks, and long, slitted eyes, very dark. As if they were empty. Until that morning in the hallway, when she looked at me."

"Of course you observed her in darkened rooms."

"Yes, I did. Even the hallway where she disappeared in the morning was quite dark. She wore her hair pulled back tight and made into a knot. And she wore a print dress almost to her ankles, and a large apron with a bib."

"Okay. The woman in your dreams."

Katie waited. She felt he had something in mind that she had not grasped.

"You were caught in unusual circumstances. Alone in the world, you might say. And something you looked at, the house, something else, unleashed something in your mind. Did you have any other experiences there that struck you strongly?"

"Yes, I did. When I was standing by the barn and looking down a little trail that disappeared into the trees, I had a strong feeling I had stood there before." Dr. Firman nodded, and now he was beginning to smile. "I thought so. Is there any chance you might actually have been there when you were a child?"

"No. Never."

"How far back does your conscious memory go, Katie?"

She tried to remember. It was true, she realized suddenly, she didn't have memories of a really early childhood.

"I was going to school. It was my first day. Mama held one of my hands, my sister the other. I was very excited."

"First grade? Kindergarten?"

"It must have been first grade. Judging by how big my sister was. She's five years older. I remember she held onto my hand when Mama left, and she told Mama she'd take care of me."

"Tell me about your family, Katie."

In a few minutes she had told it all. She never knew her father, or any of his family. They lived on the West Coast, two thousand miles away. She lived until she was thirteen with just her mother and sister. Then Doug, whom she called Pop, married her mother.

"That's all," she said. "Nothing spectacular."

"Have you always lived in this area?"

"Yes. We always lived in a small house over near where my mom lives now. Dull lives, I guess some people would say."

"Yet your memory doesn't begin until you were around six years old."

What was he getting at? Katie wished for a moment that she hadn't come. Then she remembered the horror of having reality distorted by a fear she couldn't understand. And the anxiety that it would recur at any time. Yet now, just as she felt she had figured it out, he had struck it down by making her feel her ghost was only the beginning of the hallucinations. A product of her own crazy mind, not a separate entity at all.

"I guess not," she admitted.

"Katie, I think you're experiencing flashes of repressed memories. It's my guess something terrible happened to you when you were a very small child. Something done by a mother figure. How is your relationship with your mother?"

Katie frowned. She didn't like the way this was going. "You're not suggesting my own mother did something to me!"

"It's entirely possible, Katie," he said gently. "That's why you can't remember being three years old, or four or five. Many times when there's a divorce in the family, a parent will take it out on a child. But whatever happened, it's going to have to be fully uncovered now, or those memories are going to come as they did, in dreams or in flashes, visions, hallucinations, and terrify you. I suggest you talk to your mother and sister."

He stood up, came around the desk, and took Katie's hand. Katie rose.

"We'll get through this," he said, in his soft, soothing voice. "Don't worry Katie. Shall I schedule you for next week, or would you rather come sooner?"

Katie hesitated. She brushed the back of one hand against her cheek.

He said, "Let me suggest you come back as soon as possible. I'll check with my secretary and have her call you."

Katie nodded.

She left his office feeling vulnerable and alone, wondering what she was facing on the other side of the door.

What was she facing beyond every door she opened?

CHAPTER 28

*A*fter she left the therapist, Katie sat in her car, holding tightly to the steering wheel, the people on the sidewalk moving past in a blur. She had left the office at three-thirty, and it was too late now to go back to work.

She stopped for a sandwich to go, and at home ate it while standing at the kitchen sink. She listened to the messages on her answering machine, eating slowly, with no enjoyment, looking around at the bare walls of the apartment. When she'd moved from the apartment she had shared with Ethan, she had put almost everything in storage and had just never had the heart to bring it out and try to make this a home. It was a stopover, as temporary as she could make it, on her way past grief and, she hoped, to something else, something better.

"Mrs. Rogers, this is Marshall Construction. I'm sorry, but we ran into some unexpected delays and won't be able to dig that trench for the electrical cable and gas line when we said we would. We'll let you know when we can get there."

"Oh, damn!" Katie said aloud. That meant that the scheduled laying of the lines would probably be delayed a month. She had hoped not to have to pay another month of rent here on her apartment. She considered going on out there and living with candlelight. It was still warm weather. The heat wouldn't be needed for a couple of months. At least, not seriously. And there was always the gas range in the kitchen, with its bottled propane. And, of course, the fireplaces.

The next message was from Nancy.

"Katie, I need to talk to you. Call me, please." Her voice was low and sounded vulnerable. Lately, Katie had begun feeling as if Nancy were the younger sister who needed looking after.

Katie dialed her mother's number.

Doug answered. She could hear the kids' voices in the background and a *thump, thump* as Curtis ran from one place to another. Katie smiled. Curtis couldn't just walk, he had to run. What a drag for poor Pop.

"Hi, Pop," Katie said. "What's going on?"

"Not much. How're you, Katie?"

"Okay. Are Mom and Nancy there?"

"Yeah, want to talk to one of them?"

"No, wait. I'll be over in a while."

"All right, I'll tell 'em."

Katie turned to go into the kitchen end of the apartment when suddenly the bright fluorescent light tube over the sink began a strange rubbery undulation and grew dim, dimmer, and turned dark and writhing. She was facing the dark end of a corridor that was filled with black writhing figures within the darkness. The moving darkness edged toward her.

She stood in cold terror, wanting to turn and run. Her legs grew weak. Her arms felt as if they were being stung by a million tiny, forked tongues.

She was small and helpless, clutching beneath her arm her only security. Angel wings. The dark things in the shadowed corridor were creeping toward her. Then she heard the footsteps, and saw the large figure wearing the apron.

She turned and ran in terror.

She reached a door, the knob high and difficult to turn. It slipped in her fingers. Behind her the footsteps echoed hollowly and the slithering sounds of something crawling rapidly came closer. She reached higher, and the door opened.

She was faced with an even darker corridor, but she slipped through the door and ran, her bare feet making only the softest sounds on the wood floor. She came to the tall enclosed piece of furniture and flattened herself at its end, her back against the wall.

The footsteps came down the passageway, closer, closer. Little flickers of light licked ahead of the steps. Something black coiled in the darkness of the corner beyond her, but she was more frightened of the footsteps, and the light.

The woman was suddenly there, a giant above the child, the candlelight flicking like tongues up in front of her face. The woman's apron brushed against her face as a hand clutched her arm in a rough, hard grip. A scream bubbled like blood in the child's throat, but she was too terrified to make a sound.

Katie gasped.

The light over the sink hurt her eyes. She turned away, shaking. Her legs felt oddly weak and trembly, as if she'd been running. She stood for a time with her hands over her eyes, but the images kept flickering, the little tongues of candlelight ... the apron ... the face ... the writhing, intertwining figures that were made partly of darkness, and partly of something far more sinister.

Katie ran to the bathroom, tore off her clothes, and stepped into the shower. The water, at first cold, turned hot. She let it shower down on her, on the back of her neck. She stared down at her feet, afraid to close her eyes.

Oh, God, repressed memories?

Dr. Firman had said to call him if she needed him, any time of the day or night. She felt at this moment, with terror eating at her soul, that she needed him.

She wrapped a towel around her and went to the telephone.

He answered on the fourth ring.

"Dr. Firman, this is Katie Rogers ...

"Yes, Katie."

"I'm sorry to bother you at this time of the evening—"

"It's all right. What happened?"

"I—uh—" It was so hard to explain. How could she describe such awful fear? "It was the child again. I was just walking toward my kitchenette when the light began to distort, and then the other came. The child, the black—creatures—things in the darkness, the running down a long hallway and hiding behind a tall piece of furniture. And the woman, coming after the child. But this time I was the child."

"Are you all right now?"

"I'm always left with this awful fear. Dr. Firman, I don't understand what's happening to me." She began to weep, soundlessly. She hoped he didn't hear.

"Katie, have you talked with your mother and sister?"

"No. I'm just getting ready to go over there."

"I think you should come to my office tomorrow. If nothing is solved by then, we may need to put you under hypnosis to see what it is you've repressed. Why don't you talk to your mother and sister, see if they can help you remember your past? I'll call you in the morning."

"Thank you, Doctor."

"Remember, these are only memories. They can't hurt you. You survived this early horror in your life. It would help if your mother talked to you about this."

"Dr. Firman, it isn't my mother. She never carried a candle that I recall. The woman's face—was not like—my mother's."

The face of the ghost. Familiar only because of the ghost. Dr. Firman said it was someone in her past. But who? She found herself frowning at the wall. Whose face? Had the light distorted it, too? She felt so cold and alone, so confused.

"You'll be fine, Katie. Remember, these surfacing memories are your mind's way of easing the past. Tomorrow, we can try to get to the bottom of this. Do you have any tranquilizers you can take?"

"No."

"Why don't you try a warm drink? Not alcohol, that will only make it worse. Milk, perhaps, or tea."

"All right."

She dressed quickly while the tea brewed. The fear had gone as she'd talked with the doctor, leaving the memory of it, and anxiety that it would return. She remembered, too, the strange distortion of her room, of the change in reality, as if these familiar things she looked at every day, and had always taken for granted, were not real. She had never known that reality was so tenuous. And its opposite so terrifying.

What was real? It seemed now that she was part of two worlds, two lives. The terror that was the child's, and her own strange, unreal existence.

Where did she belong?

She no longer knew.

"But Mommy," Erica argued, in the adult way she at times acquired. "There's a show on I want to watch. With Pop-Pop. He's watching it, why can't I?"

"Me, too!" demanded Curtis.

Nancy clutched two little arms in her hands and pulled both Erica and Curtis toward the front bedroom.

"It's nine o'clock, you're not staying up a minute longer. Now get into your pj's and be quiet!"

They stared at her, innocent eyes rounded. Both of them were quiet for a change. Nancy kept her amused smile to herself. That was all it would take to undo what she had accomplished with her sudden, new, stern disciplinary tactics. She had surprised everybody, even herself.

"Now listen," she said, as she helped them into pajamas; they could take baths tomorrow morning. She wanted them in bed when Katie came. "You two have been doing pretty much what you wanted to do since we've been here at Pop's and Grandma's. Now you're going to mind. You're going to go to bed by eight, or whenever I say. And you're going to keep quiet. Do you hear?"

They nodded, their eyes still rounded.

She tucked them into the big double bed. At the door, she looked back. Hmmm. It was easier than she'd thought it would be. Maybe she should have gotten sterner earlier.

"Good night."

She shut the door and stood a moment listening. Sure enough, here came Curtis's footsteps, running.

Nancy opened the door, startling him to a stop. She pointed at the bed.

"Did I tell you to stay in bed?"

He ran back to the bed and climbed in. Nancy looked at him, his little round face perfect in its beauty, and she almost relented. She wasn't meant to be a tough mother, she thought, as she closed the door again. It broke her heart.

Back in the apartment, with Perry working late so much of the time, the kids had been such a comfort. They'd all three get a blanket and cuddle together on the couch, watching television. Usually videos, Walt Disney, something the kids could see. And the kids often went to sleep there, and sometimes, so did she.

But here, it couldn't be that way.

She yearned to be alone with them. Not back in the closet-like apartment, but somewhere in a house of her own.

Katie knocked once on the open door before she opened the screen and walked in. There was something different about her, Nancy noticed immediately. She looked as if she'd hurried, as if she were worried about something. She was dressed in jeans and a tucked-in blouse. Her hair had been pinned up, and small, damp strands hung down her forehead.

Jane came in from the kitchen and sat down on a chair just inside the doorway.

"Are you losing weight, Katie?" Jane asked.

That was it, Nancy thought. Katie's on a diet. Never plump, she appeared to be even thinner than usual.

Katie took a chair near her mother. Over in the other corner, Doug turned the television down, but not off. Katie waved at him and smiled faintly.

"Don't let me interrupt your show, Pop." She looked at Nancy and said, "Hi."

Nancy, trying to sound cheerful, thinking of her own shorter, rounder, plumper self, said, "You're dieting, Katie. I thought you said you'd never diet again."

"Dieting? Not consciously." Katie looked down at her hands. "There's just so much going on lately that sometimes I don't take time to eat."

"She eats junk food," Jane said disapprovingly.

"Did you get my call?" Nancy asked.

"Yes."

Katie waited, but Nancy was silent. There was an expression on her lips of not quite a smile, but rather hesitation or indecision. Katie remembered how, when they were children, when Nancy, a protective older sister, was put in a position of indecision, she'd always smile tightly. Adults sometimes thought she was being disobedient or defiant, but Katie knew she wasn't. She could feel by the nervous tightness of Nancy's hand on hers that Nancy was more scared than defiant. Katie suspected she didn't want to talk now in front of Mom.

Jane spoke up, breaking the silence, "I think she wants to move."

"Out to Wickham House?" Katie asked, with a feeling suddenly that it was right they should. Why had they waited? The house could be wired for electricity with them in it.

Nancy said, "If it's all right with you?"

"Sure. Great," Katie answered. "But there's no electricity yet, and the way it looks, it might be weeks before there is."

Nancy shrugged. "So it will be like living back in the 1800s. It'll be fun."

Jane said, "I don't know. What about refrigeration? For the children's milk? What about that ghost Katie saw?"

Nancy giggled, a bit nervously, it seemed to Katie. "Don't you remember? Katie scared it away. All it took was one look at her."

They all laughed, but this was the opening Katie needed. She rose. "Let's go to the kitchen and have a cup of coffee or something. I need to talk to you about that."

Following, Nancy said, "First Mom said she didn't believe in ghosts, now she doesn't want me to move because of the ghost."

"That's not exactly what I said," Jane corrected, going to the stove for the coffeepot. But she didn't elaborate.

Katie said, "I've started seeing a therapist. He believes I was hallucinating."

"Um-hmm," Jane agreed. She stood at the sink, running water into the coffeepot. "I'm sure he's right. What else could it be? You probably hadn't eaten."

"There's another thing," Katie said. She felt an odd uneasiness within herself. She dreaded this question she had to ask her mother and sister. It was almost like a confrontation which she wanted to avoid as long as possible.

She waited so long to speak that Jane turned and looked at her.

"What other thing?"

"First, let me tell you why I'm seeing a therapist." She explained briefly the night dreams about the child, and then the experiences when she was awake. "Doctor Firman believes repressed memories are coming forward, Mom. He thinks something so horrible happened to me when I was little that—that I repressed it. And now—it's more or less come back to haunt me."

She sat at the kitchen table, with Nancy at the end to her left. Jane came to her seat on the right.

"Memories? So horrible you've repressed them?" Jane repeated, as if she'd said something about life on a distant galaxy. "What repressed memories?"

Nancy frowned. "That you once were a small child being chased down a long corridor by a woman?"

"Yes," Katie said. "He wanted me to ask both of you what could be in my past to cause me to remember this."

They both gaped at her in silence. Katie looked from one face to the other.

"The fear is terrible," she tried to explain, "Something is—was going to hurt me. Hurt the child. The woman seems very large, but the doctor thinks it's because I was so small—three, four, maybe five. I told him I have no conscious memories before I started school, and that's one of the reasons he feels these are memories I suppressed, because they were so terrifying."

She paused, giving one of them a chance to say something. But both remained silent, staring at her.

Katie went on, "I need to bring them out, the doctor told me, and remember what happened."

Jane drew a deep breath, looked at Nancy, then got up without saying anything and went to pour the coffee. The aroma filled the small kitchen, but it didn't give Katie the feeling of warm security that it always had before.

Nancy said, as if she couldn't comprehend what she had heard, "Your doctor thinks you've repressed memories of something horrible that happened to you? Done by a *woman*?"

Katie frowned against the dim picture swirling in the back of her mind. Like a den of huge black snakes it writhed, darkness within darkness. She put her fingers hard against her temples to push the image back.

"I think the woman was going to give me to something else," she said. "There are black figures in the darkness that I never quite see. I think she was going to give me to them. Perhaps."

Jane came back with cups of coffee. "What woman?" she asked, her face an open question.

"I don't know. I never clearly see her face in my dreams. I only see the large bib apron she's wearing, and hear her footsteps."

Jane said, "I think that things that scare a little one are probably bent all out of proportion to reality. I mean, when you're little, other people are big, after all."

"Mom, did you ever wear that kind of apron?" Katie asked hesitantly.

"You're accusing me of chasing you down a long corridor and threatening to throw you to something in the dark?" Jane laughed shortly. "Let me tell that doctor of yours, we never had a corridor of any kind, long or short, when you were that age."

Nancy was shaking her head, on and on, bewilderment on her face.

But Katie couldn't give up.

"Did we ever stay, even overnight, in a large house, or anything like that? Where someone else—did I ever have a baby-sitter in a large house?"

"No," said Jane, shaking her head firmly. "No, you never had a sitter, period, except your own sister, and your Aunt Becky. And you know Aunt Becky's house wasn't any bigger than this one."

Aunt Becky's house had been a favorite place to go. There were cousins there to play with, fun in the backyard on the swing set and in the sandbox. Katie remembered that.

"Why is it I can't remember anything with us, we three, until the day I first went to school? Nancy was holding my hand, I remember."

"We just don't remember when we were born, Katie, that's all," Jane said. "And those who claim they do are hallucinating as much as your doctor claims you were when you met that so-called ghost."

This was going nowhere, Katie realized. She looked at Nancy, and Nancy spoke up for her, questioning their mother.

"We never lived anywhere but that small house, did we, Mom?" Nancy asked. "Until we came here. After Mom started working, we went to school, or stayed by ourselves until Mom got home. Don't you remember that, Katie?"

"Yes, when I was older, but ..."

Nancy said, "Katie, Mom never wore that kind of apron. Neither did Aunt Becky. They wore only the kind that ties at the waist, if any."

Jane said, "I think that so-called therapist of yours is leading you on, Katie."

"You don't understand ... Katie started to say, *You don't understand the terrible danger the child I dream of is in, the fear of the child that I once was.*

She felt the cold of eons past cover her skin.

The child I once was.

CHAPTER 29

*J*ane sat on a lawn chair on the patio and stared up at the stars. They used to comfort her, help her feel she wasn't alone, but tonight the air seemed chilled, and she felt in her heart the distance of stars that were merely tiny specks of light after all. What could they do to help her feel less alone, less guilty?

She felt as if Katie had accused her of doing something terrible to her own baby. Nothing had happened to Katie when she was a small child. She told Katie that, and Nancy, who could remember the day Katie was born, had told her. Still, when Katie left, Jane retained the feeling that Katie was convinced that her dreams, her nightmares, her visions, were actual memories.

Nothing bad had ever happened to Katie. Jane wouldn't have allowed it. She remembered the first time Katie had lain in her arms. A warm, wiggling little creature, so much like her big sister, Nancy, who was all of five and so interested in the new baby.

Yet they were so different as years passed. Katie had seemed more adventuresome. She was the only one of them who went to college and earned a degree. She was taller, naturally slimmer, blonder. Though not any prettier than Nancy, Jane thought. They were both natural beauties, in their mother's eyes. Nancy had grown up to be more like Jane herself, interested in home and children. When she had borne her first baby, Nancy had looked so right with that baby in her arms.

The early years were still a painful memory for Jane in many ways. Her young husband, handsome, tall, blond, like a Nordic god, was too much of a womanizer to settle down, and he had left her when Katie was just three months old. They had the little house, and he at least assured her he wouldn't put her and the babies out for anything. "Why, Jane," he'd said once, when he'd come home after three weeks' absence and learned she was considering filing for divorce and asking for the house and child support, "Why do you want a divorce? The house is yours, and I'll send you money. Here, I brought you a hundred. Two hundred. Okay?"

Then he'd left again. She and the children had barely managed to squeak by. If she hadn't been breast-feeding the baby, she might have had difficulty buying milk.

A few months later she learned that her husband, and the woman he was with, were killed in a car wreck. To Jane's surprise, she found he'd been carrying insurance that would pay off the house in case of his death, and also a $15,000 policy with her as beneficiary. As she stood by his grave the day after his funeral, she murmured her sorrow and her thanks. The money, if carefully handled, would take care of her and her kids until they were both in school and she could get a job.

There were similarities in her life and Katie's. Except, of course, Katie had no children when her husband was killed, and there had been no marital problems.

So she knew positively that Katie had never been in a dangerous situation. Perhaps, she had told Katie at the last, when Katie had still not seemed convinced, the reason Katie had no memory before the first day of kindergarten, when she was barely five, was that nothing exciting had ever happened. They lived. They went to the grocery store for food. They lived, one day to the next, that was all.

The kitchen door opened. Nancy came softly out onto the patio and sat down in another of the old, saggy lawn chairs.

"What's wrong, Mom, can't you sleep?"

"Just looking at the stars. Remember when you, Katie, and I used to sit out in the backyard of our old house and look at the satellites going over? They were like traveling stars. I don't see them anymore."

"I remember. Mom, I don't think Kate meant anything by that memory stuff."

"I don't know what's happening to her, Nancy. She had a husband die. So did I. These things happen to some of us. But why would his death start her having nightmares?" It was easier to fall back on the familiar. "It's probably something she ate."

They sat still a moment. Jane wished she had both her girls here again, the way they used to be, so she could look after them, see that they wore warm coats in the winter, and ate hot oatmeal for breakfast.

"I'll bet she never has a thing for breakfast but a strong cup of coffee," Jane said. "Maybe a sweet roll later."

"Mom, she'll be okay."

"Well."

"It's okay, isn't it, Mom, that I go ahead and move out there? Maybe if Katie went, too, and we were together ..." Her voice trailed away.

Jane hesitated, looking up at the stars. So cold, so distant. Where was God? Was there a perfect place, somewhere, in those distant stars? Did God ever think of earth, and the troubled creatures who live there?

"You'll make it okay, Nancy. Maybe it would be good for both you and Katie. Maybe you can help her, even as she's helping you. What are sisters for?"

Nancy got up and kissed her mother's cheek. It felt cool to her lips, and soft. Her skin was wrinkling, like tissue paper that had been left unsmoothed, and Nancy hated to see this sign of aging, of mortality. Jane reached up and patted Nancy on the head. They said good night, and Nancy went back to the living room and her bed on the couch.

She was sleepless, too, but for a different reason, she felt. She understood that her mother might feel as if Katie were accusing her of something that had never happened. But she was too agitated about the move to sleep. She wanted to go this minute into the bedroom, where Curtis and Erica were soundly sleeping, and start packing.

She had little idea of where Katie's new house was. But at least there she'd not only have a home, but a job of sorts. She was going to be the housekeeper, at least in the beginning. "We'll work it out," Katie had said, when they'd walked out to the car and Nancy had asked if she could go ahead and move.

Katie, standing by the car, had looked up at the stars just as Jane had on the patio. At that moment Katie had seemed as far away from Nancy, emotionally, as those distant stars.

"I suppose we can live without lights, what the heck?" Katie said then. "We might as well get things started, see what we can do. Of course, we can't open the house to mothers in need until we get some electricity, but we'll work it out. You can be the housekeeper, Nan, and I'll be the bookkeeper, and well— we'll work it out."

Katie had left then. Nancy stood watching the car's taillights. Then she went out to the patio.

She could hardly wait until morning, when she would load the suitcases and the kids into the old station wagon and head for Katie's office. They were to meet at noon, and then she would follow Katie in her car to their new home.

She thought about calling Perry and letting him know where they were, and decided not to. Let him worry just a bit. He'd be calling in a few days, probably, and Mom would tell him she and the children had moved.

Let him rattle that around in his new van.

. . .

KATIE LAY IN BED, waiting for morning. Nancy had forced her into a decision, and Katie felt relieved. Although the insurance money still had not arrived, Mr. Yates had trusted Katie for the remainder of the money owed. There was an open note, for the balance to be paid on receipt. Katie had talked yesterday with her lawyer, and he had said the insurance company had claimed the check would be in the mail in a few days. There would be enough to pay the balance on the property, wire it for electricity, and help her keep it going until she could come up with a definite idea to make it self-supporting.

It occurred to her that she was unable to make plans very far into the future, even now. She thought of herself, Nancy, and the kids moving into the old mansion. She thought perhaps six months from now they might be ready to take in their first family. But she couldn't visualize the family.

It was as if something in her mind knew there would be no future in the old mansion. That its life was anchored in the past, and whoever entered there had no future.

"Oh, God," she murmured aloud, turning in bed, putting her hands to her head, closing her eyes tightly. Where were these terrible thoughts coming from?

Behind her closed eyes a scene formed. She saw the little girl, saw her more clearly than she had before. She had long, pale blond tube ringlets hanging down her back. She wore a long dress that reached almost to her ankles. It had been washed so many times it was faded colorless.

The child entered a room. Shadows hovered in the corners like a faded old photograph. She walked tentatively through another door, opening it silently. She stopped, tilting and turning her head, as if looking for someone. Or perhaps looking at a room she knew she shouldn't be in. In shadows she began to walk. There was nothing under her arm. Whatever it was that she had carried when she'd run in terror along the dark corridor was not there. The child walked through shadows. Vague outlines of furniture appeared and were passed. Then she stopped and stood looking up at something.

Suddenly Katie was the child, and it was she who stood looking up. Her heart leaped in delight. It was a beautiful doll, sitting on the dresser, its back against the mirror. It had dark, glossy hair pulled back into an arrangement that had a lovely curved comb holding it. Her eyelashes were long, black, and curled. A soft smile was permanently fixed on her lips, and dimples in her rosy cheeks. She was wearing a dress made of ivory lace, with long sleeves. Small slippers, set with pearls, peeped out from under the scalloped, lacy hem.

It seemed the doll looked down at her. Katie felt the pull of its eyes. She stood on her tiptoes. Her hands reached up, even though her mind cried a warning, no, no. Her hands, as if they belonged to some other willful and disobedient little girl, touched its waist and felt the soft body. It felt just like a real person.

No, no. She mustn't.

She lifted it. She had lifted it before. Katie, in her two minds, understood. Katie the child wanted the doll, wanted it desperately. She had never seen anything so lovely in all her life, even when she went to the stores with her mother. Even when they walked along the street and looked at the fine lady mannequins in the shop windows.

She held the doll against her heart. It was large, and its feet hung almost to the floor. She loved it with all her heart. Oh, what a fine doll. Perhaps her mother could make a new gown for the doll, so she could dress and dress it again. But no, where would she get the lace to make another gown so that it would have two gowns?

She heard the footsteps, the terror filled her. They were like the steps of a giant who walked over a hollow floor. She whirled. She saw the shadowy figure. Tall, towering, surrounded by shadows. The woman came closer, and the child's hands became useless. The doll dropped to the floor. Its head made a popping sound against the wood.

The woman in the apron stooped, picked up the doll, and checked to see if it was broken.

Katie felt the pain in the slap across the child's cheek.

The child ran, and once again Katie was the observer. She saw the pale curls bouncing, she saw the long corridor. Then, the child went down a long flight of stairs that were guarded by heavy, carved banisters. She disappeared in the darkness of a lower hall.

The vivid scene was gone. She saw only the familiar items in her apartment.

Katie stared at the faint tracks of light that came through the blind from a street lamp.

She turned on a light and sat with her hands shaking. She clenched them together, frowning at nothing, trying to understand what was happening to her.

As they'd arranged last night, Nancy arrived at noon in her old station wagon, loaded down with suitcases in the back, her kids strapped in wherever there happened to be room and a seat belt. They were quiet and subdued for a change. Nancy seemed happier than Katie had seen her in a long time. That, at least, was a comfort.

"We'll follow," Nancy laughed, "wherever you lead us. I hope your ghost hasn't materialized again."

Katie smiled, but couldn't laugh with her sister. Since her experience last night, she was beginning to feel that it definitely connected with the old mansion, where the banisters were heavy, carved, dark. Higher than a small child's hand.

"Okay. I'll try not to get separated from you, but in case I do, I've drawn a map." She handed through the station wagon window a map with the route marked through the city's south edge, and to the adjoining town that had been a town before suburbs were built.

"It's very much like being in the country outside a small town," Katie said. "As if you were a century away from a city." A century? That wasn't what she had meant to say. "I mean, a hundred miles. It's so isolated. You'll love it."

She hoped Nancy would love it. She was sure the kids would.

Katie got into her car, fastened her seat belt, and started the engine. She drove carefully, her mind replaying and replaying the scenes she had observed in the night. Trying to understand.

After his office opened, Katie had called Dr. Firman. But he had no opening today. Tomorrow, though, she could see him. She wanted to tell him the strangeness of feeling that at times she was an observer, and at other times she was the child.

She turned on the radio to keep her thoughts off the little girl. She hadn't seen the child's face. Dr. Firman felt certain the child was her. But it had occurred to her that the child's hair, always long, lovely, and carefully arranged in ringlets that hung down her back, did not resemble the pictures she had seen of herself when she was five years old and younger. Her own hair, though naturally blond when she was a child, hadn't had that platinum sheen.

IT WAS EXACTLY as she'd remembered it. The tall trees with thick, ancient trunks grew as if they had been spaced carefully at one time. As if, as was probably so, a gardener had thinned the forest, leaving room between for each lovely old oak, maple, sycamore, pine, elm, and others Katie could not identify.

The large house with stone walls and vines covering much of it, with porches whose white paint had peeled away, leaving a patina of gray, looked as if it had grown there among the old forest trees. The driveway was still visible. The old barn had turned the same soft gray, its paint peeled away in long slashes. The carriage house with the open front looked as if the whole roof sagged inward. Fix it, Katie told herself. The shack beyond the trees that edged the driveway looked warmly familiar. This was home.

A tightness went out of her chest. She hadn't been aware that she'd been holding her whole body in such a strain. Why had she waited to come back? It was here she belonged. This was home.

It was as if her life began and ended here, a place that encapsulated all that was important to her. Was this the way it felt to buy one's own house and land? This total feeling of having come home at last?

She got out of the car and stood looking around, emotions so strong, so confused, bringing tears to her eyes. She closed her eyes briefly to push the tears back, and felt the mix of unidentified emotions wane.

She had come home.

Erica watched the changes go past the car window. She saw mostly trees, at first, and then a big wall with narrow dark windows, porches, vines.

Mama guided the station wagon along the narrow road in the trees and pulled in behind Aunt Katie's car and stopped.

Erica was suddenly so eager to get out she unfastened her belt and tumbled out even before Mama turned off the switch, leaving the door standing open. She and Curtis could yell here, if they wanted to. There were no neighbors. Not for a long ways. They could run, too, all they wanted. Aunt Katie had told them so. Her footsteps pounded merrily across the boards of the porch at the side of the house.

She tried the door.

Nancy yelled, laughing, "Wait until Aunt Katie unlocks it, Erica! Don't tear it down!"

Aunt Katie came from her car, digging into her shoulder bag and bringing out a funny-looking long key.

"Actually, I don't even have a key for that door. It may never be opened. Until we get a locksmith."

"What's a locksmith?" Erica cried, coming down the steps, her loose blouse flying like the skirts of a short dress.

"Someone who fixes locks," Nancy said.

Following her mother's gaze, Erica looked up toward the peaks of rooflines, toward narrow windows on the second and third floor.

"My gosh, Katie," Nancy said. "I had no idea ..."

Aunt Katie looked scared suddenly. "What?" she asked, stopping to look back at Nancy.

'When you said it was a big house, you didn't say how tall it was!"

Aunt Katie laughed as if she were relieved about something. "I don't know how tall it is. Didn't I say three stories?"

"Not that I heard. And there's an attic on top of that, which probably has bats."

"Bats won't hurt you, Mama," Erica hastened to say. She knew all this because of nature shows she had watched, and books she had read. "They will only dive at you in the summertime. They won't hurt you."

She didn't want Mama to get scared and take them back to Grandma's and Pop-Pop's. Even though she loved them, and missed them already, she wanted to see what Aunt Katie's house looked like.

Aunt Katie led the way around to the front door. It was the biggest door Erica had ever seen, with a half-moon arrangement of spindles at the top. Erica listened as Aunt Katie explained to Mama the many attempts the builder had made to make a merely large, stonewalled house look Victorian. She fit the key into the lock and turned it. Erica and Curtis gathered close behind, and were quiet as they waited.

The door opened, silently, easily.

"What?" Nancy joked. "No long squeal of old, rusted hinges?"

Aunt Katie entered, pushing the door open. Erica followed her and stood looking.

It was like going into an old theater that had the dimmest lights and the balcony facing the wrong direction. There were no rugs on the floors. Everything looked dark.

The door opened wider and the light filtered in. Ahead was a long hallway that reached way back into darkness.

"It isn't dusty back here at all," Aunt Katie said. "Being a hundred yards or so back from a paved street, and so many trees between, there's just no dust to gather."

"Great," Nancy said. "That helps a housekeeper."

"Mama—Aunt Katie—" Erica asked, "can we look in those rooms?"

"Look wherever you want," Aunt Katie said, "but be careful upstairs. Don't crawl through the banister, don't climb them, that sort of thing."

Curtis started running, his sandals slapping the wood floor loudly. Erica grabbed his shirt tail and yanked him back.

From somewhere far away in the house it sounded like another little boy running. When Erica yelled at Curtis to wait, her voice was like many children shouting, on the second floor, on the third, returning from many rooms whose doors stood open. As if waiting for them.

"Don't touch anything!" Mama called, as Erica followed Curtis up the big stairway in the front room. "Be careful going up and down the stairs! Mind Aunt Katie, and stay away from the banisters!"

"We'll be careful," Erica promised, as she looked upward and climbed.

When they reached the funny little open room halfway up the stairs, Erica looked through the banister.

Aunt Katie was standing down the dark hall looking at the floor. Just standing and looking down, as if she had forgotten what she was doing, as if something important lay there.

But Erica saw nothing.

Just bare floor. Not even a rug.

CHAPTER 30

$\mathcal{N}$ancy's first impression of the house when she entered the tall front door behind Katie was of a smothering lack of light, of eerie shadows suggesting shapes, figures, and deeper, waiting darknesses. As she stood blinking, she had to admit to herself that she'd envisioned a house with lots of room, but lots of windows, too. The enormous foyer had two windows on each side of the solid door, but they were darkened by old velvet drapes.

"Let's leave this door open so we can see what we're doing," Katie said. "You get used to it when you're in here a while. Isn't it great, Nan?"

"Fantastic," Nancy said, although she could see nothing but a long hall reaching straight back to a series of closed doors.

This was the hall where Katie said the ghost had dropped the butcher knife. If there ever had been a knife, it was gone. Katie was not a liar, but the story she had told was too outrageous to believe. Nancy had wondered over and over what was happening to Katie. She was torn between thinking Katie was having mental problems, and believing her story. Especially now that she saw how dark and dreary the house really was.

The stairway, though, was lovely, in a massive way. It rose from the center of the foyer to a landing halfway up, before going on to the second floor. The kids at the moment were trying out an old sofa that sat on the landing, bouncing, testing, discussing.

Nancy yelled up at them, "Stop that! Those are probably antiques, and could fall apart. Erica, remember, don't touch anything!"

Overhead, surrounding the foyer on the second floor, was a balcony. The white spindles of the railing looked thin and ghostly. White? She looked again. No, they were mahogany, like the rest of the woodwork.

Nancy added to the kids, "Don't get close to the balcony!" Then to Katie, "Lord. Is it going to be worse here than it was at Mom's? Always having to watch what they do? I had no idea there were so many antiques left in the house."

"Don't worry about it," Katie said. "They'll settle down in a couple of days. Most of the furniture, anyway, is in these front rooms, I think. So far as I know. Almost as if it was for show at one time, rather than because the owner of the house loved to fill her rooms."

"Katie, don't hesitate to tell them what you expect."

"I expect everyone to be as happy as possible. Including you, Nan, so relax. The first thing to do," Katie said, "is get your luggage in. Right?"

The kids came running down from the landing, and Nancy stopped them.

"Come on, kids, help get things in. Too much of that stomping around will give that ghost a headache." Why had she said that? Erica looked at her wide-eyed. "And me, too," Nancy added.

Katie laughed. "Your mommy is just kidding, kids. There's really no ghost."

It was a relief to go back outside. Spills of sunshine through the trees, on the path, were like melting gold. Nancy just wanted to stand there and let it warm her. She dreaded going back inside.

Okay, stop this, Nancy told herself. What are you, one of those women never satisfied, no matter where you are? Perry had said so. "You wouldn't be satisfied even if we bought a house," were his exact words.

"You'd want something else."

She had shouted back at him, "That's unfair, Perry Allen, have you ever given me anything but the necessities?" She saw immediately she had made a mistake. Hit his pride right in the groin. Wrong choice of words on both sides, never to be forgotten. But maybe he was right. Maybe she really wanted to go back to school, choose a career, now that her children would both soon be in school.

Three trips later, the luggage was all deposited on the second-floor balcony, and Katie led the way to a row of bedrooms down a long hall toward the rear. She opened doors. The kids followed along, their footsteps quick and clattering on the old, darkened wood floor.

"Can I have this room?" Erica asked, looking into a room on the left.

Curtis ran down the hall to a room on the right, shouting, "And this is my room!"

"Oh, no!" Nancy said. "No! You're going to room together."

The kids came back into the hall and stood looking at Nancy with puppy-dog bewilderment, and Katie joined them.

"There are plenty of rooms, Nan," Katie said. "We've got plenty of choices."

Nancy made a vague motion with her hands. "But not just yet. Until we're really settled, I want them together, right next door to me."

They found a room with twin beds. It was a small, barren room with only a nightstand between the two beds, and one window. None of the bedrooms Nancy had looked into had more than one window, and all seemed too dark, too chilled from standing too long unoccupied. The ceilings were high, but the walls were close.

"Notice," Katie said cheerfully, "the lack of dust."

Nancy forced herself to smile.

"I think I'll go see if we left anything in the car."

She escaped outside, and went to the narrow driveway, where the sunshine speckled the flagstones and the weeds that grew in the cracks between each stone. She stood looking and listening. The sounds were so different here. The lonely cawing of crows. Occasional traffic on the two-lane highway beyond the trees. A muffled *thump, thump* beyond the walls, and faraway shouts. The kids were having a ball, now that she was out of the house. After Jane had criticized her for being too lenient, she had come down harder on them, demanding that they be quiet. Now she smiled. She hadn't known she had that much influence on them.

One thing was certain, they had taken to the place immediately. They loved it. She could see it in the open excitement on their faces. More so on Curtis's than on Erica's, but Erica liked it, too. It was probably a great adventure for them. Later, maybe, they'd have time to explore the outdoors. They had never been in the country before. The closest either child had come to nature was the nature trail in the park.

Maybe, she thought, the kitchen would be lighter, more to her liking.

She walked slowly down the old driveway. She began to notice that flat stones, such as had been used to build or surface the outside of the house, had been used for each track of the driveway. Grass grew thinly between the stones and thickly between the tracks. The driveway separated, one going on toward the barn, the other continuing on to the garage with the open front. It made a circle and joined itself again. A tree grew in the center of the circle, large, thick. It shaded most of the garage.

The first section of the garage held an old buggy. It looked tiny, narrow, the leather top and seats cracked and worn. One large spiderlike wheel had collapsed. She looked back toward the house, wishing the kids were here to see this. If she called, they'd never hear her.

She left the garage, noting there were two spots that she and Katie could probably use, if they weren't too narrow for the cars. If the roof held up. There were signs in the soft dark dirt within that a car had once been parked there. Probably long ago, when the wheel bases were narrower.

She went back to the driveway. Dirt tracks, where no grass grew at all, went past the barn and disappeared into the forest. It was like looking into an ancient English forest, and she stood lost in a kind of magic reverie. What a marvelous place Katie had found, she thought. And how fortunate, how lucky Katie was to have found it. Waiting, unsold, after all these years. Katie probably wouldn't have found it if she hadn't been in real estate herself. How odd that no one else had bought it.

She turned toward the house and saw it rising tall within the trees of its yard, and a thought struck her. It was as if Katie had been meant to get this place.

There were so many coincidences that had sent her in this direction. First, her job. Second, she had seen the property from the air. Then Ethan was killed, leaving her enough money to invest. Then ... this property, again. And here she was. She had come to it as if it were waiting just for her. The coincidences were unnerving, and had a dark quality that took away Nancy's pleasure.

She walked slowly back to the house, thinking of Katie, and the way she'd changed since she'd found this place. Her nightmares had started then, hadn't they: She had become so—so *inward,* it seemed to Nancy. Practically accusing Mom of having put her in a dangerous situation when she was a child.

Nancy walked back to the house with a sense of reluctance. She went to the path that led to the back porch. Heavy old vines grew like twisting tree trunks, or thick, brown scaly snakes, up the corners of the porch, spreading their vines on the roof, sending tendrils on up the walls of the house. Some of the vines almost covered windows of the second and third stories. The rooflines reached above the treetops, sharp and steep.

She climbed the porch steps. The boards were solid in most places. She'd have to tell the kids to watch the boards that weren't.

The porch was almost like a room, closed in by vines. Like the house, it was shadowed, and seemed permanently without enough light.

The kitchen door had a glass. There was another door, she noticed, near the far end of the long porch, but it was a solid door and the color of the stone wall and almost invisible.

She tried the door with the glass and found it unlocked.

Yes, she'd been right. The kitchen was long and gloomy and very silent. To her left was a massive black cast-iron cookstove, exactly the kind of stove a house modernized around the turn of the twentieth century would have had. Beside it, almost eclipsed by the cookstove, was a gas range, white and bright. She almost giggled at the incongruity.

To her right was a fireplace even larger than the cookstove. It had probably been used for cooking before the stove. Nearby was a window, a rocking chair, and a small table with an old oil lamp with a fringed shade.

In the center of the room was a long table covered with oilcloth. Several candles stood in the center in individual holders. Chairs had been pushed neatly up beneath the table, only their ladder backs showing.

She turned and found long cabinets reaching all the way to the high ceiling. She would need a ladder to get up there. Beneath a window looking out onto the porch was, of all things, a sink. There was even a strange, old, single faucet. The countertop was wood, like a cutting board.

She turned again, and saw several doors, all closed except the one at the end and another in the center, which opened onto a shadowy central hall. Through the one at the end she saw things that indicated a laundry room, with tubs turned sideways, an ironing board, set up, an old sewing machine, and old-fashioned dressmaking form draped with a grayed sheet.

She heard footsteps and whirled, her pulse leaping frantically. Katie came through the open door that led to the hall.

"Isn't it great?" Katie said, her eyes shining. She motioned. "Everything here. Look, there's even a cooking pot on the stove."

Nancy looked at the black stove and saw an equally black cast-iron pot about three times larger than any pot she'd ever seen before.

Nancy said, "That thing's big enough to cook a whole pig."

"God, what a horrible thing to say!" Katie cried.

Nancy looked at her. What did I say?, she wondered. People cooked pigs. Katie still had a strange look of distaste on her face. Slowly, as she stared at the pot, her features distorted, her expression changing to one of pain and fear. Her mouth opened in a childish droop as she continued to stare at the black pot.

"What are you doing?" the child enquired, looking up, standing on tiptoes, trying futilely to see into the big pot.

You silly little goose, I'm cooking. What does it look like I'm doing?"

The woman stood cutting potatoes she hadn't peeled into the big pot on the stove. Her pretty apron, a different one today, brushed against the front of the stove, but she didn't seem to notice the heat. The child could feel the heat even where she stood.

"But what are you cooking?" she asked.

"Here, I'll show you."

The woman turned and lifted her, and held her over the open pot. Hot steam bathed her face.

"See?" the woman said.

She saw in the steam of the pot the face of the pig whose belly she had scratched yesterday. It stared up at her, its eyes glazed, open, its little snout open, its tongue sticking up, thick and swollen. Its small body was curled in among the vegetables, with its skin and hair intact. Help me, it cried in silence, help me.

She began to scream and fight the woman. Something inside her heart tore away, leaving it raw and bleeding in terrible pain. She screamed, screamed, and pushed at the woman's face with her hands. She reached toward the piggy in the boiling water and felt the tips of her fingers burn.

The woman dropped her to the floor. She kept screaming, kept trying to reach the pig. The hot stove burned her arms. She couldn't reach the pig, and the woman was laughing and laughing.

She ran, toward the soft darkness of the inner hall. No matter how far she ran, she heard the woman laughing.

"Oh, my God!" Kate cried. "Oh my God!" She turned, wanting to run away, too, from the horror of the image. She kept turning, turning, feeling the pain of the child, the horror of seeing the pig's face in the big pot.

She felt someone's hands grabbing her. She fought away. *The woman, the woman with the apron. The terrible woman—she had to get away—hide somewhere.*

"Katie! Katie! What's wrong?"

Slowly Katie recognized Nancy, and clutched her close. They stood hugging each other as Katie grew less agitated.

Katie felt Nancy patting her on the back, as she would pat Erica or Curtis.

"I'm sorry," Nancy said. "I just didn't think about what I was saying."

Katie drew a deep breath, broke away, and sat down at the table.

"It was the little girl again, Nancy. It was as if I had gone back in time, and I was that little girl. A terrible, awful thing."

"Tell me." Nancy sat down, too, turning one of the chairs sideways to the table.

"It was here, she is so small. I could even feel the heat from the stove. The woman was cutting potatoes she hadn't peeled into the pot. I—the child asked her what she was cooking. She picked me up. There was a pig, looking up at me. I—it seemed to be one of a group of pet pigs. A pig I—she—the child had loved. It was horrible."

Nancy's face had turned pale, a sickly color, and Katie wished she hadn't told her.

"What was it, Katie? A hallucination? A delusion of some kind? It couldn't have been a memory!"

Katie shook her head. "I don't know. I do know I have to find out or I'll lose my mind, Nancy. That's the first time I've seen any familiar thing—like a stove—the stove, this one, and that pot. But I saw it. I was here, Nancy. I *must* have been. When I was a child." She paused. "Oh, God—it's so confusing. It's so real, the child is so real. I was her, this time. It was me. I was looking through her eyes. Feeling her feelings."

"But that's not possible, Katie." Nancy looked around at the kitchen. "It's not possible that you were ever here. I was never here before, and we were never separated."

Katie stood up, her frustration edged suddenly with anger. She slapped the table with her hand. "Why do you keep saying that? I know I was here! I know it! The—the memory was too real, too vivid. I did not imagine it. Nancy, I remember it. I remember being here, and a woman lifting me to look into that pot! It was horrible, what I saw in there!"

Nancy sat shaking her head. "But Katie ... I was with you. I remember when you were born. I tell you, I've never seen this house before. You were never away from me. Katie—"

"You're lying to me. You and Mama both, you *must* be lying to me. Everything I see here is so familiar. I must have been here when I was a child."

Katie turned away, and repeated it for the third time, knowing that in her heart she was now beginning to believe it.

"You're lying to me."

She stopped. Yet many other times, she remembered, she had seen the child as if she herself were an observer. The child had long, pale silvery blond ringlets, and she had felt then the child was not herself.

"Oh, God!" she said again, bringing her hands to her head. "I don't know anything anymore. I'm sorry, Nancy. I just don't know. I just don't know ..."

THE BED WASN'T COMFORTABLE. The mattress had been leaning on its side against the wall. The springs on the bed were old and rusted and uncovered. Nancy had helped put the mattress back on the bed, just as Katie had helped Nancy arrange her bed. Hours had passed, and all Katie had managed to do was squirm.

She wished she had gone back to her apartment. She had rent paid on it for another week. But Nancy had looked as if her eyes grew with each degree of darkness, and the candlelight had made them absolutely enormous. Katie had seen Nancy's nervousness. She wouldn't have been able to spend this first night alone here with only the kids, and not even a telephone yet.

The telephone company had promised to be out tomorrow to install a temporary line. Katie knew what construction promises amounted to. But for Nancy's sake, particularly, she hoped the telephone was put in.

She thought of the front bedroom where she had slept briefly once before. Had she imagined having the tatted, or crocheted, spread pulled over her face? She knew that bed was made up with sheets and quilts, and the room was large and furnished, probably with the original furniture, while the other rooms were like half-draped skeletons.

But she couldn't have gone back to that room. She had no desire to go where a woman, it had seemed so vividly, had pulled the bedspread up over her face. For a creation of her own mind, the woman had certainly seemed real.

As real as the child.

Dr. Firman was so convincing. "Your own mind, Katie—the mind is so strange and so powerful, and so protective of repressed memories. It will give them up bit by startling bit."

She felt the soft waves of sleep beckoning, and covered her face with her arm gratefully.

The two kids were safe, together, in one room, Katie thought as she drifted away. And Nancy, in the next room. They were sandwiched between the adults, like birds that sit side-by-side on a limb at night, the four of them had gathered closely in a house where numerous bedrooms waited to be seen.

In her dreams, Katie heard the laughter of the woman. Once again she was the child running, running, hearing the laughter of the woman behind her. Fear choked her. No matter how far she ran, down long, shadowy corridors, seeking a way out, the laughter followed.

Katie woke, trying to breathe, and for that instance of wakening the laughter continued, coming from somewhere within the thick walls of the house.

ERICA OPENED HER EYES.

Someone was laughing—it was a scary, eerie sound, like a witch might make. At first she thought it was on television in the darkened living room where Pop-Pop watched after bedtime. Then she saw a candle burning on the table between her bed and Curtis's, and remembered where she was.

She lay still, listening, and the laughter faded.

But it left a feeling in the house that made her want to cry out for the warm protection of her parents.

"Daddy—Mama—" she murmured under her breath, just moving her tongue, so dry and thick feeling. Making no sound, not even a whisper.

Daddy ...

CHAPTER 31

*K*atie walked into the doctor's office, relieved to be here at last, and yet nervous and uneasy, the way she'd felt since the experience in the kitchen, seeing the dead pig, hearing the laughter in the night. Dr. Firman rose from behind his desk, as always, and came around to take her hand.

"Are you all right?" he asked.

She made an effort to smile. "Yes, I'm all right." They took their places, he behind the desk with the tape recorder, and she in the chair. She had not yet used the recliner he had offered in the beginning.

"You've moved into your new house," he said, as if trying to make a bit of small talk. "You must be feeling very good about that."

She hesitated. Her feelings were still so confused.

"I feel at home there. Though there are rooms I haven't seen and doors I haven't opened yet. I really don't know what most of the house even looks like. I haven't even been on the third floor."

"Sounds like you've got quite an adventure ahead."

"I hope I don't find the floors have fallen through or something. I have a dread of discovering a leaky roof."

"You don't have a telephone yet, you said."

"No, but that's one thing we're going to be getting right away. They're coming this afternoon to string a temporary wire in. We'll have a phone in the foyer, at least. Then, when the trench is dug for the other cables, the telephone cable will be buried, too. Maybe we can get phones in other parts of the house."

"It all takes a lot of time."

"Yes, there isn't enough competition." She settled back, comfortable with this topic, so common at the office. "The construction company keeps putting me off. It'll be another few weeks, they say now. But," she added, "we'll have a telephone. And the kids are having fun in the house."

"Oh, yes, your niece and nephew."

"Yes." She looked down at her hands.

"Tell me about what happened in the kitchen."

She described the scene she had called him about. She attempted to describe the horror of being lifted to look down into the big, black cooking pot, the horror of seeing the little pig's face, its body. Hearing it cry out to her in its awful silence.

"It was vivid," she said in a low voice, hearing its tremble. "I know I was not dreaming this up. I'm sure I wasn't. I was that child. I saw that little piggy face. The woman lifted me. I felt her strong arms. And I dreamed of her laughter, all night. I kept waking, hearing that laughter."

"You spent an uncomfortable night."

"It wasn't—wasn't good. I'd go to sleep, and hear that laughter and wake up. It was as if it were in the house somewhere, echoing."

"Your sister was with you when you had the vision the memory in the kitchen?"

Katie nodded. "She said it wasn't possible that I had ever been there. She remembers those early years that I don't. She is adamant that I was never in the house. We were never apart, she says."

"What do you think?"

Katie hesitated. "I accused her of lying." Katie looked down. "Of course I immediately apologized."

"You know, she's only partly correct," Dr. Firman suggested softly. "Since she is five years older, she was apart from you when she went to school, right?"

Katie looked up. Why hadn't she brought that up to Nancy? "Yes."

"Let's say she started school, first grade, at age six, as most children do. She would have been away from you all day. For the next four or five school years, you were separated during the day."

Kate drew a deep breath.

"Do you know where you were while she was in school?"

"With my mother."

"But you don't remember any of that."

"No."

Kate sat looking at her hands. She no longer felt she could trust anyone. Nancy hadn't lied to her. But had Jane tried to hide something?

She had been in that kitchen, she was positive! Even now she could see the face of that pitiful little creature in the black cooking pot. She could feel the heat of the stove, and the rising steam.

"I was in that kitchen, Doctor. The big woman who wore the apron held me up to look in at the pig. She laughed at me because I cried."

"All right," he said, "let's talk about that woman for a moment. She's the same one you saw as a ghost?"

"Yes."

"The apron represents a mother figure. The woman is someone you've been in the house with, alone, many times. The house is large, or at least seemed large to you. The corridors are long. But what does this mean to you?"

Katie shook her head. "I don't know. I don't understand."

"The pig—the face of the pig—have you ever had a pet pig?"

"No, not that I remember. Not at all. It's as—as if this little girl is sometimes me, and sometimes someone I'm only observing. Once I saw her hair. It was long and pale blond, platinum blond, almost silver. It was carefully arranged in long ringlets that hung almost to her waist."

"You *saw* this?"

"Yes, and I looked at old pictures of myself, Doctor, and my hair was not like that. My mom has pictures of Nancy and me ranging back to infancy. My hair was not that long, nor was it that color."

Dr. Firman looked puzzled. For a silent moment they looked at each other. She felt as if he were trying to look into her mind.

He said, "Would you be willing to try hypnosis, Katie?"

"Yes," she said, after a hesitation. Hypnosis was merely intense concentration, in which memories were not shrouded by some psychic curtain. Dr. Firman had already assured her of that.

He stood up, came around the desk, and put his hand on the back of the recliner.

'Just try to get comfortable here, with your feet up. I want you very relaxed."

She moved to the recliner and leaned back. The footstool rose, lifting her feet to a comfortable angle. She felt his hand on her forehead. It was cool, the touch light.

'Just look at the spiral hanging in the corner, Katie. I'll turn on this little fan —and the air will cause the spiral to rotate. Just relax, watch it carefully ..."

His voice was so soothing. She had not noticed before the spiral hanging from the ceiling. It appeared to be made of thin golden ribbons that undulated as it moved, turning one way, then back the other. Turning, turning ... unraveling ...

Dr. Firman's voice behind her was as gentle and soothing as the trailing ribbons of gold.

"You're very relaxed now, Katie. You're a child, five years old ..."

She was going up the steps to school, her hand in Nancy's. She had waited a long time to start to real school. Last year she had gone to nursery school, and had learned to sit at a table with other children, in chairs that were made for little kids.

"What do you see?" the soothing voice asked.

"I'm going to school. Nancy's holding my hand."

"Just relax, Katie, we're going back farther, farther. You're younger now. Four ... three ..."

She saw a playground with lots of swings, slides. She ran to a slide and looked up. "Mama won't let me. She's coming after me ..."

"Yes, Katie. Why is she coming after you?"

"The ladder is too high. She says I'm too little to climb, to use this slide." The memory was pleasant, even as her mother took her hand and urged her away.

"Is your mother wearing an apron, Katie?"

"No. No. Jeans. Shirt."

"Relax, Katie, farther, deeper. We're going back ..." Katie slipped through childhood backwards, feeling the world grow huge and mysterious. Feeling the softness of blankets, and a warm, comforting cradling of mother's arms. She slipped backwards rapidly, as if being drawn more and more swiftly into a long, dark tunnel.

Then suddenly she stood in light. Dappled sunlight came through the trees. She crawled through the wood rails of a fence, calling. "Edward? Edward? Where are you, Eddie?"

"Katie," a voice said from far away, touching only a part of her mind. "Where are you?"

"I'm ... at ... the barnyard. I'm looking for Eddie. I call Eddie ... he can't answer. But he can hear me."

"Eddie? Why can't he answer?"

"He—can't—talk. Eddie can't talk. I love Eddie. Eddie's good."

She saw Eddie through the railings of the pigpen. He was squatting in the midst of the three pigs. Smiling, he motioned to her. She went to him, and sat on her heels, just as Eddie was doing. The three pigs lay sprawled, grunting, *uh, uh, uh*, in lazy pleasure. She began to scratch their tummies ... they stretched, their little fat legs straight up in the air. *Uh, uh, uh* ...

"The pigs—the pigs—"

"Where are you, Katie?"

The scene changed. She was in the shadowed room looking again at the beautiful doll. She had brought Eddie to see it. "*It's Miss Theodora's*" she said. "*Once she let me touch it, hold it.*" she told Eddie. Eddie nodded soberly. But then she saw he made a face. He didn't like the doll? He made motions she didn't understand. She watched him closely. He pointed down, underground.

209

Then he motioned with the flat of his hand, short, shorter than she. Little people, from underground. Bad, ugly. What did he mean?

He pulled her away from the shadowed room, away from the doll.

In a way, he was like her mama. When she had told her mama that once Miss Theodora had let her hold the beautiful doll, but now she got angry when she even looked at it, Mama had not been understanding. Stay away, she had said. If Miss Theodora doesn't want you to touch the doll, you stay away from it.

"Where are you, Katie? What is it Miss Theodora let you touch?"

The voice seemed more penetrating, but the part of her brain that heard it was paralyzed, numb, asleep. *Katie? No, not Katie. My name is not Katie …*

The scene changed again, rapidly. She was squatting beside Eddie, watching. His long fingers worked quickly, putting the rags together, forming a rounded top, tying a strip of cloth to make a neck. He had turned flowers on the face so they made round eyes, and a funny mouth that was a large red nose. She laughed, holding out the side strips of the doll.

"An angel. It makes an angel with wings. It will keep me safe, always. Safe from the Bad Things."

"What bad thing, Katie?"

"The Bad Things."

"Katie …"

No, that wasn't her name. Not Katie. No one had ever called her Katie. The voice she kept hearing was calling someone else.

The scene changed again.

She was in a corridor, the rag doll under her arm. She reached the end, where the tall wardrobe stood, and looked at the closed door. She listened. She could hear a movement beyond the door, on the step.

"Eddie?" she spoke aloud, timidly.

There was no answer, but the movement paused, as if whoever was beyond the door had stopped to listen. Eddie couldn't answer. Then it moved again, brushing the door. Her skin prickled and strained across her forehead and the back of her neck. If Eddie had gone into the room beyond the door, was he dragging something? She only wanted to peek. An order flitted through her mind. *Never open a closed door,* her papa had said, *always knock first and wait to be invited in.*

But Eddie couldn't invite her in.

She stretched up, stood on her toes to reach the doorknob. The knob was larger than her hand. She needed both hands to open the door. She would have to lay her angel doll down, and use both hands. She didn't want to lay Angel down. She never laid Angel down. Maybe if she called again, Eddie would hear her. If Eddie heard her, he would open the door for her. She paused to listen. The soft movements had begun again. *"Eddie? Is that you, Eddie?"*

She waited, but the door didn't open.

Maybe he didn't want her to come in. Maybe it was Miss Theodora ... maybe ...

She only wanted to peek.

She had seen the door close, as if wiping out a long strip of darkness, just as she opened the other door at the end of the long, shadowy corridor. She stood looking into a place she had seen only one other time. She had seen the door shut slowly and quietly.

She laid her angel dolly down and stretched up, using both hands.

The door opened upon its strip of darkness with no sound. Stone steps led down from the door into total dark. Something slid across them toward the narrow opening made by the door.

Black figures moved upward. A black, flat head with cold slits for eyes darted forward. The snout opened and a long, forked tongue shot toward her. Its tip stung her hand like a poison nettle.

She cried out and whirled away, running, leaving the door standing a few inches open. Terror filled her, surrounded her. But she had left Angel ...

... Left Angel.

She had to go back and get Angel.

She turned back, running. Her doll lay in the shadows between the door and wall, its bright colors like a crushed flower on the dark floor. Beyond it the Bad Thing moved, rising higher in the doorway, coming up the steps from the dark below.

She had to get Angel.

"Katie! Katie!"

She had to get Angel.

"Katie! Wake up, Kate! Katie, wake up!"

Terror drove her heart, pounded in her temples. She gasped for breath, aware of a change in her surroundings. She turned her head from side to side. She was cold, yet her face felt damp.

She became aware that someone was putting a cold, damp cloth on her face. She looked up and saw the face of a man. His cheekbones were prominent, his forehead broad. Dark hair slipped down toward his eyebrows. But his eyes were kind, concerned ...

She blinked rapidly and recognized Dr. Firman.

His face had blanched to the color of some of the old, old sheets she had found in the dresser drawers at Wickham House.

"Are you all right?" he asked.

She nodded, gasping for breath, the memory of her experience vivid in her mind.

"Thank God." He looked faint for a moment, then color rushed back into his face. "I thought for a minute—" He stopped, measured her pulse at the wrist. "Your pulse is surprisingly slow. Are you sure you're all right?"

She nodded, and leaned forward so that her chair came up and she was no longer reclining. Dr. Firman moved back to sit on the edge of his desk. He watched her closely.

"Doctor," she said, seeing and feeling the fear of the child who had run back after her rag doll, "Is it possible that I've lived before? That I lived two childhoods?"

CHAPTER 32

$\mathcal{K}$atie heard a clock ticking in the silence of the doctor's office. She had never heard it before. He had moved again and stood somewhere behind her chair. She couldn't see him.

She wanted no more of hypnosis. Perhaps it was only intense concentration, a delving into the depths of a mind, but how far back did the mind reach? She rose and returned to the chair in front of the desk.

"I thought I was losing you," Dr. Firman said. "I admit, I felt I had lost control."

She shook her head, and then a terrifying thought came to her mind. "What would have happened?" she asked. "If you—if I—hadn't been able to return?"

He went to his chair, sat down, took a drink of water. Color was returning to his face full force, making him look flushed. He poured a glass of water for her.

"I've never had a patient I couldn't wake up. You were the most difficult, Katie. But your pulse was slowing, becoming dangerously slow. Since your blood pressure wasn't being monitored, I have no way of knowing if that was dropping, too. But I would guess it was. Another heartbeat and I would have called Emergency. You scared me."

"You didn't answer my question."

"There is no record of a patient remaining in hypnosis. It's impossible. Hypnosis is only a deepened state of relaxation.

"If that's all it is," she said, "why were you so concerned?"

"Because—it was as if you had gone over an edge. I'm a psychoanalyst, not a psychiatrist. I admit, you caused me to feel I should have sent you to a psychiatrist. And perhaps—"

"No. You still didn't answer my question."

He looked at her, silent. His skin was mottled. She wondered if the hypnosis had drained him of energy, as it had her.

"The question I was referring to, Doctor, was, is it possible that I have lived two childhoods?"

They engaged in a staring contest. It seemed again to Katie the doctor was trying to see into her brain before he dared make a decision. Then he spoke slowly.

"I have never known of a proved case of reincarnation. I'm not a believer. The brain, at conception, is nonexistent. It develops during the fetal stage. You know all that. How is it a fully developed brain, no matter how complex, could reach into the life of another brain that is long dead?"

She didn't bother to try an answer. Something in the air? She almost giggled, but knew if she did, she would start crying hysterically. It was no joke. Not to her, who felt the fear of the child.

"I'm beginning to believe it didn't happen in *my* lifetime, Dr. Firman."

"What, exactly, makes you believe that? Is it something visual that you see? Something that can prove another time, an earlier time?"

"The child's hair. I saw it once, as an observer. It was worn in an old style. Also, her dress was long. Almost to her ankles. She was barefoot. The apron the woman wears, exactly like the one the ghost wore that night."

"All right, let's go back to the ghost. You saw her clearly, you said. You saw her face?"

"Yes—quite—" She hesitated. "I remember her eyes were like dark slits. Heavy lidded. Sunken cheeks. Graying hair pulled severely back. Of course, it was very shadowed. Almost dark. The light was very dim. Even the next morning in the hallway when she, uh, evaporated."

"Doesn't that tell you something?"

No. "What?"

"In the light of day she disappeared. Your dream mind couldn't keep her real."

She tried to assimilate it all.

"Then you're saying none of this is real? How can something so real be unreal? If I made up the ghost, then I am probably also making up the child. And all the horrors that child is seeing and feeling. I also made up the boy, Eddie, who doesn't speak. Everything."

"Possibly. I would be more inclined to think your mind created it all, possibly influenced by the old house, than I would believe in reincarnation."

"You know, I don't think I told you something I felt. When the ghost disappeared—just before she disappeared—when she looked at me, she saw me for the first time. I had been in the house all night, but she hadn't seen me. Then, in the hallway, she looked straight at me. And fear came to her face. She opened her mouth as if she were screaming. That's when she evaporated. My feelings about that were an incredulous, *she recognized me!*"

"Recognized you?"

"And that scared her."

"That's why she ceased to exist?"

"That's—uh—yes."

Dr. Firman asked that question that was beginning to irritate Katie, "What does that mean to you?"

She felt like yelling at him, *I'm here to find out from you, don't you know that? I want answers from you, not questions.* Still, she knew why he was doing it. He was trying to make her think, answer her own questions, dig into the depths of her own mind.

"It doesn't mean anything to me," she said. "It was an experience I never expected to have. Ghosts are fun things that happen on Halloween. They're not real. Meeting one when you're alone and in a strange old house is unnerving as hell, and finally, Dr. Firman, I'm getting tired of you telling me I didn't see a ghost. I know what I saw."

But to her surprise he smiled. She half expected him to stand up and tell her she should terminate her visits.

"Katie," he said in a soft, kind voice that brought tears to her eyes, "I'm only trying to get you to see reality, that's all. I can see how frightened you are. When you were under hypnosis, you had me worried. I won't be putting you under again, at least, not until we understand this better. And certainly not without a hospital setting."

"I'm sorry," she murmured, brushing away the tears.

"Don't be. It's okay if you get angry at me."

"Well—I tried to think that maybe the ghost was just part of my imagination. And the child, too, and all the rest. Like the vivid—visions—I have while I'm awake and aware of other things, too—at least, in the case of the ghost. But I can't separate the two. I really can't. The other seems so real."

"That's why I believe you're having memories of your own early childhood, Katie. We just need to open this up so your memories are more understandable to you, and when they are they'll become less frightening."

She stared at him, aghast. "A pig cooking in a pot, without ever having been—been skinned? Its face intact and staring at me? As if it were still alive? How could that become less frightening? How could that even be a memory? My God, how could that have ever happened in *my* lifetime?"

"All right, let's say it didn't happen."

"I saw it!"

"You dreamed it, perhaps."

"I—I was awake—standing—" She felt like collapsing. She was scared, she found, in a different way. "Am I losing my mind, Doctor?"

"No, you're not. Let's just look at what you saw in a different way. Let's say it was a symbol of something else that happened in your own lifetime."

He was silent, letting her do the thinking again. She felt tired, exhausted. "What?"

"It's symbolic, Katie."

"Symbolic! Pardon me, Doctor, but symbolic of what? The horrendous habit people have of eating other animals?"

She stopped, stunned at what she had said. What was she headed for? It had not occurred to her not to eat animals.

"What do you think it might be telling you?"

She tried to smile. "Maybe—not to eat other animals, they're too close. No —I'd never thought of that. Not really. You don't understand, Doctor. It *happened*."

Saying it made it true. She knew that scene had happened. Sometime, in that house. She felt as if she were part of the webs that wove the house into the past. The webs that were not in the house, but surrounded it. Invisible, but real.

She couldn't stand any more of this. She turned her face away.

"The telephone is being put in today," she said. "The kids like the house. It's great to see those two happy faces. No matter what part of the house they're in, you can hear them, because their voices carry and echo, and their footsteps on those uncarpeted floors ... " She stopped.

"You're tired, Katie."

"Yes, I am."

"Why don't we end this session? Sometime during the coming week, if you feel like delving into symbols, do so. Talk with your sister and mother. Ask them if they knew a boy named Eddie, who couldn't talk. Ask them if they ever took you to a farm. You know a three- or four- year-old child sees things from a different reality. Something that wouldn't frighten you now at age twenty-five might have terrified you at age three or four or five."

"The child is always the same age," Katie said. "She seems to be four or five. She's smaller than Erica. Smaller than Curtis, I believe. She's five." She said this with utter conviction, and frowned. Where had that knowledge come from? She was no longer comfortable with her own mind.

"Oh, yes—" she said. "And her name is not Katie." She frowned.

There was a pause. Dr. Firman asked quietly, "What is her name?"

Katie said slowly, "I don't know."

. . .

"Erica?" Curtis had turned around and she was gone. Suddenly, he was all alone in this strange room up high in the house, and he was getting scared.

"Erica?"

They had come into this room, where it was almost dark, to see what was there, in the corner. At first, it had been fun. There was a funny old bag of straw on the floor in the corner, and Erica told him it was a straw mattress, like the kind people used a long time ago. He jumped on it, and dust fogged up into his face and made him sneeze. Erica had said, "Stop it, Curtis." But he jumped on it again.

Then, when he turned to look for Erica, she was gone.

He peered cautiously around a tall chest. Sometimes they hid in places like that. But Erica wasn't there.

"Erica! Where are you?"

The tall door was closed. He was so scared now he was about to pee in his pants. He grabbed his pee-pee and held on to it so that it wouldn't wet his pants, and ran to the door. With one hand he struggled with the knob.

It was so dark in the room with the door closed.

Behind him came a sound. Erica, sliding along the wall. Scaring him so much he began to wet.

He turned and looked back.

The darkness moved. Something within it formed a shape, like a black pencil making a mark on black paper. It drew a head that sloped into a long snout. Its eyes were long slits. An arm raised, rounded, but no elbows, no hands, only long, thin fingers of different lengths. In the increasing darkness more and more of them formed and began to ooze toward him, like mud in a pond.

He hunched against the door and began to cry.

The door pushed against him suddenly, and light flowed in. Erica grabbed his arm and pulled him into the hallway.

"Why didn't you follow me, Curtis?"

Then she stared. From his face to his pants.

"What's wrong?" she asked.

He tried to tell her, but his voice kept breaking into bits and pieces. "There —there—monsters, Erica."

She frowned, but didn't laugh. He tried to describe them to her. Strange, long fingers, like jointed worms. Something like lizard fingers, only very, very long. He sobbed and tried to talk even as she pulled him down the hall away from that room.

They went down the stairs from the third floor and paused on the landing halfway down where there were two chairs with padded seats. Erica looked up toward the third floor. This was the first time they had gone up there.

She whispered, "Don't ever go up there again, Curtis."

He shook his head. His pants were all wet now, between his legs and down the inside of each leg. They felt stiff and miserable. His sister took his hand.

"We won't tell Mama," she said, pulling him on down the stairs. "Nor Aunt Katie."

With his hand in hers, she pulled him on into their new bedroom. She dug into his chest of drawers and got a fresh pair of jeans. She tossed them to him.

"Put those on. Normally," she said in her almost important voice, "we would never keep a secret from Mama. But this time we will. We can just put your wet pants down in the laundry room."

He pulled off his wet jeans and pulled on the dry. His undershorts were wet, too, but he endured them rather than changing again.

They left the room, with his jeans rolled and carried in Erica's hand. The hallway was growing darker, it seemed.

He asked, "Erica? Do you like this house?" He paused, but she didn't answer. "I don't like this house, do you?"

Erica waited a long time before she answered. He was ready to ask her again.

"No," she said. "But that's our secret, too, Curtis. Don't tell Mama."

"Why not tell Mama?"

"It would hurt her feelings. And Aunt Katie's. They like this house a whole lot."

"Mom?"

"Nancy? Where are you?"

"I'm here, at home, I guess you could say." It didn't feel like home, this huge old house with all these useless rooms. But with the just installed telephone, maybe she wouldn't feel so trapped. "The telephone man just left. We now have one phone, in the foyer. How about that?"

"You don't sound very cheerful."

"I don't? I was making a real effort, Mom."

"I can hear *that*, which means you aren't. When are you girls going to learn you can't fool Mama? Hmmm?"

Nancy tried to think of something to say in answer, and failed. She drew a deep breath.

"What's wrong?" Jane prodded.

"You mean other than nothing going right? Well, let me give you this phone number first, then I'll tell you all about the house." She gave the number, and heard her mother repeat it slowly as she wrote it down.

"How're the kids?" Jane asked.

"Going wild with freedom. They love it here. All these rooms, and most of them with at least some furniture. It's incredible. Why do you suppose people want what they call a mansion? Just for prestige? Think of Windsor House, a thousand rooms. What do people do with a thousand rooms? Forty or fifty or whatever is here seems to go on forever. I haven't seen the third floor myself, nor some of the second."

"I wouldn't know. I never had a chance to consider whether I wanted a mansion or not. So what don't you like about it? Too much to clean? It must be a mess, being empty since when?"

"I'm not sure. I think people lived in it off and on over the years, trying to buy it, but something always went wrong."

"Went wrong?"

"Well, you know, money."

"Oh. I thought it was such a bargain."

"Really, it is. For the amount of land, as well as the buildings. Katie said the price was just never raised from the original."

"How is Katie?"

"I haven't seen her long enough to find out today. She didn't even eat breakfast. We went downstairs together—the only bathroom is on the ground floor—and made some coffee, then she took off. Said she'd get something somewhere else."

"Probably a doughnut."

"Mom ..."

"I know, leave her alone. She's an adult. But you young ones need to start a good diet early. Saves a lot of anguish later on."

"When are you coming out?"

Jane paused, then said, "I went back to work yesterday, Nancy. It was so quiet here, I just went over to the nursing home and asked them if they needed me, and they gave me a part-time job. Four or five hours a day."

"Doing what?"

"The same thing I did for fifteen years. Nurse's aide. Taking care of the old ones. It kind of scares me now, thinking of what's coming up for Doug and me." Nancy listened as Jane told her about a few of the patients, people she had known from her visits to the nursing home after she'd quit work two years ago. As if Jane over the years had begun to feel at home there, working with people she had known for years, she had gone back regularly as a visitor.

"So many of them are so pathetically glad to see any visitor," Jane said. "They either don't get many visits from relatives—relatives often can't bear to see their loved ones like that, so they put off coming—or they can't remember seeing them."

"You went back to work because we left?" Nancy asked. "I thought you'd be glad to have some time to yourself."

Jane laughed. "I thought so, too." She sobered. "Perry called, madder than a wet wasp that you had moved."

"Well, tough shit," Nancy muttered.

"What?"

"Nothing. What did you tell him?"

"What could I tell him? I told him you'd moved into a house Katie is buying, about an hour's drive away. I couldn't even tell him where."

"Well, he wouldn't come there to see us, he probably wouldn't come here either."

Jane sighed, then asked, "Do you think Katie is going to be all right there, Nancy?"

"Of course, Mom, why not?" Nancy ignored the little pulse of doubt that slipped through her heart like a murmur. "It certainly will keep her busy."

"I hope it's good for her."

"Sure it's good for her." She listened, and heard the kids' voices coming faintly from somewhere above. "What are your hours at work, Mom?"

"Afternoon from twelve-thirty until four-thirty, today. It will vary from day to day. I'll go mainly when they need me, fill in at busy times for nurses who have the day off."

"Then you'd just gotten home when I called."

"Barely came in the door. I'm relieved you have a phone. How far are you from shopping centers?"

"I could walk if I had to. It looks very rural right here, but there's a small town just a few blocks away. A convenience store, that sort of thing. School is okay, too. A bus will come by and stop down on the street at the end of the driveway. Katie found out all this stuff."

"I hope she'll be all right and stop having those nightmares of hers."

Nancy hesitated in answering. What useful purpose would it serve to tell Mom that it was more than nightmares disturbing Katie? That in Nancy's presence, Katie had what she described later to Nancy as a vision of some kind, a vivid memory? Yet it had to do with the pot on the stove, and there was no way it could have been a memory. As long as Nancy lived she would not forget the trance-like stillness of Katie's body. It was as if she froze, looking at the pot on the stove. She would never forget that look of absolute terror on Katie's face, in her eyes. Nor her own sense of helplessness when she'd tried to bring Katie out of it.

"Mom, did you ever have a large black cast-iron cooking pot, with a wire handle?"

"Good Lord, no. Why do you ask?"

"Uh—well, there's one here." She stopped, getting in deeper than she'd planned. "It just—uh—looked familiar."

That was a lie. It didn't look at all familiar to her. It was Katie who had cried, after the trance, the "memory" as she called it, the vision, whatever it was, "I've seen that before! I've seen it before, Nancy! Long ago, when I was small."

Nancy had searched her memory during the night as she lay sleepless. She had never seen one exactly like it before, not even in antique shops where she liked to browse, or in flea markets. It was almost as large as the cast-iron tubs that had years ago been used to boil clothes on washday, the kind used in backyards with a fire underneath. Those tubs had nothing on the rims. This cookpot had a bail handle for carrying.

"What is it, Nancy? Is something wrong?"

"Nothing, Mom. When are you coming out?"

"In a couple of weeks. We'll let you get good and settled. Doug's sister and husband are coming next weekend, so we'll be busy with them."

"Good. That sounds like fun. Well, gotta go. Have to light some candles, it's getting dark. I have to start cooking something to eat, too. Any suggestion? Quickly?"

"What do you have on hand?"

"Not much. We haven't gone shopping."

"Potatoes? Onions? Milk? Meat?"

"We don't have a fridge, Mom, remember? No electricity."

"Dear Lord, you've dropped back a hundred years, honey."

"I have to light those candles! 'Bye, Mom."

"Make potato soup! Be careful with those candles, Nancy!" Jane yelled, as if trying to bridge the distance in case she had already hung up. "They could start a fire!"

"I'll be careful. Bye."

She hung up quickly, before Jane could start putting together something to be worried about.

It had become darker than she'd noticed. The front door, standing open since the telephone man had left, let in the dying light of day. But the hallway leading back into the depths of the house, and all the useless rooms that opened from it, had grown uncomfortably dark.

She yelled up the stairs, "Kids! Time to come down!" She didn't wait for an answer. Before she closed the front door and shut out what was left of the light, she had to light the candles. And in order to do that, she had to go to the kitchen, which seemed half a block away from the foyer, and get some matches. In this house, she thought to herself, it would be a good idea to wear something with a pocket in which she could carry matches. *Like an apron.* The thought came like a whisper in her ear, unbidden.

"Where are you, electric company?" she muttered, as she went back toward the kitchen. Her soft-soled slippers made almost no sound on the hardwood floors.

She heard the other soft sounds just as she walked past a closed door, the last one before she reached the door into the kitchen. It drew her to a stop. She listened. For a moment the house seemed filled with silence. Then, as softly as before, something moved on the other side of the closed door.

It was one of many doors she had not opened. She didn't know what lay beyond. A room, with an antique piece of furniture, perhaps a chair, a lamp that was useless. One window on the distant end that was covered with a drapery. Like so many of the rooms in the old mansion. "They will make good bedrooms," Katie had said eagerly.

Nancy pressed her ear against the door, listening, chills making goose bumps on her arms, and pulling tight the hair on the back of her neck. Her kids were upstairs. Katie hadn't come home yet.

After a space of silence, she heard the sounds again. Undefined. Movement, something sliding along the floor, or wall, or something being dragged.

Perhaps it was Katie, home after all, Nancy thought with sudden hope. Maybe she had come home and into the back of the house.

Nancy turned the knob quietly, unsure of herself. The door opened inward, as did all the doors along the hallways. She thought of calling out 'Katie, are you there?', but didn't.

A wall appeared just to the left of the opened crack of the door. A long tunnel of darkness stretched away into infinity, it seemed.

She eased the door open wider. A hallway, she realized, one of those many hallways that led to rooms or porches. There was nothing here. No one.

Yet ...

In the darkness there was movement, and again the soft sounds. It was nothing she had ever heard before, nothing to which she could put a definite name. She stared, frowning intently, and began to see in the darkness the darker shapes. Black upon black, in shades that varied. She could make out a body, it seemed, upright, yet somehow not human. It undulated, wavered, changing the shape of the darkness.

It seemed to be sliding rapidly toward her.

She pulled the door shut, her heart racing in fear.

CHAPTER 33

*N*ancy stood breathing in gasps. Afraid to be heard. Unable to slow her intense reaction of fear to whatever it was she had seen.
What had she seen?

Darkness. A kind of coiling darkness.

"Damn!" she muttered. What she'd give for a light switch. How unappreciative she had been of light switches when she'd had all she needed. How she had taken for granted such a thing as light. How she had taken for granted so many things! How unappreciative, how childish, how greedy. But no, slow down, she told herself. Don't grab the kids and run home to Perry yet. Not yet. If she gave in now her life would never change. She wanted more— for her kids, herself, and yes, Perry. She missed him. He would look into the dark hall for her.

She hurried into the kitchen and grabbed the flashlight out of the drawer they had already designated the junk drawer. That drawer that every household had to have, that caught things coming in, and held things needed daily. Plus nails and screws and a hammer.

She ran back to the closed door and paused, goose bumps rising on her arms again, like the hackles on an animal's back. She didn't want to open the door again. Her mind slid rapidly from her kids to their almost desperate situation, to escape. She thought again of gathering up their things and going back to the smothering apartment with Perry, if he'd let her in now. She thought of Katie here alone.

She opened the door timorously, the flashlight on.

Nothing.

The hall was long, a couple doors closed halfway along its length, another at the end. Only one piece of furniture occupied the long, empty space, and it stood near the far end. Tall, with a closed front, it looked like an old wardrobe.

The purpose of the hallway seemed to be the door at the end.

If there had been anything in the darkness just minutes ago, it was gone now. Possibly into one of the rooms whose doors were closed or through the door at the end. More than likely, nothing had been there. In order to be comfortable in the house, she had to believe nothing had been there.

There was a strange smell, unpleasant, almost like decaying flesh or vegetation, or some other underground decomposition. But that wasn't unusual in the house. She had opened quite a lot of windows to air out that smell, which permeated the whole thing. In most rooms it was faint, thank goodness. She hadn't said anything to Katie, not wanting to walk into her new-old house and immediately wrinkle her nose and say, "Phew!"

She closed the door and looked around. Some light still came in the open door at the front, but she had to do something about the growing dark. Her kids were pounding down the stairway from upstairs. She didn't want them going into that side hall. Even if nothing had crawled there.

She looked for something to block the doorway.

Thank God for all the useless chests and chairs that sat at intervals along the front hall. The closest one looked like an old dry sink. On its top was a candle holder with three candles.

She struggled with the chest, moving it inches at a time. She finally got it against the door. It was tall enough to hide the doorknob, and keep her curious kids from opening it.

"What are you doing, Mama?" Erica asked, as she and Curtis came running down the hall.

Curtis asked, "Are you going to light the candles now?"

"Yes."

"Can we watch?"

They both spoke at once, in a kind of offbeat harmony, their voices eager, excited. Erica grabbed Nancy's hand.

"Mama, do you like it here?"

Nancy smiled down at her kids. Their faces were perfect, she thought as always, perfect features, perfect beauty in innocent eyes, the way with all children. Puppies, kittens, baby goats and calves, baby everything— all had that perfect beauty and innocence in their eyes. She loved it.

"Yes, I like it, it's fun," she carefully lied, smiling. "Now let's go light all the candles."

Curtis hopped, danced, and squealed. "Can I help, can I help?"

· · ·

KATIE HAD DREADED COMING BACK. She had felt while she was grocery shopping after work that it would be so easy just to go back to her old apartment and stay there. So much easier than this, than getting onto the expressway that circled the city, finding the unfamiliar exit, finding the unfamiliar highway, the town where one town blended into another, then head into the country with its backdrops of mountains and forests.

She had misjudged the time it would take to leave the office, do the shopping, drive home. She should have called information to find out if the telephone had been installed and there was a number where she could reach Nancy. But maybe Nancy wouldn't be nervous. Alone in the house? Kids were never counted, Katie thought to herself. No one ever considered the kids, the impressions those young brains were getting, their peculiar fears and terrors.

She didn't know what had happened to her when she was very, very young. Was it possible she had seen a movie that had formed these impressions that now came out as dreams or visions or memories, whatever they were? She'd ask Dr. Firman. It was a possibility she hadn't thought of before.

Driving into the narrow lane that led to the house, she breathed a sigh of relief. She didn't dread coming home now. Now that she was here, it seemed natural, as if she had lived here forever.

She recalled her first feelings here. The feeling close to love, of finally having come home. At the corner of the barn that first day, looking down the little road into the forest, her feeling of having stood there before was so strong it had been frightening.

The headlights of the car made an arc through the trees, and shone for a moment on the old shed where she had found the nearly rotted rag doll.

The rag doll! *My God.*

She felt her face blanch, as if ice water had been thrown on her. She had forgotten the doll. What had she done with it? Put it on the floorboard of the back seat? Yes. And then forgotten it.

Except ... she had brought it forth and added it to her strange memories.

She had to talk to Nancy about it. She wouldn't be seeing the doctor until Friday, three days away. She would talk to Nancy. She had talked to Nancy all her life about things she couldn't discuss with her mother. Boys. Sex. She'd asked questions she needed to ask but was reluctant to ask her mother. Nancy's advice had kept her a virgin until she was married. Until she had fallen so solidly in love with Ethan that she knew he was the only man in the world for her, and knew he returned her feelings with total commitment. The commitment of marriage. She had not regretted it one moment. Nancy had admitted to Katie that her advice came from experience. She'd never told anyone, but she'd been pregnant with Erica when she'd married Perry. It had caused her to wonder if he'd have married her otherwise.

Lights were on in the house. Dim, yellow. But lights. There were even lights visible in three upstairs windows. The kids' room, Nancy's, her own. Lined up on the side of the house above the driveway. Three little warm places in a large, otherwise dark house. Katie had not gone again into the larger front bedroom that had the bedding, where she had tried to sleep that first night. Where the ghost, or whatever it was, had pulled up the covers over her head. Dr. Firman had given a rational explanation, even for that.

"The mind is interesting and extremely complex," he had said, so comfortable with his beliefs that in memory, it irritated her. "Obviously you were dreaming. Sometime in your past that woman covered you in bed. Or, someone whom she represents. The mind is very creative. It can take one person and make another person out of her. But there will be signs that will show you the real person behind the creative process."

Katie pulled in close to the back of the house and turned off the car lights. A dim light made a track from the kitchen door across the dark porch. At that moment, preceded by long, wavering shadows, the kids came running out, yelling.

"Aunt Katie! Aunt Katie! Guess what we've been doing!"

Nancy followed them, carrying the flashlight. Its beam cut through the candle-glow path like a laser.

Katie went to the trunk and inserted the key. She had filled the whole trunk with groceries.

"My gosh," Nancy cried, "what have you done, bought out the closest store?" She shined the flashlight on the bags of mostly canned goods.

"Stuff that can be kept without a refrigerator. Things in cans and things in boxes."

Curtis yelled, "Any cookies, Aunt Katie?"

"Guess what we've been doing," Erica said again, possibly for the third or fourth time. Everyone talked at once, it seemed to Katie, but at this moment, she loved the confusion.

"We've been cooking!" Erica yelled, her voice going over Curtis's, who was still wanting to know if Aunt Katie had brought cookies.

Nancy's voice came through. "We thought you were never coming home."

Katie tried to answer them all. "Yes," to Curtis, "Great, I'm hungry," to Erica, and to Nancy, "I'm sorry. I didn't realize how long it would take me to shop and get home. I had to work a little late to make up for being away for a while this afternoon."

They carried in sacks of groceries and piled them on the cabinet. Curtis climbed on a chair to look for the cookies. Nancy made him get down and took both kids into the laundry room to wash their hands.

Katie opened the pantry door and shined the new flashlight she had purchased into the cave-like darkness. It was a room at least large enough to store food for a convention. At the moment it looked bare. The table needed a new cloth to replace the worn oilcloth. The shelves were mostly empty, but some canned goods remained, grouped together like frightened lambs.

Nancy entered the room behind her, bringing a sack of groceries, which she placed on the table.

"It looks like someone's been living here, Katie."

Katie shined the flashlight on cans of corn, beans, mushrooms, even a few cans of dog food.

"Probably the last people who tried to buy the place. Mr. Yates said they'd left some stuff."

It was obvious it hadn't been left for a very long time. The cans hadn't rusted or bulged. Nancy examined one.

"Canned in 1990." She set it on the table. "Do you suppose it's still good?"

There was a closed door on the other side of the room. A familiar sight in this house. The time would come, Katie supposed, when she would know what lay behind all the doors. But for tonight, she was only interested in rest.

"It's been a long day, Nan," she said, turning away from the closed door, and the whip of a memory that came like black wings. Came and left, all in less than a thought. She didn't want to know what lay beyond that closed door. Not tonight.

"There's one more thing," she said, as she walked back into the kitchen.

Erica and Curtis came running, shouting, "What? What?"

"It's in the car," Katie said. "Want to come with me?"

With the brilliant beam of the new flashlight making a path for them, they went back out to the car. Katie opened the back door and looked in.

The old rag doll lay like fungus on the carpet. She picked it up. Erica backed away.

"Yuk!" she cried. "What's that?"

Katie held it tenderly, feeling a slight annoyance at Erica's reaction. There was something precious about the doll, the nearly rotted rags she held in her hand. "Yuk!" Curtis mimed with less disgust than Erica. Nancy said, "Oh hush."

Katie thought to herself, *Thank you.* But by the time she reached the back porch, her sense of humor had returned and she was able to laugh at the look on Erica's face, and Curtis's attempt to look as disgusted, though it was obvious he didn't know why.

In the soft candlelight in the kitchen Katie turned off the flashlight and set it down by the inner hall door.

She straightened the rags, pulling the skirt down so that the face was visible.

"It's a doll!" Erica said in a breath of awe, as if to herself. That changed everything. She no longer drew back from its soiled and rotted skirts.

Nancy asked, with a half-laugh, "Where on earth did you find that?"

Curtis crowded closer, stretching to see.

Katie sat down on one of the straight-backed antique kitchen chairs and arranged the old doll on her knees.

"See, Curtis," she said, resisting an urge to touch his round babyish face. "Somebody once made—"

Eddie made it. In her vision she had seen Eddie making the doll for the little girl.

A very old doll, now ragged, tattered, caked with dirt, mud, darkened. She became aware that Nancy was talking to her. "Katie? Katie? Something wrong?"

Katie shook her head. "No, no. See," she said, her words half choked. "The flowers make the face on the doll. It's faded, but there's the—"

"Eye!" Curtis cried, putting a finger smack in the middle of the doll's flower eye.

Erica stuck her elbow in his ribs. "Don't."

"And," Katie added, seeking hard to hold on to the reality of the moment. She felt herself drifting back, back toward the darkness of the tunnel, of that passageway down which she ran when her mind slipped into the mind of the child. "And—where's the nose, Curtis?"

Curtis leaned against her knee, looking closely at the doll's face.

"I don't see its nose," he finally said. "It doesn't have a nose. But there's its mouth." He laughed, glancing up at Katie.

Katie spread the shorter strips of cloth at the sides of the doll.

"Wings!" Curtis cried.

"Not wings, dummy," Erica said. "That's arms. Yuk. It's got black stuff on it."

"Angel," Katie said softly. "It looks like an angel, doesn't it?"

In the child's mind it had been Angel, she remembered vividly, feeling a strange deep love for this pitiful little collection of rags.

Nancy bent closer, touching the blackened, stiffened stains on the rags. She almost visibly recoiled.

"Katie, that looks like blood. Old, dried blood."

CHAPTER 34

*K*atie sat with the doll spread open on her lap, its wings extended, the black stains that had stiffened the material over most of the body from the neck down, now looking red and moist. She closed her eyes briefly to clear her eyes. She hadn't seen the dark stains as blood, but Nancy was possibly right.

Nancy turned the doll's flattened head. The back had been half soaked in blood also. There the stains were an old reddish brown, and something had eaten tiny holes in the material.

"Yuuuukkk!" Erica went backing away. "I bet there's bugs still in it. Throw it away, Aunt Katie!"

In the sudden silence, Katie heard the soft fluttering of candle flames, like moths against the window. *Throw it away?*

"You could wash it, perhaps," Nancy suggested, and Katie knew Nancy had noticed her attachment to the little bundle of dirty, stiffened rags.

Nancy put a hand on Erica's back and pushed her toward the old cast-iron sink and the one water spigot.

"Go fill the water glasses, Erica."

Katie stood up. "Go ahead and sit down and eat, I'll be back."

"Where're you going?" Curtis cried, and started with her. Nancy grabbed him back.

"Time to eat, young man. Sit."

"But I wanna go with Aunt Katie!"

"She's going to the bathroom to wash her hands, Curtis!"

Katie closed the kitchen door behind her. The long central hall was softly lighted, the candles glowing in their wall brackets and emitting just barely enough light to keep a person from stumbling in the dark.

She ran up the stairs, took the left branch, and went down the hall to her room, the doll held carefully in her right hand. Nancy had lighted a couple of candles in her room, as Katie had seen from the driveway. The light softened the height of the ceiling, and the old drapery material that had darkened at the window. As in many of the bedrooms they had looked into, the furniture was the barely essential. A bedstead, in this case iron, a nightstand that held a pitcher in a washbowl, and a tall chest of drawers. Katie opened one of the drawers and placed the doll within. She stood looking at it before she closed the drawer.

Blood on the old doll. Blood mixed with black soil. It was so obvious, so clear now that Nancy had pointed it out. Whose blood ... ?

No no no!

She turned to the bed and pulled down the blanket and sheet, folding them back, ready to be climbed into. She made herself look at the figures on the sheets, and touch the blanket, made herself feel, see, remember that these were hers, brought from her apartment. Her things.

She couldn't slip back. With effort she must stay in the present.

It seemed now, tonight, to take constant effort.

She didn't want to know whose blood had stained the old rag doll.

Angel. The child ... she ... had run back down the shadowy hall to reach Angel, to get her, to rescue her from the floor where she had laid her while she opened the door to the bad place ... the bad place ... where the Bad Things lived ...

Katie covered her face with her hands in despair. Her groan sounded as if it came from someone else, somewhere near—a voice left over from another time.

She left the room and hurried downstairs and into the bathroom. She had to get her mind solidly into the present, away from whatever it was that threatened always to pull her back ... back she knew not even when. But now it could no longer be denied. Whatever had happened, had happened here. Here, in these surroundings.

Yet her feelings of fear were mixed. She was not a prisoner here. She had the same opportunities as former potential buyers to back out of the deal.

As former buyers! Why hadn't she thought of them before? There had been more than one who had left in a hurry, as she recalled. Tomorrow, she'd look them up, and find out what had happened to them.

Perhaps it would be a way of exorcising the ghost in her own mind, so that she wouldn't have to leave. If they had had experiences similar to her own, she would also have something to tell her smug therapist!

The bathroom had been added in what was probably once a large closet or storage room. There were no windows. It was larger than the average bath, with unpainted cast-iron fixtures.

There was one candle in the bathroom. Nancy had thought of everything, even soap, towels, and washcloths. They were stacked on the shelves, low enough for the children to reach.

After Katie washed and brushed her hair back from her face, she returned to the kitchen. The kids were seated, being served by Nancy. Curtis looked sleepy, his eyes blinking slowly, as if the lids had become very heavy.

Katie kissed his cheek, then Erica's.

"Sit there," Nancy said, as if Katie were one of her children, "and I'll get you a bowl of potato soup. Want crackers or plain bread? No toast."

Katie pretended to pout. "I wanted toast."

Erica laughed with delight and Curtis grinned widely. "Me too," he said, blinking sleepily at Katie.

"What are you trying to do," Nancy said with a half smile, "destroy my teachings?"

"MOMMY," Erica said, her voice as soft and trusting as a three-year-old's, "What if I have to go to the bathroom in the night?"

Yes, it was Erica who sometimes had to get up in the night. Curtis, on the other hand, slept the night away as if he'd been drugged. He was already asleep the minute his head hit the pillow, it seemed. He had turned toward the wall when Nancy laid him down, and that was it.

Erica's bed was across the room, closer to the door. The candle on the dresser, in front of the old, filmed mirror with the hairlines cracks, threw a strange arrangement of lights toward the distant ceiling. But the light barely reached the corners where the beds were, and Erica, sitting up, was deep in shadow.

Nancy looked around. "Where are the old chamberpots that each of these rooms no doubt had in its day?"

"What's a chamberpot?"

"It looks like a fat vase with a lid, but it's sort of a portable toilet."

"Oh, Mommy! " Erica giggled, and twisted down into bed, curled, her hand beneath her cheek.

Nancy went back to her and laid her own hand against the soft, satin-smooth cheek. "If you need to go to the bathroom, you come and get me. I'll go downstairs with you, okay?"

"Okay."

Nancy hesitated. "You remember where my room is? You just go out your door and turn to the right. Remember? Aunt Katie's is to the left. I guess if you get her by mistake, she won't mind."

"I know where your room is."

"All right. Good night, baby. I love you."

"I love you, too."

"Let me see you close your eyes."

Erica closed her eyes.

Nancy stood a moment longer, reluctant to leave. Then, chiding herself for hating to leave them in a room that was only beyond one wall, she quietly left. She started to leave the door open, but the hall outside was so long, the far end in darkness. She could see, in that darkness, the suggestion of steps rising. She had noticed the back stairway, one of two accesses that she knew of to the third floor. But she hadn't gone closer to it than where she now stood.

What an adventure, she had thought during one of her highs, when she knew she had a choice now that didn't mean crawling back to Perry, on Perry's terms. What an adventure, going into an old mansion with so many rooms! But that adventure had turned sour, from the moment of her arrival.

She turned her back on the darkness where the third-floor stairway rose and went to her room. She paused. She had closed the kids' door, but she wouldn't feel good about closing hers. If Erica needed her—

She stopped and looked sharply back toward the third-floor stairway. Someone moved there. She heard the footsteps, a hollow, faraway sound, coming down the steps. Whoever it was carried a dim light. A candle, of course.

Katie?

Katie had more guts than she did, if she'd gone looking into the third floor tonight. Just minutes after they had said good night in the hall where Katie had gone into her room ...

Nancy stared at the figure coming down the third-floor stairway, her skin tightening with goose bumps. Her hand gripped the door to her room. She couldn't move.

Then suddenly it was gone, all of it. The illusion of movement, of sound. Nancy blinked, the candle in the wall bracket behind her made tiny little sounds she had never noticed before. The sounds of fire, miniscule flame doing its little thing of burning, making light.

No one was on the stairway. There was no light except that which glowed softly in the hall.

Nancy turned, and turned again, feeling now as if she were seeing things in all directions that weren't there, movements in darkness, imaginary people carrying imaginary candles everywhere. She had a moment of deep regret of ever leaving home, so deep, so profound that she felt ill with it.

She did then what she had always been instructed to do by her mother: she took a deep breath, then another. She thought of Katie, and experienced another first. She understood some of the torment Katie must have been going through.

She went past the kids' door to Katie's, and found it closed. She tapped softly. She had almost decided Katie was asleep and she hesitated to knock again and disturb her, when the door opened. Katie, looking out through the crack, reminded Nancy of Erica. Her eyes were rounded, questioning. Then she smiled and opened the door.

"Come in, Nan. Are you having the same problems I am? Finding it hard to read by candlelight? How'd they ever get along?"

"They harnessed electricity," Nancy said, as she entered Katie's room. She looked around.

The walls had been papered long ago, and might once have been a more dramatic color. But over the years the paper had mellowed and darkened and grown to look crisp and brown, like old newspaper. Edges curled. Stripes faded from gold to tan. Draperies at the window were a dark red velvet, which seemed to have been a favorite color of whoever had decorated the house. The bed was made of iron, intricately woven into a kind of filigreed headboard that reached at least eight feet up the wall.

"Not exactly something you can hang a candle on, is it?" Nancy said, lifting herself up to sit on the foot of the bed. As with the other beds, it was higher off the floor than the kind she had grown up with.

"Not exactly."

"You know," she said to Katie, as Katie got back into bed and propped herself up against three pillows, "when we were small we didn't have to worry about something being under the beds. The beds were—still are—so close to the floor we couldn't even crawl under them ourselves. But these old ones ... remember that joke about the old maid looking under her bed every night for a man?"

Katie grinned and nodded.

"I can see where that came from. A large man could have been under her bed, who knows? I think I'll start looking, too, before I get into bed."

Katie tipped her head back and eyed the ceiling. "I hadn't thought of that. I didn't look. Would you mind looking, Nan, under my bed?"

"And if I find one?" Nancy pulled her legs up and wrapped her arms around her bent knees. She leaned against the cast-iron footboard.

"Don't let 'im get away!"

They laughed.

"Feel like talking?" Nancy asked.

"What about?"

"Oh ... whatever. Things we used to do?"

Katie looked straight at Nancy. "My memories, you mean."

Nancy drew a deep breath and picked at her fingernails. She had developed a hangnail due to keeping her hands in water so much today. Even though the kitchen appeared to be clean, she went over it again herself to make sure, from the floor up as high as she could reach on the cabinets. She had even stood on the top of the counters to reach even higher. Even so, she had covered only a small portion of the kitchen.

"Well," she said, "when I was out in the hall a while ago, Katie, I could swear I saw someone on those stairs that go up to the third floor. And it occurred to me that with this candle business, the light jumps around so much, and it covers so little of the room, that it's easy to see things." She paused, but Katie said nothing. "So I wanted to tell you I understand more than I did. At first I was stunned, at the things you said were repressed memories coming to the surface, and then I was—well—not really mad, but irritated. I thought your therapist was leading you on."

"Leading me on?"

"I'm still not sure he isn't."

"Leading me on to what, Nancy? He isn't the one who's causing me to see the things I do. And they're no longer dreams. They're—they *are* memories, Nancy."

Nancy looked across the distance to Katie. They were separated by the length of a bed, but the one candle, making little fluttery sounds on a tiny table at the side of the bed, seemed to fill the space with as much shadow as light. The distance wavered, lengthened, deepened, until Nancy felt as if each of them stood on a precipice.

Katie added softly, "And that scares me, Nancy. I haven't told you half of it."

She looked toward the door, then turned her head back toward the third-floor stairway as if she could see through the walls. Nancy felt goose bumps rising on her arms, and a shiver up her backbone. It spread across her shoulders and into her hair. She hugged her legs closer.

Katie began to talk, in a voice so muted Nancy had to strain to hear. She sat in silence, listening, growing colder by the moment.

"There was a boy named Eddie. He was a teenager, older, taller. Tall, from the child's point of view. He was very kind, but he couldn't speak. He was the one who made the rag doll for the child. He lived somewhere on the third floor, I think, although I don't know exactly where because I was never in his room. The reason he made the doll was one day the child took him into a room, a nice room where she wasn't supposed to be, to look at a beautiful doll. The doll was on a dresser, or something high with a mirror behind, so that I could barely reach it, even if I climbed by putting my foot on a drawer knob. It had a white face, black hair. Real hair. Its hands were … hard … some hard substance, as was its head, but its body was soft. The—the lady ran the child away—and told her never, never touch the doll again. So the child went away crying, and Eddie wanted to know why, and I led him back to see the doll ..."

Nancy stared at Katie, who gazed dreamily at the wall across the room as she talked, her eyebrows knitted in concentration. Nancy wondered if Katie realized that she was at times referring to the child in first person. The child had become Katie, in Katie's imagination. Nancy wished she hadn't come into Katie's room, or brought her thoughts to this imaginary child. She felt she had lost Katie to her crazy, imaginary world.

"That was why he made the rag doll, Nancy," she said then, surprising Nancy.

Katie had called her by name. She knew where she was, after all, thank God. Knew where she was and whom she was with. But it only left Nancy more perplexed. "The reason ... *Eddie* ... ?"

"Yes." Katie's eyes came to Nancy's, soft, sad, almost in tears. "Don't you see, Nancy? Finding the doll proves it. It's there, it's proof. It happened. But Nan, why do I identify so closely with that child? How is it I know so much about her?"

Nancy shook her head. "Katie, you're scaring me. You're scaring me to death!"

A flicker of real concern crossed Katie's shadowed face. The candlelight played across her features like a naughty imp.

"Nancy! Why? I don't mean to. I just thought—I just thought I'd—I don't know. I don't know why I was telling you. Because I always talked to you, I guess. I'm sorry."

"No, no, no. I didn't mean that. I mean you're scaring me because you've got me really worried about you. The old rag doll you found isn't proof of anything, Katie, can't you see that? Except, a little girl obviously owned it. I'm telling you something you should seriously think about. Stop listening to your therapist a minute. It's not memories, it didn't necessarily happen at all. I mean, look at both sides, at least. *Finding the old doll is proof you made up a story to go along with the doll.* Don't you see that?"

Katie said nothing. Nancy thought she saw her lips thin and tighten, but it might only have been the changing of the dim and erratic light.

Then Katie suddenly lowered her face into her hands. Nancy hurriedly moved up beside her, taking Katie into her arms. At that instant her feelings toward Katie were similar to her feelings toward Erica. Yet added to that was a deep fear that she was losing Katie. That no matter how hard she held onto Katie, she was slipping away, and there was nothing she could do to stop the loss.

CHAPTER 35

$\mathcal{K}$atie slept as if weeping for several long minutes in Nancy's arms had drained her of tension, as if being tucked in like the helpless child that lingered in the back of her psyche had done something to Katie's mind, she slept. The next thing she knew, the alarm clock on the floor beneath the edge of her bed was making a startling racket.

She almost fell out of bed onto her face when she rolled over and reached down for it. She slammed it off, muttering, asking herself why she'd felt she might need an alarm. Her radio with the gentle wakeup music was languishing somewhere in her stuff, still unpacked, useless anyway, with no battery backup.

She opened the curtains and made up the bed. She found herself looking at it with a critical eye. A plain blue blanket didn't leave the bed looking dressed. She needed to finish unpacking her things so that she could find her bedspread and draperies. They had been packed and stored since she had moved from the larger apartment where she lived with Ethan. It was a quilt cotton-satin set, fat and fluffy, with colors of mauve, green, and burgundy in a part floral, part geometric flourish.

Miss Theodora won't like it.

Katie jerked around, looking behind her. It was as if the child had spoken, somewhere apart from her.

Miss Theodora?

She wasn't sure, but thought that was the name she had seen on the abstract. Theodora Wickham, wife of Emmett?

Katie pulled on a robe and left her room, forcing her thoughts to the mundane. The candle in the wall bracket was fluttering to an end, the holder coated with wax. How was it that a wax-less candle dropped so much wax? Give it time, and it will burn.

She drew another deep sigh, and heard it behind her as if even a sigh echoed in this endless house.

She saw that the children's door was still closed. Nancy's stood open a couple of inches, but there was no sound. Katie paused. Her sense of feeling at home here was suddenly pierced with a frightening anxiety. What if something had happened to Nancy and the children during the night?

She eased Nancy's door farther open and looked into the deep shadows of the room. Like the candle in the bracket outside the bedroom doors, the candle in Nancy's room was nearing its end. But she had left her curtains pushed wide open and a vagrant streak of real light tried to penetrate the gloom.

On the bed, where white sheets folded back over a pink blanket, Nancy lay, her dark blond hair looking brunette.

But she lay so still.

Katie started across the room when Nancy moved, stretching out her arms, turning her face. Then, with a long sigh, she slept again.

Relieved, Katie backed away and continued on downstairs to the bathroom.

Nothing like a cold shower to wake you up, she thought, as she hurriedly got in and got out with a minimum of dawdling. She, who had been addicted to long, hot showers. No more shampooing one's hair every day and blow-drying it. Here, one almost expected to go back to washing hair on Saturday, with water heated on the stove, then setting it in curlers and letting it dry. Which was probably the way it was done at the turn of the century. Or, more than likely, the girl went out into the sunshine and sat with her hair hanging long down her back until it dried enough to be braided, or twisted into a poof on top with a bun at the back.

She went out into the hall, her robe wrapped closely around her, and stopped.

The ghost woman had appeared in that doorway ...

The door stood open, the light from an east window was like a road through a dark forest, coming as far as the hallway. Katie stood, looking into the almost barren room.

Of course, people had hauled off furniture over the years, she almost told herself aloud. *Get your mind off the ghost.* In her—Theodora's?—day, the rooms would have been lavishly furnished. All of them, not just part. Theodora herself might have started selling off furniture. Perhaps money had become scarce after the stock market crash in 1929, and she had been forced to sell many things.

Katie walked past the doorway, but couldn't stop herself looking back when she reached the stairs. No one was there. Perhaps, as Dr. Firman said, no one had ever stood there. Even Nancy thought she could no longer differentiate between nightmare and reality.

Yet she had the doll.

After she dressed, she wrapped the doll carefully in a clean pillowcase. When she drove out of the driveway, it was lying on the seat beside her.

NANCY, wearing jeans and shirt, with a dish towel folded in half and tied around her waist to hold dusting cloth, a bottle of cleaner, a sponge, and a small towel for drying, went again into the central hall and screamed at the kids.

"Erica! Curtis! Where are you?"

This time she didn't get an answer. All morning, every fifteen minutes or so, if she hadn't seen them, she went yelling for them. She usually received an answer from some distant part of the house. One or two small voices responding with a *"What?"* And Nancy'd answer, "Come down closer to play."

Then she'd go back to her work without checking to see if they obeyed. They did, though, often enough for her to see that they were all right. They had managed to find dust, lots of it, somewhere in the house. It seemed that only a few of the rooms and hallways were relatively clean. A few times they had slammed through the kitchen door and gone outside long enough to come back in with a different kind of dirt added to shirts that had been clean when they were dressed this morning.

To think that the house was clean, dust-free, as Katie had said, was now a big joke. It was true that the foyer was fairly dust-free, and so was the kitchen. But the pantry wasn't, nor were the floors in odd halls Nancy had looked into. She was glad enough to keep the doors shut. For the time being.

How were they ever going to turn this place into livable rooms or apartments, Nancy wondered morosely. Because that seemed to have been the last idea. Before Nancy had gone to bed last night, she'd gotten Katie talking about the future—instead of the past—and Katie had become enthusiastic about making the place into an apartment house, at least in part. That way, the other rooms could be given free to women and children in need.

It was only a dream, Nancy felt. One of those dreams that seemed destined to play itself out. Somehow, Nancy couldn't visualize this house in any way other than its present large, dark, silent misery.

She walked farther down the central hall, wiping her hands on the small towel before she tucked it back into her makeshift caddy bag.

"Erica! Curtis!"

"What, Mommy?"

The voice came softly from right behind her.

Nancy screamed and whirled. Curtis stood looking at her with sympathy and amusement mingling on his face.

"Did I scare you?" he asked, and giggled. His hand was already peeling down the zipper to his pants. He ran suddenly, as if he could hardly wait to get into the old, large, half-dark bathroom.

Nancy heard him using the stool.

"Where's Erica, Curtis?"

"I don't know. Somewhere."

She glanced through the open door and saw a ghostly little Curtis sitting on the old toilet, his cut-off jeans hanging around his ankles. She'd have to get another candle for that room, she thought, just as the telephone rang.

Her footsteps sounded hollow on the hardwood floors, as if she walked over a cave. For the first time she wondered what was beneath the house. Not solid ground, for certain. Probably a basement, or cellar, or whatever it was called years ago. A dungeon?

She picked up the telephone expecting to hear Mom's voice, and almost dropped it when Perry started yelling.

"Where the hell are you, Nancy? I've been trying to find out where you've moved to, and all your mother says is she doesn't know. Then she told me you didn't even have a phone. What the shit kind of place is that?"

She responded, feeling her face turn hot, feeling that old urge to slam something against Perry's smart mouth. "If this isn't a telephone, Perry, what do you call it?"

"Yeah, well, okay. But where are you?"

"I'd have to draw you a map, okay? And since you wouldn't be able to see it, it wouldn't do much good, would it Perry?"

His voice became placating. "Let's not be sarcastic, Nan. Please. What're you trying to do, fix it so I can't even come and see you?"

"Well, what do you know! Now that you can't find us, suddenly you want to come and see us! What happened, did you finally discover we weren't in the house?"

"What? Oh, come on, Nancy. Listen, we got married when we were too young, maybe. Maybe we weren't grown up enough—"

"You've been talking to Mom," Nancy said, and smiled to herself.

"Well ... maybe she's right. I really do love you and the kids. Why don't you come home?"

"Ummm ... let me think about it, okay? I really don't want to leave Katie here alone yet."

"Hey, Nan," he cried with undisguised excitement. "You gotta tell me where you are so I can come and take you and the kids for a ride. You'll love the new van. We can take great vacations in it."

"What vacation?" she demanded. "You always told me we didn't have time for vacations!"

"Well, now that I've got more help," he said somewhat feebly, "Now that the business is doing better ..."

"Perry, I don't want vacations, I want a house! With a yard of our own!"

"Nancy, we will, I promise. But—"

"But you bought a new van instead."

"Nan, you could at least look at it. It'd be great for traveling. Even got its own little TV, and it's got a little sink, real water, everything. There's a seat in the back that makes down into a bed. The kids will love it, Nancy."

His voice trailed away on a plaintive note, and Nancy felt like crying. Her feelings were so torn now. She wanted to reach Perry and pull him into her arms, the way she would Curtis, and pat him and comfort him. At the same time, she wanted to scream her anger at him.

"How much, Perry?" she asked in a forced calm.

"Uh—under thirty," he muttered.

"Under thirty. Meaning twenty-nine thousand and nine hundred and ninety-nine dollars, right?" He didn't answer. "Enough to make a down payment on a house, right?"

She hung up the phone.

She went over to the front door and stood looking out. Large trees in the front yard looked like the beginning of a deep and endless forest, but she could hear a car passing somewhere beyond them. She caught a glimpse of flashing light as sun glinted on the car.

The phone rang.

She deliberately passed it and went back toward the kitchen and the pantry, where she had been cleaning shelves. Hopelessness went with her. Was she stuck here? Forever?

CHAPTER 36

*E*rica was alone in the huge entrails of the house. That was the way she thought of it, and what she had told Curtis. "Entrails?" he'd said, his eyes widening. He believed everything she said.

"Yes," she had whispered to him. "It's as if we've been swallowed by a great monster."

"A *monster?*"

"Yes, the house."

She was glad to be alone. All the other times, she'd had her little brother tagging along with her, and she didn't dare open doors that were in strange, dark places, or climb all those narrow little stairs that rose in those dark places, because he would probably fall and get hurt. And most certainly he would tell. She might not get in trouble, that wasn't what worried her. Being told on just made it no longer a secret. Actually, having Curtis always with her made secrets a little hard to have, because even when she whispered to him, "*This is a secret, Curtis,*" he most often forgot and told.

She walked along the balcony, looking down into the foyer. The front door stood open, letting in light and warm air. "This house will never need air conditioning," she'd heard Mama say in a grumbly voice, as if she didn't like it being so cold. But she was right. The warm air through open doors or windows just seemed to be— what?—eaten up by the cold air that was always in the entrails of the house.

She liked that word. It made all but the very outside edges of the house seem remote. Inescapable. Scary. But not so scary that she was afraid to open doors. Just tingly scary.

There was a door on the balcony that looked bigger, more solid, in some way, than the doors along the hall. It was darker, as if it had been there longer. The knob, too, was different. Instead of being white, like most of the door knobs, it was glass. Crystal.

Neat.

She had saved this door until sometime when she was alone, so she could have a secret that wouldn't be told.

She looked behind her. She looked down the long hall where the bedroom doors were open. On the other side of the balcony was another hallway, but it just went to four bedrooms, and she had already looked there. The rooms were almost bare, just bedsteads and bedsprings, and lots of times no mattresses.

She checked the foyer again. Curtis had wanted her to take him down to the bathroom, but she had put on a shocked face. What! You want a *girl* to take you to the bathroom? He hadn't thought of such a thing before. It was the only way she could get to be alone. Put her hands on her sides and act shocked.

It worked. He had gone alone.

But she had to hurry now, or he'd be running back.

She put her hands on the crystal doorknob. And jerked them away. It had felt warm, as if someone had just been holding it. She touched it again, and decided the first was only her imagination. It wasn't cold, like the surface of most things in the bowels of the house, but that was all right. She wasn't afraid.

The door opened without a sound, inward, onto a nearly dark room.

She entered and pulled the door closed, so that Curtis couldn't find her. She stood still, letting her eyes adjust to the darker room. It was a corner room. A large room. There was a long window in two different walls, but both were covered with long, dark red velvet draperies.

A huge bed sat against the right window wall, several feet from the window. Its headboard was dark wood and reached a long way up the wall. Two tall posts marked the foot of the bed. But most interesting were the fat pillows, and the knitted or crocheted bedspread. The room looked exactly as if someone lived in it.

The rocking chair even had a cushion leaning against the tall, straight back. The big, wide dresser with the wavery mirror had a scarf, like the bedspread, that hung down on each end. Some things were sitting on top. A candle holder that held six candles, for one. And other things that looked interesting. She wondered if anything was in the drawers. But she'd look later.

There were doors on the right, and one of them stood open. The dark interior was small, she saw when she peeked in, and there were shelves. But nothing was on them. A closet. No clothes hung on the rod.

She went quietly along the wall to the other door. Closed, it too had a crystal knob.

She opened it.

The room was darker than the bedroom, not as dark as the closet. There was a kind of tiny hallway joining the two rooms. Erica squinted. A sofa. Funny old hard thing with black wood running along the back and edges of the arms as if it were a drawing outlined with a black pencil. It had red roses the color of the drapes. There were tables, and fringed shaded lamps, and rugs on the floor. Cushions and small pillows made the sofa look softer.

Like Goldilocks, she tried out the sofa. Yes, hard, just as it looked. But the cushions were soft.

She looked up and saw a face.

A face in the shadows, white as chalk, small ... staring at her, so still, so silent ...

Erica's heart almost exploded. She was trespassing. These were somebody's private rooms, after all. She'd heard Aunt Kate say she'd thought at first that someone lived in the house, and Mama had said, it looks like someone lives here.

Erica stood up, ready to run, too embarrassed even to say, *I'm sorry.*

She stopped. The face was smiling. The face ... wasn't real. It only looked real, with the background of a mirror like a dark sky and the wallpaper reflected there, the vines curling like a halo around its head.

She went closer. It sat on a dresser chest as tall as herself, leaning slightly forward as if looking down at her.

"A doll."

Erica's whisper seemed to fill the room and make the doll's smile more endearing. The shadows eased away from its face and she saw it clearly, dark hair braided over its head, dark eyes somehow more mature than the eyes of most dolls. It was dressed in a pale gown that might have been pink, or ivory, a kind of lacy material like the bedspread in the other room. Ribbons tied the long sleeves at the wrists of the delicate hands. The fingers arched, as if pointing, and curved, as if beckoning.

"Ooooohh!"

The breath sounded as if it came from the doll as it yearned toward Erica. It was like she was saying, *Oooh, at last. You've come at last. Pick me up, little girl. Hold me. I'm yours.*

No. It was more like, *You're mine.*

For just a moment Erica drew back, hesitating. The doll was very, very old. She could tell by the white face and the eyebrows drawn with black paint, and the little mouth pursed and red. She had seen pictures of antique dolls.

She hesitated, but then she stretched up and reached one hand forward. Her fingers touched the hem of the long, crocheted gown. She stretched higher, and felt the firm, rounded toes of slippers. She grasped it and pulled gently, careful not to tip the doll over and break it.

That it was breakable she had no doubt. An old, old doll, like some she had seen in antique stores, too expensive to be owned, too precious to be touched. They sat in windows, behind glass inside the store, or in cases made of glass, sat and waited for the admiration. Poor babies. They no longer belonged to a little girl who would love them and care for them. Caged, like animals in a zoo, where they had no grass, no trees, no love.

"I love you," Erica said, and the doll tipped forward into her arms.

To her surprise, the body was soft. It filled her arms, the lovely face with the red cheeks and lips smiling at her. The eyelashes were very long and thick and black, like the hair, the eyes so dark she couldn't tell what color they were.

"Mama!" she screeched, as she began to run, "Look what I found! Can I have it, Mom?"

Her voice came back at her as if from a hollow barrel, and she remembered where she was. She looked over her shoulder as she hurried out of the room, out of the bedroom.

On the balcony that was becoming hourly more familiar, she ran, down the stairs to the landing, down the stairs to the foyer.

"Mom!"

"What?"

The answer came from far away. But she had heard her mother answering from the kitchen before, and that sound of her being in another world with a huge barrier between them was just part, she had assured Curtis more than once, just part of being in the *bowels* of the house.

The kitchen door at the end of the long central hall opened and Curtis stood holding it.

"Where've you been, Er—" he started to say, but stopped and stared, his eyes on the face of the doll. "Mommy! Erica's got something!".

"It's a doll, Curtis," Erica said, as she passed him and went into the other world of the kitchen.

How different it was in here. Though it was a long room, that had kitchen, dining, and sitting all in one, and even though the floors were just plain wood, and the old stove like a black monster, and the great fireplace like a cave, still it was the warmest room in the house. This was where they stayed in the evening after supper, and played games at the table.

She went to stand behind Nancy, waiting for her to turn around.

When she finally did, she almost screamed.

Erica laughed, delighted at the look on her face.

Nancy put her hand to her chest, the way Redd Foxx did on the old shows they'd seen with Pop-Pop. "I'm coming," he'd say. "This time it's the big one."

"Mommy, it's a doll," Erica said, still smiling.

· · ·

Nancy stared at the doll.

What is this? she thought. Everything Katie talked about, everything she said was part of her nightmares, part of something her therapist called repressed memories, eventually appeared. In a moment, the boy named Eddie would walk in the door. She could almost see him herself, kneeling, making a rag doll for a little girl who had wanted the big beautiful doll.

"Where did you get that?" Nancy demanded, more harshly than she had intended. Erica blinked. Her smile faded.

"But Mom," she said, "no one lives there anymore. It doesn't belong to anyone anymore. Why can't I have it?"

Nancy took the doll from Erica and looked it over carefully, from its underwear to its shoes, to its hair.

"Real hair," she said. "Did you know that, Erica? And long panties, the kind they used to call bloomers." Erica stood at one elbow, and Curtis at the other. They both giggled.

"Don't laugh about bloomers," Nancy teased. "I might make some for you. See, they come down below the knees. Maybe these are pantaloons instead of bloomers."

"Pantaloons!" Curtis laughed.

"Mama, don't you think I can have her?"

"Sweetheart, look. This doll has a china head and hands. Do you know what that means?"

"What?"

"It's fragile, breakable."

"But I'll be careful!"

"What about your own Susie?"

"She's upstairs in bed. Anyway, can't I have two dolls?"

"You have a dozen dolls."

"They're at home, Mama!" Erica wailed.

Nancy sighed. It was true. When she told Erica to pack only a few toys because they were going to Grandma's house for a while, Erica had left her dolls behind, except for the one named Susie. Nancy refused to feel guilty about it. The apartment had gotten too small for the kids' toys anyway, and she'd started giving them away before she left. "Lots of little kids don't have toys," she'd told her kids, and got them enthusiastic over loading up toys and taking them down to the Salvation Army.

Now Nancy said, "This doll, Erica, like everything else in the house, belongs to Aunt Katie. You have to ask her."

"But she wouldn't care!"

"You have to ask her."

"When will she be home?"

"Sometime before dark, I hope. In time for dinner, maybe."

"Are you going to cook now? Is it time to cook?"

Nancy looked at the clock that sat ticking on the mantel. It looked almost comical, a tiny alarm clock where a tall mantel clock should have been. It was so far away, its numbers so small, she had to go nearer.

"Almost time," she told Erica. Lord, how time had flown today. She had washed only a few of the shelves in the pantry, and lined them with plastic place mats so the metal cans wouldn't make marks on wood that was built to hold glass jars.

"What are you cooking?" Curtis asked. "Some macaroni and cheese?"

Nancy squeezed him and kissed his cheek.

"Sure, why not?"

"Oh, goody!" He hopped around the table on one foot.

"And we'll try out the oven," she said, "and bake potatoes. And make an apple salad with raisins. And perhaps some salmon cakes. And maybe even some corn muffins."

Erica had gone to the corner between the end of the long, high hearth and the wall. She was almost hidden, sitting on the floor, with the doll on her knees facing her. Her hands touched its hair tenderly.

Nancy found herself looking at the doll with doubt and confusion. Katie had described a beautiful doll, with black hair braided over its head. She had seen the child—who in some way she felt was herself—looking at it. Crying because she couldn't have it. Then, the boy, Eddie, had made the rag doll.

Both dolls were very old. The rag doll, of course, would deteriorate much faster than the doll with the china head. Her guess was the china doll was probably a couple of hundred years old. The rag doll ... well ...

Had Katie made up those stories about the dolls? About the boy named Eddie, who couldn't speak? The woman who'd chased the child away from the beautiful doll? It was possible she had seen the dolls, and had fabricated a story. But why? It was a chilling scene to visualize Katie going from room to room in the house and building a past to fit what she saw.

But it didn't fit the Katie she knew, scrupulously honest Katie.

Katie wouldn't do that.

She turned to go back into the pantry. Potatoes, she reminded herself, a can of salmon, crackers, eggs ...

The pantry was like walking into a large closet. She got a candle, lighted it, and set it on the pantry table. Its tiny flame wavered, moved erratically, grew and steadied. Pale light spread. Nancy looked toward the shelves, then froze.

She stared.

At first the woman seemed only a part of the flickering light and shadows. She stood unmoving at the side of the long table in the center of the room, returning Nancy's stare.

She was a tall, large woman, still straight and strong, though elderly.

Nancy's surprise turned to dismay when she saw the look on the woman's face. Anger. Fury. Hatred. Silent, dark. Her long, thin face was pinched in at the mouth, making her chin a bump of aggression, wrinkled, protruding. Her cheeks were gaunt and sunken. Her black hair, streaked with gray, pulled tightly back from her forehead. Three horizontal wrinkles crossed that narrow space.

Nancy's mind threw out a jumble of words, apologies, questions, none of them expressed. *Who are you? Where did you come from?* But most of all, *I'm sorry, I'm sorry.* Because the woman made Nancy feel as if she were the intruder.

Then she noticed the way the woman was dressed. A print dress, hanging out of sight past her knees, and over it, a long bib apron, in a different print, trimmed in gray piping.

Nancy's stare flew back to the woman's face, saw the set hatred, the anger, the—the diabolical fury.

An ancient cold emanated from the woman. She stood as still as a statue, her hand flat on the oilcloth of the table, her impenetrable black eyes staring at Nancy.

Nancy felt the cold. It came at her in waves, each wave colder than the last. It entered her, degree by degree.

Curtis came running, his footsteps pounding on the floor, coming closer, closer.

"Mommy?"

The woman disappeared.

The space she had occupied was left only with the cold.

CHAPTER 37

"*I* have something to show you," Katie said, carefully unwrapping the old rag doll.

It lay exposed on Dr. Firman's desk, looking even more crushed, more caked with dirt and ... blood?

Katie glanced at the doctor's face, and saw him staring with a dim frown at the mass of rag strips.

"It's the doll," Katie said. "I found it in the shed where I think the child lived. I think this proves something, Dr. Firman."

He continued to stare at the doll, then suddenly he rose, leaned forward, and touched the caked parts of the cloth that Nancy had said was blood. He then turned the doll over, where that same caked darkness coated three-fourths of the back of the flattened head. He touched his fingers to his jacket, as if instinctively trying to wipe away a contamination. Still looking at the doll, he sat down again.

"What, Katie?" he asked in that same, soft therapist's voice that, now, contradicted the look on his face.

"This proves that it happened, but it happened years ago."

"That what happened?"

"Everything!" Katie cried in exasperation. "Have you forgotten what I told you?"

His eyes lifted to hers.

"I haven't forgotten anything, Katie. In fact, I've been unable to get you or the things that disturb you out of my mind. What do you feel it proves?"

"It proves that the—the—" He made it so difficult for her to express her feelings. She realized she was contradicting herself, even in her mind, at times. He pulled her one way, Nancy the other, even while in certain ways they agreed. "It proves a child existed, and it's her past I see. Another child, not me. I was there, and yet obviously, I wasn't. It happened a long time ago. Something dreadful happened in that house, Dr. Firman, and this proves it. A boy named Eddie made this doll for the little girl. Then, something terrible happened. Nancy says this badly caked part of the doll, and the stains on the back of the head, are blood. I think she's right." He reached for the doll. Katie handed it over, but felt something deep within her pulling back. The child didn't want to release it.

"Do you mind if I keep this a couple of days, Katie?" Dr. Firman asked softly. "We can soon find out if it's blood."

"You'll give it back to me?"

He looked at her penetratingly.

Katie smiled faintly. "I feel divided, Doctor. The child is so strong at times. It's like she's part of me."

"Do you want to talk about it?"

He settled back. He could look so relaxed. With a motion of his wrist he turned the tape recorder off or on, and always he looked as if he had all day, though in fact she had a walk-in appointment today that would last only a few minutes. She had called about the doll, about her 'proof' of the experiences being very old.

She talked a few minutes about her feelings of gradually draining away from the person she had always been and becoming more and more drawn into the life of the child. She talked of her attachment to the house.

"I'm getting so that I don't want anything changed, Doctor. When I went into the kitchen and saw that my sister, Nancy, had rearranged some things on the counter, I had a strong feeling that she should put them back. That it was very important she put things back exactly the way they were."

"Why?"

Katie tried to think why. She picked at her fingernails, and discovered suddenly that she had picked them mostly away. The long, glossy, painted nails were more like a child's now.

Dr. Firman said, "Did you resent your sister changing things in your house?" He put an emphasis on "your."

Katie shook her head. "No, it wasn't that. It was—it made me afraid. I was afraid *she* would come and see what Nancy had done, and would be mad."

"She? Who, Katie?"

"She ... the woman."

There was a moment of silence.

Then Dr. Firman said, "Katie, would you be willing to talk to a psychiatrist?"

Katie jerked her head up, focusing on Dr. Firman. She felt betrayed. She felt her mouth droop, as if the child within her had been slapped.

"Katie," he said gently. "I'm afraid we may be getting into deeper water. I want to make sure we aren't heading toward a psychosis here."

"What on earth do you mean by that?" the part that was Katie demanded. "I am not crazy, Doctor! There's the proof. It happened! It is not repressed memories. I'm picking up someone else's experiences." She pointed toward the doll that now lay on the desk near the tape recorder.

"To me, Katie, it proves nothing. Look at it this way: you went to the old house. It's a century old, right? It has the original draperies in it, and even some of the old furniture. There are a few modern touches that buyers added and left, such as the stove, and probably the bathroom. Right? Your first experience was to conjure up the woman who might have lived there."

"The ghost."

"Yes, but we all know ghosts don't exist, right?"

Katie nodded. "Yes," she admitted. She had made herself see that something so real, then, might have been some kind of hallucination. Although there were times when she relived that night and the following morning and couldn't accept that she hadn't actually seen the ghost.

"Then you found the old doll."

"Actually ..." It was almost a pleasure to be able to contradict him. "I found it before I entered the house."

He raised his eyebrows. "Yes?"

"It was in an old shack not far from the house where obviously people had lived. The floor is dirt, and there were two straw-filled wooden frames back in two corners that must have been their beds. I found the doll there, near the door."

"You took it to the house with you?"

"I put it in the backseat of my car. And forgot it, until last night."

"But it made an impression. You see, instinctively you knew there had been a woman in the house. Once. There always is. Houses aren't built only by men, right? Houses are actually built by women, by the direction of women. So your mind, in this big empty house, created the kind of woman you imagined lived there. But—your fear indicates she is someone you yourself knew in the past, Katie. Your past, not some other child's. You are so disassociated from her, you see her as someone else. A child whose name isn't Katie."

He paused, almost pleading when he continued. "Don't you see, Katie, you have to face your real fears, before it will all go away and leave you in peace."

"My fears, Dr. Firman, are that child's fears."

"Yes, I know. I understand, I really do. And you are going in the right direction, Katie. Your mind began creating a story."

She looked at him. At least now, he and Nancy were in agreement. She waited.

"The story is fiction, with fictional characters. But they work in unfolding your fears, in opening the depths of your mind. You're working toward seeing who that woman in the apron really is. And what she did to you." Something within Katie screamed in silent anguish. No, he was wrong. If she had imagined a mistress of the house, she would have been an elegant lady, straight and corseted, with her hair in a fancy do. She shook her head.

"No?" Dr. Firman queried.

"In fact, the woman I saw looked more like a housekeeper would have, rather than the lady of the house."

"All right, perhaps she was the housekeeper. Just for the sake of my argument, let's say she was. And the finding of the doll put a small child there. A girl. No one bothers to make rag dolls for a boy, do they?"

Katie acceded he was right.

"So, we have a little girl. She's poor. Living in the shack, not able to afford a beautiful doll like the one that's bound to be in the house. Because what wealthy family didn't own at least one beautiful large doll? The little girl had access to the house. So perhaps the woman was her mother, and—"

"No," Katie said quickly. "The child is terrified of the woman."

"Very well, Katie," he said, and it seemed his voice was fading away. "If I withdraw my original idea that you are experiencing an opening to repressed memories, Katie, and these terrible fears and visions you've been experiencing are not caused by something in your own early childhood but by someone else's experiences, then indulge me just a moment. Imagine with me the things you might have seen on finding these things in the old house. From the doll to the ghost. Tell me the kind of people who lived there. Tell me, Katie ..."

... Tell me Katie ... tell me ... tell me the name of the child, the name of the child, the name of the child ...

SHE WAS RUNNING. *The Bad Things came behind her. She could hear their soft slithers as they rapidly approached her, filling the darkness. She felt something brush her arm. It was cold and damp. She had reached the tall wardrobe. She hadn't meant to come this way. She had meant to go through the pantry, and hide there beneath the table until the Bad Things were gone, and then she could slip out of the house. She had to find Eddie. Where had Eddie gone?*

She hunkered down in the dark at the end of the wardrobe. The Bad Things were a part of the darkness in the hall. They filled it. She saw them, and yet couldn't see them.

The door at the end of the hall opened suddenly, and a dim light filled the doorway. She saw the stone steps leading down. Miss Theodora rose in the doorway, as if she floated upward. The candlelight beyond made her like a paper doll, cut out of black.

251

"Stop!" she cried, and the movements in the hall, in the dark beyond the wardrobe, ceased.

The woman stared past the huddled child, then her eyes came downward.

"Ah, Katrina, " she said. She put out her hand. The candlelight outlined it. "Child, come to me."

Fear strangled Katrina. Something came up into her throat. She swallowed. I don't want to go down there.

"Come, child, " Miss Theodora said. "The time has come. "

Katrina heard movements in the hall, and glimpsed the dark figures that had no name. She heard soft mouthing noises rising from them. Katrina had to go forward to Miss Theodora, or try to run back through the Bad Things that filled the hall.

With Angel clutched under her left arm, she rose and put out her other hand. Miss Theodora picked her up and Katrina's head brushed against the top of the door frame as they went back into the cellar.

They went down the long flight of stone steps.

The dirt floor glistened. The stone wall where the candles glowed sweated cold drops of water. They glimmered in the candlelight, like tiny eyes.

There was something against the wall. A large, flat stone had been built into the wall, and some things were carved into the stone. Katrina saw the similarity between this and the altar at church, but there, Jesus stood. Here ... it was ...

Below was a long stone table, against the wall. Dark stains had run down over the stones. The blood of the dead chicken ... the blood of the piggy ...

Katrina cringed back in Miss Theodora's arms.

"No, no, no nonononono ..."

Don't put me there, don't put me there, don't ...

252

CHAPTER 38

"*K*atie! My God, Katie!"

Katie became aware that someone was rubbing her forehead with a damp cloth. Scenes merged. Stone walls dripped water that glowed like tiny eyes. Black-skinned, naked creatures with vague human form stood and swayed in the darkness beyond. In the forefront a figure emerged. The woman ... Theodora ... no, a man ... *Dr. Firman!*

Dr. Firman. He was holding her as she bent forward, his hand against her back, the cold washcloth squashed damply to her forehead. She blinked up at him, and the dark cellar receded and was gone.

She trembled, the fear that was in the child a total emotion.

"What happened?" she asked. "What did I do?"

"You seemed to go into a trance, Katie. Perhaps it was a seizure of some kind. Certainly something that I'm not qualified to handle. I was ready to call an ambulance. Are you all right now? Katie?"

She nodded.

He brought her a glass of water. Suddenly it was in her hands. She thought of the moisture on the walls of the cellar. The complete dampness of that place where she had been. The shiny, underground reptilian bodies of those creatures the child had called, or thought of, as the Bad Things. The unreal reaching of stubby arms from their upper bodies, and the growing of strange long fingers.

"I'm all right," she said, and forced herself to drink.

She heard him draw a long breath. "Katie, I would like your permission to call Dr. Swartzhoff. He's one of the best of the psychiatrists within our area, and—"

"No."

Her voice was firm. She knew what would happen. She would be talked into going into a psychiatric hospital, and she would be given drugs, and days would pass. The doctor would finally dismiss her, nothing accomplished. Or, perhaps she would just disappear into the system.

"Katie, I feel, frankly, that you need something I can't give you."

"Her name is Katrina."

"Doctor Swart—*What?*"

"The child. Katrina."

In the silence he seemed not to be breathing at all. She stared into the glass of water.

"The child's name is Katrina," he repeated.

"Was."

"The child's name *was* Katrina?"

"Yes, was." She looked up. "The child is dead, Dr. Firman. Just now I relived the beginning of her death. She was running again, not only from the woman, but from the Bad Things. The Bad Things are not human. Nor are they reptiles, although they have characteristics ... like skin. No, I'll retract that. I saw them more clearly than before, and I don't believe they have scales. They have smooth, black, eel-like skin, like something that lives or came from water, or the ground. At first they were part of the darkness, something that seemed to roll or crawl, rising in the darkness. Bodies intermingling. Then, I saw them." She paused and sipped the water. She was confusing him, she could see that. Causing him to be more than ever convinced that she should be committed.

He said nothing. She saw from the corner of her eyes that he was staring at her incredulously. Trying in his mind to make the kind of sense that his view of reality afforded.

She met his stare. "Don't ask me what those creatures mean to me. Don't tell me that my subconscious has made them up because they stand for something too horrible to remember. They have been too horrible to remember, Doctor. Or, perhaps, too horrible to forget."

"What about the woman?" he said, in a voice so calm and soft that it surprised her. She saw that he had his own glass of water.

"The woman—I don't think I've told you her name either, have I? It's Theodora. Miss Theodora. Katrina always thought of her as 'Miss.' She's the lady of the house. I think."

"Theodora? Do you know someone by that name?" He was back on his mental feet, Katie saw, and she smiled. She still trembled inside, and sometimes her hand shook when she lifted the glass to her mouth. But outwardly, both of them were playing their little parts.

"That's what this is getting to be, isn't it, Jason?" she said deliberately. "Parts. We're playing a kind of game here, aren't we?" She had never even thought of him as Jason before, but now it seemed right.

"Are we?"

"Don't give me that shit! I'm tired of being treated as if it is a game."

"Katie, I didn't mean to ever make you feel that way. It isn't a game. It's— I'm afraid it's a far more serious matter than ..."

She waited, but he seemed unable, or unwilling, to continue.

"Let me tell you what happened," she said.

He nodded, so she told him about running down the hall and becoming trapped between the Bad Things in the hall behind her, and the door at the end of the hall.

"Miss Theodora opened the door. At first I felt relieved. She picked me up. And I saw down into the cellar. The walls are of stone. Very damp. Candles were sitting along the walls on tiny stone shelves. Flat rocks turned level among the stones. There was an altar. Miss Theodora was taking me—taking Katrina—to the altar. Blood had stained the sides of the altar. It was the place where Katrina's pet chicken and pig had been killed." She felt the terror rising with the memory, and she forced it away. Drink, she told herself. Don't go back for those final moments—or hours—whatever they were.

"I'm afraid, Doctor," she said, "that one of these days, or nights, I'll relive the rest of that child's life. Her final moments. I don't think I can stand the fear, and the pain."

"Katie, was she holding the rag doll?"

"Oh, yes. Under her left arm. She always carried the doll under her left arm. She reached up with her right to Miss Theodora."

"Who is Theodora? Is she the woman with the apron?"

"Yes. Didn't I ever tell you? Theodora is the name of the original owner of the house. Theodora Wickham. Her name is on the abstract. Even her handwriting is there."

KATIE DELAYED GOING HOME. She went first to the apartment and went through it carefully, to be sure she had left nothing, then she gave her key to the manager. She had spent an hour there.

She went from there to a shopping center, and bought some things from the delicatessen. But she had to go home. She wanted to go home, yet she dreaded going there. Here, among other people, she felt as if her mind lived only for the moment. Like a robot she could move with the others, thinking, what goes well with this for dinner, or supper, or however the individual family thought of the evening meal. What's on television tonight? Oh, that same old crap? Okay, what's new on video?

Yet none of that applied to her. Also, she didn't want to leave Nancy and the children there alone. Of course, no harm would come to them. The harm had happened long ago, and one of these days it would burn out of her memory, or she would stop seeing in her mind whatever had happened, and she would be free.

She wanted, after all, to go home.

THE DRIVEWAY WAS dark when she drove in close to the back porch and parked. Pale lights glowed from the three narrow windows on the second floor, as they did every night. A pale light glowed like an enlarged firefly in the long windows in the foyer.

She expected the kids, with Nancy following, to come running out of the house across the creaky old back porch. But they didn't.

Concerned, Katie turned on the flashlight she kept in the car and shined it into the grass to find the flat stones that were almost buried. She went up the path to the porch. She saw them through the open door, and felt relief deflate her as if she'd been holding her breath. They were all right, thank God.

Of course, why shouldn't they be? They were safe here. The danger was long gone. It had died with Theodora, perhaps even with Katrina.

She had to keep telling herself that, because no matter how she loved the house, how she was beginning to feel it was hers, she didn't want to be here alone.

They were sitting at the table, and it was set for eating. But they were just sitting, waiting.

"Hi!" she called, forcing great cheer where she felt none.

Nancy got up. "Well, hey, kids, the wayward wanderer is here."

"Isn't that supposed to be wayfaring stranger?" Katie carried the grocery bag to the counter near the old gray iron sink with its one jutting faucet. She put the bag down and washed her hands under the cold water.

They weren't acting the same, she noticed. The kids weren't running to see what she had in the bag or anything.

"Am I that late?" Katie asked. "What's wrong with the kids?"

"Oh," Nancy said, "They've just been quiet too long, I guess. I've kept them here waiting."

"I'm sorry. I didn't realize I was very much later. I just wanted to get us something special from the deli."

She expected Curtis to come running, but he continued to sit at the table, his round, dimply face barely above the place setting in front of him. His eyes were large and solemn, but were blinking slowly, the way they did when he was on the verge of falling asleep wherever he sat.

Erica got up and came around the table, and Katie saw she was carrying one of her large dolls. Its hair contrasted sharply with hers, black and blond. Its gown looked like old, yellowed crocheted silk. Its feet dangled near her knees.

"Aunt Katie, I found this doll."

She turned it.

Shock washed over Katie. Her skin felt cold and tight, and then began a strange tingling. Recognition. The doll, the beautiful doll she—no, Katrina—had wanted. The doll she couldn't have. The reason Eddie had made the rag doll.

How could Jason continue to tell her this was all a dream created by her own mind, symbols of things that had happened to her, when it was here? The dolls were here.

She sighed, knowing what he would say.

But of course, Katie. You saw them, and the mind is a very creative organ. For some reason it loves stories. It loves connecting things, and making some kind of logic from them. The mind can't stand feeling that the world is chaotic. It must make sense. The old house has affected you in this way. Your creative mind connected the beautiful doll, which belonged to a wealthy child, to the old rag doll which belonged to the poor child. But Katie—the story, the fears, originated in your own childhood, not someone else's.

Except that not even Dr. Firman was trying to convince her now of these things. Instead, he wanted to wash his hands of her and hand her over to a psychiatrist, because her creative mind was threatening to go out of control.

"Can I have her?" Erica was asking.

Katie didn't reach out to touch the doll. Although Erica extended it toward her, and Katie put out a hand, she quickly drew it back. *Don't ever touch that doll!* She could hear the voice, colder than anger.

Nancy said, "I told her she'd have to wait and ask you."

Katie heard the paper bag rattling as Nancy emptied it. Always bring paper bags, she had told Katie. We need them for wastebaskets around here.

"A cream pie?" Nancy said, amusement in her voice. "What would Mom say?"

"She'd say, Why didn't you get a fruit pie? Or, she'd say, Why did you buy one, you can make such better pies at home."

They smiled at each other, and Katie saw as much strain in Nancy's smile as she felt in her own.

Katie sat down at the table, and Erica stood so close, the fragile old gown of the doll brushed against her knee.

"It has a china head," Katie remarked, adding to herself, "That's why her face was so white." In the shadows, on top of the chest where she always sat, smiling, smiling, her dark eyes almost as dark as the slitted eyes of the woman that Jason said was not a ghost, but a product of her creative mind ...

Yet here was the doll, and Katie had never seen it before. Except in those strange, realistic dreams. Visions. Nightmares. Hallucinations. Memories.

"And her hair is so black," Erica said, touching a braid. "Black and shiny."

Dulled on top a bit by dust, Katie noticed. Dust that couldn't be brushed off, but which had settled instead into the braid. Just as the gray had settled into the hair of the woman who had owned the doll.

"Take very good care of her," Katie said.

Erica looked up with excited eyes rounding. "Does that mean I can keep her?"

"Sure, why not?"

"Oh, thank you, Aunt Katie! I love you!"

Katie received the one-armed hug and kiss with deep pleasure, the lovely old doll pressed between them. Katie smelled the faint odor of age, of clothing stale and dry. She had a feeling, quick and piercing, that she should take the doll and put it back where it belonged. But she discounted it immediately. It was time she took control of her feelings. If Jason was right and she was creating everything in her mind, then she could turn it around and create good instead of bad.

Katrina could have been a happy child, who roamed the house with delight, as Erica and Curtis did. She could have finally discarded the old doll when she and her family moved on to better circumstances. The stiff, dark substance on the doll could be oil or something, so Katrina threw it away. She lived in town, perhaps, then, and went to school. She grew up, beautiful and popular, married well, and lived happily ever after. It was possible, in fact, that if she was born around the turn of the century, she could still be alive.

Perhaps Eddie had been her brother.

No, no.

Katie looked over her shoulder. The softly spoken words seemed so real.

She began to watch Erica again, as she went so proudly over to show the doll again to her mother.

Katie heard a voice again, the other voice, the one filled with rage.

Don't touch that doll.

CHAPTER 39

*K*atie heard the tap on her door, a sound that seemed part of the voices in her mind. She had been trying for hours to read, but her mind kept picking up the words, like a whisper, *No no, don't touch that doll.* The repetition had made her feel, all through dinner, then afterward in her room, that if she didn't still those voices, she would go mad. *Nonono, don't touch that doll.* Don't touch ... She was no longer sure if they were different voices, or only one.

"Katie?"

The bedroom door opened and Nancy became part of the shadows and candlelight of the hallway. Katie was so glad to see her that she laid aside her book and put out her arms.

"Come sit on the bed, Nan! I thought you'd be sound asleep by now."

"Are you reading?"

"I was trying. Have you tried reading by candlelight?" She laughed. "Didn't we discuss this last night?" Nancy gave the little half-laugh that was so much like their mother. "By the time I get to bed, I'm so exhausted all I can do is shut my eyes. But then—they won't stay shut. They keep popping open."

"Haven't you been sleeping well?"

"Until tonight. Tonight I lay there and I thought and thought, and I decided I want to talk to you about something."

Nancy sat close enough to Katie that Katie could put out a hand and touch her. She hoisted herself farther up on the high bed, and crossed her legs Indian style, her hands gripping her ankles. Katie saw her features, shaded and shadowed by the candlelight, and thought her beautiful. Each had their mother's small, straight nose, but Nancy's lips were fuller and softer than Katie's own, her face softer, rounder, always a bit childlike.

Baby-faced, Doug called her. It was easy to see he thought her very pretty, just by the way he teased her about her baby face. Katie recalled feeling some jealousy when she was about thirteen, and Nancy was a perfect eighteen. She had compared herself to Nancy, and come out gawky and boyish in comparison. Even now, she didn't have the naturally abundant breasts, the small waist, the exquisitely proportioned body. Katie was longer in bones, less curvy.

But that was okay, she had decided, when she was still a teenager. She looked fine in jeans, which happened to be her favorite attire anyway. A pair of jeans and any old top. Unfortunately, she could wear them only on weekends, and when she was showing country property that required a lot of walking through fields and woods.

Nancy's face was lowered, as if she contemplated her ankles. She wore a pair of light summer pajamas, but Katie noticed she had put on a robe, though it hung open. The house was always cool.

"I had thought I wouldn't say anything, Katie. Then—"

In the pause, Katie said, "Something happened. The roof is leaking after all?"

Nancy smiled faintly. "It probably will when it rains."

"You're wanting to leave?"

"I—I don't know."

Don't go, don't go, came the cry from Katie's heart. Don't leave me here alone. And yet, that other part of her, the part that seemed to be getting better, glowed stronger now. Yes, it would be all right if Nancy and the children left. Then the house would never have to be changed at all. No apartments made from what Nancy called "useless rooms," no electricity to mar the soft beauty of candlelight.

Nancy looked up. "I saw her, Katie. I saw her, too."

"You saw ... ?"

"The ghost."

Katie sat up straighter, snapped up so fast that one of the fat pillows behind her back slid to one side. Without taking her eyes from Nancy, she adjusted the pillow.

"You saw the ghost?" she repeated slowly. The ghost that was of her own making, of her own mind?

"She was in the pantry. At first, I thought it was someone who had come into the house, maybe even someone who had been living here in some of the rooms we haven't seen. That wouldn't be difficult to do, you know, if you just stop to think—"

"Nan! You actually *saw* her?"

Nancy nodded, meeting Katie's eyes. "In the pantry. I clearly saw the apron you mentioned." She motioned the shape of the bib. "Rounded, here, with straps about two inches wide. And pockets down here, on both sides, rounded, like the bib."

Katie nodded.

"Some kind of dainty flowered pattern. A woman with dark hair pulled back, streaks of gray. But Katie ..."

Katie waited.

"You described her as gentle and kindly. Grandmotherly. This woman—ghost—was not like that at all. The way she looked at me, Katie, even the memory chills me—it was horrible—malevolent. Worse than angry. Her eyes were like black slits, slits filled with fires of hatred and—and ill will."

"What happened?"

"Curtis came."

"Did ... ?"

"No, Curtis didn't see her. You know how Curtis is. He always announces himself. He comes yelling. Calling."

Katie felt stunned, unable to assimilate what she was hearing. Nancy had seen the same ghost-woman she had?

"So," Nancy continued as if she were running out of breath. "That ended it. I'd been thinking I was facing a real person. The candlelight was so erratic, yet I saw her so clearly, she was only across the table from me. *I saw her so clearly!* I don't understand it, Katie. It makes me very nervous."

"She disappeared?"

"Oh, didn't I tell you? Curtis's voice, calling me. That caused her to disappear. One moment I saw her, and the next there was nothing."

Katie pulled her knees up, hugged them, and positioned her chin on her arms. They sat in silence a moment.

Then Nancy said, "I wanted you to know. It's not a repressed memory, this woman and apron thing. It's not in your imagination, either. She's here, in this house. She exists."

Katie said nothing. She felt as if she were between two different ways of thinking and was able to grasp neither.

Then she heard herself asking, without planning or thinking, "Was she carrying a knife?"

Nancy looked even more startled. "Good God, no. At least, I don't think so. I ... I don't think I even saw her hands. No, they were out of sight, below the top of the table. But I saw her so clearly, I can't get over it. I saw her, and then she was gone."

"The kids don't know."

"No, I didn't tell them. I didn't even know if I should tell you."

"If you want to leave, Nan, don't stay here just for me."

"Would you go, too?"

Katie shook her head. "I'm not afraid here, Nancy. I love this place."

"But what about ... ?"

Katie knew instantly what Nancy meant. She was referring to the time in the kitchen when she'd had the vision of the dead pig.

Nancy continued, "You were terrified then, Katie. You have those ... spells, sometimes. Maybe if you were away from here, you wouldn't."

"Don't you remember? They started while I was living in my little one-room apartment. No, it's not the house that scares me. Not even the ghost. What can a ghost do?"

"You yourself said she seemed to have power over the physical."

There was another pause, then Katie asked, "Where will you go, Nancy?"

"I don't know." She slid off the bed. "Right now, I'm going to check on the kids."

Katie watched her walk to the door, pausing to pick up the candle she had placed on the dresser. At the door she looked back, smiling.

"I probably won't sleep a wink."

"Leave the door open, Nan. If you need me, yell."

"Don't worry. I'll raise the roof."

Katie sat still long after Nancy's soft barefoot steps had faded away. She heard the squeak of a door, then silence. The candle she'd hung on the head of her bed so she could read made a soft, whispery sound.

She still couldn't think. Her mind felt numbed. Oddly, too, she was sleepy. She slid down and put her hands under her cheek and watched the open door. The hall beyond was faintly lighted by candles nearby. But she knew if she went into the hall it would look endless, disappearing into black tunnels in both directions.

NANCY STOOD without sound in the middle of the children's room. Curtis's bed was in the far corner, pushed against the wall so that he wouldn't have so much falling-off room. There was a nightstand not far from his bed, with a few of his stuffed animals. A Mickey Mouse, with big, round ears. A dinosaur. And another little creature that was someone's creative masterpiece. Maybe the creator had plans for that little guy, to make him into a cartoon, make him famous. Meantime, he sat there propped up on a bulky tail, looking part lizard, part imp with pointed ears.

In the corner of the room nearer the door, also pushed against the wall, was Erica's bed. Nancy noticed the big doll was taking up the corner, sitting up. Its feet stuck out onto the bed, leaving Erica only half the space of the twin bed.

The room looked so large, and almost empty. There was a dresser, and a couple of chests of drawers they had found in another room and brought here, so both kids would have places for their clothes. Everything was folded. There were no closets in most of the rooms. Tall, dark wardrobes served for keeping clothes, and one of those stood against the wall near the window. There was one in her room also, but none in Katie's. So far, Katie was using the room across the hall for a closet. A rod, put in the corner, held her suits and dresses.

The kids were okay. But the light seemed so dim. Nancy added her candle to the two that were already burning, and went out into the hall.

She stood still, near the three open doors of the occupied bedrooms, and the open door of the room across the hall that served as Katie's closet.

She could barely see the shapes of the banister and the drop of the stairway toward the foyer. But in the other direction light faded to blackness. No light came through from open doors, uncurtained windows. It was there, she recalled, on those stairs going to the third floor, that she thought she glimpsed someone. Perhaps she had. Perhaps the ghost-woman patrolled the house at night.

Yet she had seen her during the day.

She had told Katie she wouldn't sleep a wink, but she'd been joking. Or at least, she thought she had.

She went to bed and lay facing the door, listening to every movement in the house. She heard Curtis cough. She heard the rustle of bedclothes ... or something in the hall.

She slipped out of bed and went to the hall and looked in both directions. Silence. No, wind blowing beyond the thick walls of the house. And other sounds, within. Strange, soft, sliding noises.

If she allowed herself, she could imagine she saw a tangle of black figures, down near the area of the third-floor stairway. Dark figures that, if she stared long enough, would take shape, and become like thick-bodied snakes, rising, standing on short legs, reaching with short, thick arms and long, supple fingers of varying lengths. Lizard-like.

She forced the image away and crept silently back to her bed. She had looked at Curtis's nameless creature too long, she thought.

The sound of whimpering woke Erica. She blinked at her surroundings. A strange, flickering light hovered in the dark air between her and the sound of Curtis crying. He sounded a long way off.

She sat up abruptly. Now she remembered where she was. Always when she first woke it seemed she was having a bad dream, because her little corner in the apartment with the posters on the wall above her bed were replaced by a huge darkness. And that funny little light that hopped about on the top of the candle. That little light that only showed her the outlines of the other bed so far away across the wide room.

She vaguely saw Curtis sitting up in bed, pushing away from the sides, crying louder now.

She started to get out of bed, then saw something was on the floor. It was thick and dark, and had no discernible shape, but it moved.

Then suddenly there were soft footsteps at the door, and the door was pushed open. More light came, and it surrounded Mama's head like a halo. It made her look strangely like both a ghost with no body, and an angel with a halo.

"Curtis?" she said softly, going to his bed and sitting down.

The light she carried shone on the floor where Erica had seen the black things moving. Nothing was there, not even a small rug. Only Curtis's flip-flops.

"What's wrong, baby?" she asked, taking Curtis in her arms and smoothing his hair back from his forehead.

"Mama, there's monsters under my bed."

Erica noticed that Aunt Katie had also entered the room. But she remained standing near the door. She heard her say, as if to herself, "Monsters?"

Nancy said to Curtis, "That's only a bad dream, sweetheart. Lie down and go back to sleep."

Curtis lay down and turned his face to the wall. Mama covered him, patted his shoulder, and got off the bed. She saw Aunt Katie and smiled.

"Just a nightmare," she said, in that soft voice that she used when someone was sleeping.

Erica slipped down quietly, and closed her eyes. When she felt her mother's hand touch her cheek, she lay still, as if she was asleep.

After they were gone, she opened her eyes and lay staring at the darkness beneath Curtis's bed.

A long time passed, and nothing moved.

Then, somewhere in the house, she heard someone walking. Aunt Katie, she thought. She heard her climb a stairway. Then a door closed. Just knowing that one of the grownups was awake in the house made her feel safer.

She turned over to face her new doll and closed her eyes.

Then she remembered.

Aunt Katie wore soft slippers in the house, just as Mama did. Whoever she'd heard walking was wearing shoes with clunky heels.

CHAPTER 40

*D*r. Jason Firman's office was on the tenth floor of a professional building in an area where Nancy had to hunt for a place to park. Katie used a parking lot, but Nancy didn't know where it was, didn't have time to look, and didn't want to. She finally got lucky on her fifth time around the block and pulled into a space where another driver was just pulling out. The horn of a hopeful blared at her, but she didn't even look around.

She'd had to bring the kids with her. At home this morning she had called and asked if she could see Dr. Firman. At first she was told there was no opening.

"Tell him I'm Katie's sister," Nancy said, "and it's very important. I won't take up much of his time."

After being put on hold and listening to some depressing music for a while, she was told to come on in.

She had awakened earlier to the sound of her kids' voices. Astonished, she'd sat up in bed, seen the sun shining on the leaves outside her open window. She hadn't thought she'd sleep at all, but she'd slept so soundly, at the end of the night and early morning, that she hadn't heard Katie get up and leave.

They went up in the elevator to floor ten, got out, and walked down a wide corridor that had people hurrying along in opposite directions. She should have felt good, she thought to herself, being back in more familiar territory, but she didn't. She was nervous. The traffic had bothered her. So many people around bothered her. Maybe there was something to be said for a silent ghost, even if she did look daggers at her.

"What, Mommy?" Erica asked.

"What?" She was looking for his name, Dr. Firman, on one of the pebbled glass doors. They all looked alike.

"You were smiling," Erica said, trotting down the hall on one side of her, Curtis on the other.

Had she been smiling? Today, she could smile at the thoughts of the cranky but silent ghost? She almost laughed out loud.

She found the name and opened the door.

It was an ordinary reception room, with plastic chairs covered in an array of colors, a table with magazines, and even a children's corner. The only person in the room was the woman behind the desk.

Curtis headed straight for the children's corner.

Nancy whispered to Erica, "Go with him, make sure he stays there." Those were the very words, in variation, that her mother used to say to her. Watch Katie, take care of Katie. Of course, she always did, and still felt responsible for her.

She spoke to the alert middle-aged woman behind the desk. "I called to see Dr. Firman. I'm Nancy Wynne, Katie Rogers's sister."

The nurse rose, smiling, and motioned her toward an inner door. "You're right on time."

Katie hadn't described Dr. Firman to Nancy, but Nancy's own mental picture of him was so perfectly accurate she wondered if she had seen him somewhere. He looked thinner than was healthy, and she thought of her mother, and how she would probably be inquiring about his diet.

She thought of telling him about her mother, nosy maybe, but loving. Overprotective maybe, but never abusive. But he probably wouldn't believe her. He'd want to know what she was hiding.

Nancy smiled again, from her thoughts, not the surroundings, and not the pleasure of meeting a man who she felt had been causing Katie to be more confused, rather than helping her.

A week ago she would have told this man, hey, you're messing up my sister's mind, she's getting worse, not better. There are no goddamned repressed memories. That shit never happened to her. I know, because I was with her! But of course, he'd have questioned that, too. With her all the time? Well, no, she had to admit.

A week ago, she was angry with him. Now the problem had changed entirely.

His handshake was warm and firm. She felt his long fingers touch her wrist as they parted. There was something in his eyes that she hadn't noticed in a man's eyes in a long time, but it could simply be an intense interest because she was part of a puzzle that he thought was repressed memories.

"How nice to see you," he said. "May I call you Nancy?"

Only if I can call you Jason, she thought, but smiled and nodded instead.

"Would you like to sit here?"

"Thank you."

The chair was directly in front of his desk. Off to one side, near an arrangement of windows that looked out over a park with trees, was a recliner. Katie had mentioned the recliner. That was where she leaned back when they tried hypnosis.

The park looked miniscule and distant, from this tenth floor view. People walking on the sidewalk between the street and park were miniatures heading into the miniscule park.

Had she become country acclimated so fast? She wasn't sure she wanted to come back into the city to live.

"I've been wanting to talk to you, Nancy," Dr. Firman said. "I often request that my patients' relatives, the ones who figure prominently in their past, come and see me. It helps, sometimes."

"I'm sure it does."

"How is Katie this morning?"

"Katie had already gone to work when I woke up."

"I don't know a lot about Katie's work, unfortunately. We always talk about the other, because it's so urgent."

"She's in real estate," Nancy offered.

"Yes, I knew that. Is business good now?"

"She has a client or two at this time who are keeping her busy. It's because of her work that she found the old Wickham mansion."

"You live with her, I understand."

"Yes, my children and I. And that's why I'm here, Doctor. She told us about the ghost she had seen in the house, which seemed to be one of the things that brought her to see you?"

He nodded, but didn't give her any information.

"It was something that had to do with a bib apron, and a woman who this small child was so terrified of," Nancy reminded him. "I think you had convinced her she didn't really see a ghost, right?"

"Something that appears and disappears visually is usually created by the viewer's own mind."

"Well, what happens when two people see the same thing?" She was enjoying this. "You call it mass hysteria, or something like that, don't you?"

Instead of taking the bait and giving her the satisfaction of an argument, he said, "You've been living in the old mansion, I understand, while your sister works?"

Nancy sighed. "Yes."

"Katie had told me," he said in his soft, patient voice, "that you both have great plans for the old place. It sounds fantastic. That is, I mean, it sounds great. Something that might actually work."

"Things are happening slowly, if at all," Nancy said. "No electricity yet. No way to open it up to other people, yet."

"I'd like to see it sometime."

Nancy looked quickly at him. She couldn't read that look in his eyes. Concern? Curiosity?

He said, "It might help to enlighten a few points. Katie is having severe problems, you know. Those sudden regressions could become debilitating. If you can shed any light on what is happening to her, I wish you'd tell me."

"That stuff Katie ... sees, visualizes, did not happen to her, Doctor. I was with her. Five years older, I can remember when she was born, everything. We had a very quiet life. Our mother didn't even work those early years. It's something about that house, Doctor. I saw it myself. That's why I'm here."

"You saw it yourself? What did you see?"

"The ghost."

A flicker of a frown touched the doctor's brow. He had kept it creased so much, the creases were becoming permanent. He had a high, wide forehead. Nancy saw the pulse in his temples. It was almost like watching the steady mechanisms of his brain.

Nancy said, "Doctor, you had Katie believing that she hadn't seen what she saw. I'll have to admit, I didn't think she'd seen anything, either. I mean—Katie doesn't lie. I just had my doubts that she really *saw* it."

"I understand."

"But I'm here to tell you, it's real. The ghost is there. I saw her. Yesterday afternoon. I was in the pantry, which is a large room with shelves almost to the ceiling. There's one oblong table there, with an old cracked oilcloth on it. Probably the original. No chairs. The table is—was—used for a cook table, probably, where bread and pies and things like that were made."

Dr. Firman nodded. His eyes never left Nancy's face. She felt he was searching for something.

"I had gone in for some things. It was time to start dinner. Katie would be coming home. I had called the kids downstairs. They were in the kitchen."

Dr. Firman nodded again.

"That room doesn't have a window, so you have to take a light with you. Not much light comes in from the kitchen. I had set a candle on the table. I looked up. The woman stood at the side of the table."

She paused and rubbed her arms. She smiled, and he returned the smile.

"Just the memory," he said, as if he fully understood, "gives you goose bumps."

"Yes. More now than then. Then, my first thought was, 'There's a woman living in this house, after all!' Then I noticed how she was dressed, and I began to feel very cold. Really cold, Doctor, just unreal. It was the apron. The description fit. Everything Katie had said about the woman. And there she stood, looking so real it was ... unreal."

She bit her lower lip. Alone with the kids too much, she thought. No vocabulary in a pinch anymore except the one she'd picked up from the kids. She couldn't express herself. She sighed.

"Yes?" Dr. Firman urged softly.

'There's just no way to put it into words, Doctor. It's really strange. That feeling. I could feel a horrible cold coming from her. An unnatural cold. I could feel it from her eyes. The hatred ... the awful fury ... her anger at me. *Me.* I hadn't done anything to her. None of us had."

"*She was that real?* That she emanated emotions?" Now he had incredulity in his voice.

"I understand how you feel, Doctor. I was like you, when Katie told me some of the things she saw and which terrified her. When she went into that—sort of a trance, that day in the kitchen. When she saw the dead pig. She told you about that?"

He nodded.

"I couldn't understand her fear. I could see it, but understanding and feeling it myself was impossible. So it is with the ghost woman. You'd have to see her."

"What happened?"

"My son, Curtis—he's five—when he talks he yells, especially when he forgets—he called me and came running toward the pantry. The door was open. Suddenly, before he reached the door, she disappeared."

They stared into each other's eyes for a heartbeat. Then Dr. Firman said, "How did she disappear?"

"Well, she didn't go *poof*, as Katie said she had." She smiled, almost giggled nervously. Dr. Firman remained very sober, watching her closely. "She was just gone, that's all."

"Describe it again to me. Her appearance and disappearance."

"I saw her, as clearly as I see you, except, of course, there was only candlelight. I saw her. Then, at the sound of Curtis's voice, the space she had occupied was abruptly empty. She was gone."

Dr. Firman said nothing. He seemed to be searching her eyes, from one to the other, back and forth, as if he might find some kind of answer.

Nancy said, "She was *not* a benevolent soul, Doctor. I don't know what your beliefs are, but I was raised to believe there is a God, and a devil, and an afterlife. That souls do exist and live forever. They're supposed to go to happier places when the body dies. But when I was told about—about Katie's ghost, I didn't believe it. So I guess my real beliefs are contradictory. What I want to know is, since I did see her, how real is she?"

Dr. Firman began slowly shaking his head. He opened his mouth and closed it.

Nothing. No answer this time. Nancy rose, disappointed. She had expected an answer that she could accept. Something logical. Something, perhaps, about her own mind creating in the shadows of the candlelight a character similar to the one Katie had described. A mental thing. A psychological thing. Perhaps even a metaphysical answer. Any answer.

But there was none.

CHAPTER 41

*J*ason sat still after Nancy left. He had seen her during the first half of his lunch hour. Now he remained, giving up food, coffee, just trying to relax and understand. He wished he could be as understanding as he'd tried to make Katie believe.

Giving up lunch didn't matter. He had lost interest in food, even though during repetitious moments throughout the morning his mind had often drifted to food, and restaurants, and he had idled away some private possibilities on what might be good today. It was his way of protecting himself, of slipping away mentally when a patient went on and on about the same problem. He knew he wasn't being fair, always, and so he dragged himself back to the moment, and the problem at hand.

Katie's problem had intrigued him from the beginning. At first he'd experienced the almost illicit thrill of feeling he had in his presence someone who was opening up to repressed memories. And so early in his career! In the two years he had been a counselor he had become amazed, and then dismayed, at how common certain problems were. Man disenchanted with love. Woman disenchanted with love. Over and over. Youth expecting too much from life. Elderly filled with anxieties and loneliness, so much of what was important in a life now gone. Nothing, he found, was ever very exciting in this line of work. It was dismayingly familiar.

It was sad.

They came to him searching within for some meaning to justify their existence. To find an answer, even, to the meaning of life itself. It is an inherent quality of the human mind, he had decided, to piece together order and meaning from what seems to be accidental chaos. They came to find a pattern within an endless puzzle.

The solutions usually called for getting interested in something positive on a daily basis. Forget about deeper meanings. The human mind appeared not to be that evolved. Instead, live and be happy. Have something to look forward to each day. Simple things. A game of golf for one, a lunch for another. Even a telephone call to a favorite person. But preferably, something that did not depend on other people. True independence meant autonomy. Happiness comes from within. That old adage was correct. It worked. Find it. That private happiness, or contentment that one was doing the right thing.

Then Katie had come in.

It was a selfish excitement on his part, he understood that right away. He was delighted to find a patient who had actually *experienced* something beyond disappointments in love, sex, work, or self. He *knew* he was being selfish in his eagerness, but it didn't stop his excitement. This was finally his chance to really help someone. Katie was a lovely young woman, already a widow. She had handled her grief very well, it seemed to Jason. However, her husband's death might have been the catalyst for the arising memories. The dreams, the visions. Which would mean she had in some way also repressed the grief experience, pushed it back too soon, where it had erupted in the depths of her mind and somehow pushed to the surface memories she had consciously forgotten.

Then, he began to have doubts.

If both Katie's mother and sister insisted that none of the things that terrified Katie could have happened, then what was it? There were other possibilities. Simple nightmares, which have less exotic answers, though they were sometimes harder to find. Hallucinations. Perhaps it all came from repressing the grief of her husband's death.

And in himself, disappointment that he didn't have a patient with repressed memories after all. He had to face his own weaknesses, his own selfishness, and that was never easy. He had to take his own advice. It was as bad as swallowing his own medicine. He had wanted an exciting patient, but if he was going to help Katie, he had to put aside the exotic and look for the mundane.

But this, today, with Nancy, confused him.

A *ghost?*

He had believed Nancy. There was nothing about her to suggest she was playing a game.

He rose from behind his desk, adjusted his tie, and pressed the button for his office nurse.

"Yes, Doctor?"

"Who's scheduled for this afternoon, Miss Franklin?"

She had worked for him since he had opened his office. A psychiatric nurse from a large state hospital, she had burned out on her work. She wanted to remain in mental care, but not to the degree she had been. In the beginning they had argued about what to call each other. She had insisted he call her Sarah, and he'd said no. If she insisted on calling him Doctor, which she did, then he would address her formally as well. They finally laughed about it, said it might look better in front of the patients, and settled it. Even in private they were Doctor and Miss Franklin.

She said, "James, with the in-law problems, and Clarice."

Clarice was reliving her youth, trying to find out what had caused her self-loathing, her compulsive binges and bulimia. For one moment Jason worried that canceling her appointment might set her back and cause her to give in to another binge, something she hated herself for and swore to him she hadn't done in a couple of weeks. But if what he was beginning to fear was true, it was urgent that he try to do something other than sit and listen to Katie's, and now Nancy's, questions.

"Could you call and make some other arrangements? I'll see them Saturday if they'd like. And tell Clarice if she needs me I'll see her tonight—after dinner. I'll call in later, Miss Franklin."

He left through his back door, came out into the hallway, and walked quickly toward the rear elevator. He didn't want to meet a patient.

In his car he dug out of the glove compartment the small address book he kept there. In case of emergencies it was easier to keep a book in the car than have to hunt up a desk at home, or in the office, that held the information he needed. He had addresses and telephone numbers of all his patients, and anyone connected to the patient. Rarely used, still it was one of his most important sources of information.

As he drove out of the parking lot and into traffic, he dialed on his car phone Katie's place of work. A pleasant female voice answered, announcing Yates Realty. It wasn't Katie.

"Is Mrs. Rogers in?" he asked without identifying himself.

"No, I'm sorry," the pleasant voice said, sounding happy and problem-free. "Mrs. Rogers is showing property this afternoon. Would you like to leave a message, or could someone else help you?"

"Is Mr. Yates available?"

"Yes, he is, just a moment, please."

Jason paused before edging into the traffic and considered the direction to the big city library. He didn't go there often, preferring a small branch library near his home where he could order any book he needed. This time, he wanted to see microfilm, not a book. He didn't know yet what he might be searching for. Perhaps Mr. Yates could help him clarify a few points.

"Good afternoon," a man's voice said, "This is Yates."

"Mr. Yates, I'm—uh—" He rapidly contemplated not identifying himself, but just as rapidly decided he would probably get more information if he did. "I'm Katie's friend, and I need some information about the house she lives in. Could you help me?"

There was a pause. In bemusement Jason saw Yate's point of view.

Jason added, "It seems there's a ghost ..."

"Ahhh,"' Yates said.

"Yes. Seen by two people now, which puts it in the category of being more than a figment of Katie's imagination. I wondered if I could get the background history on this property."

"I have a copy of the abstract, if you'd like to look at it."

"Would this afternoon be convenient?"

"Yes, are you in the vicinity?"

"I am. I'll be there within a few minutes. Thank you."

"I'll wait."

Jason checked the address of Yates Realty, and found it in a small shopping center. He parked nearby and walked up to the glass door. For just a moment his reflection wavered back at him, long, thinner than he really was. All he needed was a hat. Enter Sherlock Holmes.

There were several desks in the large front office, but only two were occupied. At the first desk a young woman smiled, greeted him, and left her desk just long enough to show him the door to Yates's office. By that time a small man with sparkling blue eyes had appeared in the doorway.

Jason shook his hand and sat in the chair he offered. The abstract was already on the desk. Jason picked it up. Yates went to his chair behind the desk and leaned his chin on his fists.

Jason opened the narrow booklet that had gold-colored rivets at the top. Yates sat back, his hands on the wooden chair arms.

"You'll find it's a thin abstract. There have been only two purchases completed. The original purchase was by Emmett Oliver Wickham for a section of land, six hundred and forty acres. That land was mainly used for the Wickham lumber business and lumberyard, which became part of the town. The property on which the house was built contained one hundred and sixty acres of land with only a few acres cleared. And that is what Katie bought."

Jason looked through the abstract. "It doesn't say what year the house was built, or by whom?"

"No, you have to assume it was built sometime in the eighteen-fifties or -sixties, or perhaps even later. A company based in Washington in the logging industry came into possession of the house, through the lumber companies Wickham had owned, on the death of Mrs. Wickham in 1949. The house was not sold until this year, to Katie."

Jason looked up. "It's been for sale how long?"

"Since Mrs. Wickham died, in 1949. It's been on Yates Realty books the whole time. In this case, we had an exclusive. My father, you see, owned the business before I did."

"And in all these years the property wasn't sold? How damned expensive was it?"

"Oh, very reasonable. In fact, cheap, considering. And yes, it *was* sold several times. That is, people started to buy it and backed out. Those facts aren't in the abstract simply because the deals weren't completed, no mortgages were assumed. Near sales aren't recorded." Jason took out a notepad and wrote down the name of the original owners: Emmett and Theodora Wickham.

"Didn't they have children?" Named Katrina and Eddie.

"I have no way of knowing. If they did, the children didn't survive Mrs. Wickham."

"Could I ask why the potential sales weren't followed through?"

"Sure. The house is a big one, forty-some rooms, maybe more, not counting storage rooms and such. I don't know anyone who's counted. There aren't a lot of windows. There are more hallways and stairways, it seems, than windows. So the house is dark. Everyone who intended to buy the property was allowed to move in first if they wanted to. A couple did, but didn't stay long enough to remove the stuff they'd moved in."

Jason noted Yates's smile. He was trying to hide it, but the amusement glittered in his eyes.

"The ghost, huh?" Jason said.

Yates chuckled. "Never saw it myself."

"How many have?"

Yates shrugged. "It's always the women, you know."

Uh-huh, Jason thought. A bit of chauvinism here. "Meaning they're more sensitive?" Jason suggested, though obviously that wasn't what Yates meant.

Some of the amusement left Yates's face. "Katie seems to be getting along well there. She hasn't backed out of the deal. She knows she can at any time. The way I understand it is, she and her sister, who is separated from her husband, are going to turn it into a sort of hotel for the homeless, especially mothers, a temporary shelter, with part of it for those who can't pay."

"Yes," Jason said. Katie had told him something of her dreams for the property, and he hoped it came to pass. "But first," he said, "there's a ghost that's been seen by how many?"

Yates shrugged, then seemed to understand that Jason was asking a serious question. "Well, uh, maybe half a dozen people before Katie. I remember the first time I heard of it was when my dad sold the old Wickham House back in the fifties. Some folks moved in, stayed a week, and left. Dad said the woman had seen another woman in the house, and then it turned out there wasn't another woman. She also heard things. Said she could hear laughter. That was the first time. Old houses make sounds. Let a little wind come up ..."

"Was that the first sale?"

"Potential sale. It didn't sell, obviously. People had looked at it every once in a while. The women never liked it. In real estate, you see, it's always the woman who makes the decision on the house. Almost always. There were two more families, well, men and their wives, retired couples, who moved in before their mortgage was completed, and then moved out, willing to forfeit their money."

"The ghost?"

"Yes, so they said."

"Were these sales being made by you?"

'Yes, one about fifteen years ago, and one five or six."

"Did any of these people describe the ghost?"

"No. Just said it was a woman."

"Is there any available history on the place and the Wickhams'?"

Yates shook his head slowly. "You're actually believing there is a ghost? And if there is, that it must be Theodora Wickham?"

"Wouldn't you become something of a believer after so many people saw her?"

"Women," Yates said, but he was no longer smiling.

Jason almost laughed. "I understand that. But I would like to know more about the possible reasons behind the, uh, the sightings. Whatever they are."

Yates shook his head and nodded toward the abstract, which Jason had laid back on the desk. It had mentioned very few names. Katie's was the last one. The property was now hers, no longer Theodora Wickham's.

A strange rush of concern made Jason feel suddenly depressed, anxious, worried. He rose, held out his hand. Yates shook it warmly.

"Thank you, sir, for your time."

Yates nodded. "Take good care of Katie."

Jason looked for the glitter of amusement in Yates's eyes, but it was gone. Take good care of Katie. He had meant it from the depths of his heart.

CHAPTER 42

$\mathcal{K}$ ate was right about the name of Theodora. But where did Eddie and Katrina fit in?

He felt suddenly as if he were looking through a mental kaleidoscope, where no piece fit with another. He was not comfortable with it. His thought processes had always been orderly, and his patients' problems simple, compared to Katie's. He didn't know what to do next to help her, except change his way of looking at her problem.

To look into the possibility that she might be right, and the dreams and visual scenes that were disturbing her so much might actually have happened to someone else at another time ... was that possible? He would never have thought so.

To lighten his mood, he deliberately let his mind dwell on Nancy. Through Katie he had formed a mental picture of Nancy. She was an older Katie, actually, but with a secretive look. In his image of her, she was also heavier and dowdier, and wore the hairdo she'd worn in her teens.

Wrong!

His own mind processes interested him at times, when he wasn't busy analyzing other's minds. How and why had he come up with that particular picture of Nancy? He was shocked at how wrong his mental picture was.

When Nancy walked in, something like an electric pulse went off somewhere within him. She wasn't a patient; she was coming to see him on behalf of Katie. So his sudden surprised attraction to her wasn't exactly unethical. He did, however, have to remind himself she was married. With children. Even though she was separated. He had a millisecond image of her remaining separated from the faceless man and becoming part of his own life instead. Then he snapped to reality, stood up, and shook her hand.

He had liked the feel of that hand and had wanted to hold on forever. It was soft, flexible, the bones almost melting in his hold. She had a soft look, as smooth as honey, her eyes clear and direct, her hair almost liquid in the way it fell across her shoulders. She wore only a touch of lipstick on her full lips. Her cheeks were shadowed, dipping in beneath her cheekbones. Where Katie's face was oval, Nancy's was more triangular, with a wider forehead, a narrower chin. There was only a faint resemblance to Katie. Their coloring was similar. Light brown to blond hair, fair complexion.

But the chemistry was astounding. He wondered if she felt it, too. He wondered if one person could feel a strong physical pull toward someone while at the same time repelling the other person.

Unfortunately, he knew that was true. It was almost as if one force was too strong, and instead of attracting, it repelled. History was filled with cases of unrequited love.

He was almost thirty, had been engaged once when he was in his early twenties, but the affair had fallen through. It was a mutual thing as he recalled it. At twenty-four, still in school, he had decided he wasn't ready to be married. And she was glad because she had found someone else during all those hours he spent with his nose in a book.

After that, while he was establishing his practice, he had lived for a while with his parents. Then he had rented a house, so his golden retriever could have a backyard. The next year he had decided he was wasting money just by renting, so he bought the house. Since then, time had drifted by. He was busy. He and Sam lived quiet lives, and liked it that way. Evenings were more often spent reading than with friends. Slowly, as they married, the friends were drifting away to their own interests.

And Jason was more and more involved in his work.

This was his third year, and he realized as he drove toward the library just how inexperienced he was. If he felt the need, he could consult a former teacher who'd spent years in psychotherapy before he'd decided to take the less stressful work of a teacher. Dr. Mateland still worked three hours a week at the psychiatric ward in one of the hospitals. Jason had feelings at times that Katie needed more than he could give her. But first, he had to try something else. He had to forget his own convictions, and listen to her.

Really listen to her.

At the library, he asked for help from one of the librarians. There were ten floors of information and entertainment. He had spent many hours in the room on the fourth floor where the chairs were neatly lined up by long tables and the shelves filled with books on the human mind, but he had no idea where to go to look at old newspapers.

Several people worked behind the long counter. He chose one who looked motherly and friendly, and not too busy. She smiled at him and asked, "Can I help?"

"Thank you, I hope so. Where do I look for information on events that might have happened ..." He paused. Katie had described the child Katrina as wearing a long dress, almost to her ankles. "Early in the century, perhaps, at a small town south of the city."

The librarian frowned thoughtfully. Her eyes searched the long aisles behind him. "Probably in the county seat of that town, and possibly in the library there. What's the name of the town?"

He opened his mouth, closed it. "I'm sorry. I know where it is, but I'm not sure of the name."

"Well, they surely have a library. And county records. I would suggest going there."

Of course. Why hadn't he thought of that? He nodded his thanks and left, glancing at his watch. He was wasting time. He could have gained this information by telephone.

He paused a moment longer in his car to check routes, and saw the name of the town was Deasville. He drove the closest route to the interstate that wound around the city, and took the Spring Valley exit. He drove through a rural area with scattered small farms among the modern housing developments, then into town.

Almost immediately he seemed to have dropped back in time. The streets of Deasville were narrower, the traffic slower. He came into town on a twenty-five-mile-an-hour speed limit. Large old trees adorned the town square. In the center was a statue of a Civil War general, holding his bayonet at his side, the brim of his hat a resting place for birds, one of them a bright red cardinal.

The library was on the east side of the square, a small brick building wedged between two taller buildings made of gray stone. There was plenty of parking space.

The front room of the library, up a series of gray stone steps, was no larger than the psychology room at the city library. There was an odor of aged books and wood. One woman sat behind the desk. She seemed to be alone. If anyone browsed, they were hidden down some dusty aisle.

"I don't suppose you have old newspapers," he said, and as he said it, he thought of the impossible task of looking for information that probably didn't exist, or if it did, at a time that was unknown.

He was almost relieved when she shook her head. "All of that is on microfilm. We do have a microfilm reader, if you'd like to use it."

He stared at her.

She stared back. She appeared to be in her seventies, though her hair didn't show a spot of gray. It was a soft brown and very natural. But her face had the special look of aging. She had been around a while. He did some fast figuring. If Theodora Wickham died in 1949, how old was this lady, then?

"Did you particularly want the old newspapers? You might check at the printing shop of the *Deasville Daily Sentinel*. It's been there for more than a hundred years. Had the centennial back in '75."

He shook his head and looked again at his watch. Would Nancy be home?

"Are you familiar with the old Wickham House?"

"Of course." She smiled. "I understand it has recently sold."

"Could you give me directions?"

"Yes. Just go on around the square to highway twelve. It turns off at the corner opposite here, and looks like a street. Then, just drive on out, perhaps a half mile. You'll see the house through the trees on the right if you watch carefully. There's a quite long driveway. Very narrow. Be careful when you turn. Are you a relative of the lady who bought it?"

"Friend," he said. "Were you acquainted with the former owner, Mrs. Wickham, by any chance."

"No, not personally. I knew of her, of course. I was in my teens when she died."

She was looking at him with growing curiosity. He could almost see her mind making connections. He felt a stir of encouragement. She was a native. She remembered.

"I'm looking for information about the people who lived at Wickham House, perhaps early in the century. A tragedy, perhaps, that might have happened there?"

"Oh. That's why you want the old newspapers." Even as she spoke, she disentangled herself from the chair behind the desk and went walking briskly away.

He assumed he was to follow her.

She went to a computer in an area around the corner and sat down. He stood behind her, watching the headlines of old newspapers appear on the screen.

"Do you know if she had children?" he asked.

"Not that I ever heard of. She was a recluse who showed up only at the grocery store now and then, as far as I ever knew."

"What did she die of?"

"Old age? I don't know. Oh, yes!" she cried. "A fire. A fire, at the church she attended. It was an old church, near her home. Just a minute. I can track that down quite easily because that was the year I married, and it's the kind of thing that doesn't happen often in a small town. We haven't had many fires in Deasville, and certainly not in churches."

She flipped dates and brought up 1949.

"It was in the early spring, a couple months before ... ummm ... Said it was caused by an electric storm earlier in the day, touched off old wiring, or something. Here it is."

Jason read over her shoulder. The headlines claimed, *"Deasville Loses Benevolent Dowager."*

Beneath, in a front page column, Jason read quickly as the librarian spoke aloud, explaining the contents of the article. No one else had been injured, but the church was destroyed.

He said, "It doesn't say much, does it? Just that the old lady died of smoke inhalation later at the hospital. Is there an obituary?"

It appeared the next day. It did not state her age or her place of birth, or name any survivors. It only mentioned the date and place of burial, a local cemetery, and the cremation.

"There was something else, now that I think of it," she said. "I remember hearing my grandfather talk about it. A murder, disappearances, that sort of thing. It happened when he was raising his family, so it must have been in the early 1900's."

She rapidly turned the pages back. The headlines had been going by so fast he hadn't had a chance to read them. He had seen war mentioned several times, and felt strangely as if he were in some kind of time machine that flipped him backward through the Vietnam and Korean Wars to World War Two, and the one referred to as "The World War."

She slowed the machine, then moved on, taking time to read each headline. He saw the dates. January 17, 1910. She moved it forward, mumbling.

"I thought I saw ..."

June 12, 1910.

July 21, 1910.

"Okay, here," she said, in a voice that startled him to alertness.

He saw the headlines even as she read them aloud.

"*'Local Child. Missing. Katrina Etchens is missing from her home. Searchers are combing the woods behind Wickham House.'* It goes on to say that Katrina is the daughter of Charlie Etchens, who lives on the Wickham property ..."

She turned to the following day.

"*'Child Found Dead. Edward Wickham, a deaf-mute, distant relative of Theodora Wickham's, is arrested for the brutal murder of Katrina Etchens.'* Is this the information you wanted?"

Jason was only half aware of not answering her. He peered at the print.

She turned in the swivel chair. "But he wasn't hanged, as I recall Grandpa saying, he was found not guilty, I believe." She turned back again, and moved the headlines forward. Every day, something about the trial. And then, suddenly, in large block letters,

EDWARD WICKHAM FOUND NOT GUILTY.

"There was a surprise witness named Angie Beckley. Oh, I know the

Beckleys! At least, I knew of them, and I once went to school with a couple of Beckleys. You know how it is in these small communities. You can hardly live here without knowing them."

Had Katie known of any of this? Had those names, this old tragedy, been mentioned in her presence? He could almost see her entering one of the places of business somewhere around the square and when she introduced herself as the new owner of Wickham House, being told of the murder that had occurred there long ago.

"And then ... look," the librarian said.

He forced himself to focus his eyes on the article. It was not a headline, but a few paragraphs on page two.

Missing, Angie Beckley and Edward Wickham. Although a search party had been organized to search for Angie Beckley, it was suggested that since Edward was also gone, perhaps there was no foul play.

"Let me see," she said, and turned the pages back to the obituary of Katrina Jane Etchens. "Five years old, poor baby. Barely five. Born July 10, 1905, died July 20, 1910. Survivors are her parents, grandparents, and two brothers. Hmmm," she murmured aloud. "The name is not familiar. They all must have left the area."

Jason drew back.

"And then ... no more mention of Wickham House that I can see," the librarian offered, still looking through headlines. She flipped forward to 1921,1932 ...

"That's fine, thank you very much," he said.

He was in a hurry now. He had to go out to the house, see if Nancy was home. And the kids. She had two small children. He felt an urgency he couldn't have explained had he tried.

When he left, the librarian was still at the microfilm reader, searching on, engrossed in old newspaper stories.

He wanted to drive faster than the twenty-five miles per hour allowed. He needed more information, and this time from Nancy, and Katie. How much of that story had Katie known? Was there a picture of Theodora somewhere in the house that Katie, and Nancy, had seen? Both of them had clearly described the "ghost" they'd seen. Could both of them be having the same delusions?

He realized he was reluctant to give up his repressed memories theory. That in some way Katie must be associating. Seeing the rag doll, even the house, had brought back something within her that was not yet identified.

But that didn't explain Nancy's insistence that she had seen the ghost.

He found the driveway, turned a sharp corner, and saw the interesting little trail winding through century-old trees. He felt as if he were driving into Sherwood Forest.

The house seemed a part of the woods. Behind it, in an area of more widely spaced trees, were a long, crumbling garage with several stalls, open on the front, and farther back, a barn in a more solid state that once had been red. Bits of flaked pinkish color clung in shadowed places on the barn walls. There also was a shack off to his left. It fit Katie's description of the place where she'd found the rag doll.

The house was an interesting design of mixed architectures. He recognized Victorian and Georgian or Federal. It didn't look large enough to contain the number of rooms it was claimed to have, but it was angled like a stack of blocks, and difficult to see completely even after he'd gotten out of the car and walked around to the rear.

He felt the emptiness even before he reached the door. There seemed to be a still, dark quality about the house that was forbidding in the extreme. What a difference, he thought, as he knocked and peered through the glass on the kitchen door, in people's reaction to a thing or situation. Katie had fallen in love with it instantly, and felt at home here. He was repelled by it. It was as though something had called Katie to come to the house.

She believed she might be a reincarnation of Katrina, and as he stood there, looking through old etched glass into the long, gloomy kitchen, it seemed possible ... as if all his beliefs were only the reflection of truth, the reverse side of what might be.

He wasn't ready to accept reincarnation, but he was receptive to other possibilities and new horizons. It did seem that in some way Katrina's life and death had reached Katie. All that entirely aside from the coincidence of their names.

Katie was still gone, working.

Nor had Nancy returned. There were no voices of children, no cars parked in sight.

He wrote a brief note to Nancy.

"Please call me as soon as possible."

He paused, pen in hand. He wanted to write: Urgent. But he only signed his name, adding both his home and office numbers. He folded the notepaper once and tucked it into the crack between the door and the wall where it couldn't be missed.

He drove away, hoping he'd meet Nancy driving in. At the end of the driveway, he paused for three cars to go past, and it occurred to him he didn't even know what kind of car Nancy drove.

You're too interested in this woman, he chided himself. He had to remember there was a husband, even though they were separated. The ideal situation, from a moral standpoint and for the sake of the children, was that they learn to sort out their differences and try to get along.

But ... he was still interested. He wanted to tell her he'd be there for her if her marriage didn't work out. But of course he wouldn't.

He retraced his route back to the interstate, eyeing the driver of each car he met. If he saw Nancy, he'd turn around and follow her.

The clock on the dash indicated it was close to four. On the chance that Katie might have returned to the real estate office, he dialed that number again and asked for her.

He breathed a sigh of relief when the receptionist said, "Just a moment, please."

"Hello, Katie Rogers speaking."

"Katie, this is Dr. Firman." Now he found himself facing a dilemma. How much of his own sudden anxiety should he convey to her? "Nancy came to see me this morning, Katie."

"What? Why?"

"She didn't tell you?"

There was the faintest pause. A car honked at him, and he saw he had slowed down. He saw an available slot in the slow lane and pulled into it.

Katie asked, "Are you calling from your car?"

"Yes. I've been out to your town and am on my way back. I went to your house, but Nancy wasn't home yet. Nor you, I might add."

"She came to see you on my behalf, Doctor?"

"Yes." He found himself in another crunch. If Nancy hadn't told Katie about seeing the ghost, did she not want Katie to know? He decided to let that go for the moment. "Katie, I stopped at your local library. A five-year-old girl named Katrina Etchens was murdered on that property in 1910. She was the daughter of a worker who lived on the property—"

He heard Katie gasp and say softly, "In the old shed."

"Where you found the rag doll?"

"Yes. How do you know—about this?"

"It was in the newspapers at the time, and your librarian looked it up. There was a trial. A sixteen-year-old youth was tried for the murder."

"Eddie," she said.

"Yes. Edward Wickham. He was Theodora's nephew by marriage. He was described as a deaf-mute in one newspaper, and in another as merely dumb. It seemed he could hear but couldn't speak."

"Yes," Katie said, so softly it was almost a whisper.

"Are you okay, Katie?"

"Yes, I'm all right."

He said, "I'm heading back to my office, if you want to come in and talk."

There was another hesitation while he angled toward his exit. With his attention taken for a moment by the traffic, he came back to the phone with added anxiety. "Katie?"

"I'm here. I was just thinking."

He found himself wondering if he was handling any of this right. Would she, who had somehow picked up on a tragedy that had happened years ago, be better off knowing that people she had thought she'd dreamed once actually existed? And then he remembered that it was he who thought she had created them, after he'd become doubtful that it was repressed memories after all. And now, he was no longer sure of anything. He felt oddly inadequate. This case was messing up his confidence.

"What happened to Eddie?" Katie asked. "Was he—convicted? He didn't do it, you know. Eddie didn't do it."

"No, Eddie wasn't convicted. The jury freed him."

"No that's wrong," she said quickly, in a breathless panic. "He wasn't freed. He ... he "

"Katie, Katie, yes, he was," Jason said, trying to make his voice soothing and calming. "He was judged not guilty. A young girl, Angie ... I don't recall her last name ... came forward in his defense. And the jury set him free."

"Angie?"

"The name is not familiar to you?"

He wondered if Katie might have heard or read the story of Katrina and Eddie and then consciously forgotten it. It would explain a lot. It would set his mind at ease to know she had. But it would not explain Nancy's sighting of the ghost of a woman who must have been Theodora.

"I don't think so," Katie finally said. "No—no Angie. What happened to Eddie, then?"

"He and Angie disappeared. Angie was searched for, feared murdered also. But her body wasn't found. The last article the librarian found suggested that Angie and Eddie had run away together."

"No," Katie said. "No, Eddie never left that place."

"How can you be sure, Katie?"

"I just ... have a feeling."

"Katie, will you come to my office?"

"Can I come tomorrow?"

"I don't know my schedule. I'm free this evening, if you'd like to talk."

"Thanks, Doctor, but I think I'll go home. Thanks for calling and telling me this."

"'Katie," he said, "I think it would be a good idea for you to—"

But the phone had clicked, the connection broken.

... To come on to the office so we can talk, try to understand this ...

He wanted to ask her if there was any possibility that she had heard or read about Katrina and Eddie.

But tomorrow would do. He'd make room for her, even if it took up his lunch hour.

Another thing occurred suddenly to him, with a strange chilling, as if he was just awakening to something sinister and evil.

The rag doll ... without waiting for the report from the lab, he knew the answer.

Blood.

It was blood, soaked into the old doll years ago, caked with dirt, darkened over the years.

The child's—Katrina's—blood.

CHAPTER 43

$\mathcal{K}$atie entered through the front door, and stood quietly looking into the depths of darkness that grew before her as if she were entering a tunnel. She had come home to find a stairway, if it existed, that descended into a cellar beneath the house. Before she'd entered, she had walked around the house, staying close to the walls, peering behind overgrown shrubbery and clinging vines that hid the foundation. She was looking for signs of a basement, but there was no opening, no window that she could find.

Now standing within the house, aware of the lack of sound, she felt reluctant to take a step and destroy the silence. She was afraid. Yet the house closed her in and she felt a deep longing to seek a dark corner, and huddle into it where she could blend forever with the silences and shadows.

Think, she told herself. *Remember.* Where had Katrina gone? Where had she tried to hide? In a hallway, on the ground floor. A hallway that ended at a door opening into a cellar.

She walked down the hall into the deepening shadows. To her right a door stood open, but it led into the old parlor. The second door disclosed a music room. The organ was still there, the only musical instrument in the house. There was no other furniture. Windows were vine-choked, cutting off light.

The third door revealed what must have been a dining room. A long table was still there, but all chairs were gone. Here, too, vines covered the windows. The vines grew more abundantly on the east side of the house, away from the driveway, as if they had sought a privacy of their own. Maybe the answer lay somewhere in the past, when a gardener kept the growths cut away on the west. It was as if the east side of the house had never been used.

The dining room had a door with an oval etched glass opening out onto a porch that was tucked into the walls of the house. But it was locked. She had never opened it.

The walls in the dining room were dark paneling, and as she turned back toward the hallway, she saw for the first time the door set in the paneling.

She opened the door.

In the almost total darkness she saw a narrow hallway, and directly across from the dining room door, another door, closed.

Of course! The dining room, not just the central hall, would have access to the kitchen. She knew, as if she had passed this way many times, that the door across the hall opened into the pantry.

She stepped cautiously into the hall, and felt the coldness cover her skin. To her right and left was darkness. The only light came from the shadows of the dining room. Her chest tightened, ancient warnings pulled at the hair on the back of her head. She gasped for deeper breath.

She stepped back into the dining room. Then, as if crossing a chasm of endlessness, she quickly stepped forward and opened the other door.

Her breath escaped in a sigh of relief.

Yes, the pantry. And light from the kitchen, though dim and chilled, came through the opposite open doorway.

She crossed the kitchen, hearing the hollow sound of footsteps following her. She glanced over her shoulder, but no one was there.

She had found the hallway where Katrina had crouched behind a large wardrobe, or some kind of chest that had long doors rather than drawers. But she needed a light.

She paused at the table in the pantry and lighted the kerosene lamp Nancy had placed there. The light turned the shadows a strange, soft yellow, like sullied fog.

She lifted the lamp and carried it with her to the door into the hallway. Why had she not opened that door before? Had Nancy ever opened it?

Had either of the children?

She stepped quietly into the hall. *Don't rouse the Bad Things. Walk quietly, don't let them know you're here. Go and find Eddie, tell him the Bad Things are there, there, somewhere ... he'll make them go away ...*

Katie squeezed her eyes shut and opened them again. Please God, not again. Don't let me revert now to that child!

There was something she had to do. She couldn't give in to the cries of the child, the memories, the visions, whatever they were. She must understand fully what she was doing here, what she must do to end this.

She stepped into the hall and paused, looking toward the door at the end. A few feet nearer stood the tall wardrobe, something she had seen only in vague shadows during the dreams and visions. The child had crouched there, more than once, hiding in the dark cast by the wardrobe even as light from a candle bobbed nearer.

Katie drew her thoughts back, away from Katrina. She couldn't allow herself to be taken over.

She stared at the door. There were stone steps there, beyond a landing of stone that was barely wide enough for a person to stand upon. She had seen it in her final vision of the child. The child had been carried down those steps. Katrina. "Katrina," she whispered to herself. Not someone created by her mind, but someone who had actually existed.

What was down there? Where did those steps lead?

And the woman, what part had she played in it? And those horrible creatures that were never fully visual, but seemed parts of perpetual darkness. *What were they?*

Did they still exist in that world down those cellar steps, perhaps to come up into the house and roam the hallways at night? Erica had heard something, and Curtis embellished it by claiming he had seen something. Why hadn't she asked him to describe it?

She heard her own footsteps. A few hesitant steps, then a long pause. The sound seemed extraordinarily loud in this long closed space. She found herself glancing back, but there was only the long hallway, its shadows yellowed by the lamplight but not completely dispersed. Never completely dispersed. Like heavy cobwebs, the shadows clung to the corners of the high ceilings, especially in the hallways, those long, narrow, high passages that seemed like trails made through the walls by something that wanted to slip by unseen.

She approached the door timorously, her heart beginning a rapid thudding. *Dear God, stay with me. Don't let me lose myself in the child.* She could feel the pull of memories, not her own, but Katrina's. She could feel the strong urge to creep into the darkness on the other side of the tall wardrobe and try to squeeze behind it, while down the corridor came the hollow footsteps of Miss Theodora, closer and closer. And something else ... a movement, movements, barely heard. The slithering steps of something that struck pure terror to her mind. *The Bad Things.*

Katie turned abruptly and looked back. The sounds ended. The footsteps behind her evaporated. Shadows danced with light from the lamp. The black movements were high in the corners and along the ceiling, writhing beyond the reach of the light. Something dark crawled up the walls—or down. Coming down. No, no, it was the shadows, thrown by the lamp.

Katie drew a deep sigh. She heard it and wanted to pull it back. Be silent, something within her warned. Be very, very quiet. She wasn't sure if the warning came for her, or for Katrina.

She stood directly in front of the wardrobe now. Lamplight touched an old carved relief on the face of the wood, and followed the line of the doors down to four drawers at the bottom. A porcelain knob was missing from one of the drawers. The wood was in bad shape, the varnish long sucked away by the dampness in the corridor.

She turned and stepped closer to the door. It was tall and narrow, with a black porcelain knob.

She put her fingers out, and saw them trembling. The child fought for control suddenly, and visions flashed in Katie's mind. Like light and darkness slipping past she saw the child lifted. She felt the child's terror. She felt the rag doll clutched desperately beneath her arm. She saw the door open. The stone steps ... going down ... to darkness ... no, not to darkness, but to a strange, flickering light ... the walls glistening with dampness and the touch of the Bad Things against her skin was smooth and oily and cold ... she saw the eerie, long stone bed against the wall, and the rivulets of blood seeping down between the cobblestones, the blood of the chicken, the pig, and of ...

Katie drew back, unable to open the door. Pushing away from memories that were too painful, she longed to run and run.

It happened so long ago, she told herself. Yet it was still here, surrounding her. Here, too, within her.

She couldn't open the door.

She backed away and stood looking at the door.

No one must ever open that door. Not Nancy, not the children.

Never, never the children.

They roamed much of the house. They had seen more of it than even she. But they must never open that door.

She didn't know if the cellar and the altar to evil really existed. She would never know.

She set down the lamp and then tried to move the wardrobe. It was heavy, and seemed to be grown in place. Yet she could see that it had been moved out on the side toward the door a couple of inches. Almost as if Katrina herself, in trying to wedge behind it, had caused it to move, a fraction of an inch, an inch.

Katie braced herself against the wall, put her hands behind the heavy piece of furniture, and concentrated her strength. It budged suddenly, as if the glue that had held it to the floor had broken loose. It moved out about six inches.

She should empty it, she decided breathlessly, as she stood with her hand over her pounding heart. It was probably filled with God only knew what.

She opened the doors. At the top were hooks, probably for hanging clothes, but nothing was there. She closed the doors and opened the drawers.

One old tablecloth. Yellowed linen. It had been folded carefully and placed in the bottom drawer. She put it back and closed the drawer. There was nothing else.

She had noticed that about the dressers and chests in the house: almost all were empty. It was as if they had never been filled. Theodora Wickham had lived frugally, as if her interest in life did not include the small things like sheets, dresser scarves, towels. Or, perhaps, people had gradually carried away the small things. Only the kitchen had been left fully furnished with dishes, cutlery, tablecloths. Katie suspected it was Theodora who had not filled the drawers, rather than items being stolen.

For the first time, she considered the man who'd built the house. What had he wanted with a house so large, so many levels, entrances, rooms, hallways, and stairways? A large family? Guests?

Katie realized the child had left her. She felt the emptiness almost as if she had awakened from a deep sleep. For the moment, even the fear was gone. She was left with curiosity.

She looked again at the door. Perhaps now, safe in her own psyche, she could see if the stone steps, the dirt floor, and the altar were actually there.

She put her hand out again, and just as quickly drew it back.

No.

She struggled again with the wardrobe. It moved, again, another inch, two, in jerks and starts. She angled it across the corridor, then tried to push it back against the door. As if caught on a rise in the floorboards, it refused to move more than a fraction of an inch.

Exhausted, she finally left it. She would look for another way to close off this corridor.

She picked up the lamp and went to the door at the opposite end of the hall. It should, she calculated, open onto the central hall. The door opened inward. But it was blocked by a dresser or chest of drawers. She remembered seeing it in the hall. Had Nancy pushed it there?

She retraced her steps down to the dining room door and went into the dining room, closing that door behind her. There was a keyhole, but she didn't know where the key was. There were so many things about the house she didn't know.

She followed the lamplight out into the central hall, carefully closing doors behind her, aware of the stillness in the house and the growing darkness.

Where were Nancy and the kids?

She took the lamp to the kitchen and left it on the table. Carrying a lighted candle, she went down the central hall to the foyer, lighting candles in the wall brackets as she came to them. When she reached the telephone, she dialed her mother.

Forcing cheerfulness into her voice, she chatted a few moments with her mother, then asked, "Is Nancy there?"

"No, she left probably an hour ago. She said she was going to stop at the mall."

Katie felt suddenly very tired, she was so filled with relief. For the first time she had a sudden wish that Nancy would decide to take her kids home, to the apartment, back to their daddy.

"Then I think I'll take a long, soaking bath," Katie said. "I'll have to heat some water, but what the heck? At least I have a gas stove."

"You still haven't heard from those contractors who are supposed to wire the house?"

"No, not yet. Well, Mom, gotta go. Tell Dad hi." She hung up before her mother could start asking more questions that were getting more difficult to answer. It was almost as if something ... something was keeping the contractors away from the house.

She put a kettle of water on a gas burner to heat, then went up to her bedroom just long enough to collect pajamas and robe. She went back downstairs and stopped at the gas stove, waiting for the water. When it began to steam, she carried it into the bathroom. The candle glowed softly on the marble top of the short counter.

She poured a capful of bubble bath into the old cast-iron bathtub and turned the water on, letting cold mix with hot. It was the most comfortable bathtub she'd ever sat in, but very slick. Nancy had pasted some plastic daisy treads on the bottom to keep the kids from slipping. They helped Katie sit where she could lean back into the deep slope at the end of the tub.

She closed her eyes and wriggled her toes in the water, relishing the heat in this perpetually chilly bathroom.

CHAPTER 44

"**A**unt Katie's home," Nancy said, as she climbed the steps to the back porch. A board creaked as Curtis ran up and passed ahead of her. She warned, "Be careful, some of these boards might be rotted."

"I'm careful, Mama."

He spoke distinctly, without a lisp. Both of her children had been early, clear talkers.

Behind her Erica came carrying the old doll with the china head and hands she had found in the house. Light from an early risen moon angled in spots across the porch floor, and seemed to move even as she approached, fading, disappearing, obstructed by trees and the roof of the porch.

Nancy tried the kitchen door to see if Katie might have left it unlocked, but it wasn't. She transferred the small flashlight from her right hand to her left and dug for the house key in her purse.

Something small and light in color floated down.

"What was that?" Curtis cried, and got down on his knees in the darkness at Nancy's feet.

Nancy stepped back and Erica joined Curtis on the floor.

"It went through a crack," Erica said, peering with her head tilted.

Nancy had barely glimpsed it. "It can stay there," she said. "I don't want either of you crawling under the porch. Get up."

As they moved out of her way, Nancy unlocked the door and entered the kitchen. The light on the table was a welcome sight. The kids hurried to the table. Erica found a chair for her doll. The two children spread open the new coloring books they had bought at the mall, and began an argument over the few crayons in the small box.

It was all they'd been able to buy, but they were happy, Nancy assured herself as she watched them a moment. She reminded Erica to divide the colors equally, and then share as needed.

Katie came in as Nancy was peeling potatoes. Her hair was damp and pulled back from her face with a headband, her face clean of makeup. She wore pajamas with a cotton terry knee-length robe. They smiled at each other.

"Anything great happen today?" Nancy asked. Tonight, after the kids were in bed, she'd tell Katie about her visit to Dr. Firman. Until then, they'd be sure to talk about nothing that might arouse the curiosity, or the fear, of the children.

"Sure did. Sold that house I showed this morning. A great commission."

Katie began working on the salad, shredding carrots on the old grater they had found in a kitchen drawer. "How about you?"

Nancy shrugged. "Went to see the folks. Stopped at a supermarket on the way home. Very exciting."

They laughed. Katie bit off a chunk of carrot and crunched it noisily.

Erica asked, "Can I have some?"

"Now see what you started," Nancy said, "Everybody will be filled up on raw vegetables before dinner is cooked."

"Something fell down through a crack in the porch," Curtis said as he came from the table.

"What?" Katie asked, still crunching. She cut off bites for both children.

"I think it was a little bitty ghost," Curtis said.

"A ghost!" Erica squealed. "I can't believe you sometimes, Curtis! Ghosts are a lot bigger than that."

Curtis said defensively, "Well, it might have been a baby ghost."

"A baby ghost of what? A mouse?" Erica asked with big-sister contempt.

There was a brief silence as Curtis thought. "A bird, maybe," he said finally, giving in.

NANCY CHECKED AGAIN on the children, looking into the shadowed bedroom, tiptoeing quietly from one bed to the other. They both lay very still. Curtis breathed deeply. Erica stirred slightly as Nancy eased away.

She had bathed them, put them to bed, and then gone back downstairs for her own bath. Thank God for small blessings, she had murmured to herself. She had never appreciated such a thing as a bathroom before. And it had never occurred to her to give thanks for electric light before she'd come here to live in Katie's mansion.

Katie's, or the ghost's?

She felt like an intruder as she paused in the hall outside the kids' bedroom door. She felt observed, too, ever since she had seen the ghost. She looked toward the stairway at the end of the hall, where dark steps writhed upward into a third floor she had not yet seen. She stood still, looking, half afraid the woman would appear and come toward her.

She passed on down the hall and stopped at Katie's door. It was closed. She tapped lightly on it. If Katie was asleep, she didn't want to waken her. What she had to say could wait until morning—and perhaps should never be shared. Katie seemed more her old self this evening. Would it be better to say nothing about her own growing nervousness? She wondered suddenly if she should just move on back to the apartment with Perry. But no ... how could she leave Katie here alone? Her resolve to hold out against Perry was weakening fast. Despite their problems, she still loved him. And she missed him, too. She was ready to turn away and go back to her room when Katie answered, "Come in."

Nancy opened the door. Katie was sitting up in bed, looking as small as a child. She was propped against two large pillows. Several candles glowed in a copper holder on the table at the bedside. She let the paperback book she'd been reading drop when Nancy entered.

"Reading?" Nancy asked, as she came to the chair Katie had pulled close to the bedside.

"Have you noticed how much more time there is without television? Hours pass more slowly. Days pass slower." She paused as Nancy sat down. "Kids asleep?"

"Yes." She looked down at her hands. "Katie ..." When they were children, they dressed up every Sunday and went to Sunday school. But as they got older, they dropped away from church. Nancy took her kids to Sunday school sometimes, but not faithfully. She didn't belong to a church, nor did Katie. She felt a need at times, but it seemed more a need to go into the woods and feel nature surrounding her rather than to go into a church where she didn't feel as if she belonged. Yet here she was about to suggest something—something Katie might laugh at.

"What, Nan?" Katie prompted.

Nancy looked up. Shadows flicked constantly across Katie's face, and in that first glance she didn't look like Katie. Her face seemed softer, rounder, her hair lighter. Nancy glanced away and back again. This time she saw Katie, with the high cheekbones, the sculpted look.

"Have you thought about getting a priest to exorcise the ghost from the house?"

Katie didn't laugh.

KATIE WALKED out into the hall with Nancy, using the excuse that she needed to go down to the bathroom. They had talked for about thirty minutes and reached no conclusion. Katie, sitting in bed, had felt a need to be alone, to have Nancy asleep like her children, where, she felt, she would be safer.

She waited until Nancy had checked on Erica and Curtis once more, then gone on into her room and closed her door, saying softly just before she closed it, "Good night. Want me to go down with you?"

Katie smiled. "No. Thanks anyway. I'm not afraid." That wasn't true. She was more afraid now, knowing that the "ghost" actually existed, if that was the word for such an ethereal substance. Yet in the most logical portion of her mind she doubted even that. Certainly she doubted that it was harmful. How could it be? Such a thing defied logic. She'd have to remember to ask Dr. Firman tomorrow if it could be possible that the ghost had in some way been superimposed into the walls of the house, so that her image only seemed to be seen. Then she remembered she had seen her walking, moving about, closing doors, even carrying a knife that was certainly real. That lay, even now, in a drawer in the kitchen.

She hadn't wanted to go to the bathroom. She'd only wanted to get away from Nancy, and go alone into the rooms where Erica had found the doll. The bedroom she had slept in, that first time. She hadn't been back into that room since.

With a candle in her hand she left the hallway of the bedrooms and stepped down onto the balcony. A candle burned feebly in a bracket on the stairway landing, a tiny spot of light in a huge area of darkness.

She heard sounds of creaking, an old house moving in the winds of the night.

Wait until tomorrow.

She didn't want to wait. She was awake, and her conversation with Nancy about the ghost urged her on. She had told Nancy about her telephone conversation with Dr. Firman, that he had learned that Katrina and Eddie had actually lived eighty-three years ago. That Katrina had been murdered then, in 1910, and Eddie had disappeared.

She wished almost immediately she hadn't. She had felt as if she were breaking a confidence. She didn't understand it. Something to do with Katrina —she wasn't sure.

"Katrina," Nancy had said softly. "That's a very odd coincidence, Katie."

"What is?" Kate didn't understand.

"Your name—her name."

They only looked at each other. Katherine was her given name, shortened before she could remember to Kate. Her father, she'd been told by her mother, had named her. Katherine Jane.

She wanted suddenly then to be alone. She was glad when Nancy said good night. There was something she had to understand, and she had to be

alone to give her thoughts and feelings freedom. And to be receptive to
whatever the child was trying to tell her.

To be receptive to Katrina.

The urgency to look into the rooms that must have been Theodora's grew.

Tonight it must be done, whatever it was she had to do.

She passed by the stair landing, and walked around the balcony.

One door centered the wall along the balcony, separating that section of the
house from the rest. A colonnade shadowed it. The door was closed.

She opened it, and a faint smell of old perfume or incense moved through
the oppressive air. The door to her left led to the bedroom. It was open, and
she glimpsed the large mirror on the massive dresser and the reflection of the
miniscule flame of the candle she carried. But she had not seen a photograph
on the walls of that room, and that, foremost, was what she wanted. She
wanted to see a picture of Theodora Wickham. Later she would check the room
again, the drawers in the dresser, the chests, the tall wardrobe. But tonight she
was going into Theodora's sitting room, where Erica had found the doll. Erica
had described the room as "a living room, with couches and things, up there
on the balcony."

In the small entry to the suite a second door was closed. This was it, the
door Erica had opened.

It opened quietly, as if the hinges were kept oiled. Without moving forward
Katie pushed the door back, arm's length. She remained standing in the suite
entry, expecting to see the woman there, angry at this intrusion.

She saw instead the outlines of an old sofa, the back outlined with wood,
dark and polished, catching the light of the candle and reflecting it like animal
eyes. The material of the couch looked like velvet, with large, blood-red roses.
It was placed several feet from the wall. Behind it a heavy, dark red velvet
drapery hung closed on a window. Tables at each end of the sofa held lamps
with fringed shades.

There was a rug on the floor, Persian, perhaps, very old.

Katie stepped into the room, staying on the wide strip of bare floor outside
the rug. Her bare feet made no sound as she walked slowly into the room.

Against the wall on her right was another of the chests of drawers that
furnished so many rooms of the house, and even some of the hallways. An
antique dealer would have a name for it, but Katie was interested in it because
that was where Erica had said she'd found the doll. A gold-framed mirror
hung on the wall above it.

"It was sitting there on top of the chest, its arms out, like it wanted me to
pick it up. Can I have it, Aunt Katie?"

Katie placed the candle on top of the chest, then began opening drawers.
Nothing. Whatever it once had held, there was nothing now. No old letters, no
photographs.

Either Theodora had not kept those things, or someone who had thought to purchase the house had cleaned out the drawers.

There was one painting on the wall. Katie went close, holding the candle up.

It was the face of a young woman with shadowed cheeks and long, narrow, dark eyes. Her dark hair fluffed around her forehead and disappeared into the shadows of the setting.

Katie stared at the face.

There was a name, so finely drawn Katie could barely see it. *Theodora.*

It could be ... it might be a young Theodora.

But the date, drawn by the thin tip of a brush in black oil, read 1793.

It wasn't possible that this was the Theodora who had died in 1949. Not physically possible.

Unless she lived, and lived again. Unless she was part of something not often seen and never acknowledged in the present world.

CHAPTER 45

*E*rica.

Erica snapped awake, blinking. Someone had called her. It sounded like Curtis. He had sounded as if he were a long way off. Erica sat up and looked toward his bed. She saw his face, soft and round in the light of the candle that burned on the tall table between their beds. She saw his arms over his head, curved, as if he had raised his hands to show the shape of his head, round, big. He slept that way a lot, with his arms over his head.

Maybe it was Mama who'd called!

Erica slid out of bed and ran toward the door. The bare floor felt cold to her feet. She heard her own footsteps, and finished her walk on tiptoes.

She opened the door and looked out. The hallway disappeared into darkness far down on her left, and was only dimly lighted to the right. She felt as if she should rub her eyes, to make them see better.

There was one candle in a bracket across the hall. She could hear the tiny sputter of its burning. It was half gone. That meant it was very late in the night. In the morning it would be burned down almost to the holder, the way the candles were every morning. Erica had heard Mama and Aunt Katie talking about it, about how expensive it could get, using candles if the electricity didn't hurry up and come.

Her mother's door was open a few inches, and so was Aunt Katie's. After standing a moment in the fluttery shadows of the hall, Erica pushed Nancy's door farther open. She looked into darkness.

"Mama?" Erica asked in a whisper, going into the room. She stood still at the side of the bed, and gradually the outlines of furniture became visible.

She heard Nancy breathing, softly.

No, her mama hadn't called her.

Maybe no one had. Maybe it was just a dream.

She went back out into the hall and stopped abruptly. A long shadow lay across the floor. Erica looked up.

A large, tall woman, her face spattered by angles of light from the candle, stood in the hall. Her face was tight with anger. Her eyes glittered, as if they had absorbed the candle flame.

Erica gasped and drew back, staring up. The woman's hair was pulled back from her narrow forehead. Her skin seemed very white, yet dark, too, as if tanned too long in places, and sunk to wrinkles in the hollows of her cheeks. She wore a dress with little figures of print, and an apron that reached high over her chest and long in the skirt.

The ghost?

The ghost won't hurt you, her mama had said. If you see it, don't be afraid. It will disappear when you move.

Erica stared, silent and numb with terror, unable for a while to move. Then she edged toward the doorway to her room, her hands against the wall. The ghost woman stood just beyond the door. She didn't disappear.

The dark slits of eyes with the darting candlelight stared at Erica as she edged closer to her bedroom door. Then, just as Erica reached the door, the moment before she darted within, she noticed something she had not seen before.

The ghost woman had taken the china doll. She held it in her left arm.

Erica closed the door, and stood against it. She wanted to scream for her mother, for Aunt Katie. But her mouth was dry, and her throat empty and silent. After a while she was able to lick her lips, but her tongue, too, seemed thick and dry.

She tiptoed toward her bed, pausing to look back. The door was still closed. Curtis was still sleeping, but he turned even as she looked at him, bringing his arms down from over his head.

Erica reached her bed and climbed in, drawing the sheet blanket tightly up beneath her chin. She lay on her side, staring at the door, afraid the ghost woman would open it and walk in. Afraid, too, that she would suddenly appear in the room, tall and terrible, to stand there between the beds and look down at her. And at Curtis.

She wished she hadn't taken the doll.

She wished she had never seen it.

She wished she was at home in their little apartment, in her own bed, with her daddy close. So he could hold her and tell her it was all a bad dream.

Erica licked her lips again and found there still was no moisture. Her skin felt tight and cold. She lay with her legs drawn up against her chest, her hands in fists beneath her chin, her fingers cramped on the blanket. She stared at the door.

The sound reached her as sounds had before in the house. As if they grew from the walls. As if the house took a slow breath, and the sounds came, and separated, and became something that oozed along the hallway outside the door. Something that slid along the wall and left slime.

One morning she had looked, and the wall was damp. But she didn't tell anyone, not even Curtis.

Now it was there again, sliding against the door.

She drew tighter into her knot, staring at the doorknob. It had never turned, when those sounds flowed softly back and forth in the hallway. Never before had the knob turned.

It was white. Like white glass. And now, it began to turn.

It turned part way, and turned back. The sound moved, sliding, oozing against the wall like giant snails. Then there came footsteps. A person with shoes.

Mama!

The doorknob turned again, and the latch clicked. Erica stared, her mouth open, dried and silent. Mama would come right on in. Mama wouldn't be wearing shoes tonight that made hollow, clunking sounds on the floor. Mama would open the door quickly, she wouldn't just unlatch it and then leave it, only cracked open.

Erica couldn't breathe. She felt her eyes getting larger and larger, as if they were going to explode in her head. She began to weep in silence.

The door eased open. Something black slid into view on the floor, like darkness from the third-floor stairway coming down, swelling, rising up to stand almost as tall as the ghost woman. Darkness, as black as all of outer space, swirled into the room with that sound. It writhed, and separated, and Erica saw eyes with narrow slits for pupils, in faces that glittered in the weakening candlelight. Faces that were almost formless, long and thin and shiny black and slimy. Dark tongues darted from narrow snouts, and the slanted and soulless eyes searched the room and then found her.

They came forward, one, two, more, blending, separating ... and behind them, in the doorway, stood the ghost woman.

Curtis saw them in his dreams. They came up from a black hole in the floor, and they had long, lizard-like fingers on arms that were short, thick, black snakes. Their heads tapered down to long snouts from which forked tongues darted. Their eyes were long and set on a slant, and they stared forward in a strange, set way. They had to turn their heads to look around the room.

Looking ... for Erica ...

He wasn't dreaming, not now. Erica lay limp in the monsters' arms. The terrible long fingers curled around her body. Her arms dangled, as if she was dead.

They were in the doorway, there, with the darkness, and then they were gone.

He was dreaming. *He was dreaming.*

It wasn't real. There were no monsters in real life. Mama had told him so. Even Erica had told him so.

But Erica was gone.

Her bed was empty.

The monsters had carried her away.

Curtis began to scream.

CHAPTER 46

*W*hat Nancy dreaded most was happening. Not until she heard one of her children screaming did she realize how persistently within her that anxiety lingered. Curtis's scream woke her, after, it seemed, she was already running, her short, thin nightgown twisted from her half-conscious tumble out of bed. She had barely reached the door of the children's room when she saw Katie, wild-eyed in her doorway, coming too to the aid of the child. It was more than a nightmare cry; it was a scream built of unadulterated terror.

After she was in the bedroom and gathering Curtis into her arms, she thought of the hall candle. It had burned out, and the hallway was dark.

Curtis clung to Nancy, his arms so tight around her neck she couldn't breathe. She felt him trembling, clutching, still screaming, a deafening sound in her ears. Yet she heard Katie's shrill cry. *"Where's Erica?"* Curtis gasped, coughed, sobbed, his body jerking. His arms trembled around Nancy's neck. She turned with him, and saw in the candlelight the empty bed, the blanket pulled hallway off the bed onto the floor. With one hand freed, she pulled one of Curtis's arms from her neck and pushed him away far enough to look into his face.

His lips were white, his eyes wide and terrified. He clutched again at Nancy with the hand she held in hers. He seemed too frightened to answer the question, his chin jerking, his eyes glazed with fear.

"Curtis, where's Erica?

"Curtis!"

He sobbed, his voice stumbling over an unintelligible answer.

Katie had started looking around the room, as if Erica must be there somewhere. Nancy saw her look even under the bed. She went out into the dark hall then, disappearing from view.

"*Curtis, where's Erica?*" Nancy tried again. "What's wrong, Curtis? What happened?"

Crazy things went through her mind. Someone had kidnapped Erica. Someone had been living unseen in the house, a bum, a psychotic madman. He had carried Erica away. No, *she* would have screamed. She was only down in the bathroom, perhaps.

Carrying Curtis, Nancy went out into the hall. A white figure wavered in the darkness at the end of the hall. A ghost. A different ghost, not the woman ...

Then it turned, and Nancy saw it was Katie.

"Someone put the lights out," Katie said.

She came back to the door of her room, and disappeared. Nancy became sharply aware of the darkness in the hall, in the house. Her child was in that darkness, somewhere.

Then she became aware of the soft cries tumbling from Curtis.

"Monsters ... monsters ... they took her ... they took Erica ... *monsters.*"

Katie came back into the hall, preceded by long fingers of light that splayed across the hallway floor and climbed the dark wall. She went to the candle in the hall and lighted it again.

"Curtis," Nancy tried to put sternness in her voice, yet heard it shaking. "*Curtis,* listen—talk clearly to Mama."

She pulled his hands down from his face and turned his chin so that he had to look at her. She held him straddling her waist, his legs scissored tightly against her. Katie had come back, holding the candle from her bedroom. Its light accentuated the whiteness of Curtis's lips.

"*Monsters,*" he cried on a sob. "*Monsters took her. Black.*" He motioned toward his mouth. "Long mouths. Tongues that came out. They carried her away."

Katie turned quickly, and the flame danced away from the candle as if separating permanently from it, floating one way while the darkened candle was carried the other. She headed toward the balcony.

"I'll look downstairs, Nancy. You stay here with Curtis. Maybe she only went to the bathroom."

"No, I'm going with you."

Nancy hurried to catch up, to stay with Katie and the miniscule light. Curtis had grown silent in her arms.

"*Erica!*" Katie called, and the sound of her voice came back from distant rooms, *Erica, Erica, Erica* ... "*Erica!*"

Nancy hurried ahead of her, down onto the stair landing, as Katie paused to light each candle. All of them had been snuffed out, even the two downstairs, leading toward the bathroom.

Nancy knew before she looked into the bathroom that Erica was not there. The room was dark. Erica would never have gone down without taking a light. She could feel the lack of her child, of her presence.

She could feel the absence of her child all around her. The rooms tonight, closed doors, empty spaces, long windows, high ceilings, dark corners, as dark as an underground pit, were filled with that emptiness, that lack of presence of her child. She clung to Curtis, holding him as close as she had ever held him since he'd left her womb. He leaned against her, his arms around her neck again. He was silent, his eyes large and dark.

She went through the hallway and into the kitchen. Katie came behind her, the small amount of light from the candle outlining doorways, cabinets, table. Katie paused and lighted the kerosene lamp on the kitchen table. Its light spread, golden but cold.

Nancy checked the back door. It was still locked. The glass was intact. No one had broken in here. But of course, there were other outside doors in other room, and many windows.

She took the key down from the hook on the end of the cabinet and opened the back door. Calling, she went out.

"Erica!"

Behind her, she heard the echo of Katie's call. Like a faint mocking sound. Erica, Erica, Erica ...

Why, she wondered in some corner of her mind, did echoes in this house always repeat three times?

The night was still, except for wind in the tops of the trees. She felt the breeze against her legs, pushing her short nightgown against her hips. She felt Curtis pull away from the darkness at the edge of the porch. The path of light from the kitchen lamp ended, and Nancy stopped there.

Erica, Erica, Erica ...

The echo again, dimmer, more distant. Katie's call farther away, too, as she went somewhere deeper into the house.

"I want my daddy." Curtis's voice was a soft little cry, as if he had cried that wish often to himself.

Nancy whirled back, returning to the house. She was across the kitchen before she thought of the back door. She hadn't closed it. She didn't pause. The open door didn't matter.

"Katie!" she called.

Katie came from the hallway that branched to the right from the central hall. In that direction was the back stairway. But the door to the hall was always closed. Nancy asked, in that corner of her mind that seemed detached from her dread and her worry, that protective corner that was like a second voice, why are they always closed? It was as if even when she opened a door to let other rooms air out, the door closed itself. The children closed them, she had thought. Wasn't it a natural reaction to that constant demand, *Shut that door!*, which they had heard from her at Grandma's house?

For a moment of silence Nancy stood, returning Katie's stare. Nancy's arms felt numb suddenly, weak with having held Curtis now for how long?

Katie said, "I'm going up to check the third floor, Nan." She went into the narrow hallway that led to the rear stairway to the second and third floors, still carrying the candle from her bedroom.

Nancy hurried back toward the kitchen to get the flashlight in the junk drawer. There were many rooms she hadn't seen in the old, tall house, but tonight she was going to search them, dark corner to dark corner, stairway to stairway.

"The monsters," Curtis sobbed softly, as if talking to himself. "They took her. They had black mouths, and tongues that came out."

Snakes, she thought, he was describing snakes. Yet when had he ever seen a snake except in the reptile house at the zoo? Why should he have this crazy idea that snakelike monsters had taken Erica? Later, when he calmed, when the whiteness left his mouth and his eyes lost that glaze of absolute terror, she would question him again. But of course, by that time they would have found Erica. They would have found that Erica had only gone ... where?

The dread burst into pain, as if her very heart were torn and bleeding. Erica wasn't in the house. Nancy felt that. Erica would not have gone into another room and stayed there. She would have answered the call for her, a call that entered the top floor and was returned by the emptiness there.

Erica is not here.

Maybe Perry had come and gotten her. *Please God, let it be that Perry had come and kidnapped his own child!*

She whirled back without going on to the kitchen and the flashlight. She ran down the long central hall to the foyer, and the blessed sight of the telephone. Still holding Curtis, the light from the newly relighted candle in the bracket on the stairway not enough to let her see the numbers on the telephone, she counted them one by one and slowly dialed Perry's number.

Be home, Perry. Say you've come and taken Erica. But even as she prayed, she knew it wasn't so. Perry didn't even know how to reach the house.

He answered sleepily, but became alert when he heard her cry his name. "Nan! What's wrong?"

She felt hysteria rising. Her voice quavered. "Perry, Erica is missing."

"Missing!" he shouted. "What the hell do you mean?"

"Curtis woke up screaming, Perry, that Erica had been carried off by monsters. We can't find her. She doesn't answer when we call. The back door was still locked—the windows are locked—but we can't find her."

"Where in the hell are you? Wait a minute. Give me directions, I'll get there as soon as I can."

She gave him the name of the town. She couldn't remember, at this moment, the numbers of the highways except for the one out of town. And the distance. One-half mile. Watch carefully for the driveway.

"I'll be there." He hung up.

"Daddy's coming," she told Curtis. "It's okay, Daddy's coming. But we need a light. We need more light than this—these candles."

She hurried back to the kitchen to get the flashlight. She put Curtis down when she opened the junk drawer and removed the flashlight. Her thumb found the button and snapped the light on. She heard Curtis say something, but it was a moment before it sank in and she grasped the meaning. Her skin turned frigid, and her heart sank.

"What did you say?"

Curtis's face looked up at her, a white, round softness. "There was a woman with the monsters."

CHAPTER 47

he ghost!
     A new, different fear struck Nancy, sending shafts of ice through her heart. Dear God, what were they dealing with?

She clutched Curtis's small hand, felt it wriggle, and became distantly aware she was holding it too tight. She turned. The walls of the kitchen grew dark, the doorway lengthened, narrowed, as if the house were growing taller, narrower.

Pulling Curtis with her, she went into the hallway leading to the back stairway. The flashlight beam penetrated the darkness narrowly.

"Katie!" she screamed, but received not even the answer in echoes. Her voice sounded stifled in the narrow, tall space of the hall.

Katie had told her, tonight, other nights, of dreams, or visions she'd had of the little girl. The child who she thought was herself, and then knew to be someone named Katrina.

Katrina Etchens, she had told Nancy tonight, while Nancy listened in disbelief, not fully accepting, even when Katie had told her Dr. Firman had traced the name and found the little girl had actually existed.

But now Nancy remembered part of Katie's soft, almost whispered conversation of one of her most frightening visions. It came back to her, dismissed then as a strange nightmare, screaming in her mind now.

"They picked her up, and carried her into the cellar. The ... the Bad Things, Katrina thought of them—I thought of them. I saw this, Nancy. I was that child. The Bad Things—they were black, slimy, with long, sloping, pointed faces; they stood on short

back legs, and they had arms—and long fingers of varying lengths ... I could see parts of them so clearly—"

"Sounds like a nightmare to me, Katie, not a vision."

"They carried her down stone steps, into an underground area. A cellar—something—I found the door, but I didn't have the courage to open it. There's a tall wardrobe there that Katrina had hid against. I tried to push it over to cover the door. The children must never go there. "

And now Curtis was whimpering, on and on, as if to himself, "The monsters took her. They took Erica." *They had long snouts, and two tongues that jumped out—* Nancy turned away from the third-floor stairway. Now she knew where Erica was. None of it was nightmare; it was real. Erica had been taken into the cellar.

She crossed the hall to the chest she had pushed in front of the door. It was in that hallway, she remembered, that she had seen something moving in the darkness, as if the darkness itself were made of separate entities. She too had seen them—glimpses, dark glimpses—whatever they were.

She picked Curtis up and carried him, hurrying back through the kitchen to the large pantry. Her flashlight beam traced the outlines of the door that was closed. She opened it and stepped cautiously into the hall.

At the far end her flashlight touched the sides of a tall piece of furniture. But it was not in front of the door at the end of the hall, as Katie had said; it was back against the wall.

Nancy put Curtis down.

"Go into the kitchen, Curtis. Stay there, wait for Daddy."

"No! No!" he cried. "Don't leave me, Mama."

"It will only be for a minute," she said sternly. "Now, do as I say."

She looked back as she went down the hall, and saw that Curtis was following several feet away. She hesitated. Ahead of her was the door that Katie had feared, that the child, Katrina, had feared. If there actually were steps leading down ...

She would only look. Then, she would go back with Curtis to wait for Perry.

"Stay there, Curtis. Don't come closer. Mama will be back."

He stood in the edge of the darkness. Light from the kitchen fell meagerly into the pantry and across it to the open door, the hallway, where Curtis stood silhouetted against it. She glanced back again when she reached the tall wardrobe. Curtis hadn't moved. She had to believe he would be all right. He had to stay away from the cellar door. Katie would be coming down from upstairs. Perry was coming. He should be here within the hour. She knew that at this time of night, with traffic light on the expressway, he would travel fast. Perry loved his children. She had always been secure with that. He would come, he would find Curtis.

But she—she had to find Erica.

She looked back once again. Curtis was a small, shadowy figure in the darkness of the hallway, light tracking dimly across the floor behind him. He hadn't moved.

The flashlight beam picked up the doorknob, glistening like black oil. Vaguely she noted the difference. The rest of the doors had white porcelain knobs. Why was this one different?

The door was not quite shut. She turned the flashlight off, and saw a faint streak of light along the edge of the door.

Behind her came a plaintive cry, soft and distant: "*Mama.*"

Ahead of her, revealed as she opened the door slowly, was a flight of stairs, leading down. The steps were made of stone, and they glistened damply in dim light that fluttered somewhere below.

She stepped forward. A rush of cold air mingled with smells of earth and depth. She saw candles arranged on rocks that jutted from a wall. On the wall was a large flat stone, with geometric diagrams in which drops of moisture glistened.

Beneath it, against the wall, was a long table built of stone, as if it grew naturally from the wall of stone, as if it had been excavated eons ago, long before the house was built. As if the house itself had been built purposely above this monument to evil.

A small figure lay on the stone table as if she'd been thrown there. One arm hung limply off to the side. Her face was turned toward the wall, and her hair flowed over the side like strands of gold.

"*Erica!*"

Nancy rushed down the steps toward her child, peripherally aware of moving figures in the darkness beyond, and of the ghost woman, coming nearer. In her hand the candlelight played like imps across the long blade of a knife.

There was no blood on Erica. Nancy scooped the unconscious child up into her arms.

"Mama!"

The cry was close, behind her, liquid. Nancy spun round.

Curtis was running toward her down the cellar steps.

The door swung shut behind him.

CHAPTER 48

*J*ason hadn't been able to stay at home. He had walked the floor, then made up his mind to study Katie's tapes. After that, he had lingered only long enough to change into a pair of jeans and a loose pullover. Then he had snapped the leash on Sam, his golden retriever, and with the dog happily trotting at his side, he'd gone through the side door into the garage.

He drove through a fast food pickup, ordered a hamburger for Sam, plain, and a fish sandwich, fries, onion rings, large Coke, chocolate milkshake, and nachos with jalapeno peppers for himself. When he settled down to some hard thinking, he liked to snack. He needed plenty of food on hand. He felt only a guilty twinge at eating the ocean fish. Though he fed animal flesh to his dog, he rarely touched it himself. On moral grounds.

He drove back to his office building. It had a strangely haunted look, most of the windows dark, the streetlights spilling out into a fog-like atmosphere, few cars passing. He checked his watch with the car clock.

He parked his car in the office garage, where only a couple of other cars were now parked. Sam rode up with him in an elevator that stopped for no one. Together they went down the hall to the office door.

In his office he sat back, Sam contentedly at his feet. Jason put his own feet up on the desk and slipped the tape that held Katie's visits into the recorder.

He listened, from the beginning, hearing her describe her dreams.

They had started out as recurring dreams. Dreams disturbing, frightening, growing more frightening as they kept coming. The woman in the apron ... the long hallway. Running, trying to escape the woman.

Then, almost embarrassed, Katie told him again of the ghost woman. He heard his own voice prodding her on, asking what had happened in her life recently, hearing about the death of her husband. Then, her visit to the house.

She had seen the house from the air, the one time she had gone for a ride with her newly licensed pilot husband. He had been killed a week later. Then, six months after his death, she had looked for the house, found it available.

Jason frowned at the opposite wall. There was a painting there, a seascape, its colors soft and soothing. For the first time he thought of the coincidences in the story that was unfolding on tape.

She had seen the house with her husband. They had flown over it, but then she had forgotten it. Consciously, she had forgotten it. Then, suddenly, after six months, it was in her mind. With the insurance from his accident, she might be able to buy the available property, and do something with it, and thereby, with her life.

As if it had been meant to be, she was going to the house.

The ghost woman had meant only one thing to him: repressed memories. She was a symbol. If she wasn't actually Katie's mother, then she was someone else who had traumatized Katie.

He was dismayed now at the narrowness of his own thinking. When Katie had asked him if he believed in reincarnation, he had flatly said no. Then, when Kate had begun to have visions, threatening her daily life, her sanity, he still did not see beyond the repression theory. The child in her visions of terror acquired a name: *Katrina*.

Katrina, who had been murdered, perhaps in the very house Kate had purchased and moved into.

Moved into with two small children. Nancy's children.

He shut off the recorder, picked up the telephone, and punched out Katie's telephone number.

It rang, rang, and kept ringing, while he grew more and more agitated. It was now midnight.

"Get out of that house, Katie," he muttered aloud. "All of you, get out of that house! *Get those kids out of that house!*"

Sam lifted his head at the sound of Jason's voice. The fur along his spine rose stiffly.

After the fifteenth ring he hung up, stood up, and took Sam's leash.

"Let's go, Sam. Maybe they've left, but I have this feeling something is wrong. Let's go see."

KATIE HAD NEVER BEEN on the third floor before. She had climbed the front stairs to the third-floor landing once and had seen an entirely different world. The banisters were plain, and looked as if they hadn't been polished in many decades, if ever. Tonight she went on, preceded by candlelight thrown forward by its oblong copper backdrop meant to keep the light out of the carrier's eyes. Ahead of her was one long narrow hallway. Whatever furniture had come into these rooms was not the massive kind found below.

She knew Erica had not come up here. There was a feeling of emptiness like none anywhere else in the house. Old rooms, long closed, perhaps never used. Briefly her dreams for the house flicked into mind. Perfect rooms for temporary guests. A woman alone, or with a small child or two. Some of the rooms turned into bathrooms, the others with a couple of small beds, a small chest, a mirror, a television, perhaps ...

But the dream dissolved like the shadows in the approaching candlelight.

"Erica!" she called, feeling a need to hurry and get back downstairs with Nancy and Curtis. "*Erica!*"

Erica would not be here in the darkness. A crack of light showed nowhere. She had to check, though—every room.

The first small room on her left was empty. The floor was dusty, uncovered. She went down the hall opening doors. In two rooms she saw the frames of a bed, but folded and leaned against a wall. She retraced her steps, opening doors on the other side of the hall, leaving them open. Each room had one tall, thin window, no shades or curtains. If the walls had ever been painted, it was lost now, turned a dusty golden in the candlelight.

The last door she opened, on the right above the back stairway, showed signs that it had once been used. There was a bed with a lumpy mattress that was probably stuffed with straw. The bedstead was wood, but it had never been painted. There was a nightstand. Hooks on the wall held an old pair of overalls. A boy's, or a young man's, and a dusty shirt that looked as if it had been a work shirt.

Eddie's room, she thought immediately. Eddie's clothes, left behind. Beneath the bed were even a pair of old shoes.

Had the police looked here, she wondered, after Eddie's disappearance? If they had, they'd have known he hadn't run away.

As if suddenly, and for the first time, she saw the house objectively, a cry rose in her mind. *What kind of evil lives in this house?* And she not only had moved into it herself, but she had allowed her sister and the children to move in, too.

She ran down the back stairs, the steps creaking beneath her weight. "*Nancy!*" she screamed as she ran, her thoughts searching, searching ... Who could help them?

Could anyone help?

In the lower hall she saw that the kitchen door stood open. She hurried in. The kerosene lamp stood in the middle of the table. Its wavering light stretched from the old black cookstove to the blackened interior of the large fireplace. But Katie felt the same emptiness, the same lack of life she had felt on the third floor.

"Nancy!"

The back door was wide open. Something thumped against the screen and then flew away into the night as if it knew this was no place to linger.

Kate turned, and turned again, her eyes searching for some clue to where Nancy and Curtis might have gone. She saw the pantry door open.

She crossed the kitchen to the pantry. The room was dark except for the track of light from the kitchen lamp, a pathway from one open door to another.

They had gone into that closed hall, the hall with the door at the end which she had struggled to cover with the old wardrobe.

She entered the hall. The light from her candle inched away from her hand in the long space of the closed corridor and reached the wardrobe.

It was against the left wall, in its original place. The door at the end stood half open.

Oh God, Nan, no, Katie cried in silence. She went toward the open door.

She turned the candle so that its light was shaded from the door into the cellar, and she saw the other light, the one below. A cold, dancing light, pale, as if it glowed against moisture-laden walls.

She paused, hearing only the fluttering of the candle flame. Nancy had not moved that wardrobe. It had been moved by someone—something else.

She walked to the door. The stone steps were there, as she, as Katrina, had seen them. They glistened dully in the light from candles somewhere below, in the underground world. An odor of dampness and rot wafted upward, as cold as winter. The silence was even more profound than on the third floor. Here, not even a board creaked.

She entered, and stood on the stone landing from which the long flight of steps dropped. The stone altar against the far wall was not unfamiliar. Nothing surprised her, not the darkness off to her left, nor the candles along the wall, nor the dark stains of old blood that had made meandering trails through the stones beneath the altar. She stared at the dark trails. Katrina's blood was there. But it was old, and long dried.

The altar was empty.

Empty and waiting.

CHAPTER 49

a s Katie descended into the underground, she felt the pull of the child. As if she were a shell for Katrina, the panic of the child burst within her. Katie steeled herself against giving in. She had to find Nancy and Erica and Curtis, the children of this day, this night, before it was too late.

She became aware of the size of the area she was in: it extended far beyond light. Natural caves reached back and down, perhaps to endless tunnels beneath the surface of the earth. She felt an intense fear of that darkness, and the sense of the ground sloping sharply down.

She turned toward the altar, and the feeble candlelight. The flames of the four candles that were arranged on flat, jutted stones danced toward the darkness, drawn by the cold pull of air into the caves.

Her eyes touched upon the table of stone, and the darkened rivulets of old blood. She stood transfixed, unable to move as she envisioned Katrina carried downward over the stone steps, in the arms of one of the Bad Things.

Katie stood silent, struggling to draw back from the past, but the scene unfolded vividly from long ago. She became both observer and terror-filled child.

It was a procession, led by Theodora, who carried in her left hand a fifth candle, and in her right the butcher knife.

Katrina whimpered, looking upward into the face of that which carried her, mesmerized by horror.

Its skin shimmered with damp, it strode on reptilian legs with clawed feet, its long fingers of uneven length easily held the child, as if they were made of a substance stronger than steel. Its long snout opened and closed, revealing both razor-sharp teeth and a forked tongue that darted constantly, as if testing the air. The eyes sat on a slant, cold and without soul. Yet its body was upright, muscled, like a human male's. Against it, behind it, were others, mingled together in the darkness that flowed from them.

The child struggled suddenly, jerking to life. She pulled her eyes away from the face of the Bad Thing that carried her, and wrenched her body free. She fell to the floor and scrambled to her hands and knees. Miss Theodora screamed. A sound of fury repeated over and over in the caves beyond.

Long, cold fingers snatched at Katrina, and she dropped her rag doll. Crying, she freed herself again. There were no dark bodies, no legs, no hands, between her and the steps upward. But she couldn't leave her doll. She turned, feeling on the damp floor in the darkness.

"Put her in place!" Miss Theodora screamed. "Do you hear me? Put her in place!"

The curling, segmented fingers grabbed Katrina, and jerked her up at the moment her fingers found the tattered skirts of her doll. She pulled away again, reaching for her doll. She had to have the doll. Her Angel doll. It would protect her, make the Bad Things go away.

"Stand back! Get back, fools, let me have her!"

Miss Theodora's hand closed on her arm, lifted her from the floor bodily as if she were a doll, and threw her onto the stone table. Katrina felt the crack of the hard surface against her shoulder, her head. Pain dazed her. The faces blurred. The light dimmed. Something clouded her eyes. She clung to her doll.

Crying, calling the names of those who would help her if only they knew she was here, Katrina fought, kicked, struck out with her fists, and rolled and fell again to the floor. "If ever you need something when I'm gone," her mama had said, "you go to Miss Theodora, she will help you."

Katrina reached for Miss Theodora's long apron, and her fingers tightened on cloth. "Help me," she begged, looking up through the fog that now seemed to fill the cellar. Pain shot through her eyes.

She saw Miss Theodora looking down from far, far up, her face drawn strange and ugly. She saw Miss Theodora's hand raise, and a candle flame reflected for a brief flash on the blade of the knife.

Miss Theodora screamed, "Now you've ruined it all, you fools, couldn't hold a mere child! Now she will have to be thrown into the woods like an animal! The sacred burial grounds will not do for this miscreant!"

A *miscreant*, Katrina thought, in a strange, chilled part of her mind. *What's a miscreant?*

"She shall die! Like an animal!"

The knife came down. Katrina felt it strike and jerk her body around. There was no pain at first, only fear, only the awful disbelief that Miss Theodora would hurt her. Miss Theodora, who had patted her hair, and her cheek, and even sometimes held her on her knees. Miss Theodora, who let her feel for goodies in her apron pockets after she had been to the store. Miss Theodora, who made her afraid, and chased her from her beautiful doll. But also the Miss Theodora who had given them a shed to live in, and who even gave her papa and mama work and paid them money. Miss Theodora, who often scared her, and laughed at her, but who had never hurt her.

She struggled to hold to Miss Theodora's apron tail, to clutch her even though she saw the blood making a trail down her arm and soaking into the material.

"Help me," she pleaded. "Make the Bad Things go away!"

As if it was not Miss Theodora, but the Bad Things, that wanted her dead. Why did they want her dead?

She felt herself being lifted. Then she was thrown again onto the stone table. She heard the back of her head strike the stone, as if the essence of herself had now risen from her body and floated up, looking down.

"There," Theodora said, no longer screaming in anger. "She's yours. Take her."

KATIE STOOD STILL, shocked by the scene of the murder. She stared at the old dried rivulets of blood that stained the stone sides of the table. Katrina's blood, the blood of how many others?

But the blood was old. There had been no sacrifices tonight. Nancy, Erica, Curtis—where were they? They were here, somewhere in the darkness beyond. She sensed their presence. Restrained. Held. Waiting to be sacrificed to Theodora's evil?

Or had they been used as decoys, for something Theodora wanted far more? Someone else ...

She felt the eyes in the darkness, the waiting of the creatures Katrina had seen. She saw the darkness move, shuffling, reorganizing.

Katie knew suddenly and without doubt they were of Theodora's making. Spawned by her own mind, they existed to carry out her wishes. They were her elementals, made of the lightless earth, the underground, created by Theodora's lust for power and evil. Created to do her bidding.

What was she gaining for herself but a kind of soulless immortality? Though her physical body had died, she existed, timeless, capable still of doing her evil. What was she seeking?

Katie slowly faced the darkness again, the underground cave that sloped away beneath the house. The sacred burial ground of successful sacrifices, somewhere, there, perhaps down a pit made of natural rock formations. There, too, the home of the elementals. And here, all around, the evil of Theodora.

At present she seemed restricted to this place, this time. But if she was allowed to continue to exist, what forms would she be capable of taking?

Suddenly Katie knew what she had to do, as if a silent voice beyond the darkness and the evil of Theodora spoke to her. The sacrifice of Katrina had failed. Now the sacrifice must continue. It wasn't Nancy, Erica, or Curtis whom Theodora wanted at this point, but Katrina. First, it must be Katrina.

It was Katrina whom Theodora had recognized during that meeting in the hallway.

The fear within Katie now was her own.

They were there, in the shadows, watching her. She could hear the eager grunts of the elementals, those others that were physical components of Theodora. She knew her destiny and trembled in the face of it. Deep within her a cry rose for the life she had tried to make for a soul that was not fully her own.

Inadvertently she had drawn into this horror three innocent people, and now she had to set them free. As Katrina faced her destiny, Katie, too, must face her own.

She drew a last, deep breath that long ago had lost the sweet taste of freedom. She thought of her mother, the father she had never seen, and her stepfather, Doug. She thought of Ethan.

Katie went forward, to the altar.

She turned and faced for a moment the darkness at the end of the cellar, where the cave entrances began. Eyes—long, narrow, like slits cut into the night of hell—blinked reflections of the candle flames. Katie heard a murmur, a command. As soft as the flow of cold air from that netherworld, which pulled the candle flames. It held them back.

She turned to the altar and lay down, her hands palm down on the slab of stone at her sides. Death is coming, she warned herself. Shut your eyes against it.

Yet she saw the approach of Theodora. Her body tensed against this destiny. Her eyes opened fully and she stared into the face above her.

The skin had grown dark and swarthy, like the skin of a mummy. But the eyes glowed suddenly as if they lived. There was a look of satisfaction. No questioning of this yielding sacrifice, of Katie's offering of her body.

Theodora raised the knife. Katie's eyes followed the blade, seeing it vividly, its wide, long blade, and the tapering needle point. She felt her muscles stiffen against it.

Relax, she told herself, relax, and it won't hurt so much.

The knife came down swiftly, driven by something she saw only the edges of. Something of which Theodora was creator.

Katie heard the entry into her body, the tearing of tissues, the scraping of bone. She curled around it, as had Katrina, as would an animal, giving in to its power against her, its cruel and unholy invasion of her body.

She saw Theodora staring down at her with her strange eyes, with an excitement that lit them as if they were apart from her, alive and filled with triumph. She had completed, at last, the sacrifice of Katrina.

Katie heard the rattle of her last breath, and she lay still in an awareness that drifted above the pain, pulled by something that had lived within her since long before her birth. And the strength of Katrina grew.

Even as the blood stopped flowing, and the sacrifice was made, and the elementals began to prance nearer for their feast, Katrina rose.

Katie had known, finally, that they were one. Her destiny must be fulfilled. Katrina had returned to earth for a purpose.

She stared into Theodora's eyes and saw the horror growing there, the fear, the backing away. She heard the cries of the elementals rising, echoing, as she slowly rose from the death stone, and Theodora saw what she had done.

Katie, Katrina, had crossed over into Theodora's world, the only way to destroy her and her elementals.

Their wails rose, as once long ago the wails of the Bad Things had risen when Eddie and Katrina had listened to the terrible sounds. But now they rose in their own vague fear, fear transferred to them by Theodora, fear they didn't understand.

Katie felt herself guided, up from the cellar, up to the second floor, and into those rooms Theodora had kept.

The doll Erica had taken had been put back in its place. It sat smiling on the chest, its back outlined in the mirror, black hair in a copy of young Theodora's in a knotted braid on the head. Theodora had returned it. Katrina knew these things, the importance of the doll.

She reached for it.

For a shocked moment Katie glimpsed her own reflection in the mirror. The long hair falling loose over her shoulder. The face pale, drained of blood and life. And the knife—the dark wood handle—protruding from her chest, blood soaking the front of her nightgown. Darkness surrounded her, yet she saw.

She picked up the doll and turned away from her image.

She descended the stairs, the doll held carefully in her arms. It must not be broken or mutilated; not yet. She felt herself moving, going downstairs; she saw herself, as if the being of Katrina still moved within and without.

Then, as from a great distance, she was aware of voices.

Voices ... men's voices.

In a fading part of her awareness she knew the voices. She heard the pounding on the front door, and the calls.

"Nancy! Nancy!"

"Katie!"

Dr. Firman, she thought obscurely. She knew him—she thought. Why is he calling my name? I must go now, Doctor ... Doctor ... I ... must ... go.

She moved on, down the hall, to the door that was blocked by a chest of drawers.

She paused to edge the chest aside, then found to her surprise that she moved through it. Then she went down the dark hall to the cellar door.

Carrying the doll carefully balanced on both hands, she descended.

They had gathered beyond the altar.

Theodora's strange, dead eyes watched Katie as she carried the doll to the altar and laid it in the pooled fresh blood that was Katie's own. The blood soaked the silken fabrics of the dainty dress, turning it dark.

It lay smiling upward, the candlelight playing on its still, white face.

Katie clasped the knife handle and slipped it easily from her drained heart. She lifted it over her head, both hands holding it firmly.

Theodora made a sudden mad rush for the doll, whatever it meant to her. The elementals stirred, confused. Their wails rose to screams.

Katie held the knife poised over the doll. Theodora fell back, her mouth open in her silent horror.

In the darkness of the cave Katie saw them. Nancy, Erica, Curtis. As if they were likenesses carved from the stone wall, they huddled together, eyes blank, in a state of suspension.

Theodora saw the direction of her attention, and seemed calmed by it. She was gaining control. Katie felt herself weakening. Blood flowed from her heart again, through the open wound in her chest. She was no longer sure whether she lived.

"Let them go," she said, and heard her silent voice speaking. "Let Nancy and the children go."

Theodora moved nearer, and the wails of her elementals softened. They followed closely, waiting her commands.

"Let them go!"

Then she understood the power was hers. The power to destroy Theodora. It was that for which Katrina had returned. Katrina had known, in physical death, the importance of the doll to Theodora.

Katie lifted the knife higher and plunged it hard into the soft middle of the doll.

The doll curled, its placid face holding the mask of serenity, yet its body responded. Theodora screamed, her voice blending with the rising screams of the elementals. The eyes of the doll flared, matching the fire of the candle flame, burning briefly upward at Katie before the light went out.

She removed the knife from the doll. Gray bits of stuffing stuck to the blood on the blade. Theodora froze, her eyes grayed with terror, her mouth opening in silence. She lifted her hands as if against attack.

Katie picked the torn doll off the altar, and in her moment of pause, Theodora began a wail of grief as if she understood Katie's intentions. Katrina's aim.

She lifted the doll high and threw it over Theodora's head to the restless black figures behind her.

The doll disappeared into a tumbling, snarling mass.

Theodora screamed, her voice muffled in grief, her commands ignored as the elementals tore the doll to pieces and then turned on Theodora.

She disappeared into their midst, into the snarls, growls, whines, howls of satiation. Their voices lifted in strange harmonies as they fed.

Katie heard the sounds, the cries of destruction of Theodora. They rose into the house like whistling, shrilling winds from the depths of the netherworld.

Theodora struggled helpless against those she had created. With her fingers torn away by sharp teeth and poison fangs, she clutched at the skirts of the doll. As the elementals dragged her into the dark of the caves, she tried to lift the doll into arms that could no longer hold it.

The elementals howled in eerie harmonies their freedom.

CHAPTER 50

"*My* God, what's that sound?"

Perry grabbed Jason's arm, drawing him to a halt. They had been running, stumbling in darkness peripherally lit by the lights of both automobiles. A darkness that seemed even more profound in contrast to the splay of car lights.

Jason had no breath with which to answer, nor did he have an answer. He listened to the cries, the screams, those inhuman sounds that might have been made by dozens of owls far away in a strange wood, or by something of the devil, or the house itself. With each cry a fresh warning surrounded his body like a protective layer of ice. *Go away,* his inner self warned, *get away from here. Whatever it is, leave them alone.* In Jason's car, Sam scratched on the closed window, adding his own whines and howls.

"My God, man," Perry cried, his voice going hoarse with having shouted and shouted, "my kids are in there! Nancy's in there!"

They started running again, searching for a way in. They left the side porch, ran on around the house. Lights from the cars passed the house uselessly, fading at the barn.

They ran up on a darkened back porch, where a pale light glowed a cold, distant welcome in the open door.

Perry wrenched the screen door back. The top hinge broke and the door fell in an angle against the wall. Jason heard a grunt of frustrated satisfaction as Perry ran into the kitchen.

They were in the center of a long room, lighted by the kerosene lamp on the table. They stopped.

The sounds were somewhere beneath them. Cries softening, growing farther away. Screams unearthly, growing dimmer as they faded, as if whatever it was moved deeper into the earth.

Perry was running again, screaming hoarsely for Nancy, Erica, Curtis, Katie ...

Jason paused, breathing hard, trying to quiet his breath so he could hear beyond his own noises. Perry had run out of sight through a door that revealed only a long passageway dimly lighted by a couple of candles in wall brackets. Beyond, at the distant end, Jason saw the wider area of the foyer, and one newel post of a stairway.

But the sounds came from below, not above.

He saw a door across the room that opened onto darkness. The pantry where Nancy had seen the ghost? He entered a room with a long table in the center, and shelves on the walls. The bit of light from the kitchen revealed outlines, like the old bones of long-dried skeletons.

He had almost forgotten the flashlight in his hand. But an inner warning stopped him from turning it on. There was a hollow sound beneath his footsteps, and he knew he was over the cellar, if it existed. Now, he believed it did.

Across the room was another door, and a suggestion of light came from somewhere. When he crossed the room to the door, the sounds of unearthly wails grew more distinct. Though still fading, they were nearer, to his left, below. He quickly crossed the room.

He recognized the hallway Katie had told him of, the hallway where Katrina had hidden behind a tall wardrobe.

It was barely touched by the light that came through the open door at the end of the hall.

He hurried forward. Stone steps led downward to dimly flickering lights. He ducked under the floor joists above the stone steps, then stopped, staring at the wall made of stone, etched with symbols so old that the moisture had leached them thin.

A monument to ... an altar against a wall, with ancient carvings it would take an anthropologist to figure out, and even then, it was perhaps impossible. An altar to something, something that even now screamed dead cries in the black caves that descended beyond.

Someone was lying on the altar. A woman. Her face was turned away.

Nancy ... or Katie?

He ran down the steps.

He stopped, horrified, stunned, unable for a moment to understand at all what he saw. Unable ever to understand it fully.

Katie lay as if asleep. Blood soaked her chest and streaked down her sides. Her hands cupped the wood handle of a knife whose blade was buried within her. They held it in a strange, almost loving way. There was a look of peace on her face, as if she was merely asleep. Sleeping a sleep filled with pleasant dreams.

He touched her wrist. Her skin was growing cold.

Jason became aware of another person, someone on the steps. A quick glance showed him Perry, coming hesitantly, slowing, stopping.

He started to speak, then simply stared in stunned horror at Katie.

Jason shook his head, indicating in his own silence that Kate was dead.

The world had grown silent. Whatever it was that Kate had seen in her last moments was gone.

NANCY BECAME aware of her surroundings. As if awakening from a nightmare beyond her ability to face, she was here, suddenly, in a peaceful, lovely woodland. Tall trees grew upward and made an umbrella against the sky. Yet touches of moonlight sifted through, and glowed upon a narrow little road that meandered away. Sounds of summer surrounded her. Katydids, crickets, the buzz of cicadas. A whippoorwill called far away, as if beckoning her to follow the road.

A voice called, and drew her back.

"Mama!"

Tearful, frightened still, as if he, too, had just awakened from a nightmare he couldn't remember.

Curtis, then Erica.

"*Mama!*"

Nancy went toward the sounds of their voices, their tearful, waking sounds. Where were they? Was this real, or was this part of the dream? She could hear them, but she couldn't find them.

"Erica! Curtis! Where are you?"

"Mama! Mama!"

Moonlight touched the bright hair of her children where they stood tearful on the little road. She rushed toward them. They were real. Not part of a dream, a nightmare she couldn't recall. She remembered looking for Erica. Curtis's hand had been tight in hers. She didn't remember coming out here, being separated from both of them. It didn't matter, they were here, safe. She felt their solid little bodies in her arms, smelled their distinctive scents, kissed their satin cheeks.

"Mama, Daddy has come," Erica said.

"Daddy ... ?"

"I heard his voice."

Nancy became aware of other sounds. Of men's voices calling.

Perry had come, and someone else.

The night lightened. The moon moved and found openings and lighted the small road.

"Mama," Erica questioned in a hushed voice, tugging on Nancy's hand. "Who's that?"

Nancy followed Erica's gaze. Two young people, a boy and a girl, walked along the path toward the calling whippoorwill, oblivious to the shouts of the men, or to Nancy and her children standing so near the road. In front of them, skipping through pools of moonlight, ran a little girl, smaller than Curtis. Moonlight turned her long hair silver.

A moment of moonlight, bright upon them, and then shadows, and they were gone.

Nancy felt a ripple run up her spine and into her hair. She wasn't sure what she had seen.

She felt Erica pull away, then Curtis. She turned to see Perry running toward them, and the children toward him.

EPILOGUE

S ummer was gone, the children were back in school.

Nancy had kept busy, being mother, wife, and homemaker, enrolling in college, studying nights. Perry was with them; they were a family again. They had always been, and always would be. It had been four months since Katie's funeral.

The official ruling on Katie's death had been suicide. Her prints alone were found on the knife handle.

There were times when Nancy could believe that perhaps Katie had been so affected by her husband's death that she'd lost touch with reality and killed herself.

The medical examiner said it appeared to be suicide. Nancy tried not to think that it was otherwise. She accepted that Katie was disturbed.

Yet a vague memory plagued her. She remembered going down the stone steps into the cellar beneath the house, that dangerous area that was said to connect to underground caves. She remembered seeing her child lying on a stone altar.

Then her memory began again in the woods. They were safe, the children, herself. Perry was there, and Dr. Firman. But Katie was dead. On the altar where Nancy's memory stopped.

She made the appointment three times, and canceled each time hours before. Remembering won't bring Katie back, she told herself. They would soon be moving into a new house. Perry had decided to rearrange his priorities, and he and Nancy were getting along much better.

But the memories of going down the steps ... of seeing the altar ... kept plaguing her. The odd thing was that she vaguely remembered seeing Erica on the altar—not Katie. How did that fit with them being in the woods outside the house and cellar?

The fourth time she made the appointment, she kept it.

At ten o'clock that morning Nancy walked into Dr. Firman's office. He rose from behind his desk, tall and slightly stooped, as if to come closer to her level. His hand was large and warm. Nancy remembered that Katie had come to him for help, and he hadn't been able to help her.

She sat down, adjusting her skirt carefully over her crossed knees. He hadn't been able to help Katie, but now she was here, asking him to help her.

"How have you been, Nancy?"

She looked at her hand smoothing her skirt. "It's never easy losing someone you love," she said. "Katie was very dear to me."

He nodded, and she glanced up to see a sorrow of his own revealed for a moment in his eyes.

"I have a memory gap, Jason—Dr. Firman," she said. "I remember going down into that terrible place, seeing that altar—the night Erica was missing, the night Katie died—and Erica was lying on the altar. I ran toward her. She was unconscious, asleep ... I was afraid she was dead. Then Curtis called me and I turned. I had told him to stay in the kitchen, but he'd followed me, and he was coming down the steps. We weren't alone down there—I couldn't see them, but I knew they were there. The—whatever it was that had carried Erica there. To kill her. I was certain of that."

She drew a deep breath. "Then suddenly we were all in the woods. It was later. The moon was shining. Then we were with you and Perry."

Still the doctor said nothing. He watched her, waiting.

"Dr. Firman, I want to know what happened. Would hypnosis restore that part of my memory?"

He shook his head, then said, "Perhaps. But Nancy—let it go. Leave the buried memory alone. Go on with your life, go on with today, tomorrow. Mourn for Katie as you need to, but leave the buried memory alone. I wish, you've no idea how much I wish, I had told Katie the same. But I can tell you. The mind buries memories for a reason. Please take my advice, and don't try to remember."

He rose and held out his hand, and Nancy saw he was dismissing her.

SHE DROVE SOUTH. For several minutes she didn't realize where she was going, and then she knew.

There was a chain up now across the driveway, fifteen feet from the road. A sign hung on it, swaying gently in the autumn wind. *No Trespassing.*

She parked the car and stood looking down the driveway. The house stood

large and gaunt, its narrow windows reflecting the bare branches of the trees
that scraped against them. A black bird flew up and away from one of the tall
chimneys. Grass growing along the driveway, no longer crushed by the tires of
her car and Katie's, stood tall again, as brown and lifeless as the house.

She ducked under the chain and walked down the drifting road that drew
close to the house, curled in a circle in front of the open garage. The old buggy
was still there, sitting less sturdily, soon to fall to the ground.

The house had never really belonged to Katie, she had learned. The final
papers hadn't been signed. She had lived there just long enough to die there.

Nancy walked along the driveway, looking up at the house, at the porches
with their locked doors, doors never unlocked during their stay. She had no
desire to enter the house.

Erica seemed to have no memory of what had happened to her, either, and
for that Nancy was thankful. She prayed Erica's memory was forever blank,
from the time she was taken from her room until she woke in the forest. It had
seemed so easy for the children to make the transition, to go home as if they'd
never left. Both children had gone to Katie's funeral, though, after a long
discussion with both sets of grandparents, with Perry and herself taking first
one side and then the other. At last they'd decided that the children should
understand that their aunt Katie was gone.

Nancy walked past the barn and into the woods. It had been night, with
patches of moonlight. The children's voices had awakened her. She had a
feeling that some part of herself lingered here, in the woodland. If she could
only find the spot where she had stood, perhaps she would understand
something of what had happened.

The little road looked as if it went forever on into the woods. The forest was
old, tree limbs thick and reaching toward the sun, sometimes dipping almost
to the ground before they rose again. Evergreen vines and ferns grew lushly
around the trunks. The ground was soft with old leaves.

There was an air of peace here within the woods.

Children's voices ... again ...

But not Erica or Curtis's.

At first it seemed that she was only imagining the happy voices, but then
she saw the children.

Three children. Two of them were tall and slender. A third was much
younger, no more than four or five, skipping along the path ahead of them.
Strains of musical laughter drifted back as they walked along the road, deeper
into the woods.

A flash of recognition slipped into her mind. A boy and a girl, holding
hands, teenagers perhaps sixteen years old.

And the little girl, whose hair had gleamed silver in the moonlight, now white-blond in the sun. Shadows crossed over them like stitches on fabric as they playfully ran out of sight along the road.

They were gone, yet something of them lingered.

Nancy breathed again, and felt her sadness ease away.

The child had looked familiar. Not her face ... Nancy hadn't seen her face. But in the way she'd held her head. The sound of her voice.

Then she knew.

Katie, when she was small.

Katrina.

OTHER NOVELS BY RUBY JEAN

1974 The House that Samael Built
1974 Seventh All Hallows' Eve
1974 House at River's Bend
1975 The Girl Who Didn't Die
1978 Child of Satan's House
1978 Satan's Sister
1978 Dark Angel
1982 Hear the Children Cry
1982 Such a Good Baby
1983 The Lake
1983 MaMa
1985 Home Sweet Home
1985 Best Friends
1986 Wait and See
1987 Annabelle
1987 Chain Letter
1988 Smoke
1988 House of Illusions
1988 Jump Rope
1989 Pendulum
1989 Death Stone
1990 Vampire Child
1990 Lost and Found

1990 Victoria
1991 Celia
1991 Baby Dolly
1992 The Reckoning
1993 The Living Evil
1994 The Haunting
1995 Night Thunder
Pending Bear Hollow Charlie
Pending Cry of the Soul
Pending Pride of Bella Terra
Pending Animal Backtalk